## ALSO BY RACHEL LYNN SOLOMON

*You'll Miss Me When I'm Gone*
*Our Year of Maybe*
*Today Tonight Tomorrow*
*See You Yesterday*

# We CAN'T Keep meeting Like THIS

RACHEL LYNN SOLOMON

SIMON & SCHUSTER BFYR

NEW YORK · LONDON · TORONTO · SYDNEY · NEW DELHI

SIMON & SCHUSTER BFYR

An imprint of Simon & Schuster Children's Publishing Division
1230 Avenue of the Americas, New York, New York 10020

Text © 2021 by Rachel Lynn Solomon
Cover illustration © 2021 by Caitlin Blunnie
Cover design by Laura Eckes © 2021 by Simon & Schuster, Inc.

For information about special discounts for bulk purchases, please contact
Simon & Schuster Special Sales at 1-866-506-1949 or business@simonandschuster.com.
The Simon & Schuster Speakers Bureau can bring authors to your live event.
For more information or to book an event, contact the Simon & Schuster Speakers Bureau at
1-866-248-3049 or visit our website at www.simonspeakers.com.
Also available in a SIMON & SCHUSTER BFYR hardcover edition
Interior design by Hilary Zarycky
The text for this book was set in Adobe Garamond Pro.
Manufactured in the United States of America
First SIMON & SCHUSTER BFYR paperback edition May 2022
2  4  6  8  10  9  7  5  3  1
The Library of Congress has cataloged the hardcover edition as follows:
Names: Solomon, Rachel Lynn, author.
Title: We can't keep meeting like this / Rachel Lynn Solomon.
Other titles: We cannot keep meeting like this
Description: New York : Simon & Schuster Books for Young Readers, 2021. |
Audience: Ages 12 up. | Audience: Grades 7–9. | Summary: Wedding harpist Quinn and
cater-waiter Tarek develop feelings for each other, but while Tarek is a hopeless romantic,
Quinn is not sure she believes in love, especially since the same boy she might be
falling for spurned her the previous summer.
Identifiers: LCCN 2020038930 (print) | LCCN 2020038931 (ebook) |
ISBN 9781534440272 (hardcover) | ISBN 9781534440289 (pbk) |
ISBN 9781534440296 (ebook)
Subjects: CYAC: Love—Fiction. | Family-owned business enterprises—Fiction. | Weddings—
Fiction. | Jews—United States—Fiction.
Classification: LCC PZ7.1.S6695 We 2021 (print) | LCC PZ7.1.S6695 (ebook)
| DDC [Fic]—dc23
LC record available at https://lccn.loc.gov/2020038930
LC ebook record available at https://lccn.loc.gov/2020038931

*For Jennifer Ung.*
*You make every book feel grand.*

Were I to fall in love, indeed, it would be a different thing!
but I have never been in love; it is not my way, or my nature;
and I do not think I ever shall.

—JANE AUSTEN, *Emma*

# 1

At this point, I should be strong enough to resist a cute guy in a well-tailored suit.

I knew my ex would be here. In the wedding party. Wearing a tux that would undeniably accentuate the bold lines of his shoulders. And yet when I saw him enter Carnation Cellars, a garment bag slung over one arm, a wire in my brain sparked and a neon sign flashed DANGER, QUINN BERKOWITZ, and the next thing I knew, I was shoving myself into a broom closet and shutting the door behind me.

It's possible I'm not great at confrontation.

Someone coughs. My heart leaps into my throat as a single light bulb flicks on, illuminating my sister.

"What are you doing in here?" I ask.

Asher's in her wedding planner uniform: black blazer, black pants, dark hair in a topknot. I'm only a little dressier in a gray sheath and navy tights. When I'm behind the harp, plucking away at Pachelbel's Canon during the processional, I'm meant to be part of the scenery. Pretty, but not too pretty. Decoration.

"Pregaming." Asher takes a sip from a flask designed to look like a compact. "Just a sip when things get stressful. Calms me right down."

"Mom and Dad will kill you if they see that."

"And I value my life too much for that to happen," she says. "What brings you to my closet?"

"I, uh, know someone in the wedding party," I say, trying to banish the image of him leaning over me in his car last month, but my anxiety-brain grabs hold of it, shines a light on it, hits repeat. "Intimately."

"Who is it?" she asks. "Will? Corey? Theo?"

"That list is really not painting me in the best light." I lean back against a row of chardonnay and press my lips together in a firm line before letting his name slip through. "Jonathan."

"Jonathan Gellner! As in, brother of bride Naomi Gellner. Right. He was . . ." She trails off, as though searching her memory for an adjective I used when describing him to her.

*Sweet. Jewish. Probably pissed at me.*

We met at a BBYO party, and though I'd joined the Jewish youth group to feel more connected to my religion, I didn't anticipate this precise kind of connection. He was a cardboard cutout of a hot guy: dark hair, blue eyes, one perfect dimple when he smiled. We hadn't talked about making the relationship official, but I worried it was heading there. This is the first time I've seen him since, well, our first time. Everyone says the first time can be painful, but mostly I just felt awkward—so awkward that I ended things via text the following day, three weeks ago. It would be easier if he never had to see me again, if we never had to talk about it. If I never had to think about those twelve minutes in the back seat of his car or the bruise on my hip shaped like the gearshift of a 2006 Honda Civic.

"A bad decision," I finish for her.

"We've all been in uncomfortable situations." Asher reaches up to keep the light from swaying. "It's part of the job. Do you think I loved planning the wedding of the teacher who gave me a C in freshman algebra? No, but I kept things professional."

As my mom always says, we're in the business of the most important day of people's lives. *Nothing less than our best*—that's her motto.

"I'm trying," I insist, even as my mind remains set on mapping out the most disastrous ways this wedding could end. Jonathan confronting me on his way down the aisle and demanding an explanation. Jonathan reciting our text history in lieu of a toast. Jonathan requesting a harp rendition of "Like a Virgin."

Asher holds out the flask, and I take a sip I immediately regret. It feels like swallowing nail polish remover. For a moment I'm convinced it's going to come back up, but it slides down my throat and settles in to war with the anxiety in my stomach.

"Thanks," I say. "I love it when you condone underage drinking."

She rolls her eyes, stashes the flask in her back pocket, and opens the door. The light catches the diamond of her engagement ring, or maybe she just knows exactly the right angle to position her hand. Her fiancé messaged me about a dozen ring options before he proposed, wondering what she'd like.

What I didn't say: they all kind of looked the same to me.

Asher pulls out the phone she keeps clipped to her belt. On days I'm playing the harp instead of playing my parents' assistant, I make sure whatever I'm wearing has deep pockets. A moment later, our group chat buzzes against my right thigh.

B+B Fam

**Asher:** Just finished placing name cards.
Bridesmaids/groomsmen status check?

**Dad:** Guys looking 🔥 and almost ready for 📷

**Mom:** Need help in the bridal suite. Asher, Quinn?

**Quinn:** Be there soon

Before the Jonathan sighting, I was on my way to retrieve a glass for the groom to break during the ceremony, so I swing through the kitchen and grab one, exchanging waves with the husband-and-wife owners of Mansour's, the catering company my parents have partnered with for years. Then I wrap it in a cloth napkin, deliver it to the rabbi outside under the chuppah, and race to catch up with my sister.

We've done weddings at Carnation Cellars before, but this is our first one of the summer. The rustic winery thirty miles east of Seattle has high ceilings, fairy lights wrapped around rafters, and rows of white chairs in the garden, where the ceremony will take place. The whole wedding cost about a Tesla and a half. It's not that I can't see the magic, because it's hard not to when the venue is this stunning and the sweet scent of lilies and gardenias hangs in the air. It's that it feels a little less magical after doing it a few hundred times. After knowing how many breakdowns and fights about color schemes and meddlesome in-laws happened along the way.

The bridal suite is up a spiral staircase and at the end of the hall, with a sign that says FUTURE MRS. GELLNER-BRIDGES hanging on the door. Asher knocks with two knuckles.

"Come in!" calls my mom.

As far as bridal suites go, I've seen worse. The six bridesmaids are positioned in powder-pink upholstered chairs, none of them dressed yet. A makeup artist is sweeping blush onto the cheeks of the bridesmaid nearest me, who's filming an Instagram video. Makeup and hair products cover the vanity counters, suitcases spilling their contents onto the floor—extra clothes, chargers, tampons, water bottles, jewelry. I even spot a strip of condoms peeking out from a garment bag.

Naomi, wearing a white robe with #BRIDEBOSS printed on the back, stands in the corner with my mom, who's bent over a heap of ivory fabric and lace. "Is it going to look too obvious?" Naomi asks. Her long blond hair is braided down one side, and she has the end of it gripped between two manicured nails.

"Not at all," my mom says smoothly as she runs a needle and thread through what looks like a broken zipper. "This happens all the time, believe it or not. And everyone's going to be looking at the gorgeous smile on your face, not your lower back."

"Unless they're Jonathan's friends," one of the bridesmaids puts in, and they share a laugh while Naomi mimes retching onto a barely touched charcuterie board. How anyone can leave a hunk of Brie just sitting there is beyond me.

"How can we help?" I ask, putting on my peppiest voice. I'm safe in here. And today is about Naomi, as my mom would be quick to remind me, not the history I have with her brother. Hashtag bride boss!

"Quinn, sandpaper, please." Mom delegates without looking up from her sewing. "And, Asher, steam the dresses?"

I've never known someone who draws so much energy from the chaos around them. Mom's suit is pressed, not a hair in her bun out of place, her cat-eye glasses making her look somehow both retro-cool and fifteen years younger. Asher is her carbon copy, already leaping into action across the room, plugging in the steamer and holding it up to the first mauve bridesmaid dress, a chic Grecian halter with a floor-length skirt. They're often mistaken for sisters, so it makes sense that she followed in Mom's footsteps, studying business and officially joining Borrowed + Blue after graduating college three years ago.

I unzip my mom's emergency kit and extract two sheets of sandpaper. Dad carries one too, but Mom's could double as an apocalypse preparedness kit. It's a rolling suitcase filled with beauty products, first-aid items, at least five kinds of tape, breath mints, gum, and Listerine strips, bug spray, deodorant wipes, a hot glue gun, protein bars, bamboo skewers to prevent any cake-toppling, a spool of ribbon in case a bride forgets her something blue, and about a hundred other things guaranteed to solve any wedding catastrophe. When I was little, it mesmerized me. I wanted one just like it, and for my fourteenth birthday, she gave me my own, a miniature version of hers with my name embroidered in gold floss. I didn't have the heart to tell her I'd already decided by then that wedding planning wasn't my future career.

The bride's and bridesmaids' shoes are lined up like little patent-leather soldiers. It took only one bridesmaid slipping down the stairs and spraining an ankle for my parents to learn to scuff their shoes before the ceremony. I scrape each pair of shoes enough times to ensure no bridesmaids will be plunging to their deaths today, then finish them off with hair spray.

"I love these dresses." Asher runs her hand down the length of a mauve skirt. "They're elegant, but they feel like they'll be easy to move in. And this beading along the neckline . . . gorgeous."

"Naomi did a mitzvah, picking out these dresses," says the maid of honor.

"Are you sure you don't tell everyone that?" Naomi asks Asher. "Even the ones in ruffles and shoulder pads?"

A bridesmaid shudders as she grabs a cluster of grapes. "Don't talk to me about shoulder pads. I'm still recovering from Tiffany Schumacher's wedding, and that was five years ago."

I gesture to Asher, Mom, and me with my can of hair spray. "Wedding planners are excellent liars. I'm sure we would have been all over those shoulder pads."

"I might even have some extras in my emergency kit," Asher says. "You never know when you're going to need to relive an entire decade's worst fashion choices."

Mom gives us a judgmental shake of her head, but I can tell she's fighting a smile. "Please excuse my daughters. They're still learning basic human interaction."

"You love us," I say.

"Unfortunately."

"Pulse check," says another bridesmaid, a redhead with an orchid clip in her hair, as she reaches for a cracker on the charcuterie board, careful not to mess up her lipstick as she chews. "How are you feeling? No last-minute regrets?"

The maid of honor snorts at that. "Those would be some expensive regrets."

"I'm feeling surprisingly chill, now that I know I'm not going to be flashing my ass to my new husband's parents," Naomi says. "I'll be even better if Nana Pearl manages to stay away from the bar all evening."

She wouldn't be our first drunk grandma. I've seen every kind of wild wedding guest: friends who give humiliating toasts complete with PowerPoint presentations, parents who refuse to acknowledge the other family, even a woman who declared her love for her sister's groom when the officiant asked if anyone objected. Ever the superhero, Mom shuffled her outside, calmed her down, and kept her far away from the bride the rest of the night.

I run my palm over the bottom of the last pair of shoes. "All set."

"I never would have thought of that with the shoes," Naomi says. "You guys are amazing."

"Speaking of alcohol," one of the bridesmaids says. "Is there any way we could get some champagne?"

Mom glances up from her sewing. "There's no champagne? Isaac was supposed to make sure all the rooms were stocked."

A tiny furrow appears between her brows when she mentions my dad, so slight you wouldn't notice unless you were looking for it.

I am always looking.

"I'll get it," I say, rising to my feet so fast my knees pop. I like it in here, but I'll do anything to keep that furrow off my mom's face. "And some straws." To avoid smudged lipstick. We use biodegradable ones whenever we can.

"Quinn, shouldn't you be warming up?" Mom checks her watch. "Guests will be arriving in thirty minutes."

"I'm warm," I insist, because going outside will bring me that much closer to confronting a certain driver of a certain Honda Civic. Mom lifts her eyebrows in a nothing-less-than-our-best kind of way I know not to question.

At least she's not thinking about my dad and what he was or wasn't supposed to do anymore. Maybe the champagne seemed small, insignificant, but I should know that's all it takes to shatter something I was so sure could never break.

And because my anxiety-brain is never content to stress over one thing when it could be stressing over five, I also know I can't delay the inevitable: trying to look elegant while Jonathan stares at me, or worse, deliberately avoids eye contact. If he manages to talk to me, he's going to want to know why I broke up with him.

And I'm not sure I can give him an answer if I can't even figure it out for myself.

The harp is the kind of instrument usually associated with old ladies or baby angels in Renaissance art who are all dead behind the eyes. I learned from my grandma, who played at weddings and retirement homes and babysat me when my parents were busy building their business. Her music was the only thing that could lull me to sleep. That evolved into spending hours upon hours watching her as I grew older, and as soon as my coordination skills caught up with my fascination, she started teaching me with a child-sized 22-string. Her death when I was twelve sapped some of the joy from it, and my parents sapped the rest.

The following year they started offering me to their clients as a fun bonus—*book Borrowed + Blue and we'll throw in our harpist daughter for free!*

With everything else, I can force a smile. I can pretend I still believe in the magic of happily ever after, that the bride and groom will always gaze at each other the way they're going to under the chuppah tonight. But these days my grandma's Lyon & Healy, though gorgeous, feels like a fifty-pound weight on my shoulders.

I follow Asher back down the stairs so she can fetch the champagne while I put on a plastic grin and play scales. I have to go through the kitchen to get outside, where my harp is sitting near the chuppah, but I pause in the doorway when I hear a flurry of activity inside.

". . . didn't realize you'd be back today!" one of Mansour's staff cater-waiters says, clapping a tall, dark-haired guy on the shoulder as he buttons a black vest over a white shirt. "How was your first year?"

A low voice answers back something I don't catch because there's no way this is really happening.

*Didn't realize you'd be back.*

*No.* No no no. This was not something I ever considered a possibility and therefore didn't let myself stress about it. I would take a hundred Jonathan Gellners interrogating me about our sexual history over this. This is at the top of my Bad Decisions with Boys list, and we've never so much as held hands, unless you count the flail-dancing we did as kids.

He must have been in Seattle on breaks from school, but they never coincided with weddings B+B was working with Mansour's, and while I couldn't forget him completely, I'd finally been able to thought-spiral about him only every other week. A real victory after what happened last year.

Maybe I can go around back. Maybe I can slip outside before he sees me. I *have to* slip outside before he sees me, before—

"Quinn?"

That voice. It's a time machine of familiar longing, tugging me back to the weddings our families worked together, the days we spent stealing sweets off caterers' trays. The nights we spent in some of the loveliest places in the Seattle area, the scenery playing tricks on me, turning a childhood crush into something heavier. The email I sent last September, hazy with the end-of-summer blues, confessing my feelings to him.

The email he never answered.

Tarek Mansour is staring right at me, black tie loose around his neck, vest half-buttoned. The pleats in his slacks are crisp, like they've been freshly ironed. His eyelashes are long and his hair is longer and my lungs are tight, tight, tight.

"Been a while," he says, mouth curving up slightly. It's not even a smile—it doesn't touch his eyes. It's smile-adjacent. It shares a zip code with a smile, maybe goes to the same school and shops at the same neighborhood grocery store, but it is decidedly not a smile. There is stubble on his face, along his jawline, and he never used to have stubble like that and apparently I really like stubble if what's happening to my heart is any indication, and I need something, anything, to anchor me, to keep me from losing my grip on reality.

The first thing my eyes land on is the tray of hors d'oeuvres on the counter next to me. So I grab a tiny cube of cheese and stuff it into my mouth.

"Quinn," Asher says, voice pitched with worry, and before she finishes her sentence, I realize what I'm chewing is not the savory, cheesy goodness I was expecting. It's tart. Too tart to be cheese. "That's a mango."

# 2

t takes only a few minutes for my body to surrender to the allergic reaction. My lips swell and a rash climbs up my arms and neck and then I am being buckled into the passenger seat of Tarek Mansour's car.

"I'm so sorry," he says for the twelfth time. Asher was ready to drive me to the hospital before my mom insisted she couldn't lose both of us, and there was Tarek, keys dangling from his index finger, concern slanting his dark brows.

It's been years since I had an allergic reaction, mainly because I don't encounter mangos very often. It's not severe enough to trigger anaphylaxis—and my mom has an EpiPen in her emergency kit anyway—but because it's been so long, my parents insisted I go to the hospital. Just to be sure, they said.

"Not your fault." My tongue is swollen, so I have to force out the words. "Although I don't know why you'd put mango on a cheese plate."

"It actually goes quite well with creamy cheeses," Tarek says. "Mango has the right amount of acidity to balance out the—" He breaks off, shaking his head. "Sorry, that's probably not helpful right now."

"Not really."

I stare out the window, trying to keep my face out of his peripheral vision. It's easier if I don't have to look at him, because what I've observed so far is that college made him *hot*. Almost annoyingly so. He was always cute to me: when he grew his hair a bit too long, until he couldn't delay a haircut any longer without his parents hounding him about it, and then he'd cut it a bit too short. He was cute even during his unfortunate man bun phase two years ago. Now it's the perfect length, shaggy and curling just past his ears.

He's Egyptian American, his mother born in the United States and his father born in France, both of them with parents who'd emigrated from Egypt. When we were ten and eleven, our parents started letting us tag along to weddings. They'd ask us to entertain the other little kids during the reception, and in our tiny suits and tiny dresses, we'd dance to songs I hadn't grown sick of yet. As we got older, we took on more responsibilities. I'd retreat into the kitchen after a recessional until his parents or mine yelled at me for distracting him; he'd sneak me leftovers while I helped the Mansours clean up.

It was his love for baking that drew me to him before I had the words to call it what it was. Desserts were his favorite, and it wasn't unusual for him to walk around unaware he had powdered sugar in his hair or smelled of cinnamon. Whether he was frosting mini cupcakes or balancing a tray of tomato soup shooters with wedges of grilled cheese, he had this clear passion.

And once upon a time, so did I.

The boy I used to know slouched when he walked, a side effect of a too-early growth spurt, and tugged on his long sleeves to hide the eczema I knew embarrassed him. Sometimes he even skipped weddings because of it. *He's not feeling his best today*, one of his parents would say when I asked where he was.

Maybe it's cliché to think this, but he looks so *adult* now. There's a confident edge to his shoulders he didn't have before, a new definition in his jaw. Like he "figured himself out" in college, the way people always say they're going to do. The thought of it makes me suddenly, painfully jealous, an ache that settles beneath my ribs, pulses next to my heart.

He runs a hand over his face, drawing my attention to the scruff there. Oh yes. That too.

So I focus instead on the fight we had before he left for school and how, after I tried to make things right again, he went silent for eight months.

"Are you too hot?" he asks. I wonder if the car sat abandoned in his garage while he was away. He was so excited when he finally saved up enough for this old Ford Focus, which he plastered with stickers supporting local farms and proclaiming the benefits of eating sustainably, plus an I POWER KEXP like anyone in the 206 with decent taste. The car is so Seattle, it might as well be wearing flannel. I wouldn't be surprised if it ran on kombucha. "Too cold? Do you want to stop somewhere?"

"I'm fine. Thanks."

He's clearly trying to be a good guy about all of this, but it doesn't undo what he did, and neither does his upgraded appearance. It doesn't change the fact that he ignored me for almost a full year, and now he's sitting there with his great hair and his ridiculous jawline, asking me if the NPR station is bothering me like we're two polite near-strangers instead of friends. God, maybe he really did turn into an adult, because he never used to listen to NPR.

We end up at an urgent care much closer than the nearest hospital since my reaction is more nuisance than life-threatening. Still, Tarek rushes into the lobby and explains my symptoms to the bored-looking lady behind the front desk, and I fill out the required paperwork.

Then we wait. In one corner of the room is a boy holding a red wad of tissues to his hand, the girl next to him clutching a plastic bag with what I'm half certain is a chunk of his finger in a sea of melting ice cubes. Since I'd rather not sit next to the guy who may or may not have hacked off his finger, I pick a pair of empty seats next to the vending machine.

"You really don't have to stay," I tell Tarek. "They'll give me some antihistamines and tell me not to eat any more mango masquerading as cheddar, and I'll be fine."

"I'm not going to make you Uber home alone."

"Are you sure your parents are okay with it?" Or maybe it's that I wish my parents had been less insistent about holding on to Asher.

"They've got plenty of help." Then he holds up a hand, a patch of rough red skin disappearing into his sleeve. "It's usually me with the rash," he jokes, sounding not at all self-conscious.

I give him a noncommittal grunt in return, and then we both go quiet. I cross and uncross my legs so many times it must look like I'm doing Pilates at best and a seductive chair dance at worst.

"So . . . you're back," I say, desperate to fill the silence.

He stares down at his plain black shoes with clunky comfort soles, idly scratches at that dry skin on his wrist. I wonder if he hates his eczema as much as he used to. The joke he made would indicate otherwise. "Yep."

"For the whole summer?"

"The whole summer."

Lovely.

"Was college . . . ?" I trail off, unsure where I want to go with the question. "Everything you hoped it would be?"

He makes an odd face at this, one I can't quite interpret, and then he runs a hand through the hair I used to dream about touching in that exact way. If I'm light-headed, I blame the mango. "Even better."

"I'm glad." It kills me to say it. Picturing him at UC Davis, taking classes in their renowned food science program, so completely sure of this thing he wants to spend his life doing—it stretches that jealous ache in my chest.

"And senior year? You had a good one?"

"Definitely."

"Great."

I'm not used to this stilted conversation, this way of talking without saying anything at all. We've always bickered, and I'm stunned to realize I miss that rhythm.

Because here is Tarek's fatal flaw, the thing he has tried over and over to convince me is a feature and not a bug: he is, at his core, a hopeless romantic. And not the kind of sends-a-dozen-roses-just-because romantic or hides-a-note-in-your-jacket-pocket romantic. He's much, much worse.

To date, Tarek has been in four relationships, all of them documented in excruciating detail on Instagram.

There was Safiya, who he wooed by filling her car with balloons.

Chloe, who he rented an inflatable bounce castle for on her sixteenth birthday because she told him she'd always wanted to play in one as a kid.

Paige, who he asked to junior prom with a flash mob involving his school's dance team and an old One Direction song.

And Alejandra, who he charmed by having Mansour's deliver a different homemade snack to each of her classes. After last period, she smashed a cupcake into his face and then pulled him in for a kiss.

He believed epic, sweeping gestures were the epitome of romance. If he wasn't babbling to me about his latest flashy display, he was posting about it, interspersed with couple photos that were so clearly staged but inspired comments like *wow otp* and *omg you two are the CUTEST*. Meanwhile, I did . . . things I definitely wasn't posting about on Instagram.

This was what we bickered about: romantic gestures, the very thing keeping our parents in business. Everything Tarek did felt fake, performative, bordering on intrusive. He'd insist he only planned a gesture when he was already in a relationship or when he was certain the other person would be open to it, but I couldn't imagine the pressure of being on the receiving end of something like that. It wasn't jealousy. I swear.

He and Alejandra broke up right after graduation, which meant that last summer, he was single for the first time in ages. My feelings for him whirlpooled out of control, turning me into someone who obsessed more than usual and dreamed up scenarios that could never happen. I didn't like that person. I tried every antidote, the way I'd done for the past few years—I kissed other boys, went a full week without speaking to him, made a list of everything I didn't like about him. Nothing worked. The more excuses I made to see him at weddings last summer, the more I could ignore the mental alarms telling me we weren't right for each other.

I shouldn't have ignored them. Because after our biggest fight, a fight that didn't feel at all like bickering, I had an idea. It was obvious, really: I'd smooth things between us and let him know how I felt all at once.

So I charged forward with a grand gesture of my own. In retrospect, it wasn't that grand, but it was about as brave as I could be.

I didn't expect some poetic declaration of love when I sent that email the night before he left for school, even if I secretly hoped for one. I'd gone out of my comfort zone, broken all my rules, assigned words to the swirly sickness in my chest. If he rejected me, I reasoned, he'd be more than seven hundred miles away. That had to be the best way to speed up a heartbreak. At the very least, I thought I was worth a response.

Instead, after three weeks of unbearable silence, I sent him a text. Hey, did you get my email?

He replied almost immediately: yeah sorry been busy

That was it. I didn't even get the courtesy of punctuation or capital letters. Yeah sorry been busy. He probably thought I was this heart-eyed baby high schooler trying to nab a college boyfriend, and now he's just sitting there with his stubble and his pleated pants, an ankle resting on his knee in that trademark Casual Dude Pose.

A horrifying thought occurs to me: What if he thinks I've been pining for him all year?

I have a sudden urge to take a bath in mango smoothie.

"Quinn?" a nurse calls, and I spring to my feet.

Tarek makes a move to follow me, but I hold up a hand. Blessedly, he sits back down, resumes his CDP.

The nurse takes my vitals and tells me the doctor will be in shortly, which in urgent-care-speak means anywhere from three minutes to eternity. No one seems to take the "urgent" very seriously. Once I was here with my best friend, Julia, when she sliced her heel on a jagged rock at Green Lake, and we waited for two hours before someone stitched her up.

"I'm sorry, that doesn't look very fun," says the doctor when she steps inside.

"That's where you'd be mistaken. I'm having the time of my life." I explain to her that I'm allergic to mangos but I haven't had a reaction in forever. "Gimme the good drugs."

The good drugs turn out to be a dose of Benadryl along with a prescription stronger than what you can get over the counter, plus a topical steroid cream.

"The rash should clear up in a few days," she says, and tells me to come back or see my regular doctor if it doesn't. "Oh—and the antihistamines are going to make you a little drowsy."

By the time I meet Tarek back in the waiting room, where he's scrolling through his phone, the guy with the possible missing finger is gone. It's seven thirty, and Naomi and Paul have probably already had their first dance. We're usually scheduled to leave after the cake cutting, but with a wedding as big as theirs, we'll stay longer to coordinate transportation for the guests.

"Everything good?" he asks, slipping his phone back into his pants pocket. "You're already looking a lot better."

My face flames at this non-compliment because of course it does. "I'll survive. Just have to pick up a prescription, if that's okay."

Fortunately, there's a drugstore around the corner. My eyes are droopy and I'm all out of small talk for Tarek. This is worse than having played harp at a wedding with Jonathan, worse than fake-smiling through the ceremony and pretending all of it isn't some grand romantic ruse. It's a reminder of the time last year I felt it could have been real—until a crushing wave of reality made me realize I'd been right all along.

The drive to my house is quiet as we chase the watermelon sky. Seattle summers can feel infinite, and it's not even the solstice yet. A couple times, I catch Tarek's eyes flicking over to me, as though he's making sure I'm okay or maybe trying to make sense of this whole thing.

*I have spent the past year convincing myself I despised you,* I want to tell him. *And I'd finally gotten good at it.*

He puts the car in park. Rubs again at the redness on his wrist. *Stop scratching,* I can practically hear his mom say. *I'm not scratching. I'm TOUCHING,* he'd say back.

"Thanks for playing chauffeur," I say, unzipping my bag and removing my keys, ready to pull the covers over my head and sleep for a year. Or at least until the next season of *The Bachelor*.

"Of course." Tarek gestures to the purple lanyard on my key chain. It's a newer addition, a gift from my parents when my sole college acceptance rolled in. "Hey, congrats. You're going to UW? I meant to ask you—I never saw anything about it on social media."

I look him right in the eye and summon all my saltiness. "Yeah, sorry, been busy."

# 3

The meds send me to bed at eight thirty like the wild party animal I am. I wake up Sunday morning with our eleven-year-old cat Edith on my chest. Lady Edith Clawley—so named because of Asher's *Downton Abbey* obsession—was originally Asher's cat, but she bonded with me because I slipped her slivers of deli meat. She rewards me by regularly cutting off my air supply.

"Hi, baby," I coo at her, trying to slide her to one side. Her eyes are half closed, like it's too early for her to give a shit. Same, Edith. Same.

I roll over and grab my phone, pushing the bottle of antidepressants on my nightstand out of the way. They're for my OCD, and while they don't completely silence my intrusive thoughts, they make them a lot quieter. I reply to a few texts from Julia announcing she's returned to civilization after a camping trip and informing me I'm coming over later to get ready for Alyson Sawicki's grad party tonight. Our last grad party—or at least the last one we've been invited to.

The reality of a summer weekend hits me in a way it hasn't yet. Graduation was last week, and the next three months before college stretch ahead of me. The University of Washington is only a twenty-minute bus ride away, so I'll be living at home, which I'd be okay with if my parents hadn't already picked out my first-year business classes, a freshman business group for me to join, and a spreadsheet of other courses they think will serve the future career with Borrowed + Blue they've also picked out for me, the same way they did for Asher. Except Asher worked an after-school job that helped her save up enough to live in the dorms, while my after-school job has been practicing the harp.

It doesn't feel like I'm moving "onward and upward," like our valedictorian talked about at graduation. It feels like nothing is changing.

Thinking about college makes me think about Tarek, though, so before I can go down that rabbit hole, I push myself out of bed. His hair didn't look *that* good. It's just hair.

My room is the only one on the house's third floor. Our Crown Hill home was built in 1904, which becomes extremely clear on the hottest and coldest days of the year. The moment I saw it, I fell in love with this octagonal space on one side of the house, a small capped tower called a turret. Asher thought it was creepy, so she relinquished her oldest-kid-picks-first privileges and let me have it.

Downstairs I find a post-wedding scene I'm all too familiar with. My mom is at her laptop, her wedding bun loosened into a casual ponytail, switching between our post-wedding survey and one of her endless spreadsheets. My dad is scrutinizing the massive calendar chalked on the board that is one wall of our kitchen. Each square contains the most important details for each wedding: names, location, start time, number of guests.

"Do we have an updated guest list for the Wheatley-Ishikawa

wedding?" he asks. He's weekend-dad chic in khakis and a short-sleeved button-down, sipping coffee from a mug Asher and I got him for Hanukkah years ago that says 00 DAYS WITHOUT A DAD JOKE.

"MOB just sent it over," Mom says without glancing back at him. MOB: mother of the bride. "They're at one ninety-three, and the venue is capped at two hundred. I told her that—"

"For the fourth time," Dad fills in.

"Yep, and she swears they won't go over. Although she did ask if a child counts as a whole person or half a person."

Even I can't help laughing at that. But this is the problem with the two of them working together and from home: they are never not working. They were able to grow the business when they brought on Asher full-time, and now at any given point, there are twenty to thirty weddings in progress.

"Morning," I say, heading to the cupboard for Edith's food, which I pour into her bowl while she flicks her perfect gray-striped tail back and forth.

"Morning," Dad echoes. "Guess your new look wasn't permanent?"

I feign a gasp. "Are you saying I couldn't pull it off?"

Only a faint smile tugs at the corner of his mouth, indicating he's deeply absorbed in his task.

I refill Edith's water dish, too, uncapping the bottle of dental additive and tipping the recommended dosage into the cap. For a few seconds, I peer into the cap at the mint-green liquid. The right amount, and yet the worry is always itching at the back of my brain. No matter how many times I do this, I'm terrified I've accidentally added too much. If I give this to her, I'd be poisoning her. Which is why right after I pour the capful into her water, I turn the entire bowl over the sink and watch it swirl down the drain. I can't risk it.

Before the meds, before therapy, sometimes I'd repeat this ten times in a row. Today I only have to do it twice.

"Feeling okay?" Mom says, and I know she's talking about yesterday, not about my OCD. "I'm sorry we couldn't come with you, but you understand. We figured you were in good hands with Tarek."

"I get it," I say, because I do, and it's too early in the morning to think about Tarek's hands. I peel open a cup of Greek yogurt and take a seat with my back to the wedding calendar. Although this way I'm staring straight at a framed *Seattle Times* article about B+B that ran a decade ago. THEIR BRIDE AND JOY, reads the headline that graced the front page of the lifestyle section. Asher and I are wearing veils, midlaugh as she leads me in a dance move.

A week after that photo was taken, my parents sat us down on the living room couch, Mom rubbing an invisible smudge from her cat-eye glasses while Dad forced a smile. The stress of B+B had been a little overwhelming lately, they said, what with living in the same place they worked, and my mom was going to stay in her sister's guest room for a while.

*A while*—a phrase I assumed meant a week, maybe two.

I examine my parents' grainy newspaper faces the way I always do, but I don't see any signs of strain. And although my mom moved back in six months later, I never stop searching for the same thing in their real-life faces, even if I'm not sure what it would look like.

"I hope Naomi and Paul weren't too upset about the lack of harp," I say.

"We found a harp playlist on Spotify, but it wasn't quite the same," Mom says. "We definitely missed you."

She has this astounding ability to guilt-trip me without saying she's disappointed. If I hadn't gone to urgent care, I'm sure I would have gotten a lecture about how I'm smart enough to read an ingredients list before popping something in my mouth, how I shouldn't have done something *so risky* as attempting to eat a piece of cheese before a performance.

I become immersed in excavating my yogurt with a spoon, searching for the promised fruit on the bottom. There's never enough of it.

Dad rests a hand on the seat across from me. "Mom and I wanted to talk to you about something."

"The follow-ups?" On Sundays, I usually help Mom with post-wedding surveys, which means I also know when one of our weddings ends in divorce. Almost a quarter of the couples we've tracked aren't together anymore, and I have a theory that the pricier the wedding, the likelier the marriage is to fail.

*Divorce.* The dirtiest word in wedding planning. The thing I was certain my parents were heading toward before my mom's suitcase reappeared in the hallway, before they told Asher and me they'd been seeing a counselor and they were so happy Mom was coming home, so happy everything could go back to normal, and weren't we happy too?

"No, not that." He sits down, and the ball of anxiety that lives in my stomach tightens. "Asher and Gabe's wedding is in three months. And, well, you probably know the amount of work Asher has on her plate."

"Right," I say, the anxiety crawling up my throat now, weighing down my tongue.

"We were hoping you could step in and take on a few of her B+B responsibilities. Catering, floral, transportation, mainly. It's our busiest season, and we could really use the extra help."

"I—oh." My gaping yawn of a summer shrinks to the tiniest of sighs.

"We thought it would be a fun way to spend your summer," Mom continues. "Plus, it'll be similar to what you'll be doing in a few years anyway. Might as well get a sneak peek." She says this like it's some gift they're giving me. Like I should be thanking them.

"It's my last summer before college," I say quietly. I'm already booked for six weddings with two new songs to learn.

Mom doesn't even acknowledge this. "We've been flexible with your schedule in the past. You know how much the clients love that this is a family business. It's one of the reasons they pick us over other firms with more experience."

"And how can you resist working with your favorite people?" Dad says with a wink.

*No* is not an option. They're not asking me to do this—they're telling me this is what I'm doing.

I'm used to it, though I wish I weren't. I'll leap at any chance to avoid conflict in my family. Other kids had family game nights and beach vacations, movie marathons and weekend hikes. The Berkowitzes had weddings. That was our family bonding. I've missed parties and dances and school events, all because B+B took prece-

dence. *They'll understand*, my parents always said. *We need you.* They
made a guilt-trip sandwich out of pep and flattery, spreading a little
extra manipulation on top.

"Yeah," I say, hating myself a little. "I guess I could do that."

Their grins grow bigger. "Perfect!"

My mom's phone rings to the tune of the old song "Chapel
of Love" by the Dixie Cups. *Goin' to the chapel and we're gonna get
married* . . .

"That's Melinda Nash's mom," she says. She picks up. "Hi,
Tammy!" she says in her there's-no-such-thing-as-stress wedding
planner voice. "Oh—oh no. The maid of honor did *what*?"

And with that, she disappears into their office. Dad returns to
his calendar, whistling Mom's ringtone.

Sometimes it feels like they view me as just another vendor.
Like we are business associates instead of family. They've been so
eager to rush me into B+B that I've barely had time to figure out
what I might want instead.

What I know for sure: I don't want this job waiting for me
when I graduate from their preapproved program after taking their
preapproved classes. I want the satisfaction of truly earning something after working hard for it. And I can't tell them that without offending my sister, who's always loved B+B, who loved all her
classes, who cried at graduation when they gave her a set of business cards with her new title: associate wedding coordinator. The
idea of being trapped in this for the rest of my life sends me into
a spiral so smothering, I'm not sure how I'd be able to climb out.

But as my parents are fond of telling their clients, weddings
are in the Berkowitz DNA. They met at the wedding of a mutual

friend, when they were both stuck at what was clearly a table for randoms, since none of them knew anyone else and they were the farthest from the buffet. The way my dad tells the story, a married bridesmaid caught the bouquet at the end of the night and then passed it to my mom. The way she tells it, those hydrangeas sailed right into her arms.

A decade later, my mom's water broke at a cousin's wedding in the middle of the hora. To this day, I have a strange and otherwise inexplicable emotional attachment to "Hava Nagila." And when I was in preschool, my dad left his corporate job to help my mom, formerly an assistant wedding planner, start her dream business.

Then THEIR BRIDE AND JOY.

The talk on the couch.

Three place settings at the dining table, Dad all smiles and pretending it was normal, shutting down any time I asked about it until I stopped asking.

Weekends at our aunt's place, where I slept in the guest room with Mom and a Doberman pinscher that never stopped barking at me and "go keep yourself busy" while she and Aunt Sherie had hushed conversations in the kitchen. Sometimes I thought I heard her crying.

Asher learning to drive and spending less and less time at home.

And an eight-year-old Quinn up in a tower, wondering how two people in the business of happily ever after could have a kid who felt this lonely.

When they started working together out of our home office again, I wanted to feel relieved. But they never talked about those six months that turned my world on its axis. Everything seemingly went back to the way it was before—which meant the separation could happen again, and I'd never know it was coming.

From that point on, every argument between them, no matter how small, felt like an earthquake. I couldn't remember what had been the last straw before my mom moved out, and that made *anything* feel like it could be the last straw. I was always waiting, worrying, teeth gritted and anxiety-knot getting tighter and tighter.

They put on an act for their clients, one that became clearer the more time I spent with B+B. They'd been able to grow the business because people loved the idea of weddings planned by a couple in love. That *Seattle Times* piece had sent so many brides and grooms our way—enough to fake a happy marriage, apparently. But their grins and laughs felt false when they hadn't even been able to prevent their own relationship from crumbling.

*Nothing less than our best.* They sure took that to heart.

I'm proud of what they've built, especially after I was certain the separation would tear it all apart. But it's *theirs*, and sometimes I can't help wondering if that means I'll never be able to find something that's wholly mine.

# 4

There's a certain glamour to a best friend's room that makes it infinitely more exciting than your own. For me, that room is Julia Kirschbaum's. The walls are ocean blue, a turtle paddling to the ceiling above her bed and a beluga whale on the opposite wall. She painted all of it the summer before freshman year, and my sole contribution was a three-by-three-inch portion of coral reef near the window. She's always burning incense, but the one time I tried it in my tower, I set off the smoke alarm. Then there's the rainbow bong her parents gave her for her sixteenth birthday displayed prominently on the shelves mounted above her desk.

I lean in close to the mirror in her attached bathroom to apply raspberry-red lipstick. At the beginning of senior year, I cut my hair into a blunt inverted bob, and now my light-brown waves skim my shoulders, my bangs long enough to pin back when they get in the way, which is most of the time.

"I don't still smell like the Olympic National Park, do I?" Julia asks, dragging a brush through her straight blond hair, which hangs halfway down her back. Rapunzel hair, and it's gorgeous. I'd hate her for it if I didn't love her so much.

"Nope." I take another whiff. "You actually smell great. What is that? And what does the Olympic National Park even smell like?"

"Damp moss and my parents' organic beef jerky," she says matter-of-factly. "Mom's trying out a new shampoo recipe. Rosemary and mint. You want some?"

"Yes, please."

Deb and Dave Kirschbaum are the crunchiest of crunchy Seattle hippies. While our other friends were sneaking pot, Julia's parents smoked it openly around us, encouraging us to ask questions. They make their own soap and shampoo, which they sell at a local farmers market, and raise chickens in their backyard. We met in Hebrew school and bonded over the fact that our February birthdays were only days apart, which meant having our bat mitzvahs together, and we were overjoyed when the district funneled us into the same high school.

"My parents asked if I could take on more B+B work this summer," I say. "Since Asher's busy with her wedding."

"And you told them no?"

"My parents aren't like yours. I mean, you had to convince them that art school wasn't going to stamp out all your creative impulses. They thought *art school* was going to be too rigid for you."

Julia applied to a handful of art schools and decided on a small one in Brooklyn. She'll be doing what she loves, and sometimes it's hard for her to understand why I can't do the same. Not just because of my parents—because there's no singular Thing I love, not the way Julia loves murals or my sister loves floral arrangements. Telling my parents I don't want to join B+B would not only break their hearts but would also sever my family in a way I'm not ready to face.

After breakfast my parents went through our joint calendar and highlighted a few consultations they'd like me to join them for, a dress fitting here, a cake tasting there. It's sad times when you can't even get excited about cake.

I push off the bathroom counter and head into Julia's room, flopping down on her bed so I can stare up at the surface of the ocean. The way she painted it, you can see the sunlight glinting off the waves. I un-inside-out the pockets of my dress, tangerine with tiny owls all over it. Since I can't wear patterns or bright colors while I'm working, I tend to go all out the rest of the time.

My taste in music, too, is staunchly anti-wedding. No classical, of course. No ABBA or Bruno Mars, no "Celebration" or "Shout" or "Get Lucky." It's a mix of loud girl punk and moody indie rock that would never make it onto a reception playlist. I swipe through my phone and find a song by Mitski that seems to match my current emotions.

"Is Noelle going to be there tonight?" I ask.

"She was invited, but she hasn't RSVP'd on Facebook." She slides her feet into a pair of knockoff Toms made from hemp. "I really don't think she's into girls, anyway. She was dancing with Braden Smith at Wes Watanabe's grad party, and they looked pretty cozy."

"She could be bi. You know, like you?"

"Maybe." Noelle transferred to our school midway through junior year, and she's remained a mystery the way new kids tend to do. "Anyway, she had to be smart and get in early-decision to Yale, which is eighty miles from New York."

"Don't tell me your love isn't strong enough to withstand the distance. You send the best GIFs."

"I do, don't I?"

I check my bag, make sure I have my wallet, keys, phone. I zip it up, and then I unzip it and check it again. Wallet, keys, phone—those three things everyone needs before going out, and yet my brain takes it a step further. I know my wallet and keys are there, but as soon as I zip my bag, I question it. I start wondering whether I can believe my brain, my eyes. So I do it again. It's a strange feeling, knowing you're doing something illogical, being unable to stop yourself.

Julia waits patiently, doesn't tell me to hurry up.

"I think I'm going to take a break from guys this summer," I say, still staring at the inside of my bag. There they are. They are there. Wallet keys phone. Phone wallet keys. "With everything I'm doing for B+B, and especially after Jonathan . . ."

"You doing okay with that?" Julia asks softly. She knows we slept together, but I haven't quite been able to articulate why I felt the need to break up with him immediately after. It's probably the same reason I can't articulate any of my post-Jonathan feelings. I decided to avoid BBYO events until he is safely across the country in college, though my parents already added some of UW's Hillel activities to my fall calendar. I probably would have done it on my own, but still.

I don't tell her that the real reason I'm implementing a No-Boy Summer is because of Tarek. Because I want to make sure I don't relapse. She did enough to shake me out of it after my failed grand gesture—chocolate and sleepovers and reality TV. She blocked

Instagram on my phone, which didn't prevent me from scrolling on my laptop but helped a little, despite Tarek's lack of updates. I kept waiting for his next gesture, the girl who'd be receiving it who wasn't me. Waiting, and knowing it was going to crush me once it happened.

But it never did. Unless he managed to keep a relationship offline, Tarek's been single since last summer.

"Completely," I say, and I zip my bag one last time.

"Tell me when you're ready to go home and do sheet masks," Julia whispers as we kick off our shoes in the entryway of Alyson Sawicki's house, where photos of Alyson Sawicki beam at us from every direction.

We didn't keep to ourselves in high school, exactly—we were drifters. We had friends who were in AP classes with us, friends who did theater, friends who played sports. About a fourth of our graduating class is going to UW, going from a school of two thousand to one of more than forty thousand. And yet people are hugging and toasting each other like they're going off to war.

We're making our way to the kitchen for drinks when someone shouts, "Julia!"

Noelle Matthews, a short Black girl with natural hair, looking adorable in a denim romper and Keds, is waving at us from across the room. "I'm so glad you guys are here," she says when she hurries over.

I feel Julia stiffen at my side. "Hey, I didn't know you were coming," she says, trying to sound casual. Only Noelle can reduce my confident best friend to a puddle of nerves.

"I didn't either, until about an hour ago. We were visiting family in Portland, and the drive back took less time than we thought. Thank god, because I was about to murder my little brother for listening to Kidz Bop without headphones."

"An offense that should be punishable by law," I say, because Julia has temporarily forgotten how to word. "They're still making those?"

"They shouldn't be allowed to, but apparently. Anyone up for beer pong?"

"You guys should team up," I suggest, and Julia grips my arm with a please-don't-leave-me kind of strength. "Julia's awesome at beer pong."

"I'm not," Julia rushes to say, but Noelle's eyes light up.

"Great!" She grabs the elbow of the next person who walks by. "Corey! Beer pong? Quinn needs a partner."

Oh, you have got to be kidding me.

"Quinn, hey," Corey Esposito says, staring down at me with these sleepy, heavy-lidded eyes. "You look . . . really cute."

I offer a meager wave. Clearly I'm being haunted by the Ghosts of Hookups Past. First Jonathan, then the shitshow with Tarek, and now Corey. There's something about a rule of three, right? This has to be it, even if Tarek isn't technically an ex.

Corey and I hung out for a while junior year, a few back-seat make-outs and a homecoming dance before I started obsessing over his texts and wondering if he was thinking about me when we weren't together as much as I was thinking about him. It freaked me out, so I told him we had to stop seeing each other. *The guy you broke up with because he made you feel an emotion* is how Julia refers to him, which is not only an attack but also false. If it was an emotion, it was frustration with myself for not ending the relationship earlier.

The only emotion I feel when I see him now is that he looks really cute tonight too. And maybe that is exactly what I need to erase Tarek from my mind.

"And you sound really thirsty," I say, giving him what I hope is my flirtiest smirk.

He holds a hand to his heart, mock-offended. "Be my beer pong partner? For old times' sake?"

"Only because I'm feeling nostalgic." And then a hiss to Julia before we take our places on opposite sides of the table: "She's glad you're here!"

"Glad *we're* here," Julia says. I refuse to placate her when she's being impossible.

Corey turns out to be excellent at beer pong, and when we beat Julia and Noelle, he wraps me in the kind of hug that deserves to be capitalized and italicized. It is a *Hug*, filled with suggestion, that makes me feel things in more than a couple different places. He's been bumping my hip the whole game, winking at me, gazing at my mouth. It's the kind of attention I've always liked—people making it so obvious they're into you that you don't have to drive yourself wild with anxiety trying to decipher their feelings.

So when Julia and Noelle head off to talk to a few of Noelle's friends from the volleyball team and he asks if I want to go upstairs, I say yes.

I'm perfectly sober when we start kissing in the Sawickis' guest room—photos of Alyson with braces, at Disneyland, on a beach—and I was right: it takes away, just a little, the stress of B+B and the question mark that is college. The best way to turn off my brain. I am the one in control as I push Corey onto the bed and wrap my legs around him. It's great. Corey is great. Exactly what I wanted.

Sure, I swore off boys a couple hours ago, but since we've already hooked up, this doesn't count. It's just an encore.

"I missed this," Corey says with his mouth on my neck, and it's not *I missed you*, which is okay. Because I didn't miss him, either.

And yet it waters the seed of doubt at the back of my mind. Makes it bloom into a doubt garden with little doubt topiaries. He didn't miss me. Tarek didn't miss me. Jonathan is . . . whatever Jonathan is.

I don't understand how what's happening between us grows into something that makes you spend five hundred dollars on a chocolate fountain. And suddenly my anxiety-brain is intent on making me think it's because there's something wrong with *me*.

That must be what makes me slide off his lap, still fully clothed, desperate for air. I smooth down the skirt of my owl dress, search search search for something in the room to anchor myself. Photos of Alyson. Okay. I can focus on those. Deep breaths in through my nose, out through my mouth.

And it must be what makes me ask, "What if we went to a movie sometime?"

He looks at me like I've asked him if we can play Kidz Bop as mood music. "I . . . didn't realize you were a movie kind of girl."

I put more space between us, unsure of the implication and immediately drawing the worst conclusion. "Because there's no overlap between girls who like fooling around and girls who appreciate cinema?"

"You're funny," he says. He leans in to kiss me again, but I pull back so violently I nearly topple off the bed. "No, I mean—I didn't realize you *dated*."

"I haven't, not really, but that doesn't mean I *don't* date."

He beckons me closer, lowers his lashes to half-mast in that way he must know is catnip to me. "Sure," he says. "We can go to a movie."

It won't happen. I'm sure of it.

I want to leave him here. Every feminist cell in my body is urging me to. But even though I'm sure it won't calm me completely, I let him kiss me slow and almost sweet, then unbuckle his belt and reach my hand inside. I hate myself while I'm doing it, but I don't hate the way he fists a hand in my hair. And right now that is enough to make me stay.

After we're done—after *he's* done, because I'm nowhere near it after the conversation we just had and yeah, I'm bitter—the sense of something clawing inside me is even worse.

I find Julia on the back porch with Noelle after refreshing myself in the bathroom, thumbing away the crumbs of mascara and reapplying the lipstick I left on Corey's face. When I checked my phone, I had a half dozen texts from her. I can't tell if she's giving off ~vibes~ or if we're just gals being pals. UGH HELP.

"Hey, Noelle!" I say, fully intending to give Julia some help, even if it's not the kind of help she thinks she needs. I sit down next to them. "Julia and I usually go to the Ballard Farmers Market on

Sundays in the summer. Her parents have a booth there."

"That sounds like fun. I'd love to come if—wait, was that an invitation?" She claps a hand over her mouth. "Oh my god, I'm so sorry. I thought for a moment you were inviting me, but you were probably just casually talking about your plans, and wow, I'm going to stop now."

"We were!" I say quickly to put her out of her misery. Noelle is anxious—whether it's because of Julia or because of her brain chemistry, or some combination, I can definitely relate. "We were inviting you!"

Noelle lets out a long breath and considerably brightens. "Then yes! I'm working a few days a week at a coffee shop in Wallingford, but I'm free aside from that."

"Great," Julia says, and she nudges my shoulder in what I interpret as a *thank you*. "We'll text you the details."

The sky darkens as we continue talking on the porch, and I notice how close Julia and Noelle are sitting. When Noelle tells a joke, Julia throws back her head to laugh, and every time, Noelle twists her mouth to one side, like she's trying not to let on how much she enjoys Julia's laugh. It's the kind of thing that could almost make me believe in romance.

Almost.

# 5

know it's a lot of work," Asher says as she bends over her dining room table, calligraphy pen poised over a lavender invitation. "But this is so much more personal."

I flex my fingers. "I get it. Just don't be surprised if your hundredth invite also contains the blood from my seventeen paper cuts and counting."

"Perfect. It's more authentic that way." Asher's dark hair is loose, curling down to her shoulders, and we're both in leggings and T-shirts. We might look more alike than we ever have.

I slide a finished hand-addressed invitation for Margaret and Hal Chapin, whoever they are, to my right. Up next is Danielle Ladner, one of Asher's high school friends. Asher and Gabe's apartment is cute, a newer building in Ravenna with a view of the mountains. But she's only fifteen minutes from our parents, which I can't understand. If I had that kind of independence, I'd put at least a couple hours between us, maybe a flight.

Asher so graciously gave my mom, who has the kind of penmanship studies associate with serial killers, permission to skip this, and my dad is off on a venue tour. The save-the-dates went out at the beginning of the year, but they still have to create a seating chart, go in for final fittings and meetings with vendors, and address about a hundred little details my sister handles for other couples on a regular basis. She's had a vision board for this botanical garden wedding since she was fourteen.

"It's not too late to uninvite my cousin Moshe," Gabe calls from the kitchen, where he's cooking dinner. It's six o'clock on a Tuesday, and he just got home from work. Asher always talks about how she loves her job's flexible schedule, but her weekends are nonexistent. Meanwhile, Gabe works for an arts nonprofit downtown, is always home between five fifteen and five forty-five, and often gets free theater tickets.

Gabe is Jewish too, though much more religious than we are. His family keeps kosher and observes Shabbat, which mine never did. There's a mezuzah on his and Asher's front door, family heirloom menorahs on display. We have to dig ours out of storage every year before scraping the wax off them, and I'm sure Gabe's family never "forgets" to light the menorah on night six or seven. No one in my family has married someone who isn't Jewish, though, and I've always wondered whether it's assumed I'll do the same if I get married.

In fact, Asher only ever dated Jewish guys, which is something of an accomplishment in Seattle. In elementary school, I was usually the only Jewish kid in my class, though there were a handful of others in middle and high school. And while of course there was BBYO Jonathan, I haven't hooked up with any other Jews. Which is a weird thing to acknowledge, but there it is. It's something I think about only when someone else's Jewishness—namely, Gabe's, and I guess Asher's now too—is so clearly on display in front of me, and it makes me worry sometimes that I'm not quite Jewish enough.

"What's the story with your cousin Moshe?" I ask, placing Danielle's invitation in the "done" pile.

Across the table, Asher mimes stabbing herself in the eye with the calligraphy pen. "He's in LA, trying to become a stand-up comic. Gabe is convinced that if he comes, he'll find some way to turn it into a routine. And," she says, twisting in her chair to call into the kitchen, "I promise you, I've dealt with a hundred cousin Moshes. We'll be okay."

Gabe heads into the dining room, looking business casual in khakis and a blue button-down, his dark beard especially mountain-man-esque today. Asher wants him clean-shaven for the wedding, so he's seeing how long he can grow it out before then. "And I'm just saying," he says as he places his hands on my sister's shoulders, "I'm not into the self-deprecating Jewish comedian act, and I don't want him to be something you have to 'deal with' on our wedding day."

Asher and Gabe met in college. They kept seeing each other in their dorm elevator on the way down to the dining hall, and they'd exchange pleasantries, a bit of flirting. They Instagram-stalked each other for a while before they actually followed each other, and Gabe's said he had to stop himself from telling her he was in love with her on their second date.

I don't want to believe their relationship is doomed, but I can't help feeling jaded, thinking about our follow-up folder and the marriages that have ended in divorce. About my parents and the six months they were separated. It all looks saccharine when you see how easily something you thought was solid can shatter.

"There's just so much to do," Asher says. "Don't get me wrong,

I love it. I wouldn't be doing it for a living if I didn't love it. But it's a little overwhelming right now."

This makes me feel bad about being reluctant to step in. "I'm going to help out. You'll have more time."

"Thank you for doing that." She squeezes my hand. "Seriously. I always said I wasn't going to turn into one of those brides who needed everything to be perfect, but . . ."

Gabe isn't a *whatever you want, babe* kind of groom—I can't imagine Asher being happy with someone like that—but he's known when to sit back and let her take control. Not because she's the bride, but because this is her area of expertise.

"It's going to be perfect because it's you and me," Gabe says. Supportive Fiancé 101. "Everything else is out of our control to some degree. And we're going to be okay with that."

I'm reaching for the next invitation when my phone buzzes in my pocket. I pull it out, expecting a text from Julia, and I nearly drop it when I see Tarek's name instead.

Hey. Just wanted to see how you're feeling.

I stare at the screen. He can't just turn on his phone to text me and not see our last exchange. Ignoring it is a choice, and I guess I'm making it too. Ignoring his silence, ignoring our fight, ignoring all those swirly feelings I once had.

Everything on my face is normal-sized again, I write back, and after a moment's hesitation, add, thanks.

He must be trying to earn back some decent-human points, but I'm not sure how much credit to give him. He's always cared about me. The year my grandma died, Tarek found me crying in a photo booth, cheered me up by posing with an odd assortment of props—a feather boa, a rubber horse head, an inflatable guitar—until my dad reminded us the photo booth was for the guests and that they'd paid a lot of money for it.

I still have that strip of photos, tucked away in the back of my nightstand drawer.

I stare at the phone for a while longer, trying to decide whether I should write anything else. Wondering if he's going to.

Asher pokes me. "Less texting, more hand-lettering."

"Need I remind you, I am doing you a favor."

"I love you. Thank you. Put your phone away."

After dinner Gabe takes off for the gym, leaving Asher and me alone with a few sleeves of cookies and a quarter bottle of wine.

"Only because you're not driving home," Asher says as she pours a half inch of ruby liquid into a mug. Wineglasses are on their registry. I pout and she pours more. Our parents were never very strict about alcohol because we were around it so often, and they figured as long as we learned to handle it responsibly, we'd be okay. They were right—I've gotten buzzed but never well and truly drunk. And I can't say it's not nice to be able to share this with my sister.

"To the most sophisticated of ladies," I say, holding out my mug, and Asher clinks hers with mine.

I settle back onto the couch in her living room and snag a cookie, trying not to think about how Tarek used to make the best salted chocolate-chip. The seven years between Asher and me sometimes feel like fifteen and sometimes like nothing at all. I was eleven when she went to college, and even though she didn't go far, I cried myself to sleep in her room the night she left. When she came home on weekends with buckets of laundry because the machines in the dorm were never available, it didn't feel the same. I'd finally been able to stop worrying on a daily basis that my parents were going to split up, but any minor disagreement—how to properly load the dishwasher, which of them would call back an especially hostile MOB—took me back to the place where our home without my mom in it felt so, so quiet. And now Asher was gone too.

For the longest time, I wanted to do everything she did: wear my hair like hers, listen to the same music, hang out with her friends while they gossiped about things that made no sense to me, yet still made me feel extremely cool. Gradually, I realized there was this tremendous piece of her identity—her whole career— that I didn't want, and sometimes it feels like an invisible barrier between us.

Sitting here on her living room couch feels almost like those old times.

"I can't believe I'm getting married," Asher says, using an elastic on her wrist to tie her hair up in what I've come to view as her wedding topknot. "I mean, yes, I've been thinking about it forever, but I can't believe it's almost here. You remember that vision board I had."

"The one that was ninety percent Chris Evans? How could I forget?"

"Hey, he's responsible for at least half of my sexual awakening."

"Who was the other half?"

She levels me with a serious look. "John Oliver."

"Oh my god."

"I feel really comforted by the way he delivers the news!"

"This explains so much about you," I say, and she tosses a cookie chunk at me. I open my mouth and try to catch it, but it hits my chin instead. "Can I ask you something without coming across like a total dick? I know you've wanted the fancy wedding for so long, and I'm just wondering . . . *why*?"

As much as I want to linger in the sisterly nostalgia, it's hard not to think about how Asher's life is going to change when she's married. I'm not sure where I'll fall on her list of priorities. Most time we spend together these days is at work. We don't have nights like this very often—not that we don't want to, but when she has a free night from work, she's with Gabe or with her friends. She's been doing this slow drift since the separation, since I realized my family wasn't the solid unit we'd always been.

And if I left B+B, I'd be leaving Asher, too.

Asher, to her credit, takes my question seriously, placing an entire cookie in her mouth and chewing thoughtfully before washing it down with a sip of wine. "It's changed over the years. At first it was because I wanted the attention. I mean, I was a kid, and we grew up waiting hand and foot on brides and grooms. I wanted a massive party that would be all about me. And then I started getting emotionally invested in each couple we worked with. Being part of their day felt like the biggest honor, and I've always been so grateful for that. I'd see all the people who showed up because they cared about this couple so much, and that was what I wanted. Obviously, I wasn't going to marry the first random who showed interest. And I didn't start dating Gabe with the intention of getting married—at first it was just that I liked him, and then I loved him, and then I started picturing a future with him."

I wish her optimism didn't sound so foreign to me. "Is it weird that I never had a vision board?"

"Vision board or not, you don't have to know right now if you want to get married," she says. "Even with it being such a huge part of our lives. And you can change your mind at any time."

"I know that." Apparently, I can have an eternity to figure out the kind of love I want, if any, but my career? That's already been decided.

"Stop thinking," Asher says, shoving my shoulder, probably knowing I'm too deep in my head but, fortunately, not knowing why. Her phone lights up on the coffee table, and she snatches it, eyes going wide when she sees who's calling. "I have to take this."

Because of course B+B is always there, ruining my rare sister time like it's ruined everything else.

"Go," I say, shooing her as she answers the phone on her way to the kitchen. I hear a couple gasps, a few *wows*, and then a reassurance that we have everything under control. I'm not entirely sure whether whatever's happened is good or bad.

Asher's grinning when she gets back to the living room, a few strands escaping her topknot. "That was Victoria," she says—one of our clients, who needs only one name because she's semifamous. "Hold on. I need to process this." And then she downs the rest of her mug of wine.

My family has planned some high-profile weddings—a TV meteorologist, a governor's daughter, a local musician whose band played the reception. But Victoria and Lincoln, her fiancé, with their swanky art museum wedding happening in late August, are their most famous clients to date.

They met on a Streamr reality show called *Perfect Match* I hate-watched with Julia last year before realizing, halfway into reading my twentieth think piece about it, that maybe I wasn't hate-watching it after all. The premise: after filling out a detailed questionnaire and undergoing personality testing, contestants dated a half dozen potential partners deemed their perfect match and another half dozen who were their polar opposite. At the end of the season, they picked one person to propose to, and only after that did they find out if that person was their perfect match or not. I was definitely more interested in the drama than the romance, since the couples almost always split before the season finished airing.

After Victoria proposed to Lincoln, she found out he was her opposite, and yet they stuck it out. She designs book covers for a small local publisher, and Lincoln, an environmental lawyer, moved here after filming so they could get serious about trying to make their relationship work off camera. When they started thinking about their wedding, Victoria found my parents through the Jewish grapevine.

Finally, Asher regains her composure. "Streamr wants to film the wedding."

"Well, sure, we already knew that," I said. "I thought Victoria and Lincoln wanted to keep it private. No media."

"They offered an amount of money that was impossible to turn down, so . . . it's not exactly going to be private anymore."

"One of our weddings is going to be on Streamr?"

Asher breaks into another smile and lets out a little squeal.

"Yes. Holy shit, I can't believe it. I've dreamed of something like this for a long time, but I never thought it would actually happen. I have to call Mom and Dad. I have to call the Mansours, and the photographer, and the florist, and I have to—"

"*Breathe*," I say as the cookie I'm chewing turns to chalk in my mouth. A Borrowed + Blue wedding, available for anyone to watch at any time. My mind can't make sense of that jumble of words and what it might mean for our family.

"I'm not even mad that this wedding is overshadowing mine," Asher continues. "This could really launch us into the spotlight. Imagine if we did more high-profile weddings. If we could *travel*."

"I—wow, I can barely imagine it," I say, and at least that isn't a lie.

I want to be happy for Asher, for my parents—but I can't ignore the panic building inside me, the fear that a bigger B+B would be even harder to leave.

This must make me the worst sister, the worst daughter. The worst employee. I know I have to tell them. I just want some confirmation I'd be gaining more than what I'd be giving up, and that must be why I haven't been able to express how I really feel.

*Nothing less than our best.* It'll only be multiplied by a hundred for Victoria and Lincoln's wedding.

"You okay?" Asher asks, and I rearrange my face into something resembling happiness.

"Yeah, sorry, just overwhelmed."

For a moment I want to tell her how I've been feeling: about B+B, about college, about my black hole of a future that will drain everything that makes me Quinn. But there's no way it wouldn't offend her—she'd think her job was a handout, that she doesn't work hard. She's so in love with the idea of us continuing to do this as a family.

"That I can relate to," she says. She jumps off the couch and does a little dance. "Ooh, the place cards Gabe and I ordered arrived yesterday. Did I show you?"

I shake my head as she retrieves a box from the second bedroom, trying not to think about how it would feel to lose all of this—to lose *her*—again.

# 6

'm feeling about as out of place as I usually do as a Jew in a church, which is to say, considerably.

As the Berkowitz on the lowest rung of the B+B ladder, I'm in charge of the least glamorous things: coat check, program placement, bathrooms. And when the couple asks for it: Canon in D. I set up my harp near the pulpit and begin rehearsing the Bach piece the bride and groom requested for the recessional. Asher and Gabe are at a wine tasting, and I'm already nostalgic for the evening we spent at her place last week. I have no idea when we'll get the chance to do that again.

Asher's absence also means I'm in charge of catering and floral. I coordinated with the elder Mansours and with the florist via text, and they're already setting up for the reception. Maybe I won't need to talk to Tarek at all.

The priest seems amused by my playing the harp. "Forgive me," he says from the pulpit, where he's reviewing some notes, "but most of the harpists I've worked with are at least thirty years older than you."

"I'm actually forty. Good genes." This doesn't get a laugh. Damn. Are all priests this tough a crowd? *Fleabag* betrayed me.

While I've never felt wholly welcome in a church, I haven't yet burst into flame inside one. There's no one narrowing their eyes at me, wondering what I'm doing here, telling me I don't belong.

Except the middle-aged woman already seated in the second row, but I'm fairly certain that's unrelated to religion. She's in a sequined black dress and matching wrap, her white-blond hair cut short at severe angles. She appears older than my parents, but she has this striking, sophisticated aesthetic, and she's watching me with a look of something that might be disappointment, which is odd because I've never seen her before and therefore haven't had a chance to disappoint her.

I switch songs, from Bach to Beethoven. Still, her expression doesn't soften. Okay then. Sorry the sound of the world's most pleasant instrument somehow offended you.

There's always at least one sour person at every wedding, someone who thinks one partner could do better or is using the other for their money, or knows some salacious secret about the couple. Usually a family member, sometimes a concerned friend. Very rarely, a jilted ex-lover. I'll tell my parents to keep an eye on her.

Other guests file in and find seats. Most of the time, my hands feel as though they're moving of their own accord, up and down and over and under, the texture of the strings imprinted in the pads of my fingers. I used to love this—there's enough video evidence of that—and yet I can't find the remnants of that love when I'm up here like a harpist robot. I am meant to always look serene, which usually feels like erasing all emotion from my face. I'm not supposed to steal attention from the couple, but if people do notice me, I should look flawless.

*Nothing less than our best.*

It's not that I don't enjoy playing in front of people. It's that it's been so long since I played for myself, since before my grandma passed away. It's that I could go the rest of my life without ever hearing Canon in D, that ubiquitous wedding song everyone exclaims sounds *just so beautiful* on the harp. And sure it does, the first hundred times.

But after a while, you grow weary of beautiful.

At the venue, I swap my dull lavender dress for black pants and a button-up. Despite the low-level cynicism I carry with me like an emotional support animal, this place is a favorite of mine. It's a converted warehouse with exposed wood and high ceilings, flooded with natural light. The whole place has a chic but urban feel. Indoors, because early June in Seattle can be unpredictable, which of course means it's seventy-five and sunny today. MOG and FOG spent most of the morning complaining about this, which upset the groom, who requested I keep his parents as far away from him as possible.

"What's today's bet?" Dad asks when I return from stowing my harp dress in our van.

Even if I don't want this to be my future, I've always loved this little tradition of ours: betting on which overplayed songs will make it onto the reception playlist. "Hmm . . . let's say 'Love Shack.' This seems like a B-52s kind of crowd."

"Ten bucks?"

"You're on." We shake hands.

It's cute how excited my parents have been about the Streamr news, which soothes a little of my perpetual anxiety. I can't hate something that puts my parents in that good a mood. They toasted with champagne when Asher told them, and my dad is obsessively rewatching *Perfect Match*. I imagine my dad and I won't be making any bets at that wedding.

Dad confers with the videographer while I make a sweep through the tables. The centerpieces, a mix of lavender hydrangeas and blue gerbera daisies, are all where they should be. Place cards, table settings . . . everything looks good.

"Excuse me." There's a hand on my arm, and when I turn around to see it belongs to a fortyish man in a gray suit, I recoil. Not a fan of uninvited physical contact. "You're one of the wedding . . . people, right?" He finishes this with a dismissive wave of the hand that isn't touching me.

Certified wedding person, that's me. "Hi," I say, doing my best to project peppiness. "We're still setting up in here, if you don't mind, but we have some cocktails at the bar in the—"

"I was hoping to catch you beforehand, actually." He retracts his hand and gives me a sheepish look. "My family, we've been doing this vegetarian thing"—he says "vegetarian thing" like it's some trendy new diet no one's heard of—"since last month, so I didn't mark it on the RSVP site. I figure, there's got to be plenty of food back there and it wouldn't be an issue?"

"How many vegetarian meals would that be?"

"Five. My wife, me, and three kids. Looks like we're at table seven. Oh—and I should mention, one of them isn't the biggest fan of anything green, but if you have to put it on the plate, we can work around it." Sir, I am awed by your flexibility. "We just wanted to make sure it wouldn't be a problem for any of you."

"Not at all," I say through gritted teeth. "I'll go let the caterer know."

I stalk toward the kitchen, face forward, determined not to let my gaze linger on anyone in a caterer's uniform. The vegetarian main is soy chorizo with mole and mashed avocado. Deep breaths in through my nose, out through my mouth, ignore the tightening of my lungs. I'll ask the Mansours for the extra meals and hope there's enough food. If I have time, I can schedule a panic attack right before the cake cutting.

I pause in front of the long stainless-steel counter, where Tarek's dad is chopping hunks of rich dark chocolate. The kitchen smells incredible.

"Hi, Murad," I say, my stomach already rumbling. "Is that for Mansour's famous mole?"

"The one and only," he says in his slight French accent. He's an older, shorter version of Tarek, his black hair streaked with gray. MANSOUR'S is stitched in black over the pocket of his white chef's jacket.

On the other side of the kitchen, Zainab Mansour is plating salads: fresh corn and jicama and red pepper. "He already has a big head about it," she calls over. "You're making it worse, Quinn!"

"I only speak the truth!" I call back.

Even if Tarek and I are at odds, I've always loved his parents. Their history is what some might call romantic and what others—namely, me—might call a coincidence of epic proportions. Twenty-five years ago, Murad was in culinary school in Paris, where he grew up, and Zainab was there studying abroad for a semester. Her parents had moved to Washington State from Alexandria in their twenties, and Zainab had spent her whole life in the Seattle area. On New Year's Eve both of them were ditched by their coupled-up friends and wound up alone at the Eiffel Tower. They'd barely said a few sentences to each other before the clock struck midnight and, given everyone around them was doing the same thing, kissed as near-strangers. They spent the rest of the night wandering the city, then went their separate ways without exchanging last names or phone numbers. They didn't live in the same country, after all. It wouldn't have worked.

When Zainab got back to school in Washington, she couldn't stop thinking about him, though all she knew was that Murad was studying to become a chef and that he was born in France to Egyptian parents. Zainab had a friend who worked at a local TV station, and one evening they were low on content and looking for human-interest pieces, so Zainab went on camera and made a plea: for the Egyptian boy she'd kissed at the Eiffel Tower to meet her back there when she returned to Paris after her graduation in a few months.

The story was picked up by the national media, and when Zainab flew to Paris, a camera crew followed her—and there he was. They were engaged by the end of the summer, their story making headlines all over the world. It's wild they managed to find each other pre–social media, that they went viral before going viral was a thing. But that's all it is: coincidence. Not fate, not soul mates. Tarek has always wanted a story like theirs, though, and it's a piece of his family history he carries with pride.

"I just had a guest ask for five extra vegetarian meals," I tell the Mansours. "Is that going to be doable?"

If I waver on the last sentence, it's only because I spot Tarek out of the corner of my eye, adding spices to a giant pot while other waiters ferry ingredients back and forth around him. Black pants, white jacket hugging the lines of his shoulders. His eyebrows are pinched in concentration, but every so often he smiles to himself, like he and the food are in on a joke.

It really is amazing, the things one can observe out of the corner of one's eye.

Murad gives me a grim expression. "Five? That might be difficult. Tarek's working on the veggie mains." He calls over to his son. "Tarek, how do you feel about five bonus vegetarian meals?"

Tarek pauses his stirring but doesn't glance up. "Uh, not great, Baba."

"We have a guest demanding them," I say, trying to maintain eye contact with Murad. "Apparently, his family just decided to become vegetarians."

This is how I survive: by keeping things between us strictly business. He needs to realize we're not friends, not the way we used to be. That I haven't forgiven him. We're not going to raid the refrigerator to taste-test what goes best with his dad's leftover mole later. (Pizza, yes. Sushi, not so much.) He's not going to ask me if I've seen his new favorite rom-com or give me the smile that makes me melt like a bar of milk chocolate left in the sun.

"Sounds convenient for us." Tarek finally glances our way, his eyebrows pinched again. Yes, please make my job harder.

"We don't have time to argue about it," I say. "Please tell me there's extra food."

"Of course there's extra food. It just may not be the right food," he says. "We'll have plenty of mole, but we can't feed them that by itself. Soyrizo isn't cheap, and we ordered exactly enough for the number of guests we have. We're serving small enough portions as it is. Maybe you guys should have pushed a buffet harder."

"We always do," I say through clenched teeth. When it's in the couple's budget. "Awesome. So what do you want to do, pour some mole in a bowl and tell them it's spicy chocolate soup?"

Murad seemed content to let us hash this out, but he must have noticed our raised voices because he's standing in front of us, holding up a hand to stop our bickering. "Let's try to remain calm. We'll figure this out." His eyebrows pinch together in the same way Tarek's did. "What's going on with you two? You used to be so close."

Neither Tarek nor I volunteer an explanation.

"We'll have to make something different," Tarek says. "It won't look the same as all the other dishes, but at least it'll be vegetarian."

Murad nods. "We've done it before. No problem. There's a grocery store a few blocks away. How about we get a couple boxes of tofu, grill it up, and serve it with the mole and some Spanish rice?"

"I'll grab it," Tarek says, already unbuttoning his jacket, untying the apron around his waist. Then, to his mom: "The mole's ready for the chocolate, by the way."

Zainab's already at the stove, stirring in the dark chocolate pieces. They start melting as soon as they hit the pan. Torture. "Quinn, do you have time to make sure he doesn't get sidetracked? Tarek in a grocery store is a dangerous thing."

"I take offense at that," Tarek says, but he's grinning. The way his family controls the kitchen, anticipating each other's next move, is this finely tuned choreography. There's an ease to their interactions I don't always feel with my own family.

I tell Zainab I'll check with my parents via group chat, but unfortunately, we're ahead of schedule. "Yay," I say quietly, and if I'm not mistaken, I think I catch Tarek smiling out of the corner of his mouth.

We fall into step—or as into step as we can be with his much longer legs. Thank god the walk is only two blocks. Two sweaty, silent blocks.

"Should we get a basket, or . . ." I ask when we get to the grocery store, the AC slapping my face and arms with cold, but he's already taking off toward one of the aisles. I huff out a breath, snatch a basket, and hurry to catch up.

In the "healthy" foods section filled with tubs of hummus, vegan cheese, and all kinds of fake meat, he spends an absurd amount of time examining the ingredients on the back of various boxes of tofu.

"I'm pretty sure that's just a chunk of tofu," I say. "What else could possibly be in it?"

"We try to buy local whenever we can." Of course I knew that. It's just been a while since Tarek caring about it was so clearly on display in front of me. "I'd much rather get this one from Oregon than this one from Massachusetts."

"Your mom was right. You need supervision."

He clutches at his heart. "I'm just doing my job, Quinn."

*Quinn.* The way he says my name sends a shiver of something up my spine that could be the AC. It's just my fucking name. It shouldn't make me react like this.

"Did you play earlier?" he asks after selecting three boxes of the superior Oregon tofu, staring down at the expiration dates instead of at my face. "The harp, I mean?"

"Oh. Yeah, I did," I say, realizing he wouldn't have heard me since he wasn't at the church.

"I haven't heard you play this summer yet," he says, like it's some crucial element of the season. Sun, ice cream, Quinn Berkowitz on the harp. "I guess it doesn't feel like summer without it."

Another statement I have no idea how to process. "I'm sure the harp sounds just as mellifluous as it always does." The idea of him looking forward to hearing me play . . . I have to push it away before I start to obsess. He likes the sound of the harp. So do most people, Salty Sequin Lady excluded.

"Right." He tosses the tofu into my basket, and we head to the rice and beans aisle.

I reach for a box of instant Spanish rice, the kind with the spice packet inside, but he holds out a hand to stop me. His fingers graze the exposed skin on my arms, and I fight another AC-induced shiver. They should really turn it down in here.

"Spanish rice. Like your dad said?"

"From a *box*?" He lets out this horrified-sounding scoff. "Mansour's is not serving boxed rice."

I follow him around the store as he picks up a quart of vegetable stock, a bag of rice, and a can of tomato paste. Again, I'm struck by this easy confidence he has. This request turned me frantic, but there's none of that in the way he glides through the aisles. Maybe he's able to remain so calm because he loves this work. It's never been a chore for him, the way it is for me.

"It's going to be fine," he says while we're waiting in line to check out, as though the reason I'm so tense is because I'm worried about the food. If only it were that simple to fix what's wrong. "We've dealt with worse. Remember that couple who changed their whole menu a few days before the wedding?"

"From small plates to barbecue? I can't believe you guys let them get away with that."

"Oh, we made sure they paid for it. And sustainably raised meat is not cheap," he says with another little half smile. "Anyway. These guests probably won't even know it's different from the other veggie meals."

"That's our job, right? To make all of this look effortless, even when it isn't?" The questions slip out before I can catch them, tinged with a sharpness that seems to make him suspicious.

He gives me an odd look, his dark brows drawn together. "You make it sound like 'yes' is somehow the wrong answer."

"I—I don't know." Now we are standing too close together, and I'm feeling the same kind of feverish I did on the walk over, the sun beating down on my un-sunscreened skin. "Forget I said anything."

"Okay," he says, and then we're at the front of the checkout line.

Tarek knows I don't love being my parents' on-call harpist, but not about the six months my mom spent apart from us, not my existential college-and-beyond panic. It's been a long time since we could talk to each other like that. Maybe I could, if we'd exchanged a single word over the past year. But I'm not sure what our relationship looks like in that alternate universe. If we're close friends or if we're . . . something I shouldn't think about while standing right next to him. Something there's no way I can want when he's still hiding so much.

Last summer, after he and Alejandra broke up, it didn't take long before he found his next target: Elisa, another cater-waiter who'd been with Mansour's for a few years. I watched them joke around in the kitchen and trade smiles from across a room. A playful hand on his arm. A hug at the end of a shift. He always confided in me about his crushes, probably because we didn't go to the same school and that made it safer. I assumed the only reason he didn't tell me about Elisa was that we all worked in such close proximity. Even when he and I spent time together, my own feelings spiraling, I couldn't help wondering whether he was counting down the minutes until he could be spending time with her instead.

I had to know. It would be torture, hearing him confirm it, but it had to be a more pleasant torture than uncertainty.

So I asked him—not specifically about Elisa, but if he was working on any grand gestures. Because if he wanted to date her, that's what he would do. "I'm planning something big," he said. "Right before I leave for school."

One evening a week before he left for California, he asked me to meet him at the Shilshole Bay Marina. He was cryptic about it: "I want to get your opinion on something," he said at our last wedding of the summer.

The fight that happened there is so fresh in my mind that sometimes I swear it happened only yesterday. He and Elisa had been hard-core flirting at our past few weddings—I should have seen it coming. I showed up at the marina at seven o'clock, just like he'd asked. He looked so cute with his hair still damp from a shower. My stomach dropped when I saw the boat he rented all strung up with lights, soft jazz music playing from it, and realized why he'd asked me to meet him here.

*I want to get your opinion on something.*

I was a guinea pig for his latest grand gesture.

Of all the emotions I'd tried to curb when it came to Tarek, jealousy was the worst one. The most unwelcome. I was jealous he'd spent who knew how many hours planning this while I'd been daydreaming about him. Jealous because it was a beautiful evening, and some part of me would have loved to spend it on a boat. My parents and B+B had turned me into the worst kind of cynic—the kind who couldn't even be happy for someone else. For Elisa, who'd only ever been nice to me, who was probably going to show up any minute.

"What do you think?" he asked, so full of hope and optimism, and I lashed out.

I told him exactly what I thought. That it was over the top. Cliché. "Pretty fucking ridiculous"—choking on a laugh.

And he just stood there. Taking it. "You're right," he finally said. "This was a pretty fucking ridiculous idea." Repeated back to me, the words were much sharper. We were just bickering. Weren't we?

"You don't need my stamp of approval. You had to know what I'd think about all of this. Don't let it stop you."

The sun was starting to set. The days felt much shorter than they had even a month ago, and the way he was backlit, Puget Sound glowing behind him, was almost too lovely.

Except he looked confused, and I didn't understand why. "You make it sound like I'm the only person who's ever performed a romantic gesture."

*Performed.* Couldn't he hear himself?

"I know you're not," I said. "But do you honestly think this means anything in the long term? That this kind of gesture is going to magically make a relationship last?"

"It did for my parents." His jaw was set, and there was a new tightness in his shoulders. "They could have forgotten the Eiffel Tower. Forgotten each other. But they believed in their story. They *tried*, and they made that story as grand as they could. And they've been blissfully happy for more than twenty years."

"So everyone else just isn't trying hard enough?"

My parents tried their fucking hardest. Their entire lives were one romantic gesture after another, and it still didn't prevent them from being ripped apart. From coming back together and never smoothing out the cracks.

He shrugged, but it was far from a nonchalant shrug. It was the shrug of someone who knew he was right and wouldn't listen to any arguments to the contrary. The most naive of shrugs. "Yeah. I guess they're not. Not if they really care about each other."

The words sneaked into the spaces between my ribs and stuck. He didn't know—of course he didn't know—but that didn't make it ache any less.

"This isn't the real world," I said, flinging a hand at the boat.

"But hey, good luck. I hope this is the one that lasts longer than a couple months. I'm sure I'll see it on Instagram soon enough."

Then I turned on my heel and left.

I was cruel. We both were. And while I've been so focused on his silence, now I'm wondering if Tarek is still hurting, too.

By the time the cake is cut, all I want is a bath, a microwavable chocolate mug cake, and the new season of *Bachelor in Paradise*. There's something soothing about watching hot people yell at each other on a beach.

I've just finished toting my parents' emergency kits to the van, packing them in alongside my harp in its giant case. The van used to have the vanity license plate MTRMNY, for matrimony, until I pointed out to my mom that it looked like we were hard-core Mitt Romney supporters. She ripped it off with the kind of superhuman strength usually reserved for a parent whose kid is pinned underneath a car. But the name stuck, and we still call it the MTRMNY-mobile.

My phone buzzes against my thigh. It's a photo of Asher toasting her bridesmaids with margaritas. I send her a few choice emojis, then feel bad and add some hearts.

"Quinn?" my mom calls. She's standing at the door of the venue next to Salty Sequin Lady. "We're looking for help with transportation."

"On it." I slide the van doors shut and paste on a smile. Mom disappears back inside to do what must be her final sweep, making sure the bride and groom have everything they need before we van off into the sunset. "How can I help?"

The woman holds up an ancient brick of a phone. "I'm trying to head home, but my phone's out of battery. Probably time I replace this old thing."

I pull up Lyft and pass my phone to her so she can type in her address. "Gustav is four minutes away."

"Thank you." She shifts her small purse to her other shoulder and eyes me. "You're the harpist," she says, and I brace for either a backhanded compliment or an outright insult, given her earlier glaring. I mostly get compliments from old ladies—empty praise about how lovely I looked or how impressed they are to see someone as young as I am behind an instrument like that. "Your style is . . . interesting."

"Sorry?" I say, certain I've misheard her. "Interesting" is one of those great words that's so rarely a compliment.

But she doesn't elaborate. "How did you learn the harp?"

"My grandma played. She taught me when I was little."

"Ah, so you've never had formal training? That makes sense."

"She was an excellent harpist." Sure, I don't love the instrument the way I used to, but I'm not about to let a stranger talk about her like this.

"I don't doubt that," she says as a gray Prius pulls up to the curb. "Have a nice night." With that, she reaches in her bag for her wallet and hands me a twenty-dollar bill for the fifteen-dollar ride.

It's not until the car merges back into traffic that I notice she slipped me a business card, too.

MAXINE OTTO. EMERALD CITY HARPS.

I'm so stunned by it that I blink at the navy text a few times, trying to arrange the words into a combination that makes more sense. Maybe she's a teacher, and she thought offending me would somehow make me beg her to take me on as a student? Bizarre, but okay.

My instinct is to toss the card in the recycling, but curiosity gets the best of me, and before my parents call me over to head home, I tuck it into my pocket.

# 7

I t's one of those perfect Seattle summer days, where everyone is in a good mood, the kind of day everyone declares is the reason they love Seattle. Seventy-eight degrees, cloudless sky. You may get ten months of gloom, but then you get this: one glorious summer day.

Correction: everyone is in a good mood except Julia. Earlier this morning, she messaged me photos of three potential outfits, and she picked me up in a fourth, a maxidress with an abstract watercolor print, her long hair crown-braided around her head. I'm in a long blue skirt, a bumblebee-patterned tank tucked into the waistband. If there are tiny animals on it, I will buy it.

"Oh no, I dressed up too much," she whispers to me when Noelle meets us at the farmers market in cutoff jean shorts and a striped T-shirt. "How is she so cute in just shorts?"

"You're spiraling. You look great."

Julia makes a slightly inhuman sound before schooling her face into something more presentable. "Hi! I'm so glad you could make it. I don't normally dress up this much for farmers markets."

Noelle lifts her hand in a wave and, to her credit, gives Julia an odd look that lasts only a second. "Hey. I've never actually been to this market, but everything looks amazing."

She's not wrong. There are booths with fresh fruit and vegetables, local cheeses, artisan hot sauces, all kinds of bread. There's a girl in a cat mask playing violin, a pair of guys in old-timey clothes sitting behind typewriters with a sign that says POEMS: $2. We bought one once, and it lives on Julia's fridge beneath a magnet from her dentist.

"We always do one lap for free samples," Julia says, explaining our farmers market strategy. "And then we get a bunch of food to share."

We weave through the stalls, pausing for samples of cheeses and jams and pickles. Almost right away, I realize there's a problem. Every booth with signs proclaiming LOCAL and ORGANIC and PASTURE RAISED and WE LET THESE COWS WATCH THE GREAT BRITISH BAKE OFF WHILE MILKING THEM reminds me of Tarek. I'm sure he's been to this market, which is the best one in Seattle. I'm sure he loves it.

*Stop, brain.*

I try to enjoy this for what it is: a normal summer outing with friends. I'm not thinking about Victoria and Lincoln's wedding or her dress fitting in a few days. I'm not thinking about next weekend's wedding, which takes place on a boat and already makes me feel claustrophobic. Except the thing about telling yourself you're firmly not thinking about something guarantees it's all you're going to be thinking about.

Julia makes a valiant attempt to steer us away from Seattle Sustainable Soaps, her parents' booth, but they wave us over. She does a quick introduction, and Noelle shakes her parents' hands and samples a few lotions.

"Quinn, how's your summer?" Deb Kirschbaum asks. "We haven't seen your parents at temple lately."

Ugh, Jewish guilt. "Busy!" I chirp back. "Shockingly, a lot of people like getting married when it's nice out."

We're High Holidays Jews, and even then, if a holiday interferes with a wedding, the wedding takes precedence. Sometimes I wish we were more observant—maybe it's something I can explore in college. My parents were probably doing me a favor, bookmarking all those Hillel events for me.

"Take them some of these," Dave says, shoving some soaps and shampoos into my bag before I can protest. "Oh, and there's a Jewish bakery that opened at the market today. Their challah is . . . eh, so-so"—he wobbles his hand at this—"but the babka is to die for."

"I'll remember that," I say.

As we continue through the market, I catch Julia and Noelle flirting—a lingering glance when they think the other isn't looking, a playful nudge. And this is why I'm here: to make sure Julia feels comfortable enough to be herself around Noelle. To support my best friend.

Even if my mind keeps drifting to the one place it shouldn't.

When we've collected enough food to fill our canvas tote bags, we nab the last empty table at one end of the market. There are only two chairs, so I encourage Julia and Noelle to sit down while I awkwardly ask another table if they're using their chair, then drag it over. By the time I bite into a slice of chocolate babka, I feel I've well and truly earned it. God, I love Jewish pastries.

"Do you have an idea of what you might major in?" Noelle asks. "Julia and I were just talking about college."

"Business," I say automatically. "My parents are . . . kind of strict. They're wedding planners, and they're pretty set on me studying business and working for them when I graduate, like my sister."

Noelle grabs a handful of Rainier cherries. "But if you had the choice?"

"Ha. Great question. I'm not really sure." It's hard to know without having had the chance to explore. Even now I can't solidly land on a single thing I enjoy doing enough to major in, which gives me a whole lot of *who am I?* self-esteem feelings alongside my other daily anxieties.

Noelle nods. "I'm undecided, but I'm worried I won't know by the time we need to," she says. "The idea of picking something and sticking with it for four years is . . . daunting."

*Four years.* I can barely commit to a skin-care regimen. I'm not sure how to commit to a major.

"You liked math classes," Julia says to me. "And you got fours and fives on all your APs."

"Since when did this turn into career counseling?" I say, laughing. "But yes. I liked math classes. I liked history classes. I liked English classes. That's the problem, though—I *like* everything a decent amount, but I don't know if I really love anything. Except for Lady Edith Clawley." When Noelle raises her eyebrows at that, I add, "My cat."

"What about music?" Noelle uses a compostable knife to split a pesto pinwheel with Julia. "Am I stating the obvious here, or is there a reason you haven't considered it?"

"It hasn't been a hobby for me for a long time." It's easier than I thought it would be to admit this to her. Noelle has a very calming presence. "I've been playing for years, but it's been a while since I played for the fun of it. Lately, it's felt more like a job . . . which is, I realize, exactly what we're trying to figure out here. But I'm not ridiculous for wanting to *like* what I do with the rest of my life, right?"

"You're talking to the girl going to art school," Julia says. "So . . . no."

"I can't imagine studying something I'm not passionate about," Noelle puts in. "There's basically no guarantee of a job in *any* field these days, so why not spend all that time and all that money studying something that actually makes you happy?"

I steal a piece of pesto pastry from Julia. "What a novel concept."

"I took piano lessons for . . . eleven years?" Noelle continues. "Last year my teacher assigned me all these pieces for a recital because I'd been too busy to pick them myself, and then I was too busy to practice. And I realized that if it was something that mattered to me, I would have made time for it."

"If only I could quit," I say with a sigh. "But the harp isn't the problem, really. Harps aren't exactly in high demand. What my parents have always wanted is for my sister and me to join the business so they can expand it. And that's what my sister did, but I don't know how to tell them it isn't what I want. I know it sounds privileged, not wanting this ready-made career they're going to hand to me, but . . ."

"It's not your passion," Noelle finishes. "I get it."

We sip cups of cider and eat our fruit and bread and cheese in silence for a while, until Julia, who's been gazing at Noelle with doe eyes, blurts out, "So what do you think about Kristen Stewart?"

I choke on my cider. Julia throws me a panicked look, like she can't believe what she said either.

Noelle's brow furrows, like she's seriously considering the question. "Love her transformation. Respect her artistic choices."

"And she has great hair," I put in, trying to be helpful, and Julia kicks me under the table.

"She does." Noelle looks right at Julia. "Although your hair is pretty great too."

Julia looks like she might combust. "Mm-hmm," she squeaks out, and it's impossible for me to miss the subtle way they lean closer in their chairs.

This is what summer is supposed to feel like, and with a tug of my heart, I realize I'm not sure how many more days I'll have like this. How many more days I haven't already promised to my parents.

We spend another hour at the market before Noelle has to go to work. "So," she says as we sort our trash into the proper receptacles: compost, recycling, landfill. If you don't have all three, are you even in Seattle? "Do you guys want to do something like this again next week? I mean—I don't want to intrude if you already have plans, or—"

"Noelle, *stop*." I nudge her with my shoulder. "You are a fucking delight. Of course we want you here."

"What Quinn said," Julia adds.

She visibly exhales. "Okay. Excellent. Sorry. I have really bad social anxiety. Like . . . do you ever get home from hanging out with people and immediately start analyzing everything you did and convincing yourself all of it was completely wrong? I'm positive at any given time that eighty percent of my friends don't actually like me."

"Try ninety percent," I counter, and she laughs. "I have anxiety too. I take medication for it, actually, and I've been in therapy, too. I don't go as often anymore, but it helps."

Noelle nods like talking about therapy is the most normal thing in the world, and it should be. "Me too!" And she holds her hand out for a therapy high five. "I'm not even going to stress about how dorky it was to do a therapy high five."

"You're also not allowed to stress about whether we like you or not," Julia says. "That . . . should be pretty obvious."

"Not gonna lie, that's a huge relief. So I'll see you both next week?"

"Absolutely," Julia says.

When Noelle leaves, Julia lets out this long-suffering sigh and drops her head to my shoulder. I bite the inside of my cheek to keep from laughing and reach over to rub her back. The market is alive now, bustling with shoppers, local businesses propping up their doors to entice customers inside with the promise of air-conditioning.

"I really like her," Julia says softly. "It's not just that I want to hold her hand or make out with her, which I do. It's that I want to have long conversations with her and collect eggs from our chickens with her and go to fucking brunch with her. I don't even like brunch. Why is this so hard?"

"Julia Elizabeth Kirschbaum." I pull her forward so I can place two firm hands on her shoulders. "This is bad if you're bringing the chickens into it."

"She'd be so good with them. I can just tell." She shakes her head. "It's pointless, though. We're not going to be living in the same place in a few months. We'd have eight nice weeks of brunch, and then we'd go our separate ways. Fate is a cruel mistress."

"You're sabotaging yourself," I say. "Don't think about her leaving."

"I should have said something to her sooner," she says, "but school was always so busy. How does anyone manage to successfully date in high school?"

"No idea. All my dating took place in a car or on a couch without anyone's parents home."

Julia snorts. "So classy. That's my favorite thing about you. How classy you are."

"Classy like this?" I say, lifting a strand of her hair that's fallen out of its braid and making it into a mustache on my face.

"Yes, exactly like that. How am I going to survive without this level of sophistication next year?"

Her question wipes the smile off my face. I drop her hair, feeling like I've shrunk a good five inches.

"I can't even think about that right now," I say quietly.

Julia's expression turns serious too. "Whatever happens or doesn't happen with her . . . I'm glad you're here. I don't know if I could do any of this on my own."

"Funny," I say. "I was just thinking the same thing."

# 8

The zipper is stuck.

My zipper this time. I twist around to see it in the mirror, but I can't tug it loose. Regrets: I have them.

Last night, my parents got a call from one of the grooms after the rehearsal dinner. We were all watching *Perfect Match* in the living room and playing a game I made up during *Bachelor* marathons with Julia: I assigned each of us a popular phrase from the show, and we kept track of every time someone said it. So far Mom was winning with "this is an amazing journey," but I was close behind with "I could really see myself falling for him."

When Dad disappeared into the kitchen, I joked to Mom that it was because his phrase, "I know my husband is in this room," was losing, and she laughed and told me how much she was starting to love this game.

"That may or may not be because I'm winning," she said, tapping her nose like we were in on a secret.

This was my favorite version of my parents, open and natural and *fun*, something it seemed like they were often too stressed to have. I wanted to linger in it as long as I could.

Dad returned with a grim look on his face. A bridesmaid and groomsman had had too much to drink at dinner, and the grooms were worried about potentially having an odd number of couples in the bridal party.

"I did my best to assure Josh that there are plenty of ways the photographer can stage everyone, but he was adamant," Dad said.

Mom paused the TV. "Do they have anyone who can fill in?"

"I don't think we need to jump to that quite yet." Dad sank back down onto the couch. "I told him no one's going to be paying attention to how many bridesmaids and groomsmen are up there during the ceremony. And I was going to send them some photos of uneven wedding parties, but—"

"Is that really what they need to look at the night before their wedding?" Mom said. "If Josh wants an even number, we should be doing whatever we can to make that happen."

And just like that, the natural-fun feeling vanished. Edith jumped onto the couch next to me, as though sensing my anxiety spike.

"I'll do it!" I yelled, a little too loudly. Edith was so startled, she leaped right off the couch. "I mean, if they're still sick tomorrow and they can't find anyone else. I could fill in."

"Then I guess it's settled," Mom said, and I tried not to think about how quiet they were for the rest of the episode.

The bridesmaid and groomsman were only worse this morning. I believe "hungover AF" is the proper medical terminology. Josh and Graham were relieved when Mom presented me as the backup plan.

"We've taught you well. This is just what wedding planners have to do sometimes," Mom said as she handed me the dress, a taffeta A-line in a shade of lime that could not possibly be flattering on anyone. "We improvise."

And then she improvised herself into the kitchen, where she discovered Tarek was precisely the size of the missing groomsman.

Whoever I was in a past life really fucked things up for me.

It was perhaps not my most well-thought-out idea. *Anything to stop them from arguing*, I thought in the moment. I twist a little more, not enough to tear the dress, trying to grasp the teeth of the zipper, but it's no use. The grooms are outside, taking photos on the grounds of this weekend's winery, and the rest of the bridal party is waiting nearby. Tarek and I are supposed to join them as soon as we're done getting ready in our respective suites.

Meaning I have only one option for help.

I gather the skirt of the dress, clutching it to my chest to make sure I'm not in danger of losing a boob. I head out of my changing room, pausing in front of his. "Tarek?" I call out, knocking twice on the door.

"It's open," he calls back, so I turn the handle and step inside.

"Hey, could you help me zip—"

A shirtless Tarek is standing in the middle of the room, facing a mirror, his back to me.

He's wearing pants, thank god, but his back is all bronze skin and muscles that flex as he reaches to pull a crisp white shirt off a hanger. All I can focus on is the way his hair curls against the back of his neck, a patch of rough reddish skin beneath it. The curve of his spine. The dip of his lower back.

Then he turns around, and I have the briefest glimpse of his chest before I snap my gaze to the ceiling.

He did not look like this when we were in middle school.

"Shit shit shit I'm sorry!" I say, stumbling backward. My legs tangle in the skirt of the dress, and for a moment my life flashes before my eyes. I've had a good run, I suppose. There are worse ways to go than death by embarrassment at age eighteen. But by some miracle, I manage to neither drop the dress nor tear the fabric, though it's hanging dangerously low on my chest. "I thought 'it's open' meant you were decent!"

"Am I not?" His arms are through the sleeves now, but the shirt is still unbuttoned, leaving a long thin rectangle of skin for me to definitely not ogle. And yet he doesn't look embarrassed. There's the faintest smile nestled in one corner of his mouth, like he finds all of this amusing.

"Please avert your eyes while I get this dress back up and talk myself out of walking into Puget Sound."

He muffles a laugh as he turns around, giving me a chance to readjust.

"It's not funny," I insist.

"Okay, but it kind of is," he says, and fine, he's not wrong.

"Can you please just help me zip it up? That's why I came in here, for help with the zipper from hell."

"Sure." He walks over to stand behind me with his unbuttoned shirt, like we are two people casually getting ready for an event we did not learn we'd be part of only twenty minutes ago. "Oh—it's caught on the lace back here. Just a sec."

Then I feel the gentlest press of his fingertips on my back as he works at the zipper. That's the only part of him touching me, those few fingertips, and yet I am suddenly intensely aware of how close his body is to mine. We haven't been this physically close in a long time. I've never felt the heat of him like this, the warmth of his hands as he rests a palm and then a wrist an inch from my spine to steady his grip.

Last year's symptoms come rolling back, a tidal wave that flips my stomach and floods my brain until I'm wondering what would happen if he moved forward, closing the space between us. Or if I leaned back.

After Boatgate, I didn't hear from him for a few days. He was getting ready for school, I told myself, but I sensed an iciness in his silence. I didn't know whether he'd gone on that candlelit cruise by himself or whether Elisa had loved it and they'd been fused at the mouth all week and he didn't have the time for a goodbye. There was nothing on Instagram, which made the whole thing even more mysterious.

Still, the crush wouldn't let me go. I was this horrible combination of angry and heartsick. He'd hurt me, even if he hadn't meant to, and I'd done the same. And yet I still wanted him. It had gotten to the point where it was all I could focus on, a whirlpool of obsessive thoughts that sank me deep, deep. I had to let them out or they would drown me. Otherwise, if he went off to college and left me alone with those feelings, I'd only obsess more—over his texts, his social media, the constant mental replay of memories.

I couldn't do the kind of gesture he was so skilled at, but I could send an email. This was my running through the airport, my "meet me at the top of the Empire State Building," my kiss at the Eiffel Tower on New Year's Eve. The way his arm brushed mine when we rummaged through the kitchen for leftovers or the way his eyes sparked when he talked about his parents' love story, he made me think we could have the thing I'd grown more disillusioned with every summer. I didn't think I loved him—that word was too heavy. But if I was ever going to have the kind of romance he bundled into his grand gestures, I wanted it with him.

And he did not.

"Got it," he says in a low voice. Finally, and too soon at the same time. Logic intervenes: *he ignored you for a year.* Then he lifts my hair out of the way and zips the dress so slowly, his other hand anchored on my shoulder blade. "There."

"Thank you," I manage, letting out a long breath I hope will combat the dizziness.

He returns to the hanger with his jacket and tie. "That green is . . . a choice," he says as he loops the tie around his neck, and it lightens the mood a little.

"Ugh. I know." I bring my hands to my cheeks, hoping they cool down before the photos. "I'm starting to think your parents don't value you as part of the Mansour's operation. They sacrificed you to take me to urgent care after the mango incident, and now this?"

"Nah. They've got plenty of help today, and they love working with your parents. They want the wedding to run just as smoothly as yours do. Shall we?" he says after pinning a boutonniere to his lapel, turning to face the mirror.

I chance a look at our reflections. We match, the garish green of his tie and my dress. The wave of his hair and the swooshing thing my stomach is doing. "I suppose we shall."

I curse last night's impulsiveness one more time, and then I follow him outside.

• • •

The photographer poses us in a variety of ways: standing in a line, looking serious, then pretending to laugh, then walking a few steps before backing up and doing it again. The whole time, I'm radically aware of the guy next to me, my arm hooked through his. I try to ignore how much I don't dislike the way he looks in a tie. Most people look good in a tie. That's not exclusively a Tarek thing.

I've never thought of my back as a particularly sensitive area, but now I can't stop imagining his hands there. It makes me wonder how many girls he's touched like that. While his dating history is all over his Instagram, the flashiness interspersed with very obviously staged couple photos, I have no idea what he's done physically and with whom. Our conversations never got that personal. The thought makes me feverish, and I'm relieved when the photographer splits us up to take a few photos with just the bridesmaids, then just the groomsmen.

"All you have to do is look pretty," Mom says when she lines us up for the processional. "And *smile*." I've had plenty of practice.

"I'll make a weird face if you do," Tarek whispers to me before it's our turn.

"My mom would murder us."

"Okay, sure," he says, "but now you kind of want to do it, don't you?"

I pull my arm out of his to give him a gentle shove, but before I can, Mom is cueing us, and then I'm holding in a laugh as we make our way down the aisle. This is the Tarek who I was friends with what feels like ages ago.

I miss that version of him.

It's nerve-racking, everyone watching us as I wonder if the

dress is too short or too long or shows off more of my body than I'm comfortable with. When the grooms walk down the aisle together, the guests draw a collective breath, and I can't deny that I feel some of that energy too. If I wobble during the ceremony, it's only because my shoes are a half size too large.

During dinner, we make small talk with the other bridesmaids and groomsmen. They're all in their thirties, and while I can't relate to talk of mortgages and day care, I smile and nod when I'm supposed to.

Elisa's working this wedding, her first of the summer. I do my best to keep my anxiety at bay when she swings by our table and chats with Tarek about Mansour's and about her chemistry program at Seattle U. She's the only one able to make that caterer's uniform look chic, and her blond pixie cut is so cute, it almost makes me want to chop my hair again.

"So good to see you!" she says to me, leaning down for a hug, which I am not at all expecting, and I only barely manage to avoid flinging my braised kale salad onto her.

She and Tarek are friendly, not at all awkward. It makes me even more confused about what happened after I left the marina last year.

"My parents want me to help with dessert," Tarek says halfway through dinner, typing a message on his phone and sliding it back into his pocket. "You going to be okay here if I leave?"

"Only if you tell me what escrow is so I can have something to contribute to the conversation."

"Something to do with money."

"So helpful, thank you."

He gets to his feet. "See you," he says, dragging a hand along the back of my chair before he disappears into the kitchen.

When the cake is distributed and the dancing starts, though, I find I'm not exactly in the mood for either. Josh insists that I join them for dancing, but being out here alone doesn't feel right, and neither does the prolonged strangeness with Tarek. I played my role, but now it feels like I'm intruding, so as inconspicuously as I can, I push out of my chair and head inside.

I run into my dad in the winery's foyer. "Holding up okay?" he says.

"Barely. It's hard work being pretty."

He brushes imaginary lint from his sleeve. "Don't I know it."

"Anything I can help with?"

"You've done plenty," he says. "Just relax." He makes it sound like a big deal, but all I did was put on a dress and stand there. "We're on our way out, actually, so I was going to ask you the same question."

"I might join you."

"Before the dancing?" Tarek approaches us from the kitchen, a plate of cake in one hand. "That's a shame, because I was really looking forward to it."

"Stay," Dad urges before I can interpret Tarek's words. "Have fun."

Knowing Tarek wants me there must make me give in. After my dad leaves us in the foyer, I lift my eyebrows at Tarek. "Dancing?"

"What? You don't want to dance with me?"

I fight rolling my eyes. He can't keep pretending nothing's

wrong between us, even if part of me is nostalgic for the kids we used to be at weddings, who danced as though we didn't care what we looked like. I can't imagine being that unselfconscious now.

"You really want to dance? With all those strangers?"

"Might as well get our mileage out of these clothes," he says, and ugh, the pull of the nostalgia is too strong.

The dance floor isn't too crowded, and the breeze plays through Tarek's hair and lifts mine off the back of my neck. I give him my hand, and his other hand comes around my waist. If he was gentle when he zipped me up earlier, now he feels solid. Sturdy.

"Sorry about my hands," he says, looking down at the rough patches of skin between his fingers. "I've been . . . having some flare-ups."

There's some embarrassment in the way he won't meet my eyes, and it hurts my heart the way it used to when he stayed home from weddings as a kid. Eczema can be triggered by anxiety, and if that's the case with these flare-ups, I wonder what's been making him anxious. Even if we were close the way we used to be, I don't know if we were ever close enough for him to have told me.

"It's okay," I say, quick to reassure him.

The band is playing "L-O-V-E" by Nat King Cole, one of the few wedding songs I can tolerate. It also means I owe my dad ten bucks today. We begin to sway, first slightly out of rhythm with the song, and I have to force his feet to follow the beat.

"You're leading," he says.

"Someone has to."

Silence falls between us for a few moments, as though he's finally hearing the subtext in my words. "It might be a little overdue at this point," he says, "but . . . I think we probably need to talk."

I'm so stunned that I nearly drop his hand. "Yeah. We, um— we really should."

He shoves out a breath, and if I'm not mistaken, he looks genuinely apologetic. "I'm sorry, Quinn. For—for ignoring you all year. I can't help thinking this would be a lot more fun if you didn't find me despicable, which I can tell you do, so . . . there it is. It was shitty of me, and I'm owning up to it."

It takes a while for my mind to process his words. Enough time for the singer to spell out L-O. But this blatant admission of fault is not at all what I was expecting. Of course, I assumed his lack of response meant he didn't feel the same way. That I'd made things weird between us and now he wanted nothing to do with me. Tarek owning up to it isn't at all what I was expecting.

"Thank you. For saying that. It *was* shitty of you."

"Glad we can agree on something," he says.

The relief isn't immediate, though, and maybe it's because we still haven't talked about what led me to send that email in the first place. And the fact that I acted shitty too. Remembering how his face shattered that night at the marina is what compels me to make my own apology. "I'm sorry too. About the fight, and what I said about your past relationships. . . . I pushed things too far. I thought we were just kidding around, but . . . obviously not, since we stopped talking."

At least Tarek isn't asking me for a reason. I can't explain why I snapped at him without exposing a painful piece of my history.

On the other side of the dance floor, Elisa is balancing a stack of plates and laughing with Tarek's mom.

Tarek grimaces, but when he speaks again, he sounds nonchalant. "It's fine. I asked what you thought. You told me. I'm pretty sure that relationship wouldn't have worked out anyway," he says. "I was upset, but I should have emailed. I should have texted. I was—"

It's odd to hear him brush it off like this, but I guess we've both had a year of space. "Busy. I know."

"Right. College was just . . . more overwhelming than I thought it would be."

"In a good way, though?" I try to picture him there, attempting to cook in a college dorm, being infuriated by a hot plate. "I mean, you're going back, right?"

"I'm going back," he confirms, and it's not until we're both quiet for another chorus of the song that I realize he didn't answer my first question. And I'm not sure if it was on purpose.

I try to ignore the tiny part of me convinced this isn't the whole truth. I can accept that he's moved on from last year, but whatever the details of "overwhelming," he's clearly not ready to talk about them. Even if he handled this the wrong way—even if both of us did—I miss his friendship, too. I hate that he ignored me, but I hate even more not having my wedding ally.

"That email," I say, forcing a laugh. I have to make this clear if we have any chance of being friends again. If I brush it off, maybe it won't feel the way it did last summer: like he took the most breakable, honest parts of me with him to California. "I was probably just feeling weird about you leaving. I don't feel that way anymore. I swear. We're obviously going to have to work together this summer, and I don't want you to feel uncomfortable around

89

me because you think I'm hung up on you or anything. Whatever I felt, I'm one-hundred-percent over it. Over . . . you."

It was a good thing, in a way: his rejection confirmed my feelings about romance. Just like Corey did at Alyson Sawicki's party, with his assumption that I was someone to hook up with and nothing else. It can't sting if I won't let it—that's why I've always preferred the physical over the emotional.

I can pull my cynicism blanket tight around me again. It's cozy under here.

"Well . . . good," he says after a pause. "I'd hate to be uncomfortable. So . . . we can be friends again, then?"

"Friends," I agree. His palm on my back seems to grow less stiff, and he gives my hand a quick, friendly squeeze. Now the band is playing a jazzy, slowed-down version of "Livin' on a Prayer." "So, pal, what all do we have to catch up on?"

"I'm pretty much the same, bud. Chum. Compatriot?"

"Not true. You have a beard now. Or, like, stubble." I catch him blush, like he's embarrassed I'm pointing it out.

"Oh, that? That's called being too lazy to shave," he says. "And what about you? Your hair is different."

"I cut it at the beginning of senior year," I say. It was past my shoulders when he left for college. "It's a little grown out now."

"It suits you," he says, and I'm not entirely sure how to interpret that or whether it's a compliment, so I force my brain not to linger on it, which is a bit like forcing deep-fried butter to be healthy. We've fallen back into this rhythm so easily—I don't want to ruin it. "You and Julia, you're still close?"

"Of course. Even if the universe is intent on putting nearly three thousand miles between us next year, which, rude."

"UW's a good school, though."

It is. There is nothing wrong with it, except for my parents' fingerprints all over it. But Tarek doesn't know any of that. He never has. And it makes me instantly aware of the other things he doesn't know about: my OCD, or the medication I take every morning, or any of my past relationships. I've never been to his house and he's never been to mine. There's so much we've never talked about, never shared. We were friends, yes—but not the kind of friends I wanted to be.

I ask about his friends from high school, a couple guys I've heard about but never met. I ask if he's been to the Book Larder lately, a bookstore that specializes in cookbooks and is therefore Tarek's favorite bookstore, and he tells me it was his first stop. His face lights up as he talks about the new cookbooks he acquired, but I can't stop trying to reconcile two Tareks in my mind: the one I thought I knew and the one he's never showed me.

All I have to do is avoid silences. Any time there's a break in our conversation, I become hyperaware of his hand on my waist, the warmth of his skin through the fabric of this horrible green dress.

"They're a sweet couple," he says, nodding toward where the grooms are clutching each other, softly swaying. "Did you see Graham's face when he noticed Josh had taped a note to the bottom of his shoe? Wasn't that incredible?"

I did in fact see it, and I did not have the same reaction. "Oh no. Are we starting this back up again?" If we can laugh about it, maybe that means we're past what happened last year. Maybe we're back to bickering, which has always been so much easier.

"We have to," he says. "It's the only way for me to prove you're wrong."

I blink up at him, trying to seem as innocent as possible. "So college didn't change you at all. You're still the sappiest person I know."

His mouth twitches, his eyes bright. *This.* This is the Tarek I recognize. "While I don't take offense at the word 'sappy,' I prefer a word like . . . sentimental. Dare I say . . . *romantic.*" He says it with an overly cartoonish lift of his eyebrows, knowing how much I hate it.

"Having strangers in your wedding photos is extremely romantic. Can't argue with you there."

"It's not about the photos," he says. "It's about—okay, you see everyone here? They all came because they wanted to celebrate Josh and Graham."

"Or they wanted the free food."

"Such a cynic."

"Thank you."

"It breaks my heart, honestly, all the great things you can't appreciate. I still can't understand how you don't think the ending of *Sleepless in Seattle* is romantic," he says, resurrecting one of our old arguments.

Tarek used to beg me to watch his favorite movies, all romantic comedies, and I'd come back the next weekend with a scathing review. He'd just shake his head, and that was part of the fun too: how cute he looked when he was defending these things he loved. I never told him I thought I might like one of his movies if he'd watch it next to me, if we held hands, if I could rest my head on his shoulder.

"Because Meg Ryan is a stalker!" I say, a little too loudly, given the heads that swivel toward us. "And she breaks up with her fiancé because he has *allergies*! That movie is a blight on the city of Seattle."

"It wasn't stalking. It was *destiny*," he says. "And she and Walter weren't right for each other. She was only going along with what she was expected to do, and he was the kind of person she was expected to be with. She even says at the end of the movie that she doesn't deserve him."

"I agree, she doesn't!"

"Because she and Tom Hanks are meant to be!" Tarek's laughing now. He loves this bickering as much as I do. Or he used to, at least, and the way he leans forward, using my shoulder to muffle his laughter, indicates he probably still does. Maybe we really can slip back into our old friendship. I can feel the soft drumbeat vibrations of his laugh against the strap of my dress, a couple inches above my heart.

Tarek lifts his head from my shoulder as we move apart to clap for the band, and when they start their next song, something that doesn't sound familiar to me, he says, "I love this song," and reaches for me again.

"What is this?"

"Cat Power," he says, taking a break from mouthing the words. "'The Greatest.' This is good, but the original is better."

"I know Cat Power," I say, annoyed he recognized it and I didn't. "Just not this one. Most people go with 'Sea of Love.'" I give him my hand, slide my other up to his shoulder. He's much less stiff, but truthfully, he is a *terrible* dancer. "It's a shame your dancing hasn't improved."

"Then I guess it's up to you to make us look good." A questionable perk of working in the wedding industry—I could waltz with my eyes closed.

"Oh, I've been trying for the past fifteen minutes."

Another rumble of a laugh, and then we both go quiet again, and I try not to think about my family or college or how he smells like sugar or how, even with the sun on the verge of setting, his body heat is more than enough to keep me warm.

"You look nice, by the way." His mouth is close to my ear, as though, even with the noise all around us, he only wants me to hear. "Not sure if I mentioned that."

He definitely did not. My lizard brain would remember. He says this as a little aside, a parenthetical. *By the way.* Like he didn't spend countless minutes analyzing it beforehand. God, that new college confidence. Even if it was "overwhelming," it really did change him.

"I wish I could say the same about you," I say, reaching down to his tie and smoothing out a wrinkle, intensely aware that mere millimeters separate my hand from his chest. "Chartreuse isn't your color, I'm afraid."

"Somehow I'll live." He straightens, putting more space between his lips and my ear. "Some of the waiters and I were going to hang out after this. Do you . . . want to come? Since we're friends again and all?"

"Yeah," I find myself saying. "Okay. That could be fun."

The bandleader takes the microphone. "Ladies and gentlemen, if you'd please clear the dance floor, it's time for the bouquet toss."

Tarek's hand drops from my waist, leaving a phantom pressure behind.

# 9

I t's almost midnight, and my parents took the MTRMNY-mobile home hours ago. I changed out of the bridesmaid dress Josh insisted I keep and lingered in the kitchen, offering help where I could, though Tarek's parents assured me they had it all under control.

When the Mansours dismiss us, I pile into a car with Tarek and Harun, his cousin and one of his closest friends; Stella, an Asian girl with a vine tattoo twisting up her forearm; Bryce, a white guy I'm pretty sure has been high his whole shift; and Elisa. Most of them, I've seen at past weddings, but since Mansour's has a rotating staff, I didn't know Stella or Bryce by name until five minutes ago. They're all in college, either locally or home for the summer.

"Everyone good back there?" Elisa asks from the driver's seat.

I'm squeezed in the back between Tarek and Stella, trying my best to keep my distance from Tarek without climbing into Stella's lap.

"Perfect," I squeak as we hit a speed bump that presses my thigh against Tarek's. He's half in his caterer's uniform he changed back into, half in regular clothes, his shirt unbuttoned all the way and revealing a T-shirt with a band name I can't read from this angle. I'm trying to remember the last time I saw him in short sleeves, which makes me think back to walking in on him changing, which then makes me unable to think about anything else. Cool cool cool. Love those intrusive thoughts.

"Your cake was a hit," Stella says. "People kept asking me if I could sneak them an extra slice."

"Your cake?" I repeat.

Tarek scratches at the back of his neck. "I, uh, made the wedding cake," he says. "Well—I made the cake batter and my mom made the frosting and then assembled the whole thing. That's about as much control as my parents will relinquish. I didn't want to seem like I was bragging about it."

"That is one-hundred-percent something you should brag about," I say, impressed. "That's incredible."

"It was," Elisa says emphatically. "That cake tastes the way an orgasm feels."

"Exactly what I was going for," Tarek says, and for a moment I'm stunned by the effortlessness of this exchange between them. I cannot imagine even whispering the word "orgasm." Maybe if you've had one with someone, it gets easier to talk about. Maybe Tarek and Elisa hooked up at the end of last summer, gave each other heaps of toe-curling orgasms, and then cordially parted ways.

"That was why I left. I wanted to serve it." Tarek tilts his head toward me. "Did you like it?"

"I didn't get a chance to try it. I'm sorry." And I really am, though the word "orgasm" is still pinging around my brain. "It looked great, though."

"Next time," he says, but there's an odd uncertainty in his voice, like maybe he doesn't think there will be a next time. "I had to beg my parents to let me help out with this one."

We end up at Golden Gardens, a beach in Ballard ten minutes from my micro-hood of Crown Hill. Stella and Bryce run ahead to claim a firepit while the rest of us unload beach supplies from Elisa's car. They managed to steal a couple bottles of wine and champagne.

"I always put them in here at the beginning of summer, just in case," Elisa says as we root around her trunk for some blankets and towels, a cooler filled with off-brand LaCroix, and a stack of cups. At the winery, Elisa changed into something more casual; she's in jeans and a T-shirt with an image of a beaker telling a test tube, YOU'RE OVERREACTING.

Even in my all-black wedding-planner outfit, I feel overdressed for the beach. Still, I am determined to use this night to prove that Tarek and I can be friends again. He was the best part of my summers, and for so long, I was devastated he might not be part of this one. Now that he's here, it's not just that I need an ally at work, a buffer between my parents and me—it's that I want a friend, whether it's the friendship we used to have or something entirely new.

It takes a few attempts to get the fire going as we position ourselves on blankets around the pit. Harun pours champagne into a plastic cup and takes a swig. "I'm always surprised when there's alcohol left," he says, passing it to Stella. "I feel like they usually underestimate how hammered their guests want to get."

"They didn't even splurge on the good stuff?" Stella peers at the label. "I don't know if you can legally call this champagne."

"Hopefully that just means we'll get wasted faster," Bryce says.

"I've seen worse," I volunteer. "We had an open bar a few years ago that the couple stocked with only Manischewitz and Two Buck Chuck. There was almost a riot."

"See, I bet you have the best wedding stories," Elisa says. "While the most exciting thing that's ever happened to me was getting vomited on by a bride."

Since she's driving, Elisa declines, and when it's my turn, I pour only a small amount into my cup before passing it to Tarek, whose eyes meet mine over the lip of the bottle. Now that we're not pressed against each other in the back seat of a car, I can see his shirt says SHARON VAN ETTEN, a musician I like too. Maybe I'll ask him about her later, since Tarek and I are friends again and that is a friendly kind of question.

"Anyone up for Never Have I Ever?" Stella says. "Harun and Elisa have been here the longest—well, aside from Tarek, who was basically born into this. But I only started working here a few weeks ago."

"Team bonding!" Elisa says. "I'm game."

"As long as we don't corrupt my baby cousin," Harun says.

"You're only two years older than me."

"Two and a *half*."

We start by holding up ten fingers, taking a sip and putting one down each time we've done something. I should have known that with college kids, a game like this was bound to turn sexual *immediately*. The first round is innocent: declarations about school, work, awkward moments from childhood. "Never have I ever . . . hard-core embarrassed myself in public," Elisa says.

Tarek takes a long drink without missing a beat. "Worth it, though."

"You and your grand gestures," Elisa says with a shake of her head, and I search her words for subtext. There's no way she'd be so cavalier about this if she turned him down at the marina. At least, I don't think so.

"I maintain that the only embarrassing one was the flash mob," Tarek says proudly. "Because we all know I can't dance. Everything else, I was running on pure adrenaline."

"They're so sweet," Stella says. "The most a guy's ever done for me was ask me to prom by writing it out on a pepperoni pizza. And he got hungry on the way over, so technically he asked me to POM."

"Sure, it's sweet, but if he doesn't get at least a hundred likes within an hour, he deletes the post," Harun says.

"I absolutely do not." Tarek folds his arms across his chest. "One hundred and fifty."

Everyone laughs at this, and when I try to, it sounds more like a croak.

When it's Stella's turn, she gives the rest of us a wicked grin and says, "Never have I ever had sex in the shower."

It feels like a tremendous relief that Tarek doesn't take a sip.

Harun's turn. "Never have I ever . . . jerked off while stuck in traffic. But I've definitely thought about it."

Elisa raises her faux-Croix-filled cup high and takes a sip. "I was stuck on I-5 between Tacoma and Olympia, and no one was moving." She shrugs. "I was bored."

Bryce takes a sip too, and Stella's mouth drops open. "Bryce Terpstra, you did not," she says. "Where did you even put it when you were done?"

Elisa holds up a hand. "I don't want to know."

My face grows warm, a side effect of the champagne combined

with talking about something I'm not uncomfortable doing—though I've never done it in a car—but not entirely comfortable talking about. I can't decide if I want to be able to say I've done any of these things or if I'm content telling the truth. And what either of those impulses says about me.

It's not that I'm worried about them judging me—it's that Tarek is sitting next to me, and the idea of him knowing something this intimate feels contrary to the friendship I'm trying to resurrect. We're not there yet, and this isn't where I want to start.

As if he can sense my uncertainty, he taps my leg with his cup, drawing my gaze to him. "You okay?" he asks in a low voice. With a thumb, he scratches at his forearm, wrinkling the fabric of his catering shirt.

The firelight hangs on to the angles of his face. The curve of his brow. The cut of his jaw. Everyone must realize how lovely their friends look in the light of a firepit on a beach at midnight. It's one of the hallmarks of friendship, I'm pretty sure.

"Yep. Great." And then it's my turn. "Never have I ever . . . cheated on a test." Everyone groans at that, and I tell myself I don't mind.

"She's in high school." Elisa reaches across Tarek to pat my knee. "She hasn't been inducted into R-rated Never Have I Ever."

I'm sure she doesn't mean to be offensive, but along with the knee pat, it feels ten times more patronizing than anyone who's marveled at how young I am to be playing the harp. My parents have treated me like an adult since I was twelve. To them, I am a colleague. An employee. I've always felt mature for my age, relished the compliments when my parents' friends doled them out. At least, they always felt like compliments.

Now I'm wondering if maybe they weren't.

"Never have I ever . . . had sex in public," Bryce says, and Tarek lifts his cup to his mouth, gives this sheepish smile, and takes a sip.

The champagne in my stomach stages a revolt.

Elisa tips her cup to him. "Lucky girl."

"In my defense, it was late at night on her apartment rooftop after prom, and almost no one had access to it," he says. "And it was over very, very quickly."

Bryce shoves his arm. "Really selling yourself, buddy."

Okay. *Breathe.* Tarek has had sex. So have I. Clearly we are not the kids we once were. Tarek has had sex on an apartment rooftop and maybe other places too. He had this whole mystery year in college too—who knows what else happened.

After prom. That means it had to have been with Alejandra Agustín, the girl who had gourmet snacks waiting for her in every class period. They were together for a few months, about as long as most of his relationships. He posted photos with her at least every week, and they never looked real: the two of them on a playground, a silhouette of their linked hands, Tarek kissing Alejandra's cheek while she closed her eyes. And the parade of likes below each one. Part of me must have separated the gestures and the performative photos from real physical intimacy, even the kind that's over "very, very quickly."

Jesus, this game is dangerous.

"Never have I ever had sex in public" turns into "sex with anyone else here," which no one drinks to. Harun throws his hands up and says, "Just wanted to know!" This discredits my heaps-of-orgasms theory, but I guess they could be lying. Next is "sex in a

101

car," which sparks a debate about whether it's the same thing as "sex in public" and gives me an opportunity to take my first sip in two rounds.

Stella claps my shoulder, like she's proud of me, and when Tarek's eyes meet mine for a brief moment, I look away fast, as anxiety and regret war for control of my brain. I have to fight the urge to qualify my statement. It wasn't hot. It wasn't sexy. We were in the parking lot of a Denny's that closed a couple years ago, and if there's anything less sexy than a Denny's, it's an abandoned Denny's. And what happened in the back seat was not a Grand Slam.

I felt wanted for only a few minutes before it felt almost compulsory, this thing to get over with so both of us could check something off a list. So both of us could take a sip during Never Have I Ever.

"This shit is strong," Harun says, and wow he is right. "We should call it. Who has the most fingers left?"

"Gotta be Quinn," Bryce says. On a related note, he becomes my least favorite of the group. "She drank, what, three times?"

"Four," I say in a small voice, wagging my remaining six fingers, and I am declared the winner.

Turns out, it's not the kind of game you feel awesome about winning.

Lady Edith meows from my bed as I tiptoe into my room and gently shut the door behind me.

"I know, I know, it's late," I whisper, kicking off my shoes and sliding onto the bed next to her, reaching out a hand to scratch her head. "Not that I don't appreciate it, but you didn't have to wait up for me."

Her purr lifts some of the weight from my shoulders as I swap my slacks and blouse for a T-shirt and pajama shorts and rub a makeup remover wipe over my face. I smell like a campfire, but I'm too exhausted to shower right now. As I slide between my sheets, I realize I'm not quite ready for sleep. All my cells are on alert, like I'm back at the beach and waiting for the next question. My mind trips over what I learned about Tarek, what he learned about me, and then I'm entirely too charged to fall asleep.

So I pick up my phone and do something reckless.

I call him.

"Hello?" Tarek says when he picks up after three rings, voice thick with sleep. "Quinn? Is everything okay?"

*Shit shit shit.* Why the fuck did I call him? "Yeah, all good," I chirp back, too high-pitched to my own ears.

"It's"—a pause—"after two a.m."

"Sorry." I wince, even though he can't see me. Edith gives me her most judgmental look. "I—um. Couldn't sleep."

"I could read you one of my Philosophy 101 textbooks."

"Please," I say, but then I hear the soft creak of bedsprings, like he's about to do that exact thing. "Wait—I was kidding."

"Oh."

"That was, um. Fun tonight," I say. "Fun" isn't the right word. Dancing at the wedding, that was fun. But what happened on the beach . . .

"Was it?" he asks. Maybe he feels just as unsettled about it as I do.

"I don't know. I felt a little . . . young. Like I was crashing some big-kid party."

"You weren't," he insists. "I assure you, you don't suddenly become an adult as soon as you eat in a dorm cafeteria or get your first pair of shower shoes."

"My parents have treated me like an adult for years," I say. "And I guess I got it in my head that I had all this maturity. But . . . I clearly don't."

It just slips out. I wasn't planning on talking about it, least of all to him. I thought he'd tell me good night and hang up, leaving me in the dark with my uncertainties and swirly thoughts. This conversation is a nice surprise.

"There are probably a thousand ways to be mature other than those game questions."

"I know," I say. "I'm just not in the habit of talking about any of that. My parents' sex talk was basically 'This is a condom, always use one, any questions?'"

"Ah." More rustling on his end of the line, and I wonder if he's sitting up in bed now. "Did I ever tell you what my parents' sex talk was like?"

"You did not."

"I need to preface this by saying that when I was little, I really wanted a brother or sister. I was ten, and my parents sat me down at the kitchen table and gave what I'm sure was a very comprehensive, age-appropriate speech, then encouraged me to ask any questions I had. I told them I completely understood, but that it would be super helpful to have a visual aid. So"—he breaks off, muffling a laugh—"I politely informed them that they could go make me a sibling, I could watch, and then I'd know exactly how it was done."

"Well, sure. You were just trying to be thorough."

"They proceeded to tell all their friends about it for the next five years of my life. They still bring it up at parties sometimes."

Now we're both laughing. We've never talked like this, and the mere fact that we're talking again is something I'm still processing.

"Why are we talking about this?" I say. "This is so embarrassing."

"Maybe because we're *friends*." He singsongs the last word, breaking it into two pieces. "Wait. I don't want you to get in trouble for waking anyone up."

"I won't. I'm up in the tower."

"The tower," he says thoughtfully. "Right, how could I forget? The first time I met you, you said, 'I'm Quinn and I live in a castle.'"

"I can't imagine introducing myself any other way."

"I always wanted to see it," he says, and I might be imagining it, willing it into existence, but the weight of his suggestion hangs between us for several long moments.

"Well, let me give you the grand tour." Before I can overthink it, I'm finger-combing my hair and switching the call over to video, and after a few more seconds, there he is, a little fuzzy in the dim lamplight. His hair is sleep mussed, his T-shirt rumpled, and he's wearing glasses I've never seen before, a pair of simple black frames. I didn't even know he wore contacts. It's the first time I've seen him in a T-shirt in a very long time. There's this sense of coziness, like I could slip through the phone and fall asleep right there in his bed.

"All right," he says, a smile curving his lips. It's a really good smile. "I'm ready. Are those llamas on your shorts?"

"Or alpacas. I've never been sure." I turn the phone on my cat, who's glaring at us from the foot of my bed. "This is Lady Edith

Clawley, my cat daughter. She hates everyone but me." Then I tilt it toward my closet. "This is where I keep all my very boring dresses to wear while playing the harp." I rise from the bed and gesture to the other side of the closet with a flourish. "And these are my more exciting ones for the rest of the time."

Then I show him my desk, where Maxine Otto's business card is sticking out from beneath my mouse pad. Emerald City Harps. I'll recycle it tomorrow, I decide. Once I look her up and know for certain what Emerald City Harps actually does.

"What's that red box?" he asks.

"Oh." I pick it up, shifting it so he can see the label. "Microwavable chocolate mug cakes. I'm addicted. I have to keep them up here or everyone else will steal them."

His disdain is palpable even over the phone. "You know, that kind of thing isn't hard to make from scratch. It would probably taste a hell of a lot better too."

"But I like processed sugars!" I turn over the box and scan the ingredients list. "I like hydrogenated palm kernel oil!"

He just shakes his head, and there is something so endearing about his dessert snobbery.

I show him the painting of Edith that Julia made for me in her freshman-year art class, the one with Edith's head on the body of an eighteenth-century French aristocrat. The shelf filled with books I want to read but haven't had the time for. The floorboard that squeaks when you put any amount of weight on it. I think about showing him the strip of photos of us in my nightstand drawer but ultimately decide not to. I don't want him to think I hung on to them for any reason other than nostalgia.

Lastly, I turn the phone back to my bed. "And here's where I make ill-advised phone calls in the middle of the night."

When he laughs, it's this low, dangerous scrape of a sound. This whole thing suddenly feels wildly intimate, Tarek in his bed as I climb back into mine, his eyes heavy-lidded and his voice crackling in my ear.

"I like your castle," he says, and I don't bother fighting a smile.

Part of me wants to ask him for a tour too, but I'm not sure what that reciprocity would suggest. "It's late," I say, catching sight of the time. "Well, later. I have to be up early for a consultation with my parents."

"The wedding business never sleeps."

"Even if I must. Night, Tarek. And, um—thank you. For talking." I don't know why I feel compelled to thank him. Maybe because I woke him up, and I want him to know how much I appreciate this, how committed I am to our rekindled friendship.

"Thank you for the tour. Good night, Quinn," he says, and when we hang up, my face warm and my heart pounding, I feel even more electric than before.

# 10

t's still a little long," Victoria says as she steps out of the dressing room, holding the hem of her gown. "I'd prefer not to fall flat on my face in front of thousands of viewers. The internet doesn't need any more GIFs of me."

The saleswoman charges forward with pins and measuring tape while I endure the quiet shame of having used one of those GIFs.

At first I was anxious to meet Victoria. On TV, she was Victoria H. because there had been two Victorias the previous season, when the lead picked Victoria B. over her. Her long dark hair was straightened and shiny, her skin flawless, her clothes and makeup designed to bring out the blue in her eyes. In real life, she wears her hair curly, prefers glasses to contacts, and uses only a little mascara. I thought she'd be pristine, airbrushed. But what struck me the most was that she just looked . . . like a regular person.

I reach for a glass of complimentary champagne as Mom lifts her eyebrows at me in an expression that says, *Maybe you get away with this at home, but are you really going to pull this in public?* This is not the version of my mother who played along with the *Perfect Match* cliché game.

Grumbling, I set it back down and sink into the plush cream couch. I'm wearing my most professional and least comfortable business-casual attire: itchy gray pencil skirt, sheer blue blouse, fitted black blazer. This pencil skirt was clearly not made for someone with hips. When I walk, I have to take very small steps. Fantasizing about the perfect yellow sundress in my closet is the only thing getting me through this.

"This must be so boring for you," Victoria says as the saleswoman pins the hem of her dress. "How many dress fittings have you gone to?"

Mom isn't even exaggerating when she says, "I don't know, a few hundred?" We don't go dress shopping or to fittings with everyone, but Victoria and Lincoln are getting the white-glove treatment.

Victoria lets out a low whistle. "And it doesn't get old after a while?"

"You clearly don't know Shayna Berkowitz," I say.

"Every bride is a different puzzle to solve. She might have something in mind that's completely different from what her mom envisioned, or she might try on what she thought would be her dream dress only to discover it's not right at all. Besides, I always love having my daughter here." She nudges me, and I smile as if on cue. "We're lucky that this is something we can do as a family."

My smile is only half real. I wish I weren't torn between enjoying this time with my mom and worrying about my own future. I guess not talking about things that make us uncomfortable runs in the family too.

"I love that," Victoria says. "You must be so mature for your age, if you're already helping out like this."

"Right," I say. *So mature for your age.* Have I ever had another choice?

Victoria's maid of honor, Hannah, is browsing through a display next to the dressing room. "Are you still on the fence about a veil? Because this one is all kinds of amazing." She produces a birdcage veil, a vintage style made from white netting.

Victoria examines it. "I don't hate it," she says. "But I don't know if a veil is really *me*." I wonder what makes someone a veil person.

"To veil or not to veil," Mom says. "Statement veils have been big for a while, but a lot of modern brides go without. It's entirely dependent on your comfort level. When you imagine yourself at the altar, do you see Lincoln lifting a veil?"

Before Victoria can answer, my phone buzzes in my bag, and because we are all quietly and significantly assessing the veil, it is *loud*.

Mom's head whips in my direction, her eyes daggers.

"Sorry, sorry," I say, scrambling to turn it off.

The saleswoman takes the birdcage veil and affixes it atop Victoria's head, a look that makes me feel as though we've stepped back in time a half century.

"You know, I do love that." Mom gets up from the couch and stands behind Victoria, making a minor adjustment to the veil. "I had this thought, though, that a hair comb might look even more striking with your dark hair. Maybe something with pearls, something similarly vintage looking?"

"I have the perfect thing." The saleswoman disappears for a moment before returning with exactly what my mom was looking for.

Mom holds out her hand, taking charge, and tucks it into

Victoria's hair as she creates a makeshift updo. "Especially if you had them twist your hair on one side, a little like this?"

"That's gorgeous," Hannah says, eyes wide.

"This," Victoria breathes. "Yes. This is it."

"You've barely seen it!" Mom motions for Victoria to turn so she can properly appreciate her wedding magic in the mirror.

"I can just feel it."

My phone lets out another loud buzz.

"Sorry! I swear I turned it off. Must have hit the wrong button." It's as though my hands have turned to butter because I—can't—grasp it. My mom is going to be pissed later. I genuinely like Victoria, and I prefer she doesn't think I'm a kid who can't follow basic instructions.

Just as I'm fiddling with it, it starts ringing. In this moment, I regret picking "The Imperial March" as a ringtone, but I couldn't think of anything else to express how I feel about talking on the phone.

"You know we keep our phones on silent when we're with a client," Mom mutters to me. I'd point out that this rhymes and therefore would make a great slogan—*Borrowed + Blue: our phones are on silent when we're with a client!*—but I fear she may not appreciate it.

"Is everything okay?" Victoria asks.

"I promise, we don't usually have our phones on during meetings like this." Mom lifts her shoulders as though to say, *Kids, amirite?*

"No, I meant with whatever was going on." She nods at my phone. "It sounds like it might be important."

Another text, and I chance a look down to see it's from Julia.
"I don't mind," Victoria says. "Go ahead."

"Sorry, sorry," I keep saying, opening up my conversation with Julia.

**Julia:**  SOS

**Julia:** I'm at Noelle's work and I thought it would be idk, busy?? But I'm the only one here and it's awkward and I need backup PLEASE QUINN I'M 👶

**Julia:** I finished my blueberry muffin and god help me I might get another one just so I can have something else to do

**Julia:** I got a scone instead and it was much chalkier than I was expecting it to be? Are scones always this hard? Anyway I choked a little and Noelle was concerned and I didn't want her to think she was complicit in my death by selling me a faulty scone so I told her it was delicious and then accidentally bought another one

"It's my best friend," I say, muffling a laugh. "Romance troubles."

"Ah," Victoria says. "I remember it well. It was torture not to be able to talk to Hannah during the show."

"As soon as she got her phone back, I must have gotten . . . what, thirty texts in a row?" Hannah says.

"Closer to fifty." Victoria turns back to me. "If you need to go, I totally understand."

"Really? I mean, she could use the help, but I don't want to run out on you. . . ." I look to Mom, who's half frowning, seemingly torn between Victoria's wishes and her own.

"Of course," she says. "I can finish up here."

*Freedom.*

"Excuse us for a moment," Mom says, and walks me to the door. Something bad is coming. I can feel it. "I don't want to nag you, but you've got to make sure your phone is on silent next time. We don't want anyone to think for a moment they don't have our full attention. You know better than that."

*You know better. You're so mature.*

Now I'm wondering if maybe those compliments took something away from me. Not anything dramatic, like my entire childhood, but the ability to try things out. To fail. To venture out on my own, not as one-fourth of the B+B Berkowitzes but as *Quinn*.

But if I were just Quinn, if I somehow managed to leave weddings in the past, I might feel as lonely as I did during the worst six months of my life.

I can't go back there.

"I promise," I tell her, "it won't happen again."

"You're saving my life," Julia whispers when I get to the coffee shop, a cozy spot in Wallingford with exactly two people in it: Julia and Noelle. "Oh, and don't get a scone."

"Wasn't planning on it. Hey, Noelle!" I say, approaching the counter.

"Hey," she says. "Job interview?"

"I—oh. No." I stare down at my outfit, the skirt seams probably working overtime to keep my thighs trapped. I'll have to save that perfect summer dress for another day. "I was at a dress fitting."

"Did you ever watch *Perfect Match*? Quinn's family is doing Victoria and Lincoln's wedding," Julia says.

"Seriously? I loved that show," Noelle says. "Not enough queer couples, but then again, isn't that always the problem with reality TV?"

"Agreed," Julia says.

"What are they like in real life?"

"Victoria's . . . pretty normal, actually. Nice. Funny." I order an iced mocha, and while Noelle busies herself making it, Julia leans in close.

"Thank you. Thank you so much. I owe you."

I wave this off. "Please. You can just paint me another portrait of Edith wearing people clothes."

"Here you go!" Noelle chirps. Before we turn to go back to Julia's table, Noelle says, "Wait. Um. There's this movie I was thinking of seeing tonight. Julia, remember when you mentioned that documentary about the artist who painted those murals in San Francisco using only paint made from fruits and vegetables? It's playing at the Uptown."

Julia lights up. "I'd love to."

"I have plans!" I say quickly, not wanting them to think I'd intrude when this is clearly a date. "But you guys should definitely go."

The two of them coordinate from there. Julia looks thrilled, and I'm happy for her, even if it means I'll be coming home to an empty house.

Not for the first time, I wish Asher still lived here. The fifteen minutes between my house and her apartment sometimes feel like fifty, but I text her when I get home anyway, asking if she's free tonight.

At least I don't have to hope for too long. Her response comes back in half a minute.

**Asher:** Sorry, Gabe had tickets to Avenue Q

**Asher:** I'll see if he can get extras next time!

Sighing, I tell her to have a good time as I climb the stairs to the tower. If she were here, there would at least be someone to keep me from making any additional Bad Decisions with Boys. Because the first thing I do when I get up to my room is scroll through my thread with Tarek.

Since our late-night phone call, we've been texting again. Our messages are one step above small talk, very peppy, like we haven't reached the point in our new friendship where we're able to share anything that doesn't paint us in the best light. It doesn't feel quite like the friendship we had before, not yet. But it's good to have an ally. Anything else I felt while we were dancing was likely just my horny, overanxious imagination.

I haven't checked his social media in a while. Even after unblocking Instagram, I was making myself sick, scouring his updates for clues, wondering if he'd fallen for someone and they were laughing at my email together. Waiting for him to post a couple photo and bracing for it to destroy me.

Tonight, though, I allow myself to indulge in two things that might not be great for me: a microwavable mug cake and a little light stalking. There are a few more photos from the second half of his freshman year, photos from parties, including one he must have hosted, given the number of pastries it looks like he baked. It does something to my heart, seeing this kind of pure Tarek behavior. There are strangers commenting on how much they loved them, and here is this whole other mystery life he had.

I scroll back farther, back to his perfectly Instagrammable relationships. Bright colors and sunsets and Seattle landmarks. I didn't meet any of his girlfriends, never saw them together any-where but on this screen. Safiya and Chloe and Paige and Rooftop Sex Alejandra. They're all cute and smiley and evidently loved Tarek's over-the-top displays. Further proof he and I wouldn't work—not last year and not now, and yet no matter how fiercely I try to convince myself of this, I can't get him out of my head.

*You didn't matter enough for him to spend five minutes answering your email,* I tell myself.

And because I'm still deep in my self-hating spiral, I navigate over to Gmail. The words might as well be tattooed on my frontal lobe at this point.

**Subject: Good luck at college!!**
Dear Tarek,
Am I emailing you because I'm too much of a coward

to say this in real life? Quite possibly. If I'm being honest, though, even this feels pretty terrifying.

I hope what I said the other day didn't go too far. This summer has been a lot of fun. You've been the only thing keeping me sane at these weddings, and I can't tell you how much I need that sometimes. More than that, though . . . I'm just going to say it, because I'm not sure how else to do this: I like you.

Not just in a friend way, or in an our-parents-are-friends way, or in a semi-coworker way.

The other way.

So, there it is. It's entirely possible I'll regret this tomorrow, but for now I'm going to hit send and try not to overthink it.

College is going to be incredible, and I'm so excited for you. I can't wait to see you when you come home.

—Quinn

Dear Lord. Now that I've had distance from it, the last line sounds like a threat.

I close the lid of my laptop, only to find Maxine Otto's business card staring back at me. Ugh. Okay. I have to figure out what it is, and then I can get rid of it. At least it'll fight my aimlessness. It's not that I want to feel for someone the way Julia feels for Noelle—it's that I want *something* in my life that feels right. Something where I'm not counting down the minutes until it's over.

Googling Emerald City Harps brings me to a sparse landing page with the same phone number as the business card. The tagline: *Custom-built harps in the Pacific Northwest.* So she's a harp builder. Not what I expected, and if only because I'm desperate for a distraction, I search Maxine's name next.

This time I'm stunned by what comes up. There are thousands of results. Videos, links to albums, professional reviews. An article from a harp magazine called *The Folk Harp Journal*, musing on when she'll return to performing. She's even on Spotify, both with original music and for playing the harp on the soundtrack of a popular fantasy show.

I click one of the YouTube links, the description letting me know it was filmed at an international harp festival in Australia in 2004. There's a younger version of the woman who approached me at the wedding, her hair a more natural-looking blond. She rocks forward and backward along with the harp, focused on the instrument and not the audience. Her hands are swift, her movements occasionally harsh as she hits the strings with black-painted nails.

She's not smiling. She doesn't look peaceful, serene, soft—none of the words I've always associated with the harp. And something about that makes it impossible to tear my eyes away.

In the past, I've gone down YouTube rabbit holes, looking for harp versions of the classical pieces couples have requested. Harp YouTube is not a place I expected to find trolls, and yet there they were. I remember one video of a woman in a heavy coat and fingerless gloves playing the harp in the snow, no skin exposed except her face and fingertips, followed by comments like *try it topless* and *wonder what else she can do with those hands*. Part of it was just trash people on the internet, but the other was the realization that a girl playing this instrument might always garner that kind of attention.

When the video ends, I watch another, one where Maxine duets with another harpist. Of course I know harps aren't used only for weddings, that it's not only old ladies and baby angels who play them, but I've never heard them sound like *this*, wild and feral and *furious*. It's been a while since I cared enough to look.

Maybe it's the pressure from my parents. Maybe it's the loneliness of this weekday summer evening, my inability to grasp anything with the kind of certainty that seems to come so easily to my friends and family. Maybe it's pure curiosity.

Whatever it is, it compels me to take a few calming breaths and make my second spontaneous call of the week, which, given I'm usually too shy to order pizza, is a real accomplishment. Somehow, I get the feeling Maxine is someone who would prefer a phone call over an email.

"Hello?" says the voice on the other end.

If you are calling someone for the first time, they should be legally obligated to make sure you have the right number by confirming who they are when they pick up.

"Hi. I'm calling for Maxine Otto?" I say, cursing the question in my voice.

"Yes?" she says, sounding impatient.

I close my eyes, let out a deep breath, consider pretending to be a telemarketer and asking if she has a few minutes for a survey about her current cable provider. "My name is Quinn Berkowitz. I, um, played the harp at a wedding you were at last weekend, and . . ." It sounds ridiculous to say that I googled her and loved what I heard. "You gave me your card," I finish.

I expect her voice to change a little, but she sounds as stern as ever when she says, "I remember. It's good to hear from you."

"I watched a few of your videos. I've never seen the harp played like that before. And I saw that you build harps, and, well, I'm slightly ashamed to admit I don't really know much about it, despite having been playing for most of my life."

I don't know how else to explain it: that I feel completely lost? That harp doesn't make sense to me, not fully, but neither does anything else in my life? That the last time I felt deeply in love with something was when I talked my grandma into learning a Katy Perry cover so we could play it together, and that was six years ago? And that I'd do anything to get some of that back?

I'm surprised to hear Maxine laugh a little, like maybe that stiff exterior is softening. "Most of those are pretty old, but thank you. You're welcome to come by the workshop. It's usually open by appointment only. Are you available later this week, sometime in the morning?"

I check my wedding calendar. "I could do Thursday."

"Excellent," she says. "Come by around ten? And don't ring the doorbell—the dogs get scared."

"I'll remember that. Thanks."

And for the first time all summer, I feel something a little like *optimism* spark to life in my chest.

# 11

Maxine's house is located near the northernmost tip of Lake Washington in a Seattle suburb with more space than any of the tightly packed homes in my neighborhood. It's a one-story with a sprawling lawn and BEWARE OF DOG signs tacked up all along the fence.

We have two cars, the van and an ancient Honda we share, which I took today. I park in Maxine's driveway next to an old white van not unlike our MTRMNY-mobile, relieved when my brain lets me go after locking it once. A couple years ago, during a bad OCD week, I walked back and forth from the car to the doors of a grocery store about a dozen times because I couldn't be sure it was locked. I'd just gotten my license, and I was terrified of something bad happening to the car. I kept hitting the lock button on my key fob and the car kept honking. And yet every time I put the keys in my pocket, I worried they'd brushed the wrong way against my hand or the fabric and accidentally unlocked the car. Cue unbreakable cycle.

"Wow, you think it's locked?" a middle-aged guy asked me as he walked by.

*I have a mental illness,* I wanted to yell at him, but instead I dipped my head in shame. That was the worst part of my OCD:

when it made other people think I was doing something on purpose just to disrupt their lives.

I was only able to sneak out today because my parents left early for a venue tour in Skagit County, which gives me about three hours before I have to meet them back at home for a new-client consult. Going to see someone who insulted my playing must make me a masochist, but god help me, I'm curious. Worst-case scenario, I end up with a weird story to tell Julia.

And maybe Tarek, too, who's taken to texting me things like, good morning, friend! and you working this weekend, pal? The first time, it was sweet. After that, though . . . It's hard to explain. I *want* to be friends. I really do. But I can't shake the feeling that he's overcompensating for our shaky start this summer. It's jarring, this emphasis on our new friendship. Hopefully I'll gain some clarity at this weekend's wedding.

With a healthy amount of trepidation, I lift my hand to the door and knock as quietly as I can. It doesn't matter—the chorus of barking starts up right away. There's so much barking that I can't tell how many dogs I should beware.

I'm debating turning around and running for my life when the door opens, revealing Maxine in a worn pair of jeans, her white-blond hair tucked back with a headband. I regret my clothing choice: my wedding planner black slacks and shirt. I'd wanted to look more professional. Older, even. The opposite of what I usually want on my days off.

I'm expecting German shepherds the size of horses, huskies built like polar bears. Instead, there's a tiny corgi army held back by a gate, five of them yapping away. It's clear now that the barks belonged to small dogs; they're just so *loud*. I'm too used to Edith, whose sole act of aggression is a lazy swipe of her paw if you scratch the one-inch area on her belly she doesn't like.

"Sorry about them," she says, tossing a treat over the gate, where they descend on it like furry piranhas. "They're good dogs. They just get a little overexcited."

"With those signs, I thought . . ."

"My daughter gave them to me a while back. She thought it would be hilarious."

Maxine's aesthetic seems to be corgis and woodworking. There are a few harps in her living room, along with a wall of guitars in various sizes. I scour the walls for family photos, deeply curious about this woman. There are a couple with a boy and a girl in graduation gowns, a handful of dog photos. It's probably because I'm in the wedding business that I look for a ring on Maxine's hand and don't see one, which of course could mean any number of things, not least of which that she simply doesn't like rings.

She closes the door behind me, and the barking finally starts to subside. "I'm glad you could make it. Hopefully you didn't have any trouble finding the place?" She's warmer here than she was at the wedding or on the phone.

I shake my head. "Thanks for having me. Should I, um, take off my shoes, or keep them on or . . . ?" The awkwardness, it is strong today.

"You'll want to keep them on. Let's go out to the workshop."

She unlatches the gate for her dogs, and they paw at my legs before following her through the kitchen and outside. The workshop is a separate building out back, a brightly lit space filled with machinery, the walls lined with chisels and saws I can't begin to guess the names of and some half-finished projects on a counter in the middle. And that earthy scent of wood, a scent I realize I like quite a bit.

"This is—wow." I take a few uncertain steps forward. I'm worried about accidentally stepping somewhere I shouldn't, but the dogs don't have the same concern, chasing each other around the workshop like they've done this a hundred times before. One of the corgis, a black-and-white one, plops down near a stool and starts grooming. "All of this is for building harps?"

She nods and grins at me, her first one. "I've been doing this for almost twenty years, so some of the machines are newer than others. I imagine it looks like a lot, but there aren't very many of us in this business. Fewer than thirty in the United States, and not all of them are consistently turning out instruments."

"How long does it take to make one?"

"For me? About two and a half months. I used to be faster, but I've been . . . working on my own for a while." There's an odd pause there, one I can't interpret. "I have multiple harps in progress at a time, and I can make around thirty-five in a year."

Two and a half months. I knew it was an intricate instrument, but it's been a while since I thought about the artistry and craftsmanship behind it.

Maxine tells me she has her own production method that speeds up the process, a set of patterns that standardizes each piece she makes. Then she runs through the equipment in the workshop: the various saws and sanders, a shaper, a joiner. In the back of the shop there's a spray booth, where the harps are lacquered.

She strings and tunes them in a studio back in her house, where she takes me next. A row of harps in different colors, some of them fully stringed and some still waiting. Cherrywood, mahogany, koa. One of them with a mother-of-pearl inlay on the front of the pillar, the longest column that's farthest from you when you're playing. All of them bear a tiny silver plaque with what must be Maxine's logo, a trio of leaves with the letters *ECH*.

"They're gorgeous," I say, stating the obvious. "I'd practice every day if I had something like this."

"That's what some people think. If I just had this expensive instrument, I'd become a virtuoso. I've seen too many people buy pricey harps for children, or for themselves when they're just starting out. It isn't my business to tell them it's a bad idea, necessarily, but I do try to steer them toward something less expensive."

Almost like wedding planning. My parents have had to talk couples down from dream venues, dream bands, dream dresses when they were out of their budget.

"And you're going to sell all of these?"

"Ideally." She runs a hand along a harp's neck, as though erasing an invisible blemish. "I go to conferences a couple times a year, and I have some regular clients. It's not the kind of thing where you get a lot of walk-in customers."

"I'm guessing you didn't give me your card so you could try to sell me something," I say, even though it was my initial assumption.

"That wasn't my intention, no."

But she doesn't elaborate, and maybe that's okay because my fingers are itchy. The silky sheen of the lacquered finish, the smell of the wood, all these beautiful instruments—they're messing with my head in the best possible way.

Maxine explains that all of these are lever harps, also called Celtic harps, while I've only played a pedal harp. With a lever harp, each of thirty-four strings goes through a lever at the top, along the neck, and those levers are used to change the key. My Lyon & Healy has seven pedals at its base, one for each note. So the A pedal raises all the A strings to a sharp or lowers them to a flat, and so on.

"A lever harp gives you a little more control. You might find playing it is actually easier." She gestures to the row of harps. "You want to give it a try? Which one speaks to you?"

There's a cherry one at the end I haven't been able to stop staring at, so I inch closer, run a hand along its brand-new strings. "This one, I think."

"The instrument chooses the musician," she says. "Some people claim the sound is the most important part of a harp, but the look and the feel are important too. Well—you must know that, with all the weddings."

"My harp has been in many, many wedding photos." Most of the time, the couples standing moodily in front of it look like they're a generic indie folk band posing for their album cover.

What I also learn, once she encourages me to sit down, is that a lever harp isn't nearly as heavy. There's a new intimacy with the instrument as I tilt it back, letting my inner thigh bear most of its weight.

I run my hand along the levers, flipping a few back and forth, testing their flexibility. "I might be terrible."

"You play beautifully. I wouldn't have asked you here if I didn't believe that," she says. "When I watch someone, I'm always paying attention to their hands. Yours are never resting. They're always in motion, anticipating the next note. There's this energy there that I don't always see."

"Thank you," I say. "I honestly thought you were casting a spell on me, so that's great to know."

She snorts at that, and it's such an un-Maxine-like sound, at least based on what I know about her so far, that it drags a smile out of me. It's not something I've allowed myself to think about for a while: that what I do is anything special. It's been a job. An obligation.

Maybe it doesn't have to be.

She encourages me to play anything I want. Most of the pieces I know are classical, not exactly toe-tappers. Since it might as well be written into my DNA at this point, I launch into Pachelbel's Canon. I mess around with the levers, flipping the ones I need to get into the key of D. The smaller, lighter harp is a bit of an adjustment, but Maxine's right; it's a relatively simple one. The string tension isn't as tight, and I'm playing too strongly at first, but I manage to figure it out.

The whole time, Maxine is watching with her arms crossed, serving me that look she did at the wedding.

"What?" I ask, a little irritated. I wasn't *that* bad. At least, I don't think so.

"That was . . . safe," she says. Very much not a compliment. "You didn't have any lever changes in the middle of it. That's where it gets really tricky. Do you only play classical pieces?"

Just like that, I'm knocked off my high horse. "I play at weddings. Most couples aren't requesting death metal."

"What about when you're not performing?"

If that isn't the million-dollar question. "It's been a while since I played on my own, except when I'm learning a new piece for a wedding. Which, yes, is usually classical. My grandma helped me learn a couple fun songs when I was younger. All of it came more easily back then. When weddings were still exciting."

"You lost interest." It's matter-of-fact, the way she says it, and she's not wrong.

"A little."

"And yet here you are."

I shift the cherry harp back into its upright position. Maybe this was a bad idea. The harp, Maxine Otto, her workshop—none of this is going to fix my problems. It was absurd to think it might. "Thank you for doing this, but I should probably get going."

"The way you play," Maxine continues, as though she hasn't heard me, or more accurately, doesn't care, "your body is very stiff. Your hands are doing the work—*all* the work. You need to allow yourself to really feel the music with the rest of your body."

"I know that," I insist, though it's been a long time since I felt anything with my whole body, if I'm being honest. "Do you still play? I didn't see any recent videos online, so . . ."

"Occasionally. I don't perform as much as I used to." She sits down at the black lacquered harp next to mine, her hands moving along the strings with ease, like she could play the harp and recite Shakespeare at the same time. "I guess I've grown accustomed to working on my own these days. My kids used to help out. They'd sand, or they'd help with the stringing once the instruments were lacquered. But they live out of state now, with their own families, their own jobs." A pause. "Their own lives."

There's a wistfulness to the way she says it. I think about the house, the photos of her kids, and something clicks.

I think Maxine is lonely.

I watch her demonstrate the kind of fluidity she asserted I don't have. "Do you see how this is different?" she says. "Even the levers—I incorporate the changing of them into the choreography."

And I do.

I see it.

"If you ever need someone to help out for a few hours a week or something . . ." It's only when the words are out of my mouth that I realize the idea of leaving here and never coming back is going to make me wonder whether it really happened. A fairy tale in which a mysterious woman has devoted her life to an instrument I haven't cared about in years.

I don't have to be the poised, perfect harpist. The girl who always says yes, who always smiles. There's so much to learn about this thing I thought I'd mastered, and I'm realizing how ridiculous it was to think that at age eighteen, I was an expert in something Maxine has devoted her life to.

"It's a lot of sanding," Maxine says, almost as though she's discouraging me. But there's a smile nestled in one corner of her mouth. Like maybe this is what she wanted the whole time. "A lot of tuning. It's not the most thrilling of work, and I wouldn't be able to pay much above minimum wage. And I know you have obligations with your family. I don't want this to take you away from that."

I hadn't even conceptualized this being something I could be paid for. "It wouldn't," I rush to say. I'll make sure of that.

My parents wouldn't love that I'm here, and that makes it feel like a small act of rebellion. I'm positive this isn't a B+B-approved recreational activity, given that I can't play this kind of music during a processional. This would only distract from their forever goal: *nothing less than our best.*

But what if my best isn't the same as theirs?

"Then we just might be able to work something out. And next time?" she says, gesturing to where the entire back of my pants is covered with sawdust. "Don't wear black."

# 12

A wedding at sea probably sounds romantic. Shimmering water, a sapphire sky, city lights glittering in the distance. The reality: a wedding at sea on the hottest night of the summer is an absolute nightmare.

It's a second marriage for both the bride and groom, who chartered a luxury yacht to take them around Lake Union, and while my parents have done a few of these floating weddings, it's a first for me. Fortunately, Asher's here and I'm not playing the harp.

The ceremony itself takes place on the deck of the yacht. Mom and Dad are armed with sunglasses and sunscreen, and it's not so windy that it messes with any of the flowers we tied around the railing. It's all going smoothly until Dad runs out of the tiny sunscreen bottles he keeps in his emergency kit and learns Mom doesn't have any in hers, despite the conversation they had two weeks ago about making sure they remain adequately stocked throughout the summer.

"I thought we triple-checked everything last night," he says. "You're the one who orders these in bulk every year."

Mom unzips one last pocket and sticks her hand inside. "It must have slipped my mind somehow. Trust me, I don't want everyone walking around looking like lobsters."

"But it would make for some interesting photos, especially with the boat," Dad says, and the two of them burst out laughing.

That's . . . odd. I'm not sure how they went from admonishment to laughter in under a minute, but I seize my chance to intervene. "I'll go check if Asher has some." And thank god, she does.

Now that the newly married couple is taking photos outside and their guests are inside mingling with cocktails and hors d'oeuvres, it is a veritable sauna. I'm grateful we're only doing apps and dessert. Jackets and pashminas and even pantyhose are abandoned, shoes kicked off. People are fanning themselves, toting around bottles of water instead of the specialty drink designed for the occasion, while I keep busy fetching more water and opening as many windows as I can. My bangs are sticking to my forehead, and I've accumulated a frightening amount of underboob sweat.

An older woman flags me down. "Excuse me? It's a little warm in here. Would you be able to do anything about that?"

"Working on it," I say through gritted teeth.

As I'm struggling with another window, I spot Asher leaning against the railing, her face a concerning shade of gray. I abandon the window and head outside. "You okay?" I ask.

With her head pressed to the railing, she throws out an arm and sticks her thumb up. "I'm not seasick," she says. "I promise. I'm great. I'm . . . *sea*-perb. I'm ex-sea-ptional."

I rub her shoulders. "I don't know if I should be more worried about your health or your wordplay skills. Let me see if they have any ginger ale?"

"Love you," she calls as I slip back inside.

The yacht company has their own catering staff, but since my parents hadn't worked with them before, they brought on a few Mansour's cater-waiters: Tarek, Harun, Elisa. The kitchen—I think it's called a galley—is toward the back of the boat, a small space with stainless-steel countertops and appliances.

When I enter, Tarek and Elisa are laughing at something, standing close together, and I must have a touch of seasickness too because it sparks a strange feeling in my belly. Not jealousy. Definitely not. A major dose of *what the hell happened between them last summer*, but not jealousy.

It's the first time I've seen Tarek since our late-night call last week. The sleeves of his shirt are rolled to his forearms, exposing a bit of angry red skin. I can't imagine how warm he must be in that stiff, starched shirt.

"Hey," I say, feeling a little like I'm intruding.

They turn to face me. "Hey!" Tarek says, and I want to believe the enthusiasm is genuine, that he's not forcing his eyes to light up when they land on me. Even last year, he was never this happy-go-lucky guy—unless he was telling me about one of his grand gestures. "How's it going out there?"

"Asher's a little seasick. Could I get a can of ginger ale?"

"Oh no, poor girl," Elisa says. She opens a cooler and digs around inside before tossing me a green can. "Here you go. I hope she feels better."

I thank her and turn to leave, but Tarek catches me, hurrying over to where I'm standing in the doorway. "Quinn, wait a sec." Now his brows are drawn together in concern. He plants a hand on the wall next to me, leans down so that only I can hear him. "Are *you* okay? You seem a little . . ." He trails off, as though he doesn't know me well enough to understand what mood this is.

The truth is, he doesn't.

"I'm fine. I have to get this to my sister." I tighten my hand around the cool aluminum and make my way back to Asher.

She lifts the can to me in cheers before taking a sip. We watch the couple and the photographer, my mom supervising while my dad helps the DJ with the sound system.

"They look so happy," Asher says. "I love second marriages. Well, I don't love whatever bad shit led to the end of the first marriage, if that was the case, but couples like this, they always seem the happiest to me. They tend to know exactly what they want, and they just seem so *sure* of everything."

For a moment I want to confide in her about Tarek, get some of that sisterly wisdom, but I'm not sure I can put it into words for myself. Somehow I doubt she's had enough of this particular experience to counsel me through it.

Even if she had, we've seen so little of each other lately. I'd have too much to fill her in on.

"Hi, um—you're with the wedding planners, right?" a red-headed guy in a tux is asking me. He's the bride's son, about my age, his face full of freckles. "We have a slight problem with the cake." He runs a sheepish hand along the back of his neck. "Apparently there was an issue with one of the fridges, the main issue being that it wasn't working, and the cake is kind of . . ."

"Melting," fills in the girl next to him, laying a hand on his shoulder. She's in a lilac dress with a sweetheart neckline. "One whole side of it is melting."

"We can fix this," I assure them. Or at least, Tarek can. Another reason to go talk to my new best friend.

I lead them back into the kitchen, where Tarek is finishing off another tray of appetizers. We open up the fridge, and there's the saddest cake I've ever seen. It's falling into itself on one side, the chocolate pooling in the plastic beneath it. The leaning tower of pastry.

Tarek examines it, and the two guests lean forward, waiting for his verdict.

"Chocolate and heat do not get along," he says. "I can fix it, but it's not going to look the same as the cake they thought they were getting. I think the best thing we can do is scrape off the frosting that's left, take the layers apart, and try to re-form them before re-frosting it. Quinn, your mom has bamboo skewers in her emergency kit, right?"

I nod and slip out to grab some. When I return, he gives me this big smile.

"Thanks, friend," he says, and it's the heartiest thank-you I've heard in a long time, like I've saved him from toppling overboard instead of handing him a few sticks of bamboo. The word "friend" might as well be Edith's claws on a chalkboard. This isn't the Tarek I talked to at two in the morning, his hair rumpled, his voice soft like a secret.

This is a performance, and I'm not sure if he's doing it for his benefit or for mine.

When it becomes clear that this is going to take a while, I turn to the couple. "I'm Quinn, by the way," I say. "And this is Tarek."

"Rowan," says the girl, and the guy whose mother just got

married introduces himself as Neil. I'm not sure how long he and Rowan have been together, but they can't seem to stop touching each other. Even now, she has a pinkie tucked into his pants pocket.

"Are you guys in college?" I ask.

"Just finished freshman year," Neil says. "We're home for the summer."

"Ah, so there *is* life after high school."

"Barely," Rowan says, and Neil gives her a playful nudge. In her heels, she's taller than he is. "It's very grim."

"The wedding was beautiful." I think back to what Asher said. "I haven't seen a couple that happy in a while."

Neil and Rowan exchange a look. "It took a lot to get here," he says, and I get the sense there's a deeper story there, one that isn't the kind you tell during a first conversation with someone.

Tarek deconstructs and reconstructs the cake, stealing some berries from the hors d'oeuvres and adding them to the top. By the time it's finished, I'm not sure I'd have ever known its sordid past.

"Voilà," he says. "Franken-cake."

"Thank you so much," Neil says. "Truly. I know there's no such thing as perfect, but I really wanted this to be as close to it as possible for my mom."

That emotion tugs at the place in my heart I thought had hardened to weddings. We've dealt with so many nightmare families; it's refreshing to see the earnestness with which he speaks about his mom.

Rowan brushes her long bangs out of the way and leans closer to inspect it. "You know, I think this looks better."

Tarek blushes a little at that, but I refuse to let myself think it's cute. I can't let those feelings get in the way of whatever we restarted last week. Even if I'm no longer sure how to be friends with Tarek or what that's supposed to look like when he seems to be injected with the same kind of pep I thought my parents had trademarked.

More than ever, I'm worried we're resurrecting a friendship that was never as grand as I made it out to be.

The sun goes down, and outside, the temperature drops. Slightly.

The bride and groom don't seem to notice the cake isn't precisely the one they ordered, and now that the dancing's begun, my only job is to supervise. Wait and see if anyone needs anything.

For a couple of songs, I watch Rowan and Neil. Sometimes they dance wild, and sometimes they dance close, his hand fitting into the hollow of her lower back, her head on his shoulder. Then he dances with a smaller red-haired girl who must be his sister, which is adorable. His mom, Joelle, and her new husband, Christopher, won't stop grinning at each other. *It took a lot to get here*, Neil had said. I'm glad they made it.

Tarek is standing across from me near another open window. Any other time, I'd go talk to him, make up a game, ask for extra food. But tonight . . . I'm not sure what to say. That might make me a bad friend, but he's just going to have to deal with it until I figure things out.

"Hey." I turn to see Rowan next to me. "Stating the obvious, I know, but *wow* is it boiling in here."

"I was actually just thinking about getting some fresh air."

"I might join you," she says, and together we head to the

upper deck, where one person is playing a game on their phone and another couple is gazing out at the water. The breeze is not insignificant, but after emerging from the lower-deck sweatbox, I welcome it.

The sky is dotted with stars, and Rowan tilts her head upward, exhales a dreamy sigh. "Romantic," she says, more to herself than to me.

"Is it?" I ask, and it's not meant to sound as combative as it does. Shit—I'm not her friend, even if it felt that way for a moment down there during the great cake rescue. I'm supposed to be a professional. "I mean, sorry, I shouldn't have said that. It's a wedding! Joelle is your . . . ?"

"Boyfriend's mom," Rowan says, filling in what I already suspected. "We've been together for a little over a year now."

"You guys are really cute." Even I can admit there's something sweet about the way they interact.

"Thank you," she says. "We started dating right after high school, and then we were going to different colleges. I was worried about doing long-distance, but we made it work. We'd see each other on weekends when we could, talk almost every night on the phone. And then there was the, um, creative texting." She blushes a little at that, which convinces me even more that she's someone I could be friends with.

"What's your major?"

"English. Creative writing, actually."

"Did you always know you wanted to do that?"

"Sort of. I had to allow myself to want it, despite the judgment I knew I was going to get from other people. You're starting college in September?" When I nod, she asks, "Any idea what you're going to study, or are you completely sick of that question?"

I almost laugh. I haven't been asked that question in a long time. I glance around, make sure no one up here can overhear us. "I can tell you what my parents want me to study."

"I get the impression that's different from what you want."

"If only I knew what that was."

"This seems like the time for me to give you some sage advice"—Rowan leans against the railing, shivering as the wind lifts the hem of her dress—"that I feel entirely ill-equipped to give. Follow your heart? Shoot for the moon? Life is what happens while you're busy making other plans? I don't know if I have anything that wasn't used on a motivational poster from the nineties."

"Honestly?" I tell her. "It's just good to tell someone."

We watch the water in silence for a while, and it *is* good, I realize. I haven't felt anywhere near this peaceful in a while, and it reminds me of how I felt at Maxine's shop earlier this week. There, I made a decision. I told her what I wanted, even when it scared me.

With a jolt, I realize that's what I have to do with Tarek: tell him I want a real and honest friendship. That I need to understand why we're still so far away from it.

Even if the tiniest part of me wouldn't be opposed to doing deeply unfriendly things to his mouth.

A figure approaches from the staircase, the moonlight catching his red hair. "Cold?" Neil asks Rowan, and she scrunches her face at him. He laughs and passes her his jacket. "Brought it up for you." He tucks it over her shoulders, then uses the lapels to draw her close for a kiss.

Maybe it is romantic up here, the sea and the stars and the soft rocking of the boat below.

"I'll leave you two," I say, stepping back. "Have a great rest of your night. I really am happy for your mom." And I mean it.

# 13

I descend back into sweaty boat hell, weaving around wedding guests, heading for Tarek on wobbly legs.

"Can I talk to you?" I ask. "Somewhere private?"

A furrow of his brow, like this doesn't compute with his new idea of our friendship. "Sure. Everything okay?"

"Yeah, I just—yeah." I take a moment to collect myself as he leads me downstairs, into what turns out to be a laundry room. The noise from above-deck is mostly muffled in here, and though it's tiny, I guess it'll have to do.

"You're kind of freaking me out," he says, leaning back against a washing machine. "You know you can talk to me, right? I want to be a good friend to you, and—"

"This," I interrupt. "This is what I'm talking about. This insistence that we're suddenly *such* good friends."

"But . . ." And here he looks genuinely confused. "Sorry, I don't understand. I thought we were friends again."

"We were. We are." I wonder how many times we can utter the word "friend" before it ceases to have meaning. "But you don't need to constantly remind me of that. Calling me 'friend,' 'pal,' all this enthusiasm . . . It isn't you."

Unless it's his way of keeping me firmly in friend territory to stave off any latent feelings I might have for him. To remind me that's what I am.

"Maybe college changed me." Now he's talking to the floor as the boat sways us back and forth. If I look anywhere near as grotesque as I feel, with my clothes sticking to me in all kinds of uncomfortable places, I don't blame him.

I shove a strand of hair out of my face, though all I want to do is hide behind it. "That email I sent you. That thing we're not talking about, or the thing we're talking about without actually talking about it. I put it all out there. And I don't just do that. Like . . . ever. And maybe we'll have this great, fun summer together as *friends* and then you'll go to California again at the end of it, and we won't talk for another year."

"That's not going to happen."

"You don't know what it was like, being ignored like that for a whole *year*. I know what I said about that boat gesture, about your relationships, wasn't my finest hour. But was it so awful that you didn't want to be friends with me anymore? Because we could have talked about it. All you had to do was tell me. Whatever it was that happened last year, it hurt me, too. I felt terrible for *months*." I try to meet his eyes, willing him to look at me. "But I also don't want to push you if this isn't something you're comfortable talking about."

Finally, he faces me. It's unfair that the heat has turned me into a sweat-monster and made him somehow look . . . better? What the hell. The darkest tendrils of hair closest to his head are damp, and his tie is loose, wrinkled, like it's had a rough night too. What's changed the most, though, is his expression. The cut of his jaw is sharper, his brows twin thick slashes.

"And yet here you are, pushing me." This annoyance is the most real he's been all day.

"Because I don't know what else to do!" I say, his annoyance rubbing off on me. "Being friends again, sure, it's awesome in theory. But I don't know how to be friends with someone who's still holding so much back. Which makes me wonder if we were ever that close to begin with."

"Did it ever occur to you," he says, "that maybe the reason I'm holding back isn't about you at all? That it's not about the fight or that boat gesture? Which I didn't even fully go through with after you left, by the way. You were right. It *was* pretty fucking ridiculous."

"Of course that occurred to me." There's not nearly enough space in here. I'm suffocating. "I assume it's not about me, or you would've had the decency to send me a text longer than four fucking words all year. And—I didn't realize you hadn't gone through with it. I couldn't tell, since you and Elisa are still . . . close."

"Elisa?" He sounds perplexed. "Elisa Dawson? What does Elisa have to do with any of this?"

"A not-insignificant amount!" I force myself to take a few too-shallow breaths. "I see you laughing with her and the other waiters, or her telling you that your cake is like—like an orgasm, and I'm just—" I break off, regretting my word choice, even though I was only borrowing hers. "I'm just wondering who the real Tarek actually is, because I sure as hell don't think I'm seeing it."

"Are you *jealous*?" He takes a step closer, curiosity quirking his mouth. Still upset, but now there's amusement mixed in.

I can't decide how I feel about it. I press my feet firmly into the floor, wishing it didn't feel as rocky down here. "No," I say in a small, unconvincing voice. A lift of his eyebrows confirms he knows I'm bluffing. "Fine. Maybe I am a little jealous. I'm jealous because you and I used to have that. And now what we have—it's *weird*, Tarek, and I don't like it. I don't like it at all."

At that his eyes turn to steel. He lets out a half laugh, like he knows this isn't funny, but he's so frustrated that he doesn't know what else to do. "You want to know why I didn't answer your email, Quinn? It's not because of the fight, or the email. It's because I nearly flunked out of school."

"You . . . what?"

"I wanted to write you back. I was going to. I swear. But I knew it wasn't the kind of thing I could dash off in a few minutes. I—I wanted to take my time with it." He exhales deeply, as though letting go of the anger, and what's underneath is a vulnerability I've never seen from him. His shoulders droop as he shrinks back against a washing machine. "But the time . . . It kept slipping away from me. I would get so tired, and then I'd wake up and all I'd want to do was go back to sleep. I slept through a couple of classes, and I thought, 'It's okay, I'm adjusting.' Then I slept through a couple more—a full week. And there were all these events for freshmen, and I couldn't bring myself to go out to any of them."

Tarek alone in his dorm room is nothing like how I imagined him spending this past year. It's staggering, how wrong I was.

"Sometimes, going downstairs to the dorm cafeteria felt impossible," he says. "Even getting up to take a shower—the idea of leaving my bed, forcing myself down the hallway . . . It was overwhelming. I—" He swallows hard, like maybe he's regretting telling me all of this. "I've had this kind of thing happen before. But I was usually so busy, and my parents would be there to keep me on track, keep me working, that I was always able to snap out of it. But this time I couldn't snap out of it. The reading kept piling up. I kept missing classes. I'd avoid calls from my parents, and the couple times I did pick up, I'd lie to them, tell them everything was going great. I didn't even go back for Thanksgiving, told them I had to work on a big project. My roommate finally asked me if I'd gone to see a campus counselor. Said they'd helped him out with some of his own mental health stuff."

He scrapes a hand across his stubbled jaw, and now I am picturing a different kind of stubble that grows in after days spent in bed. I'm relieved he keeps talking—both relieved and heart-achy—because I still have no idea what to say.

"It took failing two midterms—one because I didn't go and the other because of course I hadn't studied—to get me to make that trek across campus to see a counselor. When I got there, they gave me this questionnaire . . . this depression questionnaire. And at first I thought it was almost comical, because what do I have to be depressed about? My parents are great, and I'm healthy, except for all the times I couldn't get out of bed, but I was certain there wasn't anything physically wrong with me. And I was in college, where I was supposed to be having the time of my life. But I remember filling it out and thinking I had just about every symptom on the list, and having a name for it . . . It felt like finding something I hadn't known was missing. Clinical depression. That's what it was." He twists his mouth to one side, a sort of half frown. "Well—what it *is*. Since it doesn't just go away."

He's letting me into a place I've wanted to go for so long, except what's going on inside is more serious than I could have imagined.

"Tarek," I say, regretting those horrible things I said. All that selfishness. "I had no idea. I'm so, so sorry. I'm sorry for pushing you, and I'm sorry you were dealing with this."

He gives a slight nod of acknowledgment, but I can tell he isn't done. "I think I've probably had it for a while. It wasn't sudden, but I noticed it a lot more when I was on my own. It gave the depression time to fully take control, I guess. I hadn't had a major depressive episode—that's what the counselor called it—like that before. So I started seeing that counselor regularly, and I saw a doctor, who prescribed some antidepressants, and it wasn't an immediate fix. I still had some fucking awful days. But little by little, I was able to function again. I went to class. I had to beg some of my professors for extra credit, for makeup assignments, for second and third chances. That was the beginning of December. I managed to get my grades back up to Cs, so I passed, but my GPA was shot. I finally told my parents when I was in Seattle for winter break, and they didn't want to let me go back at first. I made a deal with them—I'd make a B average in every class, or I'd come home. And I did it. I worked my ass off the next semester, and I did it. And now . . . now I'm feeling a lot better. I have a therapist here, too, and I'm not *cured* or anything, but for now I feel okay."

I try to process all of this as the boat rocks us back and forth, the softest ocean lullaby.

"I'm sorry," I say again. "You—you could've told me. I would've listened. If that's what you needed."

"I should have done a lot of things. I should have told my parents. I should have gotten help earlier. But I was so *embarrassed* at first. I was terrified of my parents finding out and wanting me to move back home. And part of me was worried there wasn't a name for what I was going through and I was always going to be that way." Slowly, I see the weight of this unhunch his shoulders, straighten his posture. "You're the first person I've told. Well, besides my parents."

Another thing I'm not sure how to respond to, except with gratitude. I was a jerk, and yet he still confided in me. If he were anyone else, I'd ask if I could hug him, but I'm not sure what we are at the present moment. I'm not sure if we hug.

So instead, I reach forward, brushing his hand with a few fingertips. A brief touch to let him know this meant something to me, too. He glances up when I touch him, his eyes full of an emotion I'm not sure I've seen before, and there's an intensity there that makes me drop my hand.

"Thank you for telling me. And I'm so glad you figured out you don't have to feel that way." I sag back against the wall before barreling forward with my own confession. If we have any chance at a friendship, he needs to know I'm in this too. That I can be vulnerable. That I trust him. "I've been in therapy too. Not as regularly anymore, but for a couple years, I was going every other week. Then every month, and now it's only when I'm really having trouble managing it. I have OCD. Obsessive-compulsive disorder. And generalized anxiety disorder, which is pretty common with OCD."

He nods slowly, taking this in. "What does that mean, exactly?"

"I—um. So it starts with these obsessions," I say, the way

my first therapist explained it to me years ago. "These thoughts I can't control. Intrusive thoughts. I'll be convinced the house will go up in flames if we leave the stove on or that if I lose my keys, I'll be stranded somewhere and never be able to get home." They always sound ridiculous when I say them out loud. "And I know they're illogical. But my brain makes me believe they're perfectly rational, and so I obsess over them and get even more anxious, and I become desperate to find a way to stop that anxiety, to make sure that the bad thing won't happen. Most of them are 'checks'—like, I have to be absolutely sure I have my phone and my keys whenever I open or close my bag. I need to know they're still in there, so I check, and then I check again, and I get stuck in a loop I sometimes can't get out of for a while. Sometimes I'll do it with locking my car, or making sure the stove is off before I leave my house, or that there's nothing on the floor Edith could get into. Those are compulsions."

"So it's not just handwashing," he says. "That probably sounds ignorant, but that's what I would have associated with OCD."

"Not for me, no. I'm actually not a very organized person, which is almost annoying—like, if I'm going to have OCD, it should at least make me better at cleaning up!" He cracks a smile at that, like he knows it's okay to. And it is. "But yeah, that's what a lot of people think. They'll say, 'Oh, you mean you wash your hands a lot?' or 'I'm so OCD, I have to have an organized locker.' It's not just wanting things to be organized. It's a real illness, and honestly . . . it can be brutal."

The worst of it was a few years ago: I couldn't trust that the front door of our house was locked, which made it difficult to fall asleep. So I'd go downstairs, check the lock, come back upstairs—before wondering if I checked it *enough*, or if maybe while checking it, I'd somehow swiped it with my sleeve or a strand of hair and managed to unlock it. If it wasn't locked, I was certain someone would break in and kill my family, and it would be my fault for not checking enough. In my mind, that was an inevitability. Back downstairs I'd go, checking it double the length of time . . . and end up trapped in a loop. It got so bad that for a full month I barely slept through the night.

What I don't tell him is that it started when my mom moved out, that I never felt safe in the house with just the three of us. Not because we needed two parents to protect us, but because the house felt *off*. There's no other way to explain it. I was stealthy about it back then, though. I didn't want my parents to have yet another thing to worry about.

And it just didn't go away, the anxiety only pushing pushing pushing against my lungs and taking up space inside my head. When my parents finally did figure it out years later, I thought they would brush it off, tell me I was acting silly, but I'd woken them up on more than one occasion, and when I told them I couldn't control it, they took it seriously. They believed me, took me to a therapist, and slowly, *slowly*, I've gotten better about living with uncertainty. I can understand Tarek's relief, knowing you don't have to let your mind betray you over and over.

"Some of the things you do," he says softly. "The keys. I've noticed. I always thought you were looking for something in your bag. I hope it's not rude to say that?"

I shake my head. "No, that's okay. Sometimes I feel weird

about people noticing, but honestly, I think it's better that they know. Therapy helps, and I take medication too. I'm not embarrassed about it or anything. Or at least, I'm not anymore."

"I'm glad you told me," he says. "We missed out on a lot this past year, huh?"

"And before that too."

He nods, and the two of us are quiet for a while. It isn't a charged, uncomfortable kind of quiet. For once my mind isn't a hundred places at the same time. If we were friends before, whatever we're becoming feels like *more* of that. Something honest and real and new.

"It kills me that you said what happened this past year hurt you," he says, and there's genuine concern on his face. "Fuck, I am so sorry. For last year, and for this summer, too. You were right—I've been overcompensating, and that was shitty. Can you forgive me? For all of it?"

"Yes," I say. There's no hesitation. "Yes." He visibly exhales, like this has been weighing on him. "You seemed so confident when you got here."

"It was hard to build myself back up over the past year. Therapy and medication helped, of course, but my pride took this massive hit. I really did like my classes, and I love the campus. Especially in the spring, it's beautiful. I'm interested in this stuff. I just . . . struggled. Being away from home was harder than I thought it would be. And—" A pause. A softening of his mouth. "Being away from you . . . was harder than I thought it would be."

*I wanted to take my time with it.* That was what he said about the email earlier. I was so wrapped up in what he was telling me that it barely registered, but now it's all I can think about.

"It was?" I say. That momentary peace is gone. Now I am all charged molecules, a spinning, buzzing brain.

The space between our bodies grows smaller. "I love Mansour's, but I also really liked seeing you at work. That was, like, the highlight of my weekend. It was always a little less exciting when we were catering something that wasn't a wedding." His long lashes—I swear I'm close enough to see every single one of them. "I missed those weekends while I was away. I missed talking to you, and I missed your weird jokes. I missed *you*."

"I missed you too," I say, my voice low and scratchy, not at all like I'm used to hearing. "I had no idea. That you felt that way."

It's too hot in this room, but I don't dare make a move to leave.

Now his eyes on me are so far from steel. They're flint, maybe. Something that could start a fire. He gives this strange scrape of a laugh, one that indicates he doesn't find this all that funny. An anxiety-laugh—the kind of laugh I am very familiar with. "Quinn, I was crushing on you last summer too," he says. "The boat I rented—that was for *you*."

I have to clutch the wall to keep from swaying. It must be the choppy water beneath us, the lullaby turning frantic, that's messing with my stomach.

"Oh." At first I can only manage a single syllable, my mind racing to fit this final piece into our relationship puzzle. "Oh my god. I didn't—I had no idea."

*For me. The boat was for me.*

That doesn't make it any more romantic, or at least it shouldn't. He didn't know me well enough to know I wouldn't have liked it, and obviously I made that clear to him. But something happens in the upper-left section of my chest that indicates otherwise. Maybe it was all performance, maybe it didn't mean anything—but it was a performance for *me*.

"Yeah," he says, a little sheepish now. "I kind of figured. My parents have friends that rent it out, and I thought it would be . . . the opposite of what it turned out to be."

"I thought it was for Elisa."

"Wait. What? Why would you think it was for Elisa?"

Ugh, now I have to spell it out. "You'd seemed close for a while. I just . . . I just assumed."

"Elisa and I are friends," he says. "Good friends—there's a certain bond you develop when you have to explain to ten kids in a row that no, we don't have any macaroni and cheese. But that's it. I've never had feelings for her, and that boat wasn't for her. Is that why you keep bringing her up?"

Slowly, I nod. I'm still trying to understand all of this. "Holy shit. I shouldn't have said those things about it. I'm so sorry."

"No, no, it's okay. I know that wasn't what you wanted, and the timing was off. Guess we wound up on a boat together anyway." I can't tell if he's inching closer to me or if the heat has made me delirious. "I never laugh more than when I'm around you. And you were—you *are* so damn cute."

*Cute*. Tarek thinks I'm *so damn cute*.

"I'm eighty percent sweat right now," I inform him. "Ten percent ginger ale, and ten percent Whitney Houston songs."

"I stand by what I said." He reaches a hand toward my forearm, and it is not the innocent, calming gesture I made earlier. It's electricity, white-hot, and it sparks up my arm and down to my toes. "I thought you knew. I thought that was why you sent that email—which I loved, by the way. That's what I would have said if I'd responded the way I should have. I would have told you I liked you." Another step forward. "That I'd been wondering what it would feel like to kiss you since last June."

He says this so breezily, like kissing is a completely normal way for the two of us to interact, as opposed to the firework it is in my head.

Now there's only a whisper of space between our bodies. He could burn me up with how warm he is, and I wouldn't care. After all this time, I need to know what he feels like. I want a hand in his hair and a thumb on his cheekbone and my hips right up against his. "Do you . . . still? Want to do that?"

"Yes." That single syllable is a demand and a plea at the same time. It turns my throat dry, pushes me that final inch toward him. The walls could be closing in on us, and I don't think I would notice.

"That's a shame, because I was actually about to go—"

He traps the rest of my words between us, his lips meeting mine in a desperate clash. For a moment I entertain the thought that No-Boy Summer has been a spectacular failure. Then I kiss him back.

There isn't a sense of longing in the kiss, at least, not the kind of longing "I missed you" might convey. It's fast, deep, punctuated by rough breaths that do little to give me the air I need. I find I don't care. His mouth is warm, and he tastes like frosting and spearmint gum and all of our past summers.

153

He places three fingertips on my jaw, gentle at first, before his hands drop to my waist, settling on my hips. I weave my fingers through his hair, that wonderful hair, run my hands along his ever-present scruff, like a razor just can't keep up with his genetics. When his fingers hook through my belt loops, he tugs me closer before pinning me against the washing machine. I have never before loved belt loops this much. A dial digs into my back—another thing I can't bring myself to care about.

"Sorry, sorry," he says with a sheepish laugh, a thumb rubbing my hip bone through the fabric of my slacks.

Before I can pounce on him again, our phones buzz in rapid succession, and we trade apologetic looks as we reach into our pockets.

"We're being summoned," I say, holding up my B+B chat. Where are you? Docking in fifteen.

He shows me an almost identical message from Harun, and I step back to give us both some space. Between gulps of air, I straighten my shirt. The messiness of his clothing sends another jolt of satisfaction through me.

"Go ahead," he says. "We probably shouldn't show up together. In case we look . . . suspicious."

"Right." With shaky hands, I do my best to re-form my hair into something resembling a style. "Okay. I'll, um—see you out there?"

When I'm back on land later, I'm still dizzy with the scent of him, the press of his fingertips lingering on my skin.

# 14

Cute or trying too hard?" Julia says, gesturing to a welcome mat that says DORM SWEET DORM. It's a game we're playing at Target. Fringed blankets, fairy lights, and succulents are calling our names.

Well—they're calling Julia's. I'm here for moral support.

"I want to say cute." I lean against Julia's shopping cart, assessing it. "But it could honestly go either way."

"Trying too hard," Julia says emphatically.

"I'm starting to think you don't value my opinion."

"Excuse me," she says, faux-offended. "I absolutely do. It's just not as meaningful as mine."

It feels like we haven't done something just the two of us since the beginning of summer. Julia and Noelle confessed their feelings after their movie date, and while I'm glad they're officially together, I've missed my best friend.

It's the first week of July, which means that in eight short weeks, she'll get on a plane to New York, and I'll drive home from the airport, willing myself not to cry. We've weathered other separations: different Jewish summer camps, the art intensive Julia did two summers ago, the three-week road trip the Kirschbaums took through the Pacific Northwest the summer before high school. But this one feels so permanent. That will be her *home*, while I'll be staying here. A prisoner up in my tower.

We pass other almost-freshmen trying to talk their parents into buying mini fridges and record players, because nothing screams college like music snobbery.

"Trying too hard," Julia whispers.

"Has Noelle done her college shopping yet?" I ask as we turn down the bath aisle.

"She said she's going to do most of it when she gets there so she doesn't have to take too much with her. Which is starting to sound really smart," Julia says as she eyes her cart.

"And you two—things are going well?"

"It's just as I feared. The more time I spend with her, the more I like her."

I clutch my heart. "My baby's in love."

"I didn't say love. Did I say love?"

"Your face did."

"Damn my overly expressive eyes." She tries to school her face into a non-expression but spectacularly fails, letting out a frustrated little whine. "I like her. A lot. Let's go with that."

"Speaking of . . . well, not love, but two people who are attracted to each other spending time together . . . Tarek and I, um, kissed on Saturday. On a boat."

I'd wanted to wait to tell her in person. I could barely sleep Saturday night, even though we got home after one a.m., and last night I replayed it so many times when my head hit the pillow that for a moment I convinced myself it all happened inside my mind. Saying it out loud reminds me it was real, his warm mouth and the press of his tongue and the way his thumb stroked my hip bone.

"Excuse me." Julia brings the cart to an abrupt halt. "We've been hanging out for a whole hour and you have yet to tell me about a *boat kiss*?"

She says this last part in a whisper-shout that draws attention from a few shoppers around us. A mother pushing a toddler in a cart gives me a look that I can't describe as anything other than *Bravo, stranger*.

I feel my face flush. "Does it make it better or worse that it was a yacht? And we were in a very small, very cramped laundry room?"

"Both." She props one elbow on the cart, fanning herself. "Wow. Okay. I didn't even realize that was still going on. You and Tarek, I mean."

"To be fair, I'm not entirely sure what's going on. I don't think either of us expected it to happen."

"Well, do you like him?"

"I liked kissing him." Truthfully, I'm not sure what I want to happen now. I haven't texted him and he hasn't texted me, and while normally that would ratchet my anxiety up to eleven, I feel oddly calm about the whole thing. Maybe because I'm still trying to process it for myself. "You've seen what his relationships are like on Instagram. We wouldn't be right for each other."

I did like kissing him. But I've seen so many miserable brides, miserable grooms, miserable families putting on a show because they think they're supposed to. I've seen the expressions my parents wear with their clients. None of it is real, and I already do enough pretending.

I learned from my parents like I learned how to bustle a wedding dress: love is a performance.

"Right, of course, how could I forget you don't do the whole emotion thing," she says. "Maybe that's what I should have done with Noelle."

"It wouldn't matter anyway," I say. "He's going back to UC Davis at the end of the summer."

"My levels of horniness don't mesh with this last-summer-before-college-everyone-splitting-up thing," Julia says. "It's like my body is trying to sabotage my brain."

Most of the time I feel the opposite. I pick up a pillow shaped like a pineapple before tossing it back in the bin. "I'm not sure how I feel about making new friends in September. It sounds hard. I just want to find some unsuspecting art student who vaguely looks like you and force them to listen to all my problems."

"For what it's worth, I'm not worried about us." She holds up an alarm clock shaped like a guitar amp. "Cute," she declares, just as I say, "Trying too hard."

After Target, we wait in line at Molly Moon's in Capitol Hill, where Julia asks to try every seasonal flavor before settling on her usual, melted chocolate. I go with salted caramel, and we take our cones and put up our sunglasses as we head to Cal Anderson Park across the street. There's a softball game in progress on one side of the park, and in the tennis courts, a group of tattooed, muscular dudes all in black are playing some game that involves Rollerblades and lacrosse sticks.

"Owning five corgis is a whole personality trait," Julia says. I've just finished telling her about Maxine and the very part-time work I'm starting next week. There's something I can focus on instead of Tarek, and I vow to redirect my anxieties as best I can.

"I wouldn't even want five cats. That's five animals thinking they're better than you," I say between licks of salted caramel. "My self-esteem is touch and go as it is."

We manage to find a patch of grass that isn't being used for badminton, fetch, or slacklining, which is a real feat on an eighty-degree day in Seattle. As we sit down, my phone buzzes, and I push away the hope that it's Tarek. I glance at it, groan, and shove it into my bag. Julia lifts her eyebrows.

"Victoria," I say, then fish my phone back out. "I should answer this. Sorry."

She texted my mom and me, and while I'm sure my mom is on top of it, I feel compelled to make up for the fitting a couple of weeks ago.

My future MIL isn't a fan of the hair comb. She wants me to wear her veil, which is so 80s it's practically singing "Take on Me." Help?

We've handled plenty of pushy in-laws. I can hear my parents' voices in my head as I type back, First, make sure she feels like she's being heard. Then, calmly explain to her that this is what you want to wear. We're happy to chat with her if you feel you need an intervention.

Exactly what I was going to say, Mom writes a minute later, and I hate the spark of pride it gives me.

Julia attacks a chocolate river dripping down her cone. "I take it you haven't told your parents yet."

"I'm working up to it." That's true, isn't it? What I'm doing with Maxine has to be a step in the right direction.

"Quinn. I'm going to say this in the nicest way possible. You cannot draw this out. The longer you do, the more upset your parents and Asher are going to be. This thing is making you miserable, and you're making *me* miserable."

Even if she didn't mean it to, it rubs me the wrong way. "Wow, sorry I'm not nonstop fun to hang out with."

"Hey." She reaches out to pull on my arm, as though shaking me out of a literal funk. "You know what I mean."

I do. I think. And she's not wrong; I just haven't decided how to broach the topic with my parents. I'm not ready for the consequences yet.

"Let's talk about something else," I say.

So Julia tells me about the roommate she picked on her school's matching site and how you can sort based on how tidy you are and how tidy you'd like your roommate to be, and I smile and nod along like I'm supposed to.

The whole time, I can't help feeling like she's moving on— moving *up*—without me.

# 15

may have done something bad last night," whispers a bride through a crack in her suite door.

Next to me, Asher goes pale. "Oh god. You didn't—"

"No!" the bride, Kaci, says quickly. "Nothing like that. I just . . . well, you're going to see it eventually." With that, she pulls the door wide, revealing her once-blond hair tinged mint green.

"You went swimming," I say, recognizing the hue from when Julia and I went to a party at the house of the one person in our grade who had a pool and she emerged with green hair. There was always that one person with a pool, and they were always popular.

Kaci nods miserably. "We have a bunch of family in town, right? So I went over last night to hang out with some cousins I hadn't seen in forever, and we were in the hotel pool until they kicked us out."

In two hours, Kaci is marrying Mariana in an outdoor cere-mony on the grounds of a sprawling estate outside of Seattle. Three hundred guests.

"I can't have green hair in our wedding photos," Kaci contin-ues, teary-eyed. "I thought about cutting it off, but I really wanted to have long hair for the wedding, and I've been growing it out for ages—" She breaks off with a sob.

And even if the idea of accidentally dyeing your hair green before your wedding is kind of funny, those tears aren't. This is a big deal to her, which makes it a big deal to us.

Asher makes this calming sound, a kind of tutting under her breath. "Kaci. Listen to me. I am not going to let you get married with green hair. Okay? But right now I need you to calm down. Breathe. Because I don't think you want puffy red eyes in your photos either, do you?"

Kaci shakes her head and lets out one last sniff.

It's interesting, the differences between Asher and Mom, who asked us to check on Kaci while she helped Mariana because the brides didn't want to see each other until they were at the altar. Asher is nurturing where Mom is no-nonsense, but my sister can be intense when she needs to be. It makes me wonder, if I stuck this out, what kind of planner I'd be. If I'd fall somewhere in the middle between Asher and Mom.

The thought of it snags my lungs in a viselike grip, reminds me what I'd be losing if I gave all of this up.

*You're making me miserable*, Julia said.

*When* I give all of this up. As soon as I figure out how.

Kaci lets us into her suite, which is all done up in white and rose gold, and Asher the wedding wizard unzips her emergency kit. "I know I have a little bottle of lemon juice in here somewhere," she says, while I pour Kaci a glass of water she accepts with a shaky hand. "Some crushed aspirin might do the job too. If all that fails— which I don't think it will!—I have a box of bleach. We're going to get through this." She holds up the lemon juice, victorious. "Aha!"

And then we get to work, sitting Kaci down, spreading a towel on her shoulders, and soaking her hair with lemon juice.

"We'll let that sit for about ten minutes," Asher says. "I'm actually surprised this is the first green hair I've ever dealt with."

Kaci laughs, and it's a welcome sound. "Happy to be your first. Hopefully I'm not the biggest disaster you've seen."

"Definitely not." I lean against the window that overlooks where the caterers are setting up the outdoor tables. Not looking for Tarek. Nope. "That would be a groom whose friends thought it would be hilarious to shave off his eyebrows the morning of the wedding."

Even if our conversations are only surface, I've missed working alongside my sister, and a task like this with an easy fix is almost soothing. The fact that it's such a large wedding means I may not run into Tarek. If I see him, I don't know how strong I'll be. He's going to be standing there with his hair and his eyelashes and his smile that knows exactly what we did on that boat, and I'll remember the heat of his mouth on mine, the sound of his breath catching in his throat. And I'll want to do it again.

We were just curious. That's the conclusion I've arrived at after a week of drafting and deleting a dozen text messages. Longtime friends who found each other attractive. A chemical reaction. Usually when I'm ready to move on, when I think the other person might want to DTR, I put as much space between us as possible. So I'll see him, we'll endure a period of awkward sustained eye contact, and then we'll be golden. I am amazing at awkward sustained eye contact.

Asher's phone timer beeps. "You're good to wash it out. Shampoo and conditioner?"

Kaci holds up a travel bag of toiletries before disappearing into the suite's spacious adjoining bathroom. A few minutes later, we hear a shriek of glee.

"I'm guessing that means it worked?" Asher calls out, and Kaci flings the door open.

"You are magic. Thank you."

As the makeup artist and bridesmaids arrive, Asher asks me to check in with the florist. This will also require avoiding Tarek, which reminds me of our first meeting of the summer when I was avoiding Jonathan. Next to Tarek, Jonathan seems harmless. Jonathan was a lit match; Tarek is a five-alarm fire. Tarek is—

"Quinn?"

—standing right behind me.

I spin around in the foyer of the estate, nearly banging my arm on a towering sculpture that probably cost more than my house. "Hey, you!" I say, too loudly. Too much pep. I sound like my mother.

He lifts his eyebrows at my strange greeting—which, fair— and one corner of his mouth turns upward. I am fine. I am great. I am the coolest of cucumbers. I have taken the chillest of pills.

"I wanted to let you know that we're all set for cocktail hour when the guests start arriving."

"Yeah, okay, got it, cool. I'll tell everyone."

His smirk deepens. "You okay?" He crosses his arms, leaning against a pillar in the entryway like this is just something he does.

"Super," I say. "You?"

"Similarly super."

"Okay then. I'm going to . . ." I mime taking out my phone

to text the group chat, nearly dropping it. Jesus. The sustained eye contact was not supposed to be this awkward.

The ceremony goes flawlessly, or as flawlessly as a ceremony can, given there's no such thing as perfection in the wedding business. For some reason, my parents didn't like that as a slogan either: *Borrowed + Blue: because there's no such thing as perfection.*

I'm in the canopied dining area, waiting to escort guests to their tables, and I swear, Tarek goes out of his way to either glance at me or walk right in front of me every time he carries out a tray of food for the buffet. Harun is here too, and I watch them joking around when they're in the kitchen, wondering if Tarek told Harun about us.

Though I guess if he's glancing at me, I'm almost always glancing back. When our eyes lock, my face burns, and it's not just because I forgot sunscreen.

This is getting ridiculous. I tell Mom I've gotten too much sun, that I need a walk and some space. The grounds are large, and it's easy enough for me to disappear without disturbing anyone.

Sprawling maple trees shade my path as I walk and walk and walk, until I let out what feels like my first deep breath since last weekend, since that microscopic laundry room, since his mouth was on mine and his fingers were grazing my hips and—

*Stop.* It didn't mean anything. It *can't* mean anything.

It's quiet out here. Calming. I've never been interested in the roughing-it kind of camping trips Julia takes with her parents, but maybe I could get into nature. I am a new and open-minded Quinn. Just leave me out here in the—shit, is that a wasp?

Of course I'm in the middle of my wasp-avoidance dance

when I hear footsteps and spot Tarek heading toward me. I freeze, offering up my skin to the bees.

"Hey, you," he says, echoing my earlier greeting in this low voice. When Tarek says it, he turns those words electric. I feel them in the tips of my toes.

I don't know how he's remotely calm. Maybe because he is a mature college student, and I am the kind of chaotic mess who, without fail, gets mascara all over her eyelids every morning and has to wipe it off and start again.

I chance a step forward, keeping a very safe few feet separating us. "Hi." My heart does this infuriating beat-skipping thing in my chest that I decide to attribute to the wasps. They are terrifying, powerful creatures.

"We can't keep meeting like this."

"You're the one who followed me here."

He steps closer, something small clasped in his hand. "So I did." The sweet, earthy scent of him blends with the trees and the flowers and the summer air, and for a moment I think I might need to lie down. Just right here in the dirt. "Rumor in the kitchen is that you de-greenified the bride's hair."

"All in a day's work. And it was more Asher than me."

"Still. For such a big wedding, it's been a shockingly crisis-free one. The brides knew exactly what they wanted. We don't always get that."

"You really like doing this," I say. "After all these years. You still love weddings."

"You don't?"

At the beginning of the summer, I was jealous—of him, of Julia, of my sister, of everyone who seemed to have their lives figured out. Now I just feel lost. Everyone is moving ahead and moving on, so solid about their chosen paths, and I'm still wondering where I fit.

Part of me wants to tell him how I feel about B+B, and while it would be easier than earlier in the summer, this isn't the right place. I'm not getting sappy about Kaci and Mariana—it just wouldn't be respectful.

"What we should really be talking about," I say, because a subject change is always easier than honesty, "is why you followed me here."

My words hit him in a way I didn't anticipate. His eyebrows jump to his hairline, his dark eyes widening. "Shit—I'm sorry. I shouldn't have done that. I just wanted to talk to you alone, and there were all those people, and . . ."

I cut him off with a laugh. "Relax. I'm just giving you a hard time."

"Okay. Because I actually did have a reason. I brought you something." He unwraps a pastel-pink macaron, the loveliest little dessert I've ever seen. Kaci and Mariana did macarons instead of a cake, an impressive tower of them. He used to do this all the time, save me desserts, and it endeared him to me so much. Now it makes me want to press my mouth to the corner of his lips where his half smile starts.

"That's adorable."

"I was going for delicious, but I'll take it." He holds the macaron out to me, and it looks so delicate I'm almost afraid to grab it for fear of breaking it.

"Are they hard to make?" Dear god, can I stop saying the word "hard"?

"In theory, no. But they're tough to master. They're extremely temperamental, really sensitive to moisture in the air. So you could follow the recipe exactly, and they could still be a disaster. But when you finally get them right, the perfect crunch to the shell and the lightness of the filling, they're heavenly."

I bite into it, and it's at once soft and crisp and sweet and tart. "Oh my god, that's perfect. Grapefruit?"

He watches me while I'm eating, like he can't relax until he has my honest opinion. "Yeah? You like it?"

"Yes. So much." I take another nibble. "But everyone's about to eat them. Can't really make any changes now."

"I don't care about everyone."

And damn it, I'm weak. And woozy. And alone in this shaded grove with a boy who fed me dessert and can help calm some of my anxiety, even just for a bit.

So I grab his vest and tug him the last few inches to me. His mouth lands on mine in a smirk, and he is sugar and salt and heat, warming me up faster than the sun. His lips are familiar, but the kiss is more intense than Saturday. Firm. Insistent. I match each slide of his mouth, each stroke of his tongue as one of his hands moves to my hair, the other to my hip. I'm not sure how much longer I can keep standing. When I free one hand to reach behind me and find a tree trunk, I let my back meet the bark, and *yes*, that's much better.

*More*, I tell him with the bite of my teeth. *Absolutely*, he replies with a hand pressed to the tree above my head. His body is flush against mine now, taut muscles and solid curves. The weight of him is enough to make me dizzy. I reach around to his back, his skin hot beneath starched fabric, as he lifts his lips to plant a kiss at the corner of my mouth. Along my jawline. Down my neck.

"Did you really need this buttoned all the way to the top?" he drawls against my throat.

I might faint. "My parents—they want us to look professional."

"Is that how we're going to look when we go back out there?" he asks, mouth tracing my collarbone. His teeth snag on my top button. "Professional?"

Slowly, he pulls back, and his gaze on mine is molten, like nothing I've seen from him before. Then, ever so gently, he flicks the button open with his thumb. One, then another.

"Are you trying to kill me?" I'm distantly aware of how labored my breaths sound. I'd be self-conscious if his chest weren't rising and falling at the same speed.

A laugh that creases the skin around his eyes. God, that's cute. "Is it working?"

"Yes. But you'll have to explain to everyone how it happened."

He's still laughing when he lowers his mouth to my newly exposed skin. Just an extra two inches, but it feels like he's ignited all my nerve endings. Not wanting to be outdone, I push my hips against his, drawing this beautiful groan from his throat. The things that sound does to me . . . Yeah, we should probably stop.

I lay my palm on his chest. "I have to get back."

Another groan, this one laced with frustration. *I know,* I want to tell him. *Me too.*

I volunteer to head back first—since he's, uh, not quite ready—and before I do, he pulls me close one more time and kisses my forehead. A soft sweep of his lips.

Somehow, that's the one that feels the most dangerous.

# 16

Maxine wasn't wrong—it's a *lot* of sanding.

It's my third time here since our first meeting, and I'm in one corner of her workshop, the sound box of a harp-to-be on the downdraft table in front of me. Heavy-duty earmuffs are clamped around my ears as I operate the handheld optical sander, the table sucking up the sawdust. The corgi club is just outside the workshop door, away from the loud noises.

Already, I know more about wood than I ever thought I would. Maxine uses a variety: walnut, cherry, mahogany, koa, bubinga, spruce.

"The harp is essentially three main pieces," she said last time, showing me each one. "The neck, which is the curved top piece. Then there's the pillar, which is the front piece, and the sound box, which includes the soundboard and the string rib."

"And what about this?" I asked, pointing to the back of the sound box.

She smirked. "We just call that the back."

The wood has to be exceptionally smooth before Maxine applies the finish, which means hours and hours of sanding. About four hours for each sound box.

And I like it, completely losing myself in the task like this.

Sometimes my mind wanders to places where I can't quite catch it, but other times I can turn off the noise—literally, with the earmuffs—and simply *be*.

I've never spent much time around adults who aren't my parents or teachers. Our vendors mainly work with my parents, and even then, we're working together. Collaborating. Here I am very clearly a student, and yet Maxine doesn't treat me like a child. There's a middle ground, I realize, between the way my parents treat me and a way I'd hate to be talked down to.

That middle ground is Maxine Otto and Emerald City Harps.

After another hour, I switch off the optical sander and head into the studio. This is our trade-off: I sand, and then I get to play around on my favorite cherrywood harp after I finish tuning.

I'm working on the Beatles' "Yesterday," which is full of lever changes. It's very obvious when the lever isn't right, especially with a song you know well, which makes this a good one to practice. You hear a natural instead of a sharp, and it's immediately jarring. If one of my levers is wrong, I back up a couple measures, determined to recapture that fluidity I love about harp music.

"Try crossing under with your second finger there instead," Maxine says next to me, pointing. The dogs react differently to music, I've learned. A couple of them curl up at the bottom of the harp to feel the vibrations, though one of them, Gregor, whose tawny fur is flecked with the white of old age, whines a bit before eventually settling down. Maxine told me he doesn't like anything in a minor key. "Otherwise you're not going to be able to get to this string with your thumb. It's all about the fingering."

I try and fail to hold in a snicker, and she shakes her head. "Sorry. I'm basically twelve."

The piece is still more staccato than I'd like, my movements a little staggered as I flip the levers. It's a new kind of choreography for my hands, and it feels . . . *powerful*. Like I didn't know my hands were capable of this, and now there's a whole new skill set quite literally at my fingertips. Sure, I could have searched for this kind of music, but I wouldn't have known anything about lever harps. I wouldn't have been able to see their versatility for myself. Watching the instrument turn from nothing into something—it's hard not to be inspired. I didn't know playing the harp could be angry, rough, complicated. What I'm realizing is that it can be so many different things.

Before I launch back into the song, my phone buzzes. "Sorry," I say, reaching into my pocket to switch it to do-not-disturb mode. A text from Asher, but I'm not in the mood to answer it. Not when I'm in my new safe space. "My sister. We, um, work together."

"Right, the family business," Maxine says, and there's a flatness in her tone I can't interpret. "My daughter, Josie, used to help out in here. Even when she was little, she could never stop fidgeting. She was always tapping her fingers on something or bouncing her legs, and I was so convinced she was going to become a musician."

It's unusual for Maxine to share so much about herself, and I revel in it. "I take it she didn't?"

Maxine smiles, but it's not entirely a sad one. "She could have been really great. She played harp until she finished high school, and she helped in the shop until she finished college, and then she was off on her own path. Graphic design. Of course I wanted her to do what she wanted, but I can't say I wasn't a little disappointed.

And Josie was always going to do what she wanted."

"Does she live here?"

"Chicago. She and her wife eloped a couple years back. You have no idea how relieved I was. Her father, though . . ." She shakes her head. "He was livid. Or he just wanted to go to Hawaii—who knows. I gave up trying to figure out what was going on in his head a long time ago." When I'm silent for a moment, she supplies, "Divorced. Fifteen years ago."

"Oh, I'm—" *I'm sorry* is what I was going to say, but what am I really sorry about? Sorry she isn't married? Sorry something she may have thought was supposed to last didn't?

Fortunately, Maxine continues, saving me from stuttering out an end to that sentence. "I love living on my own. I had the experience of being married, and I never felt like myself, to be honest. And now . . . now I can do everything I want. I don't think being married was for me. Being partnered up in that way . . . wasn't for me. I couldn't even begin to tell you how much happier I am now."

There's an earnestness in her voice, and I feel lucky she's trusting me with this information. My parents would have leaped to the conclusion that someone unmarried at Maxine's age was something to mourn. *Sorry* is something my parents would have said, and it shouldn't have been my gut reaction. The first time we met, I thought she was lonely, but I was so, so wrong. If Maxine is happier now, then I'm glad it ended too.

Maxine changes the subject, and I get the sense that this was maybe more personal information than she wanted to divulge. "Let me see if I have some more sheet music for you." She shuffles a stack of papers on a side table—hand-carved, of course. A brightly colored flyer sails to the floor, and I bend to pick it up.

ONE NIGHT ONLY, it says. ACCLAIMED HARPIST MAXINE OTTO.

"Just a little show I'm doing," Maxine says, holding out her hand for the flyer. She says this casually, like she's trying to brush it off, and I can't quite understand why.

"And I thought you didn't play anymore."

"Not very much. I'm not officially retired, but I'm mostly holed up here in the shop. An old friend asked me to be part of this charity concert at the end of the month, and I told her I would. Really, it's not a big deal."

"I've never been to anything like this. I'd love to go."

She regards me with an odd expression, white-blond eyebrows knit close together and—I think she might be *nervous*. "It's been a while since I played in public. I may not be very good." At this, a small smile forms in the corner of her mouth, like she knows that's impossible.

"I'm putting it on my calendar." It's only when I pull out my phone that I spy the date on the flyer. A Saturday. It overlaps with the Stern-Rosenfeld wedding, a glam Jewish shindig we've been planning for a year and a half.

I've never skipped a wedding, but I'll come up with an excuse. I don't know when I'll get another chance to see Maxine perform.

Now that I'm holding my phone, I see the texts from Asher.

**Asher:** Hey, where are you?

**Asher:** Why is your phone off?

**Asher:** Quinn?? Now I'm worried, call me asap.

"Do you mind if I—" I ask, gesturing to my phone, and Maxine waves a hand as I hit my sister's number.

"Quinn? Are you okay?"

"I'm fine. I'm fine. What is it?"

There's a shuffle on the other end, and then, when she speaks again, her voice is a near-whisper. "I'm currently doing a floral consult in Capitol Hill with Genevieve and Preston. Alone."

Oh. *Shit*.

"Where are you?"

I glance around the studio. "I'm—at Julia's. I had my phone off and we lost track of time. I'm so sorry, I'll be there in fifteen minutes. Twenty, max. Capitol Blossom, right?"

"We'll be done by then." Her voice is crisp. "Just don't let this happen again, okay? I looked like a total idiot telling them I was waiting for you when apparently you weren't planning on showing up."

We never talk to each other like this—but then again, we haven't talked to each other very much at all lately, not about anything that isn't wedding related.

"Okay," I say quietly, and then we hang up.

"Everything all right?" Maxine chirps.

"Yeah. I . . . should probably go." Even if I'm not needed, the guilt is enough to send me home.

"You should take it with you. The harp." When I just stare at her, she adds, "So you can practice more."

For a moment I'm overwhelmed with a feeling that soothes the anxiety of the call with Asher. "Because I need the practice, or because you're doing a nice thing for me? This is worth thousands of dollars. I mean—you know that, obviously."

"For harp makers, it's a huge compliment to have a musician they admire play one of their instruments." And then I get another rare Maxine smile.

Whatever that feeling is—I ride it all the way home, where I hide the harp in my closet and wash the sawdust out of my hair.

> **Tarek:** So that reality show couple is doing their final tasting at Mansour's this week.

> **Quinn:**

> **Tarek:** Is anyone from B+B planning to be there?

> **Quinn:** Yep, the youngest B. Aka me.
> And mainly for the food.

> **Tarek:** I was hoping. That one's my favorite.

> **Quinn:** What a coincidence, the youngest M is my favorite too.
> Mainly because of the food.

> **Tarek:** I was thinking of making some baklava, if that's something you'd be interested in.

> **Quinn:** I really shouldn't eat on the job.

> **Tarek:** So that macaron last week?

**Quinn:** I was tricked!

**Tarek:** Or that piece of mango?

**Quinn:** Do not even *think* about
mangos in my presence.

**Tarek:** 😆
I'm so sorry, I had to.

**Quinn:** Thanks for being there.
At the urgent care, I mean.
I probably never said
that, so . . . thank you.

**Tarek:** To be fair, you were too busy telling
me with your eyes to go fuck myself.
But you're welcome.

**Quinn:** 💬

**Tarek:** 💬

**Quinn:** 💬

**Tarek:** So hypothetically, if I had
some baklava sitting on the counter
at Mansour's . . . ?

177

> **Quinn:** Then I'd make sure it
> was given proper attention.

**Tarek:** Good.

> **Quinn:** Good.

**Tarek:** In case I haven't already
made it clear, I'm glad you're going to be there.
And I really liked . . . everything
that happened on Saturday.

> **Quinn:** Oh, I could tell.
> And . . . I did too.

# 17

I am leading a double life.

In one life, I am Quinn the obedient daughter. I attend fittings, consults, rehearsal dinners. I smile. I say *of course* and *not a problem* and *yes*.

In the other, I'm Quinn the stealth harpist, who rushes home to shower off the scent of sawdust, who plays the cherrywood harp only when no one is home (after nearly breaking my back hauling it up to the tower), who sneaks out of her house to a harp maker's studio whenever I can.

It's exhausting, but I love that second life so much that it's worth it.

Today I am the first Quinn, on my way to Mansour's on a Wednesday afternoon to finalize Victoria and Lincoln's menu. Instead of another torturous pencil skirt, I wear a vintage peach dress with tiny dogs on it I got on a thrift store trip with Julia last summer. I haven't worn it nearly enough. I pin my hair back on the sides and add a swipe of red lipstick I almost never wear, and I don't hate the way that looks either. Maybe it's not B+B-approved, but my parents won't be there.

Mansour's isn't a storefront, just a large kitchen space downtown with state-of-the-art appliances and pristine white countertops. Of course, when Victoria and Lincoln arrived, they asked a hundred questions about the framed articles on the walls detailing how Murad and Zainab met. There's the two of them on the set of a national morning show, pages from *People* and the *Washington Post* and *Cosmopolitan*. Then they bonded over having love stories that took place partially in the public eye, which led to a discussion about living in "the age of social media" and how "nothing we do is private anymore," according to Murad, while Tarek caught my gaze and rolled his eyes.

The upside of working today: food. The Mansours have prepared each appetizer, entrée, and dessert for Victoria and Lincoln, which they arrange on the counter in front of us. And as Tarek promised, there was baklava waiting for me when I got here.

"You have to try this," Victoria says to Lincoln, holding out a golden potato croquette. "They're so crisp but also so light? I could eat about a hundred of these."

"You guys knocked it out of the park," Lincoln agrees. I haven't seen him as much as Victoria, but he has this relaxed, easygoing personality that's impossible not to like. He's tall, Black, wearing Seattle hipster glasses and a short-sleeved button-up with tiny sharks all over it. Tiny animals will never not be the best pattern. He tries a croquette, then another. "I can't believe there isn't any dairy in these."

"Make sure you try them with a little of the sauce," Tarek says, pushing the bowl toward them. "Sweet sriracha mayo. Vegan mayo, I should say." It's a kosher menu, and Mansour's even has relationships with some of the local rabbis we work with.

"We get it. You made the sauce," Zainab says, like this is something they've been joking about all day.

Tarek flushes, and it's adorable.

"And it's excellent," Victoria says. She takes a fork to the roast chicken, one of the mains. "We're so glad you could accommodate those last-minute changes."

Zainab waves a hand. "Please. Not last minute at all. We completely understand wanting to swap out the rack of lamb for something . . . a little more attractive to be eating on camera."

"The cameras," Victoria says flatly. "Right."

"Very exciting," Murad says. This publicity is a big deal for them, too. "We really are honored to be part of it."

"It's just a lot of pressure. Not that I didn't get torn apart enough the first time I was on TV," she says with a brush-off kind of laugh.

I remember the breakdown she had the episode before the season finale, how she cried facedown on her hotel room bed while a producer rubbed her back. She liked both men so much, could see a life with each of them . . . but the one she couldn't imagine saying goodbye to was Lincoln.

Now he's the one rubbing her back, stroking her long curls, telling her it's all going to be okay. "People are going to be watching because they're happy for us," he says. "Which in itself is still surreal."

Victoria straightens and puts on a smile. "Really, I'm fine. It's just the regular your-wedding-is-in-four-weeks-and-will-be-on-Streamr jitters."

"Very common," I assure her. "All our brides go through it."

At that, I think her smile might turn real.

They don't end up making any changes to the menu, which I think is a relief for all of us.

"Five o'clock," Zainab muses once they leave, gesturing to the wall-mounted clock next to a framed photo of young Mansours shaking hands with young Berkowitzes.

"You say that as though time means something when you're in the catering business," Murad says, sweeping plates into their industrial-grade dishwasher.

"I can close up here, if you want," Tarek says. "I know it's been a while since you guys had a night off."

Zainab pauses in the middle of wiping down the counter. "You're sure? That would be wonderful. Thank you," she says, moving over to him and kissing each of his cheeks. "Wow, a night off—I'm not even sure what that looks like."

"Whatever it ends up being, please don't tell me." Tarek waves them to the door, and god, I think I love his parents.

That realization comes with a stab of jealousy. They've always been open and loving, supportive of what Tarek wants regardless of whether it's what they want too. I've never been able to figure them out—if they're faking a romance for the rest of us, the way I've always assumed my parents are, or if what happened at the Eiffel Tower really did lead to a genuine relationship. It was the grandest of grand gestures, and yet somehow it worked. And it's been working for more than twenty years.

"So thoughtful of you," I say after they're gone. "Closing up for your parents."

"I'm a good kid," he says, untying his apron and inching closer to where I'm leaning against the kitchen island. The temperature seems to jump a full fifteen degrees. "That's the only reason I did it."

I pull his face down to mine, kissing him for the first time today. I breathe him in, his laundry-fresh scent and the spices from the food.

"Are the dogs on your dress wearing hats?" he asks against my mouth, biting at my lower lip.

"Yes. They're very sophisticated."

"Believe it or not, I did have an ulterior motive for asking them to leave. But it's not what you think." I lift my eyebrows at the way he's pinning me against the counter. "Okay, it's half what you think. But—" He pushes off the island, goes over to the stack of books and binders in neat shelves on the other side of the kitchen. He extracts a sheet of paper with something handwritten on it. "I've been trying to get this recipe right. I grew up watching my mom make it, and her mom used to make it for her, and her mom's mom made it back in Egypt . . . but the recipe was never written down. I've tried a few online recipes, but nothing's quite the same as when she makes it. I eventually had to ask her to make it very slowly so I could write down each step, but she doesn't measure anything, so it can be tough to get the ratios right."

"What is it?"

When he slides the piece of paper over to me on the counter, I realize I've never seen his handwriting. The letters are cramped, fighting for space, a few stray scratches and crossed-out measurements. "They have a few different names, but my mom always called them zalabya. I've only been a couple times, but they're a pretty popular street food in Egypt. They're like . . ." He waves a hand in the air, as though struggling to describe with words something he's only experienced through taste. "Little fried dough balls, and you can soak them in simple syrup or dust them with sugar or cinnamon, or any variety of other things. So I thought that might be . . . fun? If you wanted to, I don't know, hang out for a while."

He's sheepish as he says this last part, and if the promise of fried dessert weren't already tempting, the sweetness in his expression does me in.

"I could hang out for a while."

That's all it is: two friends hanging out. With some occasional kissing. I'm not about to deny myself that serotonin boost after the summer I've had.

Before he touches any of the ingredients, he swipes at his phone to play music from the room's speakers.

"I listened to that Cat Power song, by the way," I say, hoisting myself up onto the kitchen island. In my mind, it's a sexy, effortless move. In reality, there's some grunting, some awkward leg flails. Thank god his back is turned. "'The Greatest.' I liked it. Not as much as 'Sea of Love,' but it was a refreshing reception song. And then you were wearing a Sharon Van Etten shirt a while back—you seem to have a thing for female singer-songwriters."

"You caught me. The moodier, the better. What kind of music are you usually into? That feels like something we should know about each other, but I guess I only know what you play on the harp."

"Moody female singer-songwriters," I say, and he laughs. "Lately I've been listening to a lot of St. Vincent, Phoebe Bridgers, Courtney Barnett."

A moment later, a St. Vincent song starts playing. Then he turns toward me on the kitchen island. "You look absurdly cute up there," he says, placing one hand on either side of my legs.

I kiss him once, quickly, before patting the center of his chest. "Go. Bake for me."

Tarek looks so natural in the kitchen that it's impossible not to enjoy watching him. It's not just the roll of his shoulder blades beneath his T-shirt as he grabs a baking sheet or the adorable way he squints as he scans the containers of flour in the pantry. It's the ease of those movements, something that might have made me jealous earlier this summer. Now I'm just glad he has something he loves this much.

"I used to want to be a baker," I say, tapping my feet to St. Vincent as he works. "For a solid few months when I was seven years old. For Hanukkah that year, I begged my parents for a doughnut hole maker."

"What the hell is a doughnut hole maker?"

"It's one of those kitchen gadgets that only serves a single purpose, like an avocado slicer or pizza scissors."

"If I ever start a band, I'm calling it Pizza Scissors."

"I'll play harp for you."

"Pizza Scissors has the *best* harpist," he says. Then he makes a horrified expression. "I can't get over this doughnut hole maker. That's not real baking."

"Try telling my seven-year-old self that. Anyway, I was devastated when I didn't get it, and it crushed my career dreams and set me on a path of . . . well, not that." Since I can't exactly finish that sentence, I forge ahead. "Have you always loved it? Baking? I'm not sure I've ever heard about how you got into it."

"Ah, yes, it's the thrilling tale of a boy, his favorite cousin, and a food allergy."

185

"Harun?"

He nods, whisking flour, sugar, and a few other things together in a bowl. "That was why my parents moved out here—so my dad could be closer to his brother and their kids. Harun has celiac disease, and when he was younger, it wasn't as easy to find things he could eat, or they were really expensive. So I started experimenting, playing around in the kitchen with my parents. I loved that I could do this one thing that made him happy, and it kind of snowballed from there." He adds a cup of yogurt, then another, frowning at the markings on his handwritten recipe. "I always wanted to know *why* ingredients would interact the way they did and what would happen if you did things a different way. My whole life, I've been around food, and I saw how much joy it could bring people. I saw the reactions my parents got from their clients, how food could make you content or nostalgic or any number of other emotions. It's this perfect blend of art and science. You can make a real connection with someone through your food."

"And wedding cakes are probably one of the most intense connections you can make?"

He lifts a finger as though to say, *Yes, exactly*. "Now, if only my parents would let me handle one on my own."

"Have they *tasted* your cakes?"

"Yes, and I think they're pretty fucking good," he says. "Someday. I'm gradually wearing them down. It was torture, not being able to cook the way I wanted to in college. I subjected Landon—that's my roommate—to a lot of experiments." Then he allows himself a small smile. "Maybe dorm food was the real source of my depression."

"Being able to joke about your own mental illness is a big step," I say. Then I feign a gasp, draping a dramatic hand over my forehead. "Oh god—did you have to eat Top Ramen? Or Annie's mac and cheese? The horror."

"There are a lot of ways you can dress up Annie's mac and cheese," he says, because of course there are, and of course he's done it. He pulses the electric mixer for a few seconds, and when he speaks again, his tone is more serious. "I've been getting this feeling lately, and correct me if I'm wrong, if I'm seeing something that isn't there . . . but maybe you're not loving all of this the way you used to?"

It would be easy to lie the way I have with everyone else. But if we really are friends now—albeit friends who can't seem to stop kissing—then maybe I can do this. "I . . . don't. I've felt that way for a while. My parents have always assumed I'll join B+B once I finish college. When you asked me about UW—it's not that I'm not excited about college, or grateful that I'm able to go. It's that they've already picked out all my classes. They've plotted out the next four years of my life, and I've never really gotten a say in it."

It's such a relief to tell someone who isn't Julia. I've kept these words in my head for so long, I didn't know what they'd sound like when I spoke them aloud. *If* I spoke them aloud.

Tarek is quiet for a few moments. "I'm so sorry. I thought you were burned out or something, but I had no idea it was like this." We're going down opposite paths, but he can see the view from mine just as well as his.

"It would kill them if they knew how little I'm interested in weddings these days. I don't know how to tell them that I don't want any of this. It's always been their thing. And I love that they have it, and they're good at it, but it's not mine. I want to work hard for something. To really earn it. I just feel like it's not going to feel *mine* until that happens." A flash of panic, and then I add: "Not that I think that's what you're doing!"

"I didn't think you meant it that way, don't worry," he says. "That's a lot to deal with, helping out your parents and not feeling like you can talk to them about it. Do you have any idea what you might want to do instead?"

He sets aside his mixing bowls so he can talk to me, and I don't know if it's the kind of baking that needs supervision, but even if it isn't, it's almost overwhelming, the amount of attention he's giving me. I hooked up with more than one guy who was always on his phone, nodding and mm-hmm-ing when I wanted to talk to him about something. I shouldn't be so surprised by the fact that he cares, and yet I am.

"Well . . ." I think about Maxine. "I'm not sure if this is directly future-career-related, but I met this woman at a wedding, actually, who builds harps? I started helping out at her workshop. And it's pretty amazing, seeing all the steps that go into it."

"Yeah? Tell me," he says, and there's a look of such genuine interest on his face that makes my heart do something strange and foreign in my chest.

So I do. I tell him about lever harps versus pedal harps, about the corgi club, about the whir of the machines in the workshop. "The way she plays is like nothing I've heard before. She's loud and unforgiving and *raw*, and I'm obsessed with it. Obviously harps are beautiful instruments, but seeing the way they come together . . .

Maybe this is cheesy, but it feels kind of special." I gesture to the kitchen. "Maybe it's even a little like baking."

"You'll play for me sometime?" he asks.

"You've heard me play plenty."

"Uh, excuse me, not on a *lever harp*."

"Okay. I'll play for you sometime. On the lever harp."

As I tell him this, I wonder what it would entail, Tarek coming over to hear me play. It probably won't happen, even if I don't hate the way it looks in my imagination.

"You can be honest," Tarek says as he finishes plating the zalabya. He's prepared some with simple syrup, some with powdered sugar. "You won't hurt my fragile male ego."

I don't tell him that his lack of a fragile male ego is one of my favorite things about him. I take a piece that's been soaked in syrup, and— "Oh. Holy shit. Holy *shit*."

"What?" he asks, sounding alarmed, taking a piece for himself and chewing slowly.

"It's so fucking good," I say, and he relaxes back onto the kitchen island barstool next to me, rolling his eyes.

"You're the worst."

"Thank you."

"Not quite how my mom makes them," he says, grabbing another one. "But you're right. They're pretty fucking good."

Once we've polished them off, I check my phone. "Shit, it's almost eight o'clock."

"Your bedtime?"

"Hey, I'm allowed to stay up until eight thirty in the summer.

I just didn't realize we'd been here for this long." The thing is, I don't really want to go home yet. This has been nice. And maybe, evidenced by the fact that he hasn't said anything to the contrary, Tarek feels the same way. "I guess I could head home. Unless . . ."

His whole face changes, his mouth slipping to one side. He has powdered sugar in his hair, and I'm not going to tell him. "Unless?"

I swat at him. "Oh my god. Are you going to make me say that I like hanging out with you?"

He catches my hand in his, lifts it to his mouth. When he kisses my knuckles, I have to fight a full-body shiver. Kissing a hand should not be that hot. "I was actually thinking of going to one of those movies in the park down in Fremont tonight. It starts at sundown, so we should still have time to make it."

"That sounds like it could be fun."

"There's a catch, though—you're not going to like the movie." Grimacing, he holds up his phone. *Sleepless in Seattle*. "They play it every year," he says by way of defending himself.

"So this was a trap!"

"I swear, it wasn't!"

I groan. "*Fine*. I'll go. You definitely tricked me, but I'll go."

He excuses himself to change before we leave, and I text my parents that I'm hanging out with Julia, not wanting to answer questions about Tarek. When he reappears, he's dressed in dark jeans and a graphic tee, scratching at a patch of dry skin on his elbow.

He looks really nice in normal clothes.

I clutch my chest. "Are those—are those *forearms*? I may faint."

"Guess it's been a while since you've seen me in short sleeves," he says, looking only half bashful. "Ready?"

"I will try to keep my cynicism to myself. Mostly." I hop off the barstool and shoulder my purse. "Although I'm going to remind you *one more time,* that kind of grand-gesture movie romance isn't actually real."

With a lift of his eyebrows, he indicates the framed articles about his parents. "I beg to differ."

I let my gaze linger on their photographs—his mother's long hair, contrasted with the prim bun she wears most days, the way his father looks at her like he's not sure she's real. The Eiffel Tower in the background, a reenactment of the night they met. How many couples have posed like this in front of the Eiffel Tower? I wonder. How many have this kind of photo hanging in their homes?

"You really love it," I say. I'm not trying to pick a fight with him. I just want to understand—to the extent that my hardened heart is able to.

"It's the story I grew up with." He doesn't miss a beat. Tarek lives for people asking about his parents. "It was the first I learned about love, about romance, and I was just so *proud* that we had this epic family story. That there was this proof of how much they cared about each other, that they'd gone to such great lengths to find each other again. And now I see what they do and how much they love each other, and I want something like that someday. Simple as that."

*So everyone else just isn't trying hard enough?* That was what I asked him last year. And he told me yes, asserting that grand gestures were the only way to hold a relationship together when I've seen too much evidence of the opposite.

"Right. As simple as a chance encounter at the Eiffel Tower."

He gives me a wry smile. "And sometimes the world is terrible, and love stories . . . They make it feel less heavy."

I think about the times anxiety has felt like the tightest of blankets around me, one I can never fully cast off. "I guess I can't argue with that," I say as we head outside, Seattle flirting with dusk. "About wanting something to make the world feel less heavy."

# 18

A confession: I don't actually hate the movie.

Is it a masterful cinematic endeavor? Absolutely not. Is Meg Ryan a frightening woman whose actions—using her journalism job to track down Tom Hanks's address after hearing him on a radio call-in show, spying on him and his child playing at the beach—should have been reported to the police? One-hundred-percent.

But the nineties nostalgia is fun, even though I didn't live through it. No one's clothing fits. They're walking around in paper sacks that are vaguely human-shaped. Even playing a stalker, Meg Ryan is adorable, and there are moments that make me laugh. Every time this happens, Tarek turns his head, as though curious whether we find the same things funny.

We took his car, and I made fun of the stickers on it, which I didn't feel comfortable doing back when he took me to urgent care. After we parked a few blocks away on a darkened Fremont street, we made our way to the movie, where we found a spot in the back, and Tarek spread a blanket on the grass. At first I didn't know how to arrange my body. We weren't going to be all romantically draped over each other, like some of the couples surrounding us.

When I was little, I'd see couples like that, the kinds who were all over each other and who didn't care who saw, and I wanted so badly for someone to love me like that someday. Sometimes they were B+B clients and sometimes they were strangers. Of course, I had a child's concept of love back then, the kind quashed by a separation no one in my family wanted to talk about.

Tarek and I don't even touch for the first third of the movie. It's only when women nationwide start going wild over Tom Hanks telling his story on the radio that his hand drifts toward me, grazing the fabric of my dress before landing on my calf. It's so distracting, I miss what's happening on-screen for a solid minute.

To retaliate, I slide my hand to his back, his skin warm through his T-shirt. His vengeance: his hand creeping upward, thumb drawing a circle on my knee. I counter that by moving downward until I'm tucking my fingers into the curve of his belt, my thumb beneath his T-shirt, brushing up and down along his lower back. His breath hitches, and it feels like a victory.

He leans his head down to mine. "It's good, isn't it?" he says into my ear, and for several seconds I'm convinced he isn't talking about the movie.

Shortly after, there's an intermission, food trucks all around us selling popcorn and ice cream and nachos. I make a move to get up, to stretch my legs, but Tarek places a hand on my knee.

"Wait," he says, nodding toward the screen.

I sit back down. It's one of those corny social media shout-outs they have at big events: baseball games and concerts and graduations. The whole thing looks like a PowerPoint presentation put together by a seventh grader. Who got a B on it.

SENTIMENTAL IN SEATTLE are the words floating across the

screen, along with a graphic of a boat and the Space Needle.

"So original," I say.

The screen dissolves into a message that draws *aww*s from the audience.

> To Cynthia, from Richard
> We saw this movie for the first time on our first date. You lamented you'd never be as beautiful as Meg Ryan, and I agreed. Because you were wrong: you're even more beautiful, and it's as true today as it was then. Happy 20th wedding anniversary!

"Because nothing says 'I love you' like the animation effect that makes text bounce."

But Tarek is rapt, watching the screen with a strange intensity.

And that is when my stomach drops. Because the next message that appears on-screen is this:

> Quinn,
> I'm sorry we couldn't figure it out last summer, but I'm glad you gave this a chance.
> —Tarek

I must briefly dissociate because it takes a moment for it to register that *I* am this Quinn, that this is for me. I am speechless in Seattle. And then it doesn't matter that it's only a sentence. It doesn't matter that no one knows this is us, even as they coo all around us at these cheap, cliché messages.

"That was—" I try to swallow, but my tongue has doubled in size. Which, coincidentally, is the same thing the SENTIMENTAL IN SEATTLE text is doing on-screen. "How did you—when did you—"

"I, uh, saw it online. When I went to change before we left for the movie," Tarek says. He at least has the decency to look sheepish. "I thought . . . I thought it would be nice."

It reminds me that for a moment last summer, I wished that boat gesture had been for me. The gesture I now know *was* for me.

This gesture, it comes with expectations. It says, *Quick, figure out how you feel about this* and *What are you going to do to prove those feelings?*

It says, *This is going to end one day. Badly.*

"It's okay," I say quickly, even though it isn't. "I just . . . wasn't expecting it. That's all."

He brushes it off with a laugh. "Sorry. I really didn't think you'd react this way."

"We talk about this kind of thing constantly, Tarek." I try to keep my voice down, not wanting anyone to overhear. "You know I'm not a fan."

"I know. I know. But we're usually joking around, and last year I never found out how you felt about something like this being for *you*. I tried, but . . . well, we both know how that ended."

I want to laugh this off like he did, but it gets caught in my throat. There's a warning at the back of my mind. A flashing neon sign. Maybe it's true he "thought it would be nice," but I know Tarek. What this gesture really means is that he wants this to work. He wants *us* to work, when the truth is that there is no *us* that can last for a significant length of time.

We may have talked about last summer and shed the outermost layer of our insecurities. We may be a year older. But neither of us has changed. If anything, Tarek seems more romantic than ever, and that cannot possibly be a good thing.

"I thought this might be different," he says feebly.

"And then, what, you could post this on Instagram? And delete it if it didn't get enough likes?" It's not the kindest thing I could say, and I immediately regret it.

"Only if I had your permission." His expression is so rigid, I know he means it.

People are taking their artisan food truck popcorn back to their blankets, settling in for the second half.

If we talk about this much longer, he might see there's something buried beneath my loathing of these too-public displays of affection. And I can't dig that up.

The only option is to bury it deeper. To shut this down.

"Let's just watch the rest of the movie," I say, and I never thought I'd be so eager to watch two people falling in love.

"You can't say it's not a great ending," Tarek says as we walk to his car. "It's iconic. The way the music swells when she puts her hand in his—it gets me every time."

We've just watched Meg Ryan rush to the Empire State Building observation deck only moments before Tom Hanks and his kid get in an elevator going down. Except the kid forgets his backpack, and as Meg Ryan picks it up and pulls a teddy bear out of it, the elevator doors open, and boom, Tom Hanks is back. They gaze at each other, seeming to instantly know who the other is. *It's nice to meet you,* Meg Ryan says, the last line of the movie.

"I didn't. All I'm saying is I don't buy that she's in love with him. I don't buy that it was destiny. She doesn't even have a conversation with him until the end of the movie!"

This, I can still do, this kind of bickering that feels playful, innocent, not laced with expectation the way his on-screen message was.

As though reading my mind, Tarek stops on the sidewalk, fiddling with his keys, not meeting my eyes. "I really am sorry. About that message."

"I like spending time with you," I say softly, because I don't want to fight, and I don't want this to ruin what's otherwise been such a good day. Whatever we've started feels precarious, even if it cannot go where he might ultimately want it to. "I want to keep doing that, okay? But I'm not a balloons and skywriting kind of person."

He grimaces. "Okay, then I might need to make a few calls."

I swat at his arm. "You don't have to do any of that. Not with me." I mean for this to be a good thing, but he's not laughing.

Part of it was sweet, that gesture. At least, I think my heart fluttered, or whatever it is a heart is supposed to do in response to that kind of thing, before the dread set in.

Still, I feel compelled to extend some kind of olive branch. Something to make him more of his regular self. Because truthfully, this was fun. Not just the movie, but our conversations at Mansour's and the zalabya he made, and it's not something I want to have been a onetime thing. I want another night like this, a realization that rocks the ground beneath me.

"So." I scuff at the pavement with my sandal. "The woman

whose harp studio I've been working in, she's having a show next weekend. I was going to ask Julia, but . . . maybe you want to go too?"

I deliver the invitation directly to the sidewalk. It's dangerously datelike, and I might regret it, but when I risk a glance at him, the way Tarek lights up to match the full moon is enough to ease my panic. It's both lovely and terrifying.

"I'd love to," he says, stepping closer, grazing my wrist with the fingertips of his free hand. "Thank you."

Two friends hanging out. Not a date, even when I close the space between us and kiss him, his hands on my waist and mine in his hair. This is easier. The physical always has been—no thinking, just feeling, touching, sighing. An anchor when I've felt anchorless.

He pulls back, nodding to his car. "Do you want to, uh . . . ?" A nervous Tarek is not something I'm used to seeing, and the idea that he's nervous because of *me* is almost too much to handle.

"Make out in the car?" I ask.

"I was going to say 'get in the car,' but yeah, you know what, I like the honesty. Do you want to make out with me in my 2011 Ford Focus, Quinn Berkowitz?"

"Yes. Yes I do."

When we get in the back seat, I do my best to push away my car-hookup-related nerves. Maybe it's the dark or the weight of the words we've exchanged, but it doesn't take long for us to turn frantic. I press myself close to him, his mouth hot on my neck as I pull at his hair. The scent of him clouds my senses and quite possibly my good judgment.

I don't need to do this to turn off my brain, I remind myself.

I wasn't searching for a distraction—he just happens to be one. *I am in control.*

"I'm sorry about—about my hands," he says, pulling back when he touches my shoulders. I can barely see the red of the rash in the moonlight. "I hope it's not gross or anything."

"Tarek," I say softly. "It's not. Not at all."

He lets out a breath, clearly relieved. "I'm not as self-conscious as I used to be, but it still feels like something I need to explain to people. I've accepted that it's going to be bad sometimes, even with the creams and medication, even if I still wish I didn't have it."

"You shouldn't have to explain it. It's your body." I want to tell him I've always found him beautiful. But it's not right for this moment and I'd hate for him to read into it, so I don't.

"Thank you. For saying that."

He draws me to him again, and in this tight space, it's so easy to mold my body to his, especially when I'm not in my stiff wedding planner shirt and slacks. My thin dress might as well be lingerie. There's more skin to explore, and that's exactly what he does, his hands running up my legs underneath the dress.

"I like this, by the way," he says, playing with the hem of it. "The dogs with the hats. One of your rest-of-the-time dresses?"

"My what?"

"When you gave me that tour of your room. You had your dull dresses and the more exciting ones you wore the rest of the time."

I'm stunned he remembered something like that. I'm also not used to talking this much while hooking up with someone. Sometimes I'm so wrapped up in sensation that the person I'm with almost becomes faceless, but Tarek seems intent on reminding me that it's him I'm here with.

"Yes. One of my rest-of-the-time dresses."

What he must mean is that he likes the way it bunches up around my hips, the way his fingers meet my bare thighs just above my knees. I tug him down on top of me, one leg on either side of him, kissing him deeper. He could easily pull the dress over my head, but instead, one by one, he flicks open the buttons.

When he gets the last one and I'm in my bra and underwear, he buries his face in my neck. "Give me a minute." He lets out a rough laugh, pressing his mouth into the spot where my neck meets my shoulder, dropping kisses lower and lower and lower, until he reaches my navel and I can't help giggling.

I rub my hand over the front of his jeans, and he sucks in a breath. Maybe my memory is failing me, but hooking up has never been this *fun*. I knew this would erase any lingering weirdness from earlier this evening.

"Our clothing ratio seems radically unfair." I reach for his shirt, and he helps me tug it over his head. It's cruel, really, that it's too dark for me to take in every detail of his chest, but I can use my hands to map him out.

Without my dress in his way, his hand travels from thigh to hip, free of obstructions. "Is this okay?"

"Yes," I breathe out, but as soon as his fingers skim along the outside of my underwear, I feel my body tighten up. "Wait. Stop." He immediately pulls back. The nerves take over. "I'm sorry, it's just—me and cars . . ."

"Ah. I'm not going to lie and say I don't remember what

happened during Never Have I Ever," he says, and there's enough moonlight for me to catch him blushing.

We rearrange so we're sitting side by side in the back seat. There's no way I'm forgetting he's the one I'm here with right now, but he shouldn't be doing this. He shouldn't be patiently waiting for me to explain, and I shouldn't want to.

And yet the words start tumbling out. "I'm not even sure it was the car, actually," I say. "I've only . . . had sex . . . that one time. In the car. At least, sex in the way society usually defines sex, which is outdated and heteronormative, but, um. Yeah."

He's just watching me, listening.

"It didn't last very long," I continue. "And I didn't—well, it was done when he was done." I could have said something, I'm sure. But he also could have offered. Could have asked.

Tarek looks like I just told him I let Jonathan punt Edith over a fence. "That's . . . wow. I'm sorry."

*You don't have to be sorry*, I want to say. This conversation is veering too close to relationship territory. I wanted to get in the car specifically so I wouldn't be having those kinds of thoughts. I don't know why we can't just get one of us off—realistically, him—and then go home.

Because the last time we got close to a relationship—and now that I know we were even closer than I used to think—it only hurt us both.

"We don't have to keep talking about it," I say. "If you don't want to do that, it's fine. I'm used to it. You don't have to go through the motions just because you think you're supposed to. Like, it's still fun for me, even if I don't . . . you know."

"Are you saying you've never had an org—"

I'm not sure why, but I can't bear to hear him utter the word. "With someone else?" I shake my head.

"But you've had one before, in general? On your own?"

I nod, hiding my burning face against the seat.

"Hey." He rubs circles on my back. "You do it. I do it. Why is that embarrassing?"

"I don't know," I admit.

Maybe it isn't. Maybe it isn't embarrassing, especially when he's treating it all as this very normal thing. Because as much as I want to fast-forward to the part where we're sighing against each other again, the more I talk, the more the dread turns to relief. Maybe I've needed to talk about it and I haven't found the right words.

"I've only had sex with one person too," he says. "In case you were wondering."

I was, and I'm glad he's telling me. "With other guys, when we were fooling around, there was always one clear end goal for them." I make a gesture with my hands that probably looks like that old Shake Weight commercial or opening a can of soda. The latter is possibly too on the nose. "It would take too long for me, so they'd get tired or bored or whatever, and they'd either stop, or I'd ask them to stop. Their end goal didn't always include . . ."

"You having an orgasm." He finishes the word this time, and okay. It's not the worst word in the world. Not at all. "I can assure you," he continues, a fingertip brushing my ankle, "I am not going to get bored."

When he talks about it like this is something he wants as much as I do, I'm convinced I might be made of only desire.

"Okay," I say in the smallest voice. "Then . . . that sounds like it might be enjoyable."

He grins this ridiculous grin, one that turns me inside out, and when he kisses me, I am just . . . gone.

I'm not sure how long it takes. Frankly, I'm not thinking about that. All I know is the way his breath catches when he touches me, that he's gentle and focused, that he talks to me. And then I grip his shoulders as his fingers move faster, faster, until everything else dissolves and it's just him and me and a brilliant warm intensity.

Maybe this was the difference: the fact that he *cared*, which is so unlike my past experiences that I'm not sure how to process it.

Once I recover, I return the favor, touching him until he shudders and lets out this low moan, like he's trying not to be too loud, even though we're alone in the dark out here. I want to bottle up that sound. Make it my ringtone. Learn it on the harp.

This was supposed to turn off my thoughts. It wasn't supposed to be him telling me how not-boring this was as he plants soft kisses along my ear, my jaw. And I wasn't supposed to like any of that.

I don't trust my brain and I don't have the right words, so I just hold him tighter.

# 19

Work brunch happens the last Sunday of every month. Until the laptops come out, it's the only time I have with my whole family that isn't dominated by B+B. Dad plays the local public radio jazz station, despite all of us telling him that he can stream any musician he wants, but he always insists he likes the excitement of never knowing what song is coming next. Dads gonna dad.

I take my medication and rush downstairs, worrying about poisoning Edith for only a brief moment while I refill her water dish. A good OCD day.

We each have a specialty, a dish we've honed over the years, and Asher comes over early to start cooking. I heap Dad's triple-berry pancakes, Mom's black-pepper bacon, Asher's frittata, and my chocolate-chip banana bread onto my plate and pour a glass of farmers market orange-ginger juice. It's also mandatory that we wear pajamas the whole time. I'm wearing my llamas-or-alpacas shorts and matching shirt with a long striped robe, my hair just long enough for a messy bun. Though he only ever saw them over the phone, the pajamas remind me of Tarek.

Then again, a lot of things remind me of Tarek lately. It's the end of July, four weeks until Victoria and Lincoln's wedding, six weeks until Asher and Gabe's. Seven weeks for Tarek and me to keep doing . . . whatever it is we're doing.

"I probably shouldn't say this," Dad says once we dig in, "but *damn*, this is good bacon."

"We're all terrible Jews," I agree, swiping another slice.

Mom's eyes light up behind her cat-eye glasses. "We just won't tell any of the rabbis we work with."

This is the part of my family I love so much. The part that isn't connected to B+B.

For the first time ever, Asher declines it. "I'm actually—well, with Gabe, at home . . . we keep kosher. Both of us."

There's an odd silence as we all take this in.

"Sure, of course," Dad says. He stares down at his 00 DAYS WITHOUT A DAD JOKE mug. "That's admirable of you."

"How long?" I ask, flipping through a mental catalog of the meals I've consumed with Asher this summer.

Asher shrugs, parting her serving of frittata like the Red Sea. "A few months, I guess?"

This feels like something I should know about my own sister. Except . . . I haven't spent enough time with her this summer to have learned about it. And even though I respect it, it feels like yet another thing she's doing with her soon-to-be-married life that's so separate from the life she used to have.

My family isn't my family if we're not all perky and smiling, so Dad seizes an opportunity to smooth things over. "Should we go around and share highlights?" he asks, ushering us into the work part of work brunch.

Mom goes first. "I scheduled a final venue walk-through with the film crew next Thursday, which Quinn's going to do with me. And she's agreed to stop by the museum this week so we can have a sense of what the space looks like with their new exhibit."

Dad shares about a new client, a couple referred to us by friends whose wedding we planned last year, and Asher talks about the wardrobe for a 1920s-themed wedding taking place in the fall. There's a palpable excitement in the air, mugs being waved for emphasis, mimosas flowing freely for everyone but me.

"Quinn?" Dad says. "You're up."

*Well, I've been making out with our caterer's son. He's as good at kissing as he is at cooking, and we all know he's very good at cooking.*

*I've also been taking secret harp lessons in exchange for helping build harps.*

*And I'm trying to figure out how to tell all of you I want to quit.*

"We finalized Victoria and Lincoln's menu with Mansour's," I say. "And Asher and I decided her entrance song would be Smash Mouth's 'All Star,' so I've been learning that on the harp."

"Is it too late to change my mind?" Asher says. "I was thinking we could do 'Tubthumping.' Chumbawamba's lyrics really speak to me."

"Anything for the bride."

My parents look grim, as though worried Smash Mouth or Chumbawamba will actually be played during the processional.

"You two are going to send us to early graves," Mom says. "Not that Smash Mouth doesn't have their time and place—they always get people dancing during the reception, but—"

"Mom. We're doing Etta James. Don't worry."

Mom visibly exhales, and I can't help laughing at this, too.

This kind of inside joke with my sister won't happen when I'm no longer part of B+B. Work brunch and betting on reception songs with my dad—gone.

"I can work next weekend," Asher is saying. "I'm actually feeling pretty great about where everything is? I haven't had a stress dream in at least a week. All that's left is for me to show up looking flawless."

"Oh, wonderful," Mom says. "We could use an extra pair of hands."

"Next weekend," I say, sensing an opportunity here. "That's the Stern-Rosenfeld wedding, right?" Even though it's right there on the calendar in the kitchen, the one behind my back.

"Yep," Dad says. "Should be really spectacular."

"The Salish Lodge always is," Mom puts in.

"I, um—I'm not sure I'll be able to go?"

Everyone's head whips toward me. "What?" The angle of my mom's ponytail somehow manages to look just as perplexed as she does.

And then there's this moment. An opportunity. I've had a handful of them over the years, and I've always backed away, content in my cowardice. What if I told them now? *There's this other thing that makes me happy*, I'd say. *I really want you to be happy for me.* They'd be furious, but they'd get over it. They'd have to. Sure, it would probably cast a shadow over my sister's wedding, and she might resent me for years to come, but at least it would be out there. My anxious brain wouldn't have to war over it anymore.

Even inside my head, the suggestion is absurd.

"I don't know if I'll be able to make it on Saturday?" I say, phrasing it like a question again, hating the way my voice slides up at the end.

"What do you mean, you don't know?" Dad laughs. "Should we check with your secretary?"

"No, I mean—I told Julia I'd help her with a new mural." I realize how half-assed the lie is as soon as it slips past my lips.

"Julia will understand this is important," Mom says. "She always has."

That's what they've always said. *Julia will understand. Your teachers will understand. Everyone will understand.*

Just like that, the moment is gone. The laptops come out to review Victoria and Lincoln's master timeline, and the best part of work brunch is over.

"I know what's going on with you," Asher says later, when we're washing plates in the kitchen. Our parents have moved to their office.

"Yes, it's a new shampoo from Julia's parents, and I agree, my hair looks great." I slide a bowl onto the drying rack.

"Well, now that you mention it, there's definitely a bit more volume there. But no. The reason you've been acting off lately. You disappeared for a while at Kaci and Mariana's wedding, and then the floral consultation you didn't show up to, and now this, trying to get out of a wedding? None of it's like you."

"I am an onion."

She rolls her eyes. "You and Tarek," she says triumphantly, waving a whisk and flicking suds onto me. "You're together. I've been picking up on some vibes."

"Vibes? There are no vibes. We're friends. If anything, you picked up on friendship vibes."

"I do *not* vibe like that with my friends." She wrinkles her nose. "Okay, I'm over the word 'vibe.' What I mean is, there was some tension between the two of you."

I let out a deep breath, relenting. It's much easier than telling her the real reason. "Yes. Well, we're not together, but we've been hanging out. A little."

"I love being right. You guys have always been adorable."

It's strange, Asher not knowing the whole story. Julia's the only person I told about the email, and while Asher knows some of my hookup history, my crush on Tarek always felt too tangled with work. She was such a mini-Mom that I could never be sure how she'd react. Evidently, it doesn't bother her at all.

"We're not labeling it or anything," I say, accepting another clean bowl from her. "Please don't tell Mom and Dad."

Asher sets her mouth in a firm line. "Sure. What's another secret I'm keeping for you," she says, and when I flinch at this, she says, "Wait. Quinn. I didn't mean it like that. I'm sorry."

"I know I should have been there last week. I messed up."

We never fight, and I don't want to start now. I'm not used to disappointment from her either. We've always felt like equals, but her disappointment reminds me of the years between us. That sometimes she feels more in charge than my equal.

It makes me wonder, not for the first time this summer or even this brunch, how well we know each other anymore. It's fine that she wants to keep kosher, but it's a sudden change, a clear sign that she's about to become someone new. Of course, I know "wife" won't be the sole piece of her identity. But it will be a new part of her identity, and it will be something I can't possibly understand. And, of course, I hope her marriage lasts, that it makes her happy, but that cynical piece of me that never sleeps wonders if that happiness has an expiration date.

"We're all under a lot of stress right now," Asher says, but when aren't we? Weddings are stressful. That's a simple fact.

When we finish up, Asher pats my shoulder in a way that's supposed to be sister-friendly but instead makes me feel very, very young. Then she disappears into the office with my parents, their door cracked so that I can't see them, but I can hear them. The three of them in there with this business my parents built from nothing.

Despite what Julia says, what Tarek says, maybe it would be easier to keep pretending. After all, I already know how to do that. Maybe business classes wouldn't be too terrible. Because the idea of not being part of this in the future . . . It's heartbreaking. A specific brand of loneliness I'm not sure I want to become familiar with again.

The horrible truth is this: I don't know how to be part of my family if I'm no longer part of the family business.

# 20

Two days before the Stern-Rosenfeld wedding, I tell my parents I'm sick, and yep, I hate myself for it. I was calculated in the way I worked up to it: told them I felt feverish and fatigued on Thursday but that I'd probably be fine by Saturday, thought I was getting better Friday afternoon, but couldn't peel myself out of bed Saturday morning. Mom brought up a bowl of matzo ball soup, our go-to Berkowitz cure for a variety of ailments. It slid down my throat, slicked with guilt.

It was the only way. I just have to buy a little time before I tell them the truth. I'm losing track of the number of secrets I'm keeping, and the idea of maintaining my double life beyond this summer makes me want to crawl back into bed with a vat of matzo ball soup. Or directly into the vat. I'm flexible.

I'm waiting in line outside the downtown music venue with Tarek, Julia, and Noelle, clutching a bouquet like a child unwilling to let go of their favorite toy. Julia has been teasing me about the flowers nonstop, and now that Tarek and Noelle are here, they've joined in. Yes, I spent fifteen minutes at Metropolitan Market picking out the right flowers. Yes, I took one bouquet to the self-checkout before realizing it wasn't quite right, doubling back, and selecting a different one. As the daughter of wedding planners, I should probably know more about flowers than I do. In all seriousness, I'm not sure how to explain to them how much I love Maxine's workshop, how much it's meant to me.

It's a posh, artsy crowd, and though we are not a dressy city, most people are summer formal. I'm wearing a chambray maxi-dress, my hair pulled back and half braided on one side. When Tarek got here, he pulled me close, placed his lips beneath my ear, and said, "I like your hair like this." And I felt myself melt a little bit into the sidewalk.

Not a date, not a date, not a date.

Julia leans in to adjust the thin strap of Noelle's dress, which has been on the verge of falling down her shoulder for the past five minutes. It's a simple, almost effortless little gesture, and Noelle gives her an appreciative grin before Julia slides her hand into hers.

"How long have you been dating?" Tarek asks. What he's wearing isn't too unlike his catering uniform, though he's traded his starched white shirt for one that's soft and slate gray, the top two buttons undone.

"Officially? A few weeks," Julia says. "But it probably would have been longer if I hadn't been so awkward about everything in the beginning."

"It was endearing," Noelle assures her.

They talk about college, and I try my best not to feel left out. Julia and Noelle have been stalking their roommates-to-be on Instagram, and Tarek says he's rooming again with Landon, his freshman-year roommate. From what I gather, Landon seems to be his closest friend from school. Tarek even gives them tips on how to dress up dorm food and what you should and should not attempt to make in a microwave.

There's a silent auction happening in the lobby to benefit a local music charity, two rows of items ranging from fancy gift baskets to spa trips to vacations. Maxine's even auctioning off a harp. Though I'm sure none of us can afford anything, we pretend we can.

"Ah, yes, I'd certainly bid on this trip to Martha's Vineyard if I hadn't just summered there last year," Julia says in her best rich-person voice.

Noelle adjusts the brim of an invisible hat. "It would be an embarrassment to summer in the same place two years in a row."

As we turn to the other side of the table, something catches my eye: backstage passes to the Seattle Rock Orchestra. I haven't heard of it, so I step closer to read more. "Oh wow. This one is actually really cool."

The Seattle Rock Orchestra, I learn, is exactly what it sounds like: an orchestra that plays rock music. They've done the Beatles, David Bowie, even Lizzo. I had no idea something like this existed—I assumed orchestras only played music that had been around for hundreds of years. It's wild, really, how much I don't know about music, this thing that's been in my life since I was born.

"You could try for it," Tarek says.

I peer down at the bids. "For six hundred dollars? My parents don't pay me nearly that much to play Pachelbel's Canon every other weekend."

Serious bidders have started to give us sour looks. I don't want to embarrass Maxine, so we head inside the auditorium and take our seats. The harp is already onstage, waiting for her.

"You seem nervous." Tarek places a hand on the knee I can't stop jiggling up and down. "Everything okay?"

"I mean, have you met me?" I say, forcing a laugh. But he's not wrong. Maybe it's that I know how long it's been since she performed like this and I have secondhand nerves. There are so many people here to see *her*. At weddings, I've only ever been part of the scenery.

I wonder what it would feel like to build the instrument and then play it in front of a sold-out audience like this one.

"She just hasn't played in a while," I continue. "I'm probably projecting. She's a professional. I'm sure she's extremely calm."

"But she's, like, world-famous, right? You said she played on the soundtrack of *Dragonthrone*?"

"Oh, I loved that show," Noelle says. "But I'm still bitter about the last season."

Before the curtain goes up, I get a text from Asher. How are you feeling? The guilt rolls back in like a storm cloud, and I dash off a quick a little better, probably going to sleep soon before I stow my phone.

There's no opening act, and during the first half, Maxine plays some popular, recognizable songs, including the theme to *Dragonthrone*. Then she moves on to her original pieces.

I've seen her play in videos and in her studio. I've been working alongside her for the past month. But here, I am *riveted*. The audience is holding its breath, and it's wild to see so many people on the edge of their seats for the world's tamest instrument. She's just that good. The sound is rich, warm, at times light and lovely and at others deeply haunting. Her hands, flying up and down it in a way that looks somehow both natural and precisely choreographed.

The harp she's playing—I know how it began. Several pieces

of wood, cut and sanded (and sanded and sanded and sanded) and glued and stained and strung. I know the number of hours it must have taken, the sharp smell of the lacquer when it was freshly painted, the tediousness of getting all the strings and levers just right. I know the way it might have felt when she sat down and played a song all the way through for the first time.

I know all of these things, and that makes my heart swell in my chest.

"Wow," Tarek says under his breath. His hand stays on my knee, his thumb tapping along, and I'm too entranced by Maxine to unpack what that might mean. "She's incredible."

And that's enough to fill me with pride. He sees it too. It's not just me mesmerized by what this instrument can do, what the right person can create when they're playing it. I've been performing for years, both literally and figuratively, but I've never truly *played*. Not like this.

*What about music?* Noelle asked at the farmers market earlier in the summer. Was it too obvious? she wanted to know.

Maybe it was, and I just couldn't see it yet.

"These are for you," I blurt, passing Maxine the bouquet that's now a little lopsided after sitting on the floor during her performance. I hope she doesn't notice.

"You didn't have to do that," she says as she accepts it. "Thank you."

We waited in the lobby as Maxine made the rounds, greeting people she knew and some she didn't, thanking them for coming and for supporting this cause, a local music charity. When she spotted me, her eyes lit up, as though she was surprised I'd shown up.

She's dressed in black pants and a capelike shirt that makes her look vaguely medieval. She's wearing only a bit more makeup than she usually does, some shimmer on her cheeks, a mauve lipstick. A pair of wooden earrings I imagine she carved herself.

"That was amazing. Beyond amazing. And I, uh, brought some friends." It's frustrating that I'm still anxious around her, this adult I'm trying to prove myself to. I do some quick introductions.

"It wasn't too boring for all of you?" Maxine asks. She seems genuinely touched that I brought people with me.

"Nowhere near," Tarek says. "I had no idea you could do things like that on the harp."

Maxine smiles. "That's what I try to convince people. Even Quinn."

"I'm fully a convert, don't worry."

Someone calls her name. "I have a few more people to thank, but I appreciate this so much." She raises the bouquet. "Quinn, I'll see you this week? And thank you for coming. Really," she says with a quick squeeze of my hand, and maybe she really didn't think I'd be here.

We all decide to grab some food nearby. My parents won't be home until late, so I might as well get my mileage out of this lie. Before we go, Julia announces she has to go to the bathroom. "Quinn's coming with me," she says.

"Sorry, she's not potty trained yet," I tell Tarek and Noelle as Julia drags me to the bathroom. "That wasn't subtle. Like, at all. You know that, right?"

Julia shrugs as she leans close to the mirror to brush away a stray eyelash. "I'm aware. I just wanted to talk to you. About Tarek."

"There's nothing to say." My face is flushed, and I rinse my hands before patting my cheeks, hoping to return them to their regular shade of pale. "We're friends with benefits. This is the friend part. I'm sure we'll get into some of those benefits later."

"Quinn. Sweetie. Darling. Treasure of treasures. That boy really likes you."

"You sound so surprised. I'm very likable!"

She rolls her eyes. "I'm serious. He sat through two hours of harp music for you."

"So did you."

"But my hand wasn't on your knee the whole time."

"I know what it might look like," I say, "but I don't want a relationship."

"And why is that, again?"

About a hundred reasons that sounded a lot less fuzzy in my brain a couple weeks ago. "You know why. You know what my parents went through."

"You're not marrying the guy."

"Okay, obviously. But you and Noelle—that seems to be going well?" I hope she doesn't see it as the clear subject diversion it is.

"It is. I really am bummed that we didn't get together sooner, but at least our schools aren't that far apart."

"You're changing your mind about long-distance?"

Julia gives a coy smile. "Maybe? I just feel like we owe it to the relationship to at least give it a try."

"That's great," I say, and I mean it. But it doesn't mean I need to want that for myself.

Back in the lobby, I decide to check on the Seattle Rock Orchestra tickets to see if by some stroke of luck, all the bidders dropped out and they're going for twenty bucks.

What I see on the sheet of paper instead makes me feel as though someone's run my stomach through Maxine's band saw.

*Tarek Mansour . . . $750*

"Quinn? You okay?"

Silently, I jab a finger at his bid, and Julia's eyes go wide.

"Oh. Holy shit. He really, *really* likes you, then."

"This isn't *like*. It's . . . I don't know what it is." And before I can give it a second thought, I snatch the paper and march outside, where Tarek and Noelle are arguing over where we should grab pizza.

"You can't do this," I say, pressing the paper into his chest. Thank god the auction hasn't closed yet.

"What is—oh." Realization dawns, and he gingerly takes the piece of paper from me. "I thought—you made it seem like you wanted them, and it's for a good cause, and . . ."

"I think we'll meet you guys there?" Julia tugs on Noelle's arm and says to me, "I'll text you where we end up."

My face burns. I don't want to do this in public, but that's the thing—Tarek forces these gestures to be public, which makes it impossible for any conversation about them to be private.

"Do you even have this kind of money?" I say once Julia and Noelle have sped away in Julia's car. "Because I definitely don't."

"I have some savings," he says quietly.

"I just—I don't know how you leaped to this conclusion. Regular tickets can't be that expensive. If you wanted to do something

219

nice, why couldn't it be that? Why did it have to be this—this—"

"Grand?"

"*Excessive.*" I reach to run a hand through my hair out of frustration, getting even more frustrated when I remember I attempted a hairstyle and don't want to mess it up. "Even after I told you how I felt about that message at the movie. Evidently you weren't listening."

"I'm listening," he insists. "I'm just not understanding. All I'm trying to do is show you that I like this. Spending time with you."

"Really? Because it feels like you're doing this for *you*. Not for me. Because you want me to, I don't know, fall at your feet or something." It's so ridiculous to say it out loud that I can't help scoffing.

"Of course it's for you. Why else would I have done it?" he says, holding up the paper again. "I thought it would be romantic. Clearly I was wrong. Why do you act like that's the worst thing in the world, for someone to want to be romantic toward you?"

"Because it's not real." Our old argument, except now it's much more personal. I don't know what else I can say without digging into my family trauma, opening up the wound and showing him how ugly it is. I'm back at the marina, and he's telling me my parents, who've devoted their whole lives to *till death do us part*, didn't try hard enough to keep their marriage from fracturing.

Sure, not in those words, but I can't imagine he'd change his theory if he knew the truth.

I walk over to a nearby bench and drop down onto it, hoping it'll calm my temper. He approaches cautiously, as though worried I won't want him to sit next to me.

"Quinn. I'm sorry. Okay? I messed up. I'll scratch off my name, tell them I made a mistake."

"Okay. I would appreciate that."

This is all he knows how to do. He's never not made that clear to me. This can't last much longer—or there won't be any of our friendship left afterward either.

When I speak again, my voice is softer. "We can go home, if you want. I'll text Julia some excuse."

His brow furrows. "What? Why?"

A laugh slips out. "Because we're fighting? You really want to keep hanging out with me after this?"

"Yes?" He phrases it as a question. "I'm not going to stop spending time with you because we had one argument."

I wasn't expecting that. "Well . . . okay then."

I guess . . . we're done fighting? There's no way it's that easy, but he forges ahead. "Did Julia text you where they are?"

As I dig for my phone, fighting conversation whiplash, Tarek makes a move to reach for my shoulder—maybe to wrap an arm around me, or maybe just to give me a friendly pat. On instinct, I dodge it.

It's not worth it for the way his face falls, but I promise myself I'll make it up to him in the dark later.

# 21

Pizza turns out to be supremely good at smoothing frayed nerves. Since Julia had to be up early for another Kirschbaum camping extravaganza, she and Noelle took off ten minutes ago, leaving Tarek and me alone to navigate our awkward post–silent auction feelings. Except—it hasn't been that awkward.

I stare down at my last half slice of pulled pork, pineapple, and jalapeño. "Do you want this?" I ask him from across the booth. Tarek declared this the best pizza in Seattle, and he was right; I'd never had wood-fired pizza quite like this, with gorgeous blackened bubbles on the crust, and it's a crime I can't finish it.

Tarek shakes his head. "Pork."

"Shit. Sorry. Now I feel bad for eating this in front of you." Pork products are getting Berkowitzes into all kinds of situations lately.

"Don't apologize. And please, don't stop on my account."

Tarek doesn't often talk about his religion, but now I'm wondering if it's because we've only just recently started talking about serious things. Mansour's doesn't have pork on their menu, and aside from that, they only use humanely raised animal products. The first time I realized this might be unusual for a catering company was when my parents dropped a client who said something insensitive when they suggested Mansour's. My parents refunded all their money, despite the work they'd already done. Said they refused to work with people like that.

"I don't keep kosher." I motion to the pizza. "I mean. Obviously. My sister's fiancé, he's, like, very Jewish, and I remember he was shocked when they started dating and she ordered pork at a Chinese restaurant in front of him, completely unaware. And now she observes more of the customs he grew up with, and she's keeping kosher too. Sometimes I feel like I'm letting down 'my people' or whatever. I don't know. I'm not a very good Jew, I guess."

It's not something I've ever really vocalized, and he's quiet for a moment, taking it all in. "I feel like there are probably a lot of different ways to be Jewish, just like there are a lot of ways to be Muslim. Is it something you think about a lot?"

I shake my head. "Only occasionally. But when I do, it's suddenly all I can think about. What about you?"

"My parents aren't nearly as religious as their parents were," he says. "But some things have just sort of stuck? Like, we work with a halal butcher, but not everything we eat or serve is halal. My mom drinks, but my dad doesn't, and, well, you saw me do it at the beach. And I've had sex before marriage."

"Right," I say, feeling my face heat up.

"There are some things I agree with and some I don't, but I still consider myself a Muslim. Just like you probably still consider yourself Jewish."

And I do.

We split what's left of the bill. I love this city at night, especially in the summer. Maybe that's why I was so bold after the movie in the park, because I feel it now too: this sense of heady anticipation, liquid gold in my veins. *Opportunity. Possibilities.* We're past the halfway mark, the days getting shorter, those opportunities dwindling. Tarek and I have been seeing each other a couple times a week, sometimes at a wedding and sometimes on nights like this.

Logically, I know I've got to start distancing myself before we get any deeper. But it's so hard to remember that when we're tangled in his back seat or even when we're talking about pizza.

Before we head out, I check my bag, probably spending more time doing it than usual. Checking, checking, checking.

"There's something I've been wondering," he says when we get outside. "And feel free to tell me to shut up if it sounds insensitive."

"This sounds ominous."

"I swear, it's not. Or if it is, you can be the judge. I've just been wondering—when you're doing those things, those checks, what does it feel like? I'm not judging. I just want to try to understand it."

I try not to be embarrassed that he noticed. "It's sort of like . . . getting stuck in a loop. I'll do something, but I won't believe my memory that I actually did it, even though I *know* I would hear it if I dropped my keys or phone, or I would feel it if a door didn't lock, or I would see it if I didn't turn the stove off. Like I can't trust any of my senses. So I check again, and I still don't have actual proof that it happened, or I worry I'm checking so much that I may have undone the thing I want to make sure of, so I keep doing it, and then I can't stop.

"When I was at my worst, I went through this phase where I'd take photos of things to make sure they were the way they were supposed to be. I had hundreds and hundreds of pictures on my phone of my house's locked front door, of Edith, of our stove." I'm not used to being this open with someone I'm hooking up with, but I don't hate the way it feels to tell him all of this. "It's that searching for proof and realizing I'm never going to get it. That's how my therapist talked about it. Because the photos didn't stop me from doing additional checks, or from taking even more photos. I have to be okay with the uncertainty. I have to trust myself. It's a fight with my brain, and most of the time, my brain is acting especially infuriating."

"I'm sorry." He taps the side of my head with a fingertip. "I happen to like your brain, whether it's fighting with you or not."

Tarek liking my brain feels a little too boyfriend-adjacent for comfort, so I smile and try to brush it off. "Speaking of fighting," I say. "I have the perfect idea to end this night. How do you feel about breaking things?"

Tarek is wearing goggles and a hard hat and wielding a sledge-hammer. I'm sure I look equally goofy in my protective gear, plus a borrowed jacket and pants, since I wasn't allowed to break things in a dress.

"A rage cage," Tarek says, laughing as we enter the room. "Maybe nothing should surprise me about you at this point."

"No, it's RAAAAGE CAAAAGE! You have to be aggro while saying it or it doesn't count. And it's supposed to be very cathartic."

I'd always wanted to go to a wrecking club like this. Breaking things and not getting in trouble for it? What's not to love? I didn't think it was possible to look good in goggles and a hard hat, but damn it, of course Tarek pulls it off. After we get a safety spiel from one of the employees, we're led into a graffitied, industrial-looking room set up to look like a very sad office: an ancient computer and TV, a chair with three legs, and a long desk with woodworking that would horrify Maxine, stacked with old ceramic plates.

I pick up my sledgehammer and bring it down on the chair, and a hunk of it breaks off. Then I do it again, smashing it into smaller pieces. In a Venn diagram with people who play the harp on one side and people who like to smash things on the other, I thought there wouldn't be any overlap, but nope, I am loving this.

Tarek takes his sledgehammer to the stack of plates. He's gentle at first, barely nicking one, before sweeping them to the floor in a massive crash.

"You want to do this one together?" I ask, and we join forces to obliterate a TV monitor.

I can't remember the last time I laughed this much.

After about twenty minutes of hard-core destruction, we take a break on a bench in the room. Tarek removes his goggles and hat. His hairline is damp with sweat.

"This is a great look for you," he says, pulling my hat down over my eyes. If we were a real couple, we'd probably be taking selfies. "That was quite a lot of rage. Well done. I've got to come back here with Harun sometime."

"It's been a summer." I take off the hat and fiddle with the brim of it. "Sometimes I wonder if it would really be that terrible if I kept going along with what my parents want."

He just stares at me. "And keep being unhappy?"

"I don't know! It's less scary than the alternative. It's comfortable. You're not there when they're guilting me into something. They make me feel like I can't say no to them."

I've planned it out in my head a hundred times. It starts with those words women use to qualify things so often, "maybe" and "I'm not sure if" and "I just."

"Even if it does hurt them," Tarek says, "that hurt isn't going to last forever. Isn't it better to tell them sooner as opposed to having it keep building? Wouldn't it hurt less that way, for all of you?"

"Why do you have to be right?" I grumble.

"I'm older. More educated."

I roll my eyes. "So if I told them, what would that look like? 'Hey, Mom, hey, Dad, I fucking quit. Oh, and by the way, I've been taking harp lessons because I wanted to expand on my least marketable skill.'"

"You still have to play for me."

"I will, I will," I say, unsure whether I'm lying. "It's just hard, with my parents, and even finding the time to play . . ."

He reaches over, pulls my legs across his lap. "I know. Hey. Let me try something. Don't think—just say whatever comes to mind first. Five years from now, what are you doing? Your biggest, wildest dream?"

I close my eyes. I can imagine myself with B+B, but maybe that's only because it's the default. Would I still be helping out in Maxine's workshop? Would I still be playing the harp at all?

"You're thinking," he says.

"Because I honestly don't know," I say. "You go. Wildest dream."

His smiles slides to one side. Of course he knows. "I love the idea of opening a bakery–slash–test kitchen, where people could come in and try something new every week or take cooking classes." He moves his hands as he speaks, almost like he's waving around an invisible whisk or spatula. "One week we'd do Middle Eastern pastries, and the next we'd do pies, and then we'd do gourmet grilled cheese. I'd want to test out new recipes for different allergens, too, the way I started out with Harun. I've been trying more of that lately."

"I can picture it." I can, and it sounds wonderful. When it's like this between us, it's easier to forgive his flashy attempts at romance. Easier to forget I'm not supposed to be this comfortable with him, no matter how good it feels.

"For now, though, I'd be thrilled just to get a chance to do a cake on my own. When I made the cake batter for the wedding we filled in at, even minus the frosting and the actual assembly—that was a huge deal. My parents are intense about cake. I've been wanting to do one on my own for a while, but it's one of those things that needs to be *perfect*, so they're hesitant to give up control. But if I'm going to have my own bakery someday, I'll need to be able to do that without my parents watching me as I measure each ingredient."

"You're amazing at what you do," I tell him, awed not for the first time by the differences between our parents. "They have to see that. And when the bakery happens, I'll be there for your grand opening."

"As long as my depression doesn't get in the way," he says, each word as heavy as that sledgehammer.

"Is that . . . something you worry about?" I ask. We've already dug deep today. Might as well keep digging.

He scuffs at the floor with his shoe. "All the time." He says it softly, and the raw honesty in those words shocks me. *All the time.* Even with my own issues, there are plenty of days I'm not actively concerned about them.

"It's not that I'm depressed all the time," he amends. "The therapy and medication have helped so much. It's just made me wonder if that future I've pictured . . . if it's something I'm going to eventually fuck up for myself. If I'll never get to have it for no other reason than my shit brain chemistry."

"Tarek," I say, running my hand along his arm. If he doesn't get his bakery–slash–test kitchen, I'm going to be devastated. "That fucking *sucks.* I'm sorry. I'm sorry you have to feel that way."

He nods, still not meeting my eyes. "It's a competitive industry, and college was competitive too. Everyone so full of ambition. That was part of what dragged me down initially, this fear of not being able to keep up. And I was so fucking lonely, even living with Landon. And the rest was just . . . the way I am." He turns his attention back to me. "Let's talk about something else. Or not talk at all," he says, moving in to kiss me.

I like opened-up, honest Tarek. I hope he doesn't think he said too much.

When we move apart, his eyes are still closed. "I'm going to ask you something," he says slowly, his fingers tapping out some unfamiliar rhythm on my back. "No gestures. Just me with you in a rage cage, asking a question. And I might already know the answer, but I'm going to keep wondering if I don't ask it. So. What if . . . What if we made this official? You and me?"

The room grows smaller, the air thinner, these borrowed clothes turning stiffer than my most rigid pair of B+B slacks. I like him—I can admit it. That much is clear from the pounding of my heart alone. Last year's swirly sickness multiplied by a hundred.

But that's not enough.

"This silence is doing a lot for my ego," he says with a half laugh.

"I'm sorry," I rush to say. "I want to keep doing this. Hanging out with you. But . . ."

"But not as my girlfriend."

For a moment I allow myself to imagine it, the way Tarek might romance me: dinner dates at Seattle's best restaurants, moonlit walks, flowers to mark the monthly anniversary of our first kiss. Maybe it's the oxytocin fucking with me, but in my head, it's not the worst thing in the world. I might have even wanted to hold his hand when we were in line with Julia and Noelle.

Except romance is like the harp, or how I viewed the harp before I met Maxine: a performance. He'd want something wild and grand, and I've spent my life with grand. Grand is exhausting.

I bite down hard on the inside of my cheek. "I can't."

At this, he gets to his feet and puts a few steps between us. "You can see how this might be confusing, right?" His eyebrows are creased, and I have to fight the urge to go over and smooth them out. Iron them with my lips. "You do all these things that make me think you feel the way I do. Then you tell me you don't want a relationship. And everything we've done today—it feels like a date. So I'm just . . . really fucking mixed up about this."

He's not wrong. Sitting here, comforting him the way he comforted me, it feels like he is my boyfriend. The fuzzy boundaries between us have taken a toll on him. I've been so focused on making sure I emerge from this unscathed that I haven't wondered whether any of this might hurt him, too.

I splay out a hand on the bench and stare down at it, then turn it over to see the new calluses forming on my fingers. "I'm sorry I invited you to the show. Maybe I shouldn't have." And it kills me to say it, but I add, "We don't have to do things like this. We can . . . I don't know. Keep the boundaries clearer?"

It's not what I want. I want to be close to him, especially if he's feeling this way right now, but that's selfish. I'm the one making him feel this way—I can't be the one to fix it.

He rakes a hand through his hair, this burst of frustration I haven't seen from him. It's not fun, knowing I caused it. "No, no. Forget I said anything. We can keep doing this. All of this."

"Okay," I say quietly, wondering why if I'm getting my way, if I'm getting him in all the ways I want, it still feels like we're both losing.

It's all I know how to do. He said earlier that he didn't understand, but he has to get it by now.

"Hey. I loved the show," he says, sitting back down and beckoning for me to come closer. Reluctantly, I do, closing the space between us again. He pulls me into his lap, hands on my hips. "And I loved this." He motions to the wrecking room around us. "Could you—could you at least tell me why? We've been friends for so long, and I can't remember you not feeling this way."

His voice is so soft as it invites me to tell him my secrets.

"Maybe I just really hate romantic comedies."

He scoffs at that, and I probably deserve it. "I'm sorry if I sound daft, but it seems so straightforward to me. We like spending

231

time together. We're obviously attracted to each other. I know I fucked up at the auction, and at the movie, and I'm sorry. But what am I missing, Quinn? What am I not seeing?"

In my mind, I reach farther back into the past. I am so close to letting him into this painful place. Letting him hold some of that pain with me, maybe even help me make sense of it.

"I just—" I break off, take a deep breath with my fingertips pressed hard against my temples. If it'll make him understand, I have to let him in, even if it only makes it harder to eventually shut him out. So I push myself over the edge. "My parents separated."

*Separated.* It doesn't sound like what it really is—either a prelude to divorce or a last-ditch effort to save a marriage. It sounds . . . *final.*

He blinks a few times as this registers. "They . . . what? Isaac and Shayna?" he asks, as though maybe I'm talking about my other parents.

I nod. "When I was eight. They said work had been stressful, and my mom was going to stay with our aunt for a while. It was only for six months, and then she moved back in and they pretended everything was fine."

"*Only* six months," he says, giving it a strange emphasis.

"What?"

"You said it was only six months. That's not an *only* to me. That's six fucking months. Six fucking months when you were eight years old. That probably felt like a lifetime."

"I—yeah. I guess it didn't feel like an *only* to me back then either." I move off his lap, my breaths still shaky. "We never talked about it. I tried to, but they clearly just wanted to move on and forget. Asher was in high school, and she was always so busy, and I didn't want to bother her, either. And—and when I stayed with my mom, sometimes I overheard her crying, and it all felt like . . . like all these adults were making decisions about me, but no one cared to let me know what was happening or why."

"I am so sorry, Quinn." A couple emotions flit across his face and his fingers twitch, as though he wants to comfort me but knows it's the opposite of what I'm asking for. So he keeps his hands in his lap.

"What you said last year at the marina, about couples not trying hard enough to stay together? I couldn't imagine them having tried any harder than literally being in the business of love."

"I'm sorry," he repeats. "If I'd known, I wouldn't have said that." But he might have still believed it.

"They went back to work like nothing was different. They'd just almost gotten divorced, but they were all smiles with their clients, and none of it ever seemed real. It felt like they were faking their whole marriage because it was good for business." God, it feels weird to be telling this story with an ax at my feet.

"And you think they're still faking it? Even now?" There's no judgment in his questions. He's not asking them to prove me wrong. He genuinely wants to know what I think.

I hold up my arms. "Yes? I don't know. It took me by surprise when it happened, and there weren't any signs at all. So I'm constantly waiting for something to go wrong, for any minor disagreement to be the last straw. And if I left B+B, well, I can't help feeling like that last straw would come a lot sooner."

What I don't tell him: the closest Tarek and I ever got to a relationship, it hurt in a similar way, the kind of hurt that makes the ground unsteady beneath your feet, that makes colors duller. The kind of hurt that made me feel I had one less person in the world on my side. A deep, acute loneliness.

It confirmed everything I thought was true about relationships: that they don't give a fuck about who they hurt when they go up in flames. We hadn't even started one, and already I'd been burned.

"You have to know we wouldn't be like that," he says. "For about a hundred reasons. You really think all relationships are doomed? Your sister's? Julia's?"

I shrug. "Some of them, sure. It's just statistics."

"Right." The word ricochets off the walls of the small gray room.

"You're going back to school in September anyway," I continue, because if I can't convince him with emotion, then I'll use logic. "Why does this have to be something serious? Why can't it just be fun? You are having fun, right?"

He hesitates, but then his mouth quirks up. It's such a relief to see, even if it isn't a whole smile. "I have been having a ridiculous amount of fun, yes."

"Me too. So why can't we keep having fun? We can still be friends. We'll just be friends who kiss. And . . . other things," I say.

He's quiet for a moment, processing this. I know this kind of casual relationship I'm asking for goes against every die-hard-romantic cell in his body.

"Okay," he finally says. "Then I guess we'll keep having fun."

It must be the saddest way anyone's ever talked about having fun, and it scrapes at my heart. But he'll see, when he goes back to

California and I go exactly nowhere, that this was the right decision. This way, neither of us gets hurt.

I wrap my arms around him, bury a hand in his hair, ask if he wants to go back to his car.

At least that's one thing we can agree on.

# 22

We didn't think they would be so . . . naked." Lincoln taps his chin as he stands in front of a nude oil painting that leaves nothing to the imagination. "Or so, uh, well endowed."

"My parents are going to lose their minds," Victoria says. "We can't have our first dance in front of this. Not on TV."

A producer and camera operator stroll through the exhibit, pausing by each work of art to examine it up close. Victoria and Lincoln booked the museum six months ago, and suffice it to say, the exhibits have changed.

"It's all very artistically and tastefully done," Mom says, trying to be helpful. "Right, Quinn?"

"Oh—right." I try to tear my gaze away, but it's, like, a *lot* of penises. It's taking all my willpower not to send a photo to Julia. Maybe I can snap one when no one is looking.

"Are you sure we can't move some of them around? Even just for one day?" the producer asks the curator.

"Unfortunately, that's not going to be an option. This collection is in very high demand."

Mom lets Victoria and Lincoln walk a few paces ahead of her, then whips her head toward me, lowering her voice so only I can hear. "What happened to that quick pop-by you were going to do last week? To take photos of what the art looked like in the space before the walk-through?"

Last week. Shit. Was I? When Mom mentioned the walk-through at work brunch, I assumed this was what she meant.

"It may have, um, slipped my mind," I say.

The disappointment on her face is impossible to miss. I'm not just her daughter. I'm the employee who fucked up.

"We'll play around with the setup." Mom strides into the center of the room with a binder tucked under her arm, all business. "We could do the buffet here, and the band here, and then we could get some curtains or a divider screen to cover up the more erotic pieces?"

"I like that idea," Lincoln says. "Vic?"

"Everyone's going to think we're pervs for deciding to have our wedding here," Victoria says. "My mother thinks HBO is pornography. This many dicks might actually kill her."

The producer and camera operator are discussing something in hushed tones. "I know timing is tight," the producer says, "but we're wondering if it might be better to explore other venue options at this point."

"Other venues?" Victoria squeaks. "We've had this booked for ages. I grew up going to this museum with my grandparents. There's a reason we picked it. We can't pull a new venue out of our asses with two weeks to go."

"It might actually be kind of funny if we do the cake cutting right here." Lincoln points to a painting of a man with some strategically placed desserts. "It's unconventional, sure, but we could roll with it. What do you think, hon?"

Victoria bursts into tears.

"Sorry—I just—" she says, and then she races out of the exhibit.

"I've got this," Mom says.

Lincoln holds out his arms, looking defeated but concerned. "Be my guest. I wish I could say this is the first time this has happened, but I think she's under a lot of pressure. I can say from experience that I'm probably not who she wants to talk to right now."

I place a hand on my mother's binder. "This whole thing was my fault. I can go talk to her."

A beat passes between us before she relents. "Thanks. I'll try to puzzle this out with the camera guy."

Comforting a weepy bride is the last thing I expected to do today. I've seen my parents do it numerous times, and I'm always bowled over by their patience, their empathy. Crying in public is the worst; I owe it to Victoria to try to make things right.

I can hear her sobs before I reach the bathroom. I knock on the door. "Victoria? It's Quinn. Can I come in?"

She just cries louder, which I take as neither a yes nor a no. Her pointy-toed flats peek out from beneath the door of one of the stalls.

"I'm just going to sit out here," I say, sliding onto a padded bench across from the sinks. It's a very luxe bathroom, with a sparkling chandelier that looks like a work of art itself. "If you want to talk about anything, I'm here to listen. Or if you want to not talk, we can do that, too."

A sniff from the stall, and then the sound of toilet paper unrolling. When she opens the door, mascara has spiderwebbed down her cheeks, and a few strands of hair have escaped her curly bun. I'm reminded of her meltdown the week before proposals.

"Sorry," she says, blotting at her face with a wad of toilet paper. "You must think I'm a complete bridezilla."

"We at B+B firmly reject that word. You're absolutely allowed to be emotional, and we deal with plenty of disaster grooms, too, and there's no word for that."

"Fine. A mess, then."

"No," I insist, and when she raises a single eyebrow in a way that makes me deeply jealous—my eyebrow-raising ability is both or nothing—I relent. "Well. A little. But you don't have to apologize."

"It's honestly not even about the art. I mean, hell, I work with art. Those paintings are beautiful. The dudes are hot, am I right?"

I let myself laugh at that. I'm starting to get the feeling there's something bigger going on than painted penises. Metaphorically speaking.

Victoria joins me on the bench. "All of this is just a reminder that people are expecting perfection from us. They have this idea of who we are and what this is supposed to look like, and if the wedding doesn't mesh with that, then we're going to get a lot of backlash."

"Most couples we work with want perfection," I say. "You might be in the minority who already knows it's not going to be that way."

"My parents were skeptical enough when I went on a reality show, and sure, I was too. I thought I'd get more Instagram followers, that it would be good for business. But there was a part of me that believed in the whole thing too. Part of me that wanted to fall in love."

"And you did." I saw it play out, the way her conversations with Lincoln had more depth than anyone else's, how her eyes lit up when they met for a date. She had been open to it. Open to love. And it had happened.

"Yes. But it wasn't just what the cameras picked up. It was the little things, like how Lincoln would arrange for a producer to deliver takeout if it was an especially grueling day of filming, or how he'd write notes for me to read on the days we weren't together." Maybe my heart isn't as hardened as I thought it was, because that's pretty sweet. "So the fact that we're going to be back on TV, opening ourselves up to criticism again . . . It's a lot. I tried to avoid the Twitter commentary last time, but there were entire blog posts talking about how I was shrill and annoying, anti-Semitic shit all over the internet, racists who didn't want us together . . ."

"Shit." I saw the blog posts, but not the rest of it. "I'm so sorry."

"It was what I signed up for," she says with a shrug. "That doesn't excuse it, of course, but I knew it was going to happen. I just didn't think it was going to be that bad. And it's going to happen again, so I'm trying to prepare myself."

"It's not too late to kick out Streamr."

Victoria gives me a knowing look. "Ah, but the money," she says. "I'm always worried, though, about what people are saying about us behind our backs. If they think we won't last because we met on TV or we haven't been together that long. And I *love* Lincoln. I want to marry him. I didn't even really believe in the concept of The One until I met him. But I've been on the verge of a panic attack every night this week, and now, seeing the venue, all of it feeling real . . . It sent me over the edge."

"I hear you." It's the closest to telling her "I understand," when the truth is that I can't, not fully. "Obviously I've never been in your position, but people are going to talk. People are going to write horrible fucking things. I overhear so much gossip at weddings, and some of it's terrible."

She shudders. "That's what I'm afraid of."

A couple months ago, I would have cast aside her worries, rolled my eyes and marked them unimportant. Now, even if I can't put myself in her position, I feel for her. I want to make it better. Right now, I think I see her.

"You're going to be the one up there looking fucking amazing on the best day of your life, penis paintings or not, internet vitriol or not." It's a miracle I say it with a straight face. "I've seen a lot of relationship drama, and the fact that you and Lincoln aren't at each other's throats, that it isn't manifesting into something pushing you two apart? That's a big deal. It's not about the artwork. It's not about the venue or the cake or the band or the dress or the fact that thousands of people are going to be able to stream it."

"It's a great dress, though," Victoria whispers, and I can't help grinning at that.

"My mom does this thing before every bride or groom walks down the aisle. She tells them to look at their partner, and to make sure to take some time with them away from everyone else at some point that day. And she reminds them, no matter what else happens, this event is about the two of you. We'll take care of the rest."

"Jesus. How old are you again?"

"Thirty-seven. I have great skin."

"I like you," she says. "You're going to be there, right?"

I tell her yes, and I realize—I *want* to be there. I want to see Victoria looking elegant beyond belief, and I want to see how B+B pulls off this wedding.

Most of all, I want to witness that moment Lincoln sees her dressed up for the first time. I want to see their first dance. Because despite what I may or may not believe about love, I'm rooting for them.

There's a knock on the door. "Everything okay in there?" Lincoln's voice.

Victoria gets to her feet and swipes at her eyes a couple times. "Yeah, hon, I'm just on my way out." Then she turns back to me. "Thank you," she whispers, leaning down to squeeze my shoulder.

We wrap up at the museum by ordering some velvet curtains online, express shipping, and Mom taps a crew to handle their installation.

"Hope this rain lets up before tomorrow," she says as we drive home. Tomorrow: an outdoor wedding at Alki Beach. It's impossible to make it through a Seattle summer without at least one storm like this, the kind of rain that frustrates everyone because how dare one of our perfect sunny days be compromised. We always need a backup plan, and Mom has more than one favorite tent rental company.

I focus on the swish of windshield wipers. "Mm-hmm."

After a half dozen hypnotic swishes, Mom lets out a deep breath, like she's been working up to saying something. "So. I've wanted to ask you this for a while, but . . . you and Tarek?"

A flash of panic. "Did Asher say something?"

One side of her mouth curves upward. "When you're in this business, you pick up on a lot of body language and nonverbal cues. I had a feeling that something romantic might be going on."

Jesus, my family needs some hobbies.

I want to tell her there's nothing romantic about what I'm doing with Tarek. "We're just . . . hanging out." What a euphemism.

"O-kaaay," she says in this high-pitched, very amused-sounding voice, and I fight the urge to hurl myself out of the car *Lady Bird* style.

My mom and I don't talk about things like this. We don't talk about anything of substance.

There's a weariness in her face I don't usually notice in the midst of a wedding, a droopiness beneath her eyes, a sag to her mouth. She's beautiful, she always has been—she just looks exhausted.

I wonder if it's the way she looked before she moved out. The way she felt.

For the first time, I'd rather talk more about a wedding than about this. "I really like working with Victoria and Lincoln."

"They're great," Mom says. "And this wedding could open up so many opportunities for us. We might even be able to do destination weddings. We've never had the budget or the bandwidth. But once you're working full-time, it'll be much easier for us to expand."

Any warmth I felt after helping Victoria turns cold. My chest tightens, and my brain fills with images I can't control: me at twenty, stuck in business classes, my weekends accounted for. Planning the weddings of all my classmates who stayed in Seattle. At thirty, still in the tower and working for my parents. At forty, when my parents retire and pass B+B off to the next generation of Berkowitzes, and I have to force a smile and tell them this was what I always wanted, to take over this thing they built.

"That sounds . . . wow," I say, still trying to process it. "It wouldn't be for a while, though, right?"

"Right." Mom goes quiet for a moment, and then: "The attitude isn't helping, Quinn."

If she wanted a reaction from me, she's getting one. "Attitude? Did I not just comfort Victoria in there?"

"You did. And I appreciated it," she says. "But you've been so distracted lately. I'm not upset, but I have to ask—is Tarek the reason you missed the walk-through?"

"The *pre*-walk-through," I correct. "Because of course we needed two walk-throughs. Nothing less than our best, right?"

"We needed two walk-throughs to avoid what happened today." There's an edge to her voice. My mother, the boss, chastising her employee.

I have to hold myself back from saying it's not the relationship that's distracting me. The relationship—the non-relationship—is the one thing that feels solid. Too solid, probably, but it's a life raft right now.

"Maybe I should skip tonight's rehearsal dinner." I slouch low in my seat, feeling more like a child than I ever have. "Since I have such a bad attitude and all."

"Maybe you should." It's an unexpected punch to the gut. "We'll be fine without you."

And I should want to hear that they'll be fine without me, but that's not the way it feels. It feels like my worst fear, my parents and Asher on one side, me alone on the other. Battle lines drawn. It tempts the lies to climb up my throat until my desires are on display for everyone to see.

"Great" is what I say instead, and we're silent the rest of the drive.

# 23

Tarek smells like rain and chocolate.

I texted him as soon as I saw the MTRMNY-mobile leave our driveway from my tower window, and he told me he was just getting home from therapy but he'd be over as soon as he could. If his appearance doesn't take away all my anxiety, at the very least, it makes me feel like maybe I won't have a total breakdown tonight. But who knows, the night is young and panic is my brand.

"I've been doing some experimenting," he says after I open the front door. He passes me a foil-covered mug, the ceramic still warm. "And I'm finally ready for you to try this."

"Is this what I think it is?" I peel back the foil and gasp. "You made a mug cake!"

"I did. It should have cooled down enough at this point to eat it," he says. "It sounded like you maybe needed some chocolate. And I'm not going to lie—part of me wanted to prove to you that this is better than the kind you microwave from a box."

"I really did need chocolate. This looks incredible. Thank you."

He peers past me into the house. He's wearing a T-shirt again, and the sight of his bare forearms makes me wobbly. "Not that I don't love and respect your parents, but I didn't see the van in the driveway. Are they . . . ?"

"Not here," I confirm, pulling him inside and closing the door behind him. "They're at a rehearsal dinner."

"Good." In one swift movement, he pins me against the door, trapping the mug between my chest and his. But instead of kissing me, he leans down, burying his face in my neck, his mouth fitting into the space where my neck meets my shoulder. There's something deeply intimate about it, more so than a kiss. "You always smell like wood."

"From the shop." I reach out my free hand to stroke his hair, to pull him closer. When I got home from the museum, I changed into the T-shirt and jeans I wore to Maxine's earlier in the week. "It's impossible to get the sawdust out of my clothes. I think I'm seventy percent sawdust and thirty percent human at this point. I can shower if—"

"No." He wraps my hair around his fist, a slight pressure as he pulls at it, breathing me in. "I love it."

That L-word lands heavy in my chest, but I'm distracted by his mouth moving up my jaw, kissing me beneath my ear, then my earlobe, a gentle bite on the shell of my ear. When I shiver at that, he bites down harder.

In the depths of my mind, it occurs to me that I asked him over to comfort me the same way someone might seek comfort from a boyfriend or girlfriend. And the comfort he brought that's warming my hands—that's some kind of gesture, even if it's not a flashy one. It's personal, something he made because he knows my weakness for mug-based desserts. I like it too much to ponder what it means right now.

When his lips find mine, he tastes like rain and chocolate, too.

"Come upstairs," I say, and I don't have to tell him twice. I grab a pair of spoons from the kitchen before following him.

From my bed, Edith regards him with a swish of her tail before looking up at me, as though she needs confirmation she should not pounce on him. Tarek makes a move to pet her, but I hold out a hand to stop him.

"She responds best to people who ignore her." Much to Asher's chagrin. "The cat equivalent of playing hard to get."

"Well, sure." He proceeds to stand up straight, determinedly not looking at her. She figure-eights around his legs, brushing up against his calves. "She seems to not hate me?"

"You must smell good to her or something," I say. Seeing him here in my bedroom, my cat warming up to him, makes me feel a certain way.

Maybe being a prisoner up here wouldn't be so terrible after all.

"I've never had a boy in my room," I tell him. "I've never had a boy come to my house, actually."

His mouth quirks up at that. "So I'm special."

"A little."

"Is it okay to eat in here?" Tarek sits down on my bed next to Edith, who takes a tentative step into his lap. He scratches her head, behind her ears.

"You're asking the girl who hoards boxes of processed microwavable desserts in her room. Yes, it's okay."

I hand him a spoon and sink onto the bed. I carve out a hunk of chocolaty goodness and lift it to my mouth, and . . . yeah. I could die right now and I'd only be a little mad. "It's perfect. But you already knew that."

"Never hurts to hear it," he says with a grin.

We sit in this comfortable silence for a while, our spoons clinking against the ceramic mug. The rain pummels my windows. Up here in the tower, it feels like we're taking shelter from an apocalyptic storm, like we've slipped out of summer and into another season entirely. Like I'm sitting on someone else's bed with this sweet boy who bakes sweet things.

"No pressure," he says, "but if you need to talk about whatever happened today, I'm here to listen."

"It's just work." I bury a hand in Edith's fur. "Victoria and Lincoln's wedding, the camera crew, everyone freaking out about it. I'm used to my parents treating me like an employee, but lately they've been treating me like their least-qualified employee."

"I'm so sorry." He links his fingers with mine, thumb rubbing my palm.

"I have to quit. After Asher's wedding."

"Yeah?"

I nod, feeling more certain about this than I have about anything in a while. "And then I'll start school in a month and study . . . something." Despite the calming motion of his fingers stroking mine, I let out a deep sigh. "Even if I don't have it figured out, shouldn't I at least have some idea? Am I broken?"

"No. You are *not* broken." He says this with such conviction. I want to believe him so badly. "You know you don't have to have it figured out right now, and the degree doesn't have to perfectly align with whatever you end up doing. I mean, my mom has a degree in marine biology. And your dad studied . . ."

"European history," I say.

"Which I imagine he's using every day," he says. "And you don't necessarily need a degree to do what I want to do. But I love learning. I wanted a degree to fall back on in case I change my mind later."

I get what he's saying, and it's not anything I haven't thought before. There are a hundred different majors that don't segue neatly into a career. I allow myself to wonder what would have happened if I'd applied to other schools instead of sending the one application to the one school my parents and Asher had gone to. They had rolling admissions, and I figured I'd deal with it later if I didn't end up getting in. But I did, back in December, rendering the rest of my senior year nearly pointless. I thought I'd be thrilled, but that college acceptance was just another thing tethering me to my present with no opportunity for change. Another thing keeping me prisoner in this tower.

That's what I've been chasing, too: *change*. I said yes to everything my parents wanted because it was easier to go along with what had been decided for me long ago. To grow up and grow into this role.

"I know a creative career isn't easy, if that's what I decide I want to do. And it's probably even harder with an instrument like the harp. Orchestra jobs are extremely competitive. Playing with Maxine, though . . . It's made me realize there's other stuff out there. That I don't have to keep doing something that makes me unhappy."

He squeezes my hand. "I'm glad," he says softly. "I don't like the idea of you being unhappy." We scrape at the mug with our spoons for another minute before he says, "I've always liked hearing you play. Even when we were younger. You were the cute harp-ist my parents worked with."

Gently, I shove his shoulder. "You did not think that. You're just saying that to butter me up."

He lifts his eyebrows, feigning innocence. "Is it working?" Too well, probably. "I'm serious, though. It was this massive instrument and you were this tiny thing, and I couldn't believe the way you *controlled* it. You became a different person when you were playing, and it was a person I wanted to know better."

Hearing this reminds me how I first fell in love with the harp, how I'm falling in love with it again. And it's not entirely dissimilar to how I feel with Tarek, which is accompanied by a sharp layer of dread.

Yet somehow I keep managing to push the dread away. *Not now. Let me enjoy this.*

I reach over to my nightstand drawer, rooting around inside for something I haven't looked at in ages. "Do you remember this?" I pull out the strip of photos, watching his face light up.

"You kept this?" He stares at it in disbelief. "Yes. Of course I remember that day because we got in trouble immediately after-ward." He points to the last photo. "Look at our faces. We knew we were about to get caught." He presses a kiss to the side of my head. "Worth it, though."

I lean back against him. Whatever we have here, it's something I never felt with Jonathan, or with any of the others. And maybe that's the difference, that this with Tarek is *comfortable*, even when I want to climb on top of him and kiss him until he groans deep in his throat. The way my parents treat me, it's as though I am too old for my skin, for my bones. With Julia, we've had our own language for so long. But Tarek is familiar and brand-new at the same time. My brain isn't buzzing, aside from the low-grade anxiety-hum I carry through life. With Tarek, my mind is quiet, and *god* that's a nice feeling.

Or at least, it's quiet as long as I don't think about what happens when we don't have this anymore.

When he goes back to school.

When we maybe stop talking again.

"Could you play something for me?" he asks. "You've been teasing for so long. I'm dying to hear."

Sitting in my desk chair isn't the most ideal setup, but I make it work. I tilt the cherrywood harp backward, enjoying its familiar weight, and launch into the first few bars of a song I've been practicing a lot lately.

"Cat Power?" he says, eyes bright. "You learned that for me?"

There's this dangerous sweetness in his words that nearly breaks me in half.

"I'm still figuring it out. That's all I know so far." But it doesn't stop him from grinning.

I launch into another piece, a Maxine original, and the entire time, I'm aware of his eyes on me. Lately, I've been able to shut everything out while I'm playing—but not this. Not now.

"You love it," he says when I finish, and there is something so earnest in his tone that I can't not kiss him after that.

It feels like only the two of us exist up here in the tower, and I'm thinking I would be okay if we never left.

For long, lazy minutes, all we do is kiss. Slow, slow, fast. Slow, slow, fast. Building our own rhythm. His hands on my back and on my hips and then sliding down my thighs, like there is not enough of me for him to touch.

Gently, I run a hand along the faint reddish shadow on his arm. "Hey. It isn't that bad today."

"It isn't," he agrees. I can tell he's fighting the urge to draw his arm away.

"I remember your mom used to get so mad at you for scratching."

"And I'd tell her I was only touching, not scratching." He continues to stare down at the rash. "It really doesn't bother you? We're not in the dark. You can see it all."

I shake my head, finally letting out the words I wanted to say so long ago. "You're beautiful," I say quietly, my heart in my throat. It's easier to say than *You're so easy to talk to* and *I can just be myself around you.*

He pulls me to him and just holds me for several long moments. Eventually, his hands drift up the back of my shirt, pausing when they reach the strap of my bra. I break away from him for a moment to pull off my shirt, giving him easier access.

When he sheds his shirt and jeans, I have to will my heart to slow down. He is lovely, all that deep tan skin and the dips of his muscles. He closes his eyes as I run a hand down his chest, placing his hand on top of mine. "I'm going to say something, and you have to promise not to get mad at me," he says.

"No way. I reserve the right to get mad at anything you say."

He lifts my hand to his mouth, kisses the inside of my wrist. "Fine, I shall risk your wrath." A deep breath, and then: "I really, really like you." I must have some kind of reaction because he says, "Why does that make you scoff?"

"I—I don't know. It was involuntary." I shake my head, wanting to live a little longer in that compliment, though part of me doesn't believe him. "This is such a dumb thing to ask, but now I have to know. What do you even like about me?" I have to laugh because it sounds ridiculous, and yet I keep going. "I'm just this weird, maybe-broken girl who played part of a Cat Power song on the harp and owns too many articles of clothing featuring tiny animals."

"This is a difficult question to answer when we're half naked, but I'll do my best." He backs up on the bed, putting some space between us, but he reaches for one of my hands and starts ticking items off using my fingers. "Okay. Things I like about Quinn Berkowitz. You have a fantastic sense of humor. I can open up to you in a way I haven't been able to with anyone else. You care about your family, which is why it's been so difficult for you to decide what to do about B+B. You're brave, even if you think you're not. And . . ." A flick of one eyebrow. "You're sexy as hell."

RIP me.

I don't know how to react except to push him deeper into the bed. He doesn't ask me the same question, possibly because his self-esteem isn't down in the gutter where mine apparently was, and I'm glad he doesn't.

Because then I'd have to say, *everything*.

I kiss him everywhere, the places he used to think were ugly, the skin he wanted to hide. We lose the rest of our clothes and his mouth moves down my chest slowly, slowly. It's agony. Eventually, he reaches my waist, my navel—and keeps going.

"Is this okay?" he whispers, pressing a kiss to one hip bone and then the other.

"Yes." My voice is featherlight. "But I—I haven't done this before."

"I haven't either." The words are low and breathy, and they do nothing to ease my wanting. "We could figure it out together?"

The figuring-it-out is strange at first. Then a little less strange, warm and shimmering and *yes*, my hands in his hair and his name on my tongue. And then just . . . bliss. Utter bliss.

When I pull him back up to me to kiss him, it feels different. Heavier. Maybe because we're alone, maybe because that was new for both of us and by far the most intimate thing I've ever done.

He drops his lips to my neck. "*Quinn*," he says into my skin, a little growl that sounds like both an invitation and a question. Just like that, I'm ready again.

"Do you have a condom?"

He nods. "Are you sure?"

"Very. Are you?"

"I don't think I'm doing a terribly good job hiding my enthusiasm," he says, muffling a laugh into my neck as he grows more enthusiastic against my leg, "but yes."

I have to laugh at that too, because laughing is okay, because why can't this be funny and hot and sweet and probably even a little weird all at the same time? Why did I ever think it had to be only one thing and that I'd done it so wrong?

It's all of those things and more, and as soon as it's over—for both of us—I miss the heat of him. With the sheets around our hips, we talk and we laugh and we listen to the rain *taptaptap* at my tower window. Our stormy summer soundtrack.

At one point, Tarek cups my face with his hands, his touch

gentler than it's ever been, this reverence that nearly breaks me in half. "So, how was it? Having a boy in your room?"

"Ten out of ten, would do again."

A grin lights up his face. "You're not unhappy right now, then."

"No," I say. "I'm very, very happy."

It's only once the words leave my mouth that the dread fights its way to the surface, filling my mind with all the fears I've tried to lock up tight. It makes me roll away from him on the bed, desperate for air, his light touch suddenly suffocating.

I could really fall for him. I'm convinced of that now, and it would be a catastrophe.

I should tell him to leave. Kick him out of my room. This isn't right, having him here long past our expiration date, no matter how *very, very happy* it made me. Happiness is fleeting, and any amount of it I have now isn't worth the heartbreak waiting for us on the other side. I've already made it clear I can't be the girlfriend he wants. I can't give him the story his parents had if I've never believed in stories.

The longer I let him stay, the more this is going to hurt. Somehow, I know it won't just leave a bruise this time—it will rip me apart.

And that's how I know it's time to end it.

# 24

The flowers were supposed to be royal blue," Mom barks into her phone, an unsuspecting florist on the other end. "These are *cerulean*."

The museum is a flurry of activity. Camera wires are taped down, tables are repositioned, candles are lit, centerpieces are examined to make sure not a single petal is out of place. The ivory velvet curtains hiding the most erotic paintings look rather artistic themselves, giving the reception an even more exclusive feel.

Our clothes are pressed and crisp, and Dad made us do this dorky team huddle when we got here that still somehow managed to tug at my heart. I can't help feeling jittery, despite my decision that Asher's wedding will be my last one with B+B. Or maybe because of it.

Naturally, something goes wrong right away.

"That's odd," Asher says, frowning down at something on her timeline.

"What?" I straighten out the MOB and MOG cards at the head table.

"I have a few cards here that haven't been assigned to a table." She shows me the handful of delicate, loopy-scripted cards. "Five of them, actually."

We cross-check my stack of cards with the seating chart, and it turns out I have three more without a home.

"We're lucky it's a buffet." Asher's bun is slicked back with so much hair spray, you'd need one of those infomercial knives that can cut through granite to take it apart. "We were so meticulous. You updated the RSVP list this week, right?"

I'm pretty sure I did. Didn't I? "We could add an extra chair at each table," I suggest feebly, but we have an entire family to seat, and we can't split them up.

"Let's see if we can grab another table."

"A reject table."

She taps her nose. "Yes, but only you and I will know that."

Two more weeks, and then I will break her world apart.

I swallow that down. No time for it now.

We find an extra table in the museum's restaurant and recruit a couple of producers and cater-waiters to help us tweak the spacing. My stomach does this swoop when Tarek appears in the doorway. Everything about him looks brighter, fuller today, the wave to his hair and the light in his eyes and the quirk of his mouth when he sees me.

"Hi," he says, rolling up his sleeves like he's about to do something more aerobic than simply moving tables. He grazes my lower back with a few fingertips, his hand lingering for a moment. It's a small but intimate gesture, and it makes me blush.

"Hi." And suddenly I can't stop grinning.

Too late, I catch myself. Tarek is my other countdown, but I haven't yet decided how to tell him. Ghosting wouldn't feel right, though I've done it in the past. It's probably a good thing he's going back to school soon. We can't do a long-distance relationship if we don't have a relationship. That's got to be the least messy way to end this.

"Hi!" Asher says with false enthusiasm and a clap of her hands. "Now that we've all said hello, can we keep this moving?"

The ceremony itself, which takes place on the patio, goes smoothly, except for a couple flower girls who love the petals so much, they can only bring themselves to part with one or two every few feet. Finally, one of their mothers intervenes and throws fistfuls of petals, which makes everyone laugh. Victoria looks stunning in her strapless A-line dress and hair comb, Lincoln the epitome of dapper. If I didn't know they were being filmed, I wouldn't be able to tell. They have this way of tuning out the cameras honed over a dozen episodes of reality TV.

A glass is broken and everyone shouts "Mazel tov!" and when my jaw starts feeling strange, I realize it's because I've been smiling. Guess I'm more excited than I thought for another episode of *Perfect Match*.

No mistakes at dinner, either. No dropped plates, no embarrassing toasts. I can almost feel the weight of this day lifted from my family's shoulders. The cake has been waiting in the middle of the room all through dinner, and toward the end of the meal, I head back toward the museum restaurant to retrieve a knife. This is the last cake cutting I'll be part of for a while—that's what I'm thinking when my shoe snags a camera cord and I stumble, toppling forward and flinging my arms out, grasping for anything to break my fall—

—and that "anything" turns out to be one of the velvet curtains.

It happens both in slow motion and in a single heartbeat, the tearing of the curtain from the ceiling, the shouts from the wedding guests, the gasp that might be coming from my own throat.

And the unveiling of a painting with the most well-endowed guy of the bunch.

Parents clap hands over children's faces. "What on earth?" says one little old lady, while another puts on her glasses to take a closer look. In some distant part of my brain, I hope that's the kind of old lady I become.

Somehow, I don't spontaneously combust from embarrassment, which is the way I've always assumed I'll die. With my body half beneath the curtain, I decide I shall hide under it for the rest of my life. This is my new home. The men in the paintings will be my only friends. It will be a good life, a simple life.

Except something wild happens. People start *laughing*. A few chuckles at first, but then it spreads, a wave that takes over the whole room until even Victoria and Lincoln join in.

From where they're standing near the exhibit entrance, just off camera, my parents and sister look amused too. Horrified, but amused. Maybe this will be okay. I haven't ruined the wedding—I've just turned it into a comedy.

The room is in such an uproar that no one immediately notices the smoke rising from the other end of the curtains.

At least, not until the fire alarm goes off.

Followed shortly by the sprinklers.


Miraculously, the art is safe, but the cake and most of the decorations are ruined. Months of work—gone.

Tarek and his mom run to a nearby bakery to buy out all their cakes while the guests dry off outside. The crew is still filming, despite Victoria's mother's best efforts to shut them down. Victoria waved her off, told her she didn't care if they documented this disaster. "Lincoln and I are married," she said. "That's what matters."

The curtain swiped a candle on its way down, and if there's a better metaphor for my relationship with my parents going up in flames, I would like to hear it.

"We got lucky," Dad is saying as we clean up the exhibit-slash-reception alongside the museum staff. Asher's outside with towels and extra articles of clothing she scrounged from our emergency kits, trying to keep the guests from further losing their collective shit. "Everyone's okay. Victoria and Lincoln are okay. This could have easily been much worse."

"I'm so sorry," I say for the hundredth time, guilt and embarrassment fighting for control, both intent on making me feel as shitty as possible. My wet hair isn't helping either. "I don't know what happened. I just—I just tripped. I wasn't paying attention. I'm sorry."

Mom rolls up a tablecloth so tightly, I'm worried she might use it as a weapon. "I realize mistakes happen, but something of this magnitude? You knew how crucial it was to be on top of our game today. All these people trusted us. That's what this job is—*trust*."

*Mistakes happen*. Why, then, do I get a lecture and her endless, aching disappointment any time I make one? My allergic reaction, the missed trip to the florist, the forgotten walk-through. If I were a vendor, they'd simply stop working with me. But because they can't, this is what happens. It's not just a mistake. It's the destruction of the biggest wedding of their career, and I'm the easiest person to blame. The cake could have flipped over onto my head of its own accord, and I'd still be the one getting berated.

I drop silverware into a large gray bin, each damp clang turning my guilt to anger. "Right. People trust us to make sure their flowers are the right shade of blue."

"I don't exactly see how sarcasm is helping right now." Mom attacks another tablecloth. "It doesn't matter how insignificant a request seems. It's our job to do everything we can to make it happen, and we're good at it. It's the reason we're able to put food on the table, the reason you're able to go to such a good school."

"I know that," I snap. Of course I appreciate what they do. Of course I'm grateful. "I'm glad you have this thing you love *so much* you had to have your kids be part of it."

"This is our family business." There's genuine confusion in my dad's voice. "I'm not sure I understand what you're saying."

This is it. I want to be calm, collected, professional, the perfect wedding planner they've groomed me to be. The poised and dignified harpist.

But I'm not that person anymore.

"I don't want this." My heart is pounding against my rib cage. I throw an arm out, gesturing to the wedding wreckage. "Any of this. I don't want to study business, and I don't want to join B+B when I graduate."

My parents pause their cleanup, Mom dropping into a chair and Dad letting a soggy centerpiece fall to the ground. The rest of the staff, as though sensing we're having A Moment, give us some space.

"You don't want to join B+B?" Dad says. "You . . . don't want to work with us?"

Those questions nearly break me.

I have to summon all my bravery to keep going. "It's not that I don't want to work with you. It's that all of this . . . It isn't right for me. I get that you love it, but I haven't felt that way for a while. For years, if I'm being honest. I can't get excited about dress fittings or cake tastings. I'm not the kind of person who's going to shed a tear when the bride walks down the aisle. All the timelines and calendars and vendors to organize, it's too much. I go along with it because that's what I'm supposed to do, but this isn't my passion. It's yours."

It should feel better than it does to finally tell them. I expected an immediate untwisting of all the tangled, knotted parts of me. I thought I'd be able to take a deep breath, move forward, move on.

That doesn't happen.

Dad takes a chair next to Mom, who's still speechless. He loosens his tie, swipes a hand through his damp hair. "You always seem to have fun. Maybe not today"—he even chuckles at this, as though hinting that we'll be able to laugh about this wedding in the future—"but with the betting on songs, and having Victoria and Lincoln as clients, and work brunch . . ."

The guilt comes rolling back. It's possible I went too far, convinced them I liked this job when what I really loved was my family working together. I'm not sure how to explain the difference.

"I loved that we did this as a family," I say, urging my voice to stay solid, to not collapse. "And part of the reason I held off on saying anything was because I didn't know what I'd rather be doing, only that it wasn't this. But I've been taking harp lessons this summer, and—"

"Harp lessons?" This is when Mom chooses to interject. She's ghost-pale, her eyes barely blinking behind her cat-eye glasses. Even in all this chaos, her damp hair is free of frizz and flyaways. "But you already know how to play. You don't want to be part of the wedding business, but you're taking harp lessons?"

I squeeze my eyes shut for a moment, like I could disappear and open them up in a new reality where Victoria and Lincoln are laughing and eating potato croquettes. "It's a different kind of music." My defense sounds thin. I knew they wouldn't get it, and here is the brutal confirmation of my worst fears.

"Is it really you saying this, Quinn?" Mom says. "Or is it Tarek?"

"Tarek? What does Tarek have to do with any of this?"

"You've been completely different this summer—ever since he came back," she says. "We always knew you had a little crush on him. We were worried at the beginning of the summer that he might make things tough for you. And now that you're spending time together, well . . ."

I'm certain there's nothing worse than your parents knowing you had a crush on someone.

"It's not like that," I insist. "We're—" But there is no *we're*. I made sure of that. "We're nothing. There's nothing between us." The words don't feel right. They're too sharp on my tongue, but I press forward anyway. "I haven't been acting a certain way because of him. Why is it so hard to accept that I made this decision on my own?"

Dad gets to his feet and holds out his arms, as though I am a wild animal he's trying to pacify. "Maybe we should discuss this later. All of us are a little emotional right now, and we have a lot of cleaning up to do."

"I'm not emotional." My voice cracks, betraying me. "This is how I feel. You didn't ask me to help out more when Asher was busy with her wedding. You never *ask*."

"So we've forced you, then? Your whole life, we've forced you to be part of—the horror—the most beautiful, important day of other people's lives?" Mom is all claws now. I've never seen her like this, but I shouldn't be surprised. B+B is her baby. I'm just her employee.

"Fine. Maybe you don't force me, but you sure as hell do an amazing job guilting me into it," I spit out, gaining more power now as I stalk toward them, past the table where Victoria and Lincoln were supposed to eat their cake. "You always assume I'm going to do whatever you say because that's what I've done for eighteen years. And it works out for you, because the truth is that I'm terrified of creating a rift if I say no. Because this family never fucking talks about anything."

I've never sworn at my parents. *Never*. I'm shocked to have said it, to have put words to this thing we never talk about. More quietly, I add, "Not about anything important, at least."

"What are you talking about?" Dad says, forehead crinkled with confusion.

"Hmm, maybe the six months Mom wasn't living with us?"

265

This hits them in a soft *whoosh*, their features crumpling, shoulders sagging. Suddenly they look so, so small, less like my parents and more like two people who've never had the answers.

"What does that have to do with anything?" Mom says quietly.

I try to laugh, but it comes out as this choked sound. "*Everything*. It's the reason I've been scared to tell you how I really feel about working for B+B, the reason I've been scared to leave. Because I don't want this to fall apart without me—not because I'm some integral piece of the business, but because I'm constantly worried you're going to start fighting about flowers, or candles, and there won't be anyone there to intervene. You've just—you put on this act for B+B's sake, pretending you're so in love and you have this perfect marriage, but I can see through it. I know it's not real."

"Quinn." Dad shakes his head, disbelieving. "We're not pretending. I don't know what gave you that idea, but . . . that was so long ago. We're all past that now."

"How can we be past it when you've never talked to me about it? When Mom just moved back in one day and we were supposed to pretend the previous six months weren't the most miserable of my life?" I blink blink blink to soften the pressure building behind my eyes. I won't cry in front of my parents. I won't.

My mom gets to her feet, readjusts her glasses, and squares her shoulders. Back to no-nonsense Shayna Berkowitz. "I think we've had enough. This whole circus needs to stop, Quinn. You're acting like a child."

"Funny," I say. "You've never treated me like one."

# 25

I have to find Tarek. After pausing in the bathroom to thumb away mascara smears from beneath my eyes, I race through the museum and back into the tiny restaurant kitchen, where he's helping unpack a tower of bakery cakes.

His back is to me, his shoulders stiff.

"Tarek?" I say, reaching for his arm. "What's wrong?"

I want him to tell me that this whole thing is a mess, but we're going to fix it. Even if I'm not supposed to want that from him.

I should be glad, then, when he says, "That was . . . an enlightening conversation you had with your parents."

Aware we're not alone in the kitchen, I lower my voice. "You heard that?"

"Parts of it. I'd just gotten back with the cakes, and I wanted to make sure you were okay." He must see I'm about to lose it because finally, he softens. "What you told them, about not being part of the business anymore. That was . . . a lot. Are you okay?"

And then *he* is comforting *me*, even after I said something so horrible about him.

Slowly, I shake my head. "I'm sorry. I just need to—" I break off, unable to catch my breath, unsure what I'm apologizing to him for. Tears back up behind my eyes, and I smash my hands into them, again willing them not to fall. I can only hold them back for so long.

He gets me a glass of water before asking Harun if he can cover when his parents get back and guiding me out of the kitchen and into an employees-only corridor with too-bright lighting and a geometric-print carpet that looks like a relic from the eighties. These are all the things someone would do to comfort a girlfriend, and even if I'm not a girlfriend, not his girlfriend, I don't ask him to stop.

I lean against the wall, focusing on the blue-green hexagons on the carpet and taking slow sips of water. "I—I really fucked up."

Tarek moves closer, places a hand on my shoulder. It's not enough. It's nice, but it's not enough. I want to bury my face in his chest and lose myself in him, shut out the rest of the world and my parents' demands and the daughter they wanted that I will never be again.

I'm no longer the girl who always says yes. I didn't just tell them no—I told them *never*, and it feels worse than I imagined.

"They're your parents. They'll forgive you," he says into my hair in this steady voice that makes me want to believe him. "They'll understand."

Sure, they might understand I want to find something I'm passionate about. But this will forever alter my relationship with my family, Mom-Dad-Asher on one side and me, all alone, on the other.

Another thought occurs to me. "Please tell me I haven't completely ruined things for your parents too. No, I don't deserve that. Let me have the worst of it. Tell me how bad it is."

"You haven't ruined anything for anyone," he says. "My parents are fine, and your parents are going to bounce back. They're good at what they do. People will understand that this was a mistake. It could have happened to anyone."

"Maybe." A future in which B+B doesn't exist is too terrible to contemplate, regardless of how much I've wanted to separate myself from it.

"This is going to be the worst part. You're in the thick of it now, but it's going to get better. And hey—you finally did it. You ripped off the Band-Aid."

"I just have to hope the wound doesn't get infected."

He cracks a smile at that. "Not sure how much longer we're going with this metaphor, but hey, even if it does, I'll get you some antiseptic."

God, he's too good. "I can't believe they had the audacity to suggest the reason I haven't been 'myself' this summer, or the version of myself I've been pretending to be for all these years, is because of *you*."

Tarek's eyebrows draw together a little too tightly. "But you told them I'm not the reason. That I'm—that I'm nothing."

He heard that, too.

*Fuck.*

"Tarek. That's obviously not—you're not—I mean—" I stumble over my words, trying to backtrack. "I said there was nothing going on between us. Not that you're nothing. You're—you're not." I can't even give him a compliment.

He pins his shoulders to the opposite side of the corridor. "Right. A huge difference."

"You don't know my parents like I do. This is everything to them. To Asher. They thought it was because of you that I haven't been fully invested at work this summer. I had to tell them it's how I've felt for a while, that it wasn't you, so they wouldn't get the wrong idea."

"Wouldn't want that to happen."

I'm not used to hearing this kind of sarcasm in his voice. I want to go back to that night in my room, wrap those rain clouds around us like a blanket.

But this was never a wrapped-in-a-blanket kind of relationship.

"I've had fun with you," I say carefully. *Having fun.* That's what we said we were doing. Images flash through my mind, the two of us on the yacht and at the rage cage and in my bed with his home-made chocolate mug cake. Beneath my sheets. "Fun" isn't the right word anymore, but it's all I can come up with right now.

"I have too," he says. "More than fun. I've had . . ." He breaks off, scrubs a hand through his hair. Nervous Tarek is still so foreign to me. "Jesus, Quinn. I told myself I wasn't going to do this."

"You weren't going to what?"

A vigorous shake of his head, as though he's convincing himself he's not going to do it. "We couldn't get it right last summer, and I know that was partly my fault. I've been trying to make it up to you. Trying to show you that this could be something real. And I just thought, if you changed your mind, wouldn't it be great to have this amazing story about us?"

"Is that the only thing that would make it meaningful? Having a story like that?"

He scuffs the geometric carpet with his shoe. "I just . . . don't know what else to do. How else to make it feel that way."

Truthfully, I haven't hated everything he's done: the mug cake, the time we spent in the Mansour's kitchen, the movie in the park. But I can't bring myself to mention any of that right now.

"I never asked you to be my boyfriend. I made that clear."

"I know. I know. And I thought I was okay with it. So it's clearly my fault I'm feeling this way. But . . ." He says this next part so quietly, I have to strain to hear it. "I like you, Quinn. I like you so much."

The words are as soft as the highest notes on the harp, the "so much" wrapping around my heart in this unexpected, unwelcome way.

*I like you.* He said the same thing in the tower. It's not that most dangerous of L-words, but it's close.

"Please don't say that."

"Why not? Is that really such an awful thing, to be liked?" Again, he shakes his head, and then he repeats it. "I like you. And I thought maybe you felt the same."

There have been times I thought so too. Those shimmering, faraway-seeming ideas I pushed to the back of my mind. "For a while, I thought I could," I say. "Last summer, I was ready to go all in with you. I even did that grand gesture of my own, with the email. Maybe it wasn't as cinematic as anything you've done, but it was all I could think to do. And it didn't work out. It always works out. In every movie you told me to watch. I watched them all, Tarek. And—and it always works out." I squeeze my eyes shut. When people cry in romantic comedies, it's only because they're guaranteed a happy ending afterward.

271

"But it can," he says. "That's what I'm telling you. We can figure this out together." He reaches out, twines his fingers with mine, and for a moment it sounds like something I might be able to say yes to. That's how ingrained romantic gestures are for him—they've made me question what I really want.

"There's nothing to figure out."

That's all it takes for him to draw his hand back. "Okay. Let me get this straight, then. You wanted me to comfort you, but you don't want a relationship. You tell me I make you happy, but you don't want me to be your boyfriend. You want all the perks of a relationship without the actual commitment, because god forbid you let someone hold your hand or open a door for you."

"Tarek . . ."

"I'm not wrong, am I?"

He is. He's so incredibly wrong, but I'm losing the will to defend myself.

"If relationships are so great, why haven't your other ones worked out?" It's a low blow. "You made them seem so perfect on Instagram, but those gestures—were they one-sided? What did your girlfriends ever do for you in return? And what was your record? Three months?"

"You can't call it a record," he says. He has every right to be angry with me, but he's soft, so soft, the way he always is, and that's what makes his words cut even deeper. I can feel how badly he wants this like it's a living, breathing thing in the hall with us. "It's not some competition. Maybe . . . Maybe I'm not good at relationships without the flashy stuff. Maybe I'm still trying to figure out how, exactly, to navigate that. But I'm good with *you*."

The fact that he's still so invested in us when I am clearly upsetting him is further proof of what I've believed for so long. I was scared of us hurting each other, but the truth? We already are.

I have done so much more damage than I thought possible.

As though it'll make me more confident in what I'm about to say, I straighten my posture, though the wall is still holding me up. "Fine. Here's the real reason I don't want to be in a relationship with you. The reason I *can't*. It's because the last time we got close, the closest we'd ever been, you hurt me. And I know I hurt you too—that I hurt you first—before that. I know we've apologized. I thought we'd moved past it, that I was over it, but even if I'm not actively hurting every moment I'm with you, it's still there, underneath everything, no matter how close we get. That's what relationships do to people. Every time you do one of those gestures, it makes me realize we're going to end up back there again. It reminds me that it's inevitable."

That inevitability is the electric current running beneath all our encounters this summer. My good old anxiety-brain, finally stepping up and protecting me.

I thought we were so different from who we were last year, but maybe we haven't learned at all.

"Quinn," he says, but I'm not done.

"You don't know what it was like when my parents separated. How fucking lonely those six months were. Half a *year*, Tarek, and it didn't 'heal with time' or any of the things people say about shit like that."

This seems to only make him angrier. He tugs at the tight sleeves of his uniform, shoving them up so he can scratch the dry skin on his wrist. "You think you can avoid being hurt just because you don't put a label on it? Because I have news for you. We're *in* a relationship. We have been all summer. You can call it whatever you want or you can call it *nothing*"—he puts a sharp emphasis on that word—"but that doesn't make you exempt from getting hurt. We're *all* hurting, Quinn. In different ways, some that we can treat with medication and therapy and some only with time. And some in ways that might never heal. Sometimes the good outweighs the bad. Sometimes those great times are so fucking great that they make the bad times a little easier to handle."

"Or they make them worse." I've hunched back down, my shoulder blades wearing grooves in the wall. "Did you know that even after my mom moved back in, I couldn't sleep at night for months? But I guess you wouldn't be able to relate since your perfect parents have their perfect little story."

"My parents are far from perfect."

"I've never seen them fight."

"Oh, just because you don't see them do it when they're *at work*, that means they don't?" he says. "I'm sorry about your parents. I can't imagine what it was like to go through that, and it's shitty they never talk about it. But couples fight. You and I did."

I scoff at that. "You can't pretend that's some sign we're meant to be together."

"No, but it doesn't mean we're doomed, either. Sometimes couples fight. It doesn't mean they're not right for each other—it means they're trying to work something out. Together."

"That's what I'm trying to tell you," I say. Even with as much conviction as I can muster, it's only a whisper. I make myself stronger, urging certainty into my voice. "I don't want to try."

At that, his face just . . . shatters. That's the only way to describe it. It shatters, and I'm the one holding the sledgehammer.

"Okay," he finally says, all the feeling drained from his voice. "Okay. I get it now. It should have been clear to me before, but I guess I was too much of a fucking optimist to see it. There's no way we can make each other happy." He breaks off, takes a deep breath, as though working to keep his emotions at bay. When he speaks again, there's a roughness to his voice. "If you were doing this to save yourself from being hurt, well, congratulations. Let's just end it right now so you don't have to suffer any more than you already have."

I've broken him.

This sweet, romantic, optimistic boy, and I've broken him.

He turns to head down the corridor, and I have to rush to catch up.

"Tarek, wait—that's not what I—" I try to reach for him, but he shrugs me off. I was supposed to be in control here.

"What did you say it was? Inevitable?"

I did. I did say that. "Please," I whisper to his back, unsure how this went so wrong and how to make it right. I don't even know what I'm pleading for, only that I don't want to be alone right now, and I'm scared of what that means. "Tarek. Please."

He just walks right into the kitchen, leaving me in the silent corridor with my brain the quietest it's ever been.

# 26

For the next three days, I don't leave the tower, except to sneak down to the kitchen when I'm positive my parents are out of the house. On day two, even Edith gets fed up and goes in search of someone who will do something other than cry into her fur. I listen to Cat Power on repeat, though it only makes me sadder.

I can't even bring myself to talk to Julia. Her most recent text says, hey hi making sure you're alive, and I manage to type back, yep, just busy, sorry.

It's too similar to Tarek's text from last year, which of course only sinks me deeper into this mess I've made. I hate how similar *I* am to that girl I was last year: weepy, hollow, half of myself. The last time I couldn't control my emotions around Tarek. The last time I let someone get close enough to leave a mark.

This was supposed to be the easy way out. It was what I wanted since our first kiss, but it's getting harder and harder to remember why.

It's not just Tarek I've lost this time. Somehow, I managed to wreck all my relationships in a single day. It aches, imagining my parents downstairs, ushering couples into their office, my dad scratching things out and scribbling over the kitchen calendar. It took a lot of apologizing, but they should manage to get past this

nightmare unscathed. They offered every guest at the wedding discounts for their services and for some of their vendors. Victoria
even seems to have moved beyond caring what people think about
her and Lincoln, since they're letting Streamr move forward with
it next month.

I've seen the trailer. It promises to deliver just as much drama
as the show did.

I shouldn't be surprised that my parents have handled it all
like pros, that they've smoothed out my mistake and washed away
the evidence. That they've cut me out of B+B, exactly the way I
wanted. And yet a few times, I'm compelled to race downstairs, tell
them I didn't mean any of it, beg them to let me back in.

But I don't. Despite the way it happened, everything I said
was true.

Day four of wallowing coincides with Asher's bachelorette party. A
party bus pulls onto our block and honks to the tune of "It's Rain-
ing Men." I've had enough men for the time being, thanks.

"It's here!" Asher shouts from downstairs, where she and her
friends have been getting ready. Because we are Just That Kind of
Family, our mother is coming too.

The last place I want to be right now is on a party bus with a
half dozen screaming women, but it's for my sister. I don't want
to ruin the party for her, not after I've already ruined so much. I
wasn't sure if she still wanted me there, but when I texted her last
night, she said of course she did. So I put on my shortest, tightest
dress, paint my face, and meet the rest of them in the hallway. It
should be clear I'm not myself: I'm wearing black.

It turns out that a party bus is precisely as terrible as it sounds. It's outfitted with neon lights, sticky plastic seats, and a ridiculous amount of alcohol. There are two poles at either end. For . . . dancing? Yes, I learn as a couple of bridesmaids start grinding against them. Yes, that is exactly what they're for.

"Quinn!" yells maid-of-honor Whitney, a third-grade teacher and Asher's best friend from high school. "Dance with us!"

"I'm good," I call back, sipping a sparkling water.

Asher's wearing a frilly white romper with a pink sash over it that says OFF THE MARKET. She rolled her eyes when one of her bridesmaids, Brianne, presented her with it, but she put it on anyway. Her hair is down, her waves doused with so much mousse they almost look crunchy.

The music is loud, and that keeps me from spiraling. Keeps me present. Asher's friends ask me about my summer, about college, all seemingly innocuous topics that make me borderline hyperventilate. Still, I try to answer with as expressionless a face as possible.

Despite the bus, it's not a raucous, *Magic Mike* kind of bachelorette party. Our first stop is dinner at an upscale Italian restaurant with trapeze artists performing above the tables. I order the cheapest thing on the menu and poke at it for an hour and a half, not unaware that my mom is watching me the whole time.

Afterward, we drive through the city blasting all my least favorite reception songs before ending up at Whitney's place for dessert and games. I sit on the couch with a half-eaten cookie on a napkin in my lap, laughing when I'm supposed to, unearthing embarrassing stories about Asher when the mood calls for it.

"Thank you all so much for this," Asher says during a rousing match of Pin the Sweater on Chris Evans. "Really. I can't imagine getting married without all of you here. Yes, even my mom."

Brianne reaches across the couch to give her a sloppy hug. "You gave me my dream wedding. It's only fitting for you to have yours."

Karina, another bridesmaid, shoves up her blindfold to gauge the space between her sweater cutout and the poster of a smoldering, shirtless Chris Evans. "Damn it," she mutters, passing the blindfold to my mom. "I was *this close*."

Mom's sweater lands on Chris's left foot. I'm up next, and as she holds out the blindfold, she says quietly, "I know you're not speaking to us right now. And you have every right to be upset."

That surprises me. "Mom, I—"

She cuts me off with a shake of her head. "I know this isn't the place to get into it. But . . . we're here. Whenever you're ready."

"Hey, who's next?" Whitney asks.

I take the bandanna from my mom. "I think Chris Evans is getting cold."

"I'm just trying to understand." Her voice is so soft now, I'm not even sure if she wants me to hear. "I want to understand you."

And if that doesn't make two of us.


With the exception of my mother, everyone opts to spend the night at Whitney's. Most of them pass out early, until eventually Asher and I are the only ones awake.

"This reminds me of crashing your sleepovers when I was little," I tell her as we set up blankets in the living room. "Except I didn't understand half of what you guys were talking about."

"For good reason. You would have been traumatized."

"You do *not* want to see my search history from that point in my life," I say. "You had a good time tonight?"

"Amazing. Thank you. It was everything I wanted." She nods to the Chris Evans poster. "I'm getting that framed." Then she sits down, and I slide to the floor next to her. "We should talk, though. About everything that's been going on with you."

"I don't want to ruin your party."

"I've partied an adequate amount. You're not ruining anything."

"Mom and Dad probably told you what happened. What we fought about."

"They did. But I wanted to hear it from you."

So I settle in to tell her the whole story—about my parents and B+B, yes, and about Tarek, too.

"I wish you'd told me this sooner," she says when I'm done. She's put her crunchy waves back into her usual topknot.

"I wanted to. But I was worried you'd think I was offending you, saying I didn't want this free ticket into B+B."

Asher snorts. "I did not get a free ticket."

"What do you mean?"

"I had to *beg* them to let me help out when I was younger. I was always getting in the way, and I think it took them a while to realize I was genuinely interested in wedding planning."

"Ah, so *you're* the one who fucked things up for me, with them assuming I'd join the family business too."

"Guess so. Sorry, kid."

I swat at her with one of Whitney's seventy decorative throw pillows before turning serious. "We also haven't been . . . as close as we used to be this summer." I grab another pillow, fidget with a stray thread. "I've always assumed you'd be on Mom and Dad's side." Like her love was conditional on me being part of B+B, the way I thought my parents' was. "It's this one thing we all do as a family, which sometimes doesn't leave any room for us to do anything else."

"I'm so sorry." She stares down at her nails, painted white to match the romper she wore. "I want to say it's because I've been wrapped up in the wedding, but that's not an excuse."

"That's what I've been worried about too. That you'll be married, and your work is all about weddings, and I wouldn't be part of any of it. I just—I don't know what our relationship is like if we don't have that connection."

Asher's face falls. "I had no idea. Oh my god. Quinn, I—I'm sorry," she repeats. "I'm not becoming a different person just because I'm getting married. I still have hopeless crushes on both Chris Evans and John Oliver. And you're going to be part of my life whether we're working together or not. Sure, that's easier when we're working for B+B, but that doesn't mean we'll stop seeing each other now that you've left. Which, if I'm being honest, is still hard for me to wrap my mind around." She offers a small smile. "I'm working on it, though."

I want to believe her—that we won't stop seeing each other. Even if logically, I know we won't, it'll still take time before we feel as close as we once did.

"I can't help thinking about how it felt when Mom and Dad separated. That's the other reason I held on for so long."

Something strange flutters across her face, and it takes me a moment to realize it's recognition. And that's a shock, since the separation is so often on my mind. "Right. The separation," she says. "Sometimes I forget that even happened."

"I guess you weren't around very much."

"Shit. I'm sorry again."

"I get it. You were fifteen. The last thing you wanted to do was comfort your little sister. But . . . we never talked about it, Asher. *No one* talked about it, which made it a thousand times more confusing."

She's quiet for a while, taking all of this in. "You need to talk to Mom and Dad about it."

"Like they'll want to."

"Trust me. Ask them about it."

I do trust her, so I promise I will.

After a few moments, she lies down, tapping my ankle with her toes. "Should we talk about Tarek?" she asks.

"I think I've deeply fucked it up, so there's probably no point in thinking about it." I hold a pillow over my face, muffling my words.

"You don't think all couples fight? Last week, Gabe and I argued for twenty minutes about the proper way to load the dishwasher."

Tarek said the same thing, but I don't know how to explain to her that it felt worse than a fight. The look on his face, the knowledge it was my fault . . .

"I wouldn't know how to fix it, even if I wanted to," I say, but as the words leave my mouth, I'm not sure they're true. All I know is I don't want to *not* be with him. "I've spent so long convincing myself that romance isn't real."

To her credit, Asher doesn't bat an eye. "Even me? With Gabe?"

"Well . . ." I trail off, unsure how to respond. "You don't feel like you're performing, in a way?"

"Quinn. We're *all* performing. Like, all the time. You think I act the same way around you as I do around Mom and Dad? Or that Whitney pole dances in front of her third graders?"

"One would hope not."

Maybe what I've been most scared of is really *wanting* the kind of love I've been around all my life and not receiving it in return. I chose hookups so I could convince myself that was what I wanted: to not be loved. Any time those relationships flirted with emotion, I ran. Over and over, I put myself in these situations that guaranteed I'd get an outcome that confirmed what I already believed: that I didn't want romantic love.

Except with Tarek, I wanted more. For the first time, I let myself have a taste of it, and then once again, I sabotaged myself. I was so close to that feeling in his favorite movies, the one where you lock eyes with someone across a crowded room like they're the only one there. The one where you just *know*, the way Meg Ryan and Tom Hanks do at the end of *Sleepless in Seattle*.

And now I'm certain he wants nothing to do with me.

"How do you convince yourself that it's worth it?" I ask, voice shaking. "Even knowing it might end in disaster someday?"

"You take a chance," she says simply, like it really is that easy to close your eyes and leap. "And you hope the other person takes the same one."

# 27

An unexpected upside of having attended hundreds of weddings over the course of my life: I know exactly how to crash one.

You want to wear something that helps you blend in. Bright patterns will get you noticed by the guests and wedding coordinators right away. Larger weddings are, of course, easier to crash, easier to lose yourself in. You don't want to catch anyone's attention, either—no rushing the dance floor when your favorite song comes on.

We've dealt with our share of crashers. Most of them, my parents have politely asked to leave, though at one wedding, the bride and groom were so amused, they let them stay.

It's another one of those perfect Seattle summer days, ideal for a brunch wedding reception. By the time Julia arrives, I've narrowed my list down to three venues holding weddings today, based on some late-night social media sleuthing. It would have been too easy if Mansour's had been catering one of ours. My parents would be horrified if they knew what I was doing, but since it's in the name of romance, maybe some part of them would be pleased.

"I feel like we're undercover," Julia says in the car. "Can we have code names? I want something badass. Like . . . Lilith Copperstone."

"Why do I feel like you've been waiting to use that name? You came up with that way too quickly." I check my mascara in my rearview mirror. I'm wearing one of my harpist dresses, ideal for blending in, my hair loose and wavy. "And no, we are absolutely not using names that might make us stand out in any way. You're still Julia."

The idea came to me last night, when I was in the middle of an intense mope session after texting Tarek. I can't even begin to explain how sorry I am, I wrote. Do you think we could talk?

He didn't reply. There had to be a way to show him I wasn't the person I was last year, because, of course, he wasn't either. I had to show him I'd finally figured it out. Tell him he's never been nothing to me.

And then it hit me. The biggest—dare I say grandest—way to show I've changed.

"What do we say if someone asks who we know?" Julia says.

"Hopefully they won't. But 'family friend' is probably the easiest, or that our parents are friends with the POGs or POBs," I say. "We're more crashing the wedding *vendor* as opposed to the actual wedding."

"Not nearly as exciting."

"Have I said thank you enough yet? Because seriously, thank you."

"A few more times wouldn't hurt."

Our first attempt is a winery out in Woodinville, but when there's no Mansour's van out back, we move on. The next one is a hip event space in Capitol Hill. We get there right as guests are arriving, and Julia squeezes my hand as I square my shoulders and charge forward, using any amount of confidence and elegance I've gained over the past eighteen years to pretend like we fit in.

We fall in line behind a family with two young kids, one of them complaining about how long the ceremony was. "You'll get to have cake soon, I promise," the father is saying.

When we get inside, most people are checking their sweaters and bags, making their way toward the hand-lettered seating chart to see where their table is. Instead, I drag Julia down a skinny hallway, where I'm guessing there's some kind of prep area for the caterers.

"Do you want me to stay out here? Keep watch or something?" Julia says.

"Sure," I say. I've needed the moral support, but I need to do this next part on my own. "Thank you."

On the other side of a glassed wall, waiters swarm around trays and plates and pots of hot food. My stomach turns over when I spot Harun, and then Tarek's mom, and then Tarek, busying himself with a platter of what look like mini quiches.

It's been only a week and a half, but he somehow manages to look both different and painfully familiar, his hair slightly longer, his jawline scruffier. If his posture indicates anything less than his usual confidence, I must be seeing things, wishing them into being.

I'm about to open the door when he heads toward it with the tray of quiches. And suddenly this whole thing seems like a terrible idea. He's *working*. There's barely enough time for me to flatten myself against the wall as Julia flashes me a panicked "What are you doing?" look. I motion to the door just as it swings open, and then I close my eyes and hope he doesn't see me.

"Quinn?"

Slowly, I open one eye and give him a pathetic little wave. "Hi," I say as an anxiety-laugh slips out.

He doesn't seem to find it funny. "What's going on?" From the expression on his face, dark brows pinched, it's clear I'm the last person he wants to see. "What are you doing here?"

"I needed to talk to you, and you weren't answering my texts, and—"

"Huh. Generally, if someone doesn't respond, it means they don't want to talk to you."

"That's what I thought for a year. But we both know that wasn't true." I take a step closer, and he seems to soften for a moment before shaking himself out of it.

"I'm working," he says, bouncing the quiches. I spy a patch of red on his wrist. A flare-up. "I have to take these out."

"Wait. Wait. Just hear me out. I promise, I'll be fast." I didn't plan this far ahead. I assumed he'd be so swept away by the gesture that he'd wrap me in his arms, tell me he saved a slice of cake for us. But, ugh, I guess grand gestures tend to be accompanied by grand speeches. And I have no idea what to say. "I screwed up." I have to show him I can do the kind of romance he wants. That I can be in a relationship—that I *want* a relationship. With him. "I'm so, so sorry. I shouldn't have said those things about you—*to* you. I don't feel that way at all."

"How *do* you feel, then?"

"I . . . want a relationship." There it is.

He snorts. Not the reaction I was expecting. "Really," he says, deadpan. "Why? Why now?"

"Because I miss you. I care about you." I fling an arm up, motioning to the venue around us. "Why else do you think I'm doing this, this grand gesture?"

At that, he just blinks at me. "So that's what this is." He switches the tray to his other hand. "A grand gesture is supposed to be this earnest, selfless declaration of love. This just feels like a performance."

"And everything you did for me wasn't?" I say. I didn't want to fight with him, but I'm not the only one who messed up. Again and again, he didn't listen to me.

"I know. I can see it now, and I'm sorry." He sounds genuine. As though realizing he's made mistakes too, he leans against the wall, draws a deep breath. "I've been thinking about it a lot lately, and you're right that this was all I knew how to do. I wanted my relationships to look a certain way from the outside, and maybe that's why none of them lasted longer than three months—my record, as you so kindly pointed out. Underneath all the gestures, they were superficial."

Some of the tension in my shoulders eases. He's opening back up.

"Not entirely superficial," I say gently. I don't want him to be this hard on himself. They were coming from a good place—I know that now.

"And what you said before, about wanting you to fall at my feet? I was horrified when you said it, but I think that's because, in a way, part of me did want that. And that wasn't right at all. I thought if I did enough gestures, you'd eventually realize you wanted a relationship with me, despite how often you told me you didn't. I wanted what my parents had so badly, and I guess I thought I could, I don't know, conjure it for myself."

"Force it, you mean."

He grimaces. "That's one way of looking at it. Maybe they were a performance, but . . . I don't know, I still want to believe parts of them were genuine. That they were sincere, even though I know they weren't. And I only know that because of what I had with you. But you showing up here, while I'm working . . . I don't know, Quinn. It isn't *you*. I don't know what this is supposed to mean, aside from potentially pissing off a bunch of people who paid a lot of money for this day to be as close to perfect as possible. *This* is the performance."

"It's not. I swear," I say, but maybe he's right. I thought I could waltz in here, declare I'm ready for a relationship, and he'd want me back.

"Okay. Then tell me how you feel about me."

I stare at the floor. "I like you," I say in a small voice. I'm not sure I'm ready for what comes after that. The other word is too foreign, too grand. "You know I like you. Why can't that be enough?"

"Because I—I *loved you*, okay?" He presses his lips together, like he didn't mean to say it.

*I loved you.*

That word does something to my heart.

*I* loved *you*. Past tense.

"I loved you for a while, knowing you didn't feel the same way," he continues. "Then, when I thought there might be a chance, you confirmed over and over that you were never going to return those feelings. You went out of your way to tell me, even when we were doing all these things that made us feel like a couple. It was a mindfuck, Quinn."

"I'm sorry," I whisper. "Tarek. I'm so sorry."

"I forced myself to be fine with it, but I'm not anymore. And I'll gladly accept some of the responsibility here. It's my fault too. I wanted too much that you weren't going to give, and I've accepted that. Maybe we can even be friends again, one day. But right now I can't be around you."

With that, he walks forward, and a bearded man in a suit approaches me, a stern expression on his face. "Excuse me, miss," he says. "Are you supposed to be back here?"

"Don't worry," Tarek says. "She was just leaving."

And as Julia and I are ushered outside, I finally know exactly how I feel about him.

Brokenhearted.

"I won't ask if you're okay," Julia says. We're sitting on top of the big hill at Gas Works Park, watching the boats on Lake Union.

"Appreciate that. Appreciate *you*." I grab a fistful of fries, swipe them through ketchup, and stuff them into my mouth.

After we left Capitol Hill, Julia rushed us around to pick up what she declared were all the best breakup foods: fries and chocolate milkshakes from Dick's Drive-In, sloppy slices from Ballard Pizza Company, and nachos from a nearby taco truck. We haven't said anything in a good twenty minutes, and that's one of the things I love about this friendship. We've known each other so long that our silences aren't uncomfortable.

"I know it's hard," she says after a while. "I'm sorry."

She doesn't just mean what happened with Tarek, but with my parents, too, and everything this summer that's made me both more and less uncertain about who I am, about what I want. Tarek, who loved me. Who doesn't anymore.

"I've felt so lost this summer." I try to laugh because it sounds so melodramatic, but nothing comes out. I take a slurp of milkshake.

"What do you mean?"

"Everyone I know has found their passion so easily. You with painting, my parents and Asher with weddings." *Tarek with baking.* "And it doesn't have to just be one thing, either. Even now, I love what I'm doing with Maxine, but maybe I want to keep it as a hobby. I'm not sure."

"You have *time*," she says, and I'm trying so hard to believe that. She rests her head on my shoulder. "Maxine came to you when you were least expecting her. Maybe this will too."

"I'm sorry I've been invisible these past couple weeks," I say, and she lifts her head. "I just . . . shut down. I didn't know how to process it except to, well, not process it, apparently."

Julia's quiet for a moment, then: "Yeah. About that. I need to say something." She rakes a hand through her long hair, pulling it over one shoulder. "I needed you. When you were being invisible."

Her words shock me into sitting up straight. "Shit. Oh my god, Julia, I am so sorry. What happened?"

"Nothing major," she says, holding up a hand. "I'm fine. Mostly fine. It was just, Noelle left. For an early-summer start. And even though we're doing long-distance, I had some doubts, I guess. About whether it was the right thing to do. I needed to talk, and I couldn't get ahold of you. We're okay, and I'm okay now, but I had a few rough days, if I'm being honest."

I should have been there for her. She was here for me, and I've been an idiot.

"I'm a trash best friend. I am so sorry, Julia."

"You can spend the next few weeks making it up to me."

"Done." I reach over and hug her. "Do you feel like telling me what happened?"

And she does. We talk and we eat and we laugh until her phone chirps on the grass next to her. "It's Noelle," she says. "We had plans to FaceTime. I can stay a little longer, though, if you need it . . . ?"

I shake my head. "*Go.* I'll be okay here."

And maybe I will be.

But I also don't think I'm done fighting quite yet.

# 28

've graduated to drilling holes. Seventy-two holes on the neck, three different sizes. This piece requires more work than anything else on the harp, and I love seeing it come together little by little.

Maxine is in the spray booth, but she trusts me enough to leave me alone out here with the drill press, which is significantly more powerful and more precise than the handheld power drill I've seen my parents wield during wedding disasters. Operating heavy machinery requires all my focus, and I can't let my mind slip without risking losing a finger. The way this work anchors me—I've never felt that before.

What I've learned, among many things, is that the harp is a living instrument. Over time, wood warps. Maxine has clients who bought harps from her a decade ago who still come back for adjustments. I like that, too: this instrument's ability to change. I used to think the harp was stuck in time, a relic of the past. And that's just not true. It can innovate. It can evolve.

Maybe I can too.

"This might be a weird question," I say when Maxine emerges from the spray booth, leaving behind the outfit that looks more like something a beekeeper or an astronaut would wear than a harp maker. She gives me this look, like she's come to not just anticipate weird questions from me but to enjoy them. "But why did you take me on? You didn't know me. You didn't have to do that."

At first I don't think I'll get a real answer, but she leans against the counter, drawing a fingertip along the smooth wood of a half-finished harp. "It had been a while since I'd had anyone else in the studio, I suppose. It can get pretty quiet in here, which may sound strange because it's usually so noisy. I love living alone, I do—but that's part of the problem when you live where you work. I missed having a coworker."

"I think I'm touched." I read her so wrong during our first meeting, when I thought she was lonely because her kids had moved out and moved on. She wanted someone in the studio with her, and it fills me with a sense of belonging I never felt with B+B to realize *I* am that someone.

That earns me a smile. "You know," she says, "one of my regular conferences is going to be down in Portland in December. You wouldn't be interested in tagging along, would you?"

I just stare at her. "Are you serious? Yes, one-hundred-percent yes. Thank you. Thank you!"

"It might be boring," she warns. "A lot of old people, a lot of old instruments."

"I'm sold."

Maybe this won't ever be more than a hobby. Maybe it won't be my future career. Maybe I'll look back on it when I'm older as something I did for a summer, a fun story to tell. Whatever it becomes, I don't have to know yet what it means. I have *time*.

Everyone's been telling me I have time to fall in love, to discover who I want to spend the rest of my life with.

But it's not just a *who*. It's a *what*, too.

No matter how much I love working at Maxine's, the moment I leave, the ache in my heart returns, taunting me on my drive back home. It's been a week since the blowup with my parents and with Tarek, and I thought the ache would have dulled by now, but it's only deepened, a new hollowness that lives next to my heart.

The first person I want to tell about everything that happened today, the conference and the drilling—which I'm sure one or both of us would make a dirty joke about—is Tarek. And I can't.

I'm expecting an empty house, the loneliness I've gotten so used to over the past week. I'm not prepared for my parents waiting for me in the living room, reminding me of the night they told us about their separation and all the talks we never had after that.

"You're not with a client?" I ask, slowly sliding my bag to the floor.

"We were thinking it might be time for us to have a talk," Mom says. She exchanges a glance with my dad. "A talk that's probably very overdue."

"Oh," I say quietly. Part of me wants to ask what happened to the *whenever you're ready* she promised at Asher's bachelorette party, but the truth is, I may never be ready. "I've been wanting to talk to you, too."

Dad motions to the couch, and I sit down next to Mom while he takes the armchair.

"I feel like we need to start with the separation," Mom says.

295

Oh my god. "Is it happening again? Are you separating? Or—"

"*No*," she says emphatically, leaning forward to pat my knee. "We're not. Sorry, I should have phrased that better. What I'm trying to say is that I think we may not have handled it the best the first time around."

"Or at all," I say.

Mom cringes. "We probably deserve that."

"We thought we were these progressive, empathetic parents," Dad says. "We were in counseling, and then you were in therapy for your OCD, and we were all working together. . . . We really thought everything was okay. But we made a mistake."

"That's . . . a relief to hear out loud," I say. Adults acknowledging they fucked up: not something I'm used to hearing. "Because it was kind of a terrible time for me. If I'm being honest."

"Quinn." Mom looks like she might cry. "I want to make this right. We both do."

"Can you just tell me *why*? I've been so anxious about it happening again because I never understood why it happened the first time. And then when you moved back in, everything was supposed to be back to normal, and I didn't understand that, either."

Dad takes a deep breath. "When your personal life and your work life have that much overlap, it's a challenge. And 'overlap' isn't even the right word, really—our personal life *was* our work life, and vice versa. We kept nagging each other, sniping at each other, and then when we stopped working for the day, we'd be bitter with each other."

"But you're still doing it. You're still living and working in the same place."

"You may not remember, but we actually rented an office space for a while," Mom says. "Later that year. And we preferred working out of the house so much more. With this job, you're always on the move. It didn't make sense to pay all that money for a space we weren't going to be using all that often."

She's right: I don't remember that at all.

"So what changed? When you came back, what was different? It's still stressful—that much is clear."

"The thing is, we already knew how to make our marriage work," Mom says. "We'd been doing that. What we didn't know was how to make our business work alongside that. That was a lot of what we talked about in counseling. Learning to understand and work with each other's communication styles."

"And we didn't tell you because, well, it was painful for us, too, that time apart. We just wanted to move forward. It's clear now that it wasn't the right decision, and we're very sorry about that."

I tuck my feet up on the couch. "All this time, I've been waiting for the last straw, every time you fight about something, no matter how small it is."

"It's normal and okay for there to be conflict in a relationship," Mom says, as everyone lately seems intent on making sure I know. "I think all of this actually made the two of us stronger as partners. Because we struggled through something together."

"And it still brings you joy?" I ask. "This kind of work?"

They exchange a look. "When you love it," Mom says, "it doesn't always feel like *work*."

"This may seem like an odd thing to say, given what we do . . ." Dad trails off. "But if we were really that unhappy, it would have been better to have split up. That might have been what was best for the family. We've seen it with our friends, and we've seen it with couples we've worked with—sometimes divorce isn't actually failure."

And that makes sense too.

"I want to apologize too," I say. "Again. Whatever I was going through, it wasn't fair to let it affect my work this summer. For that, I'm sorry."

My parents are quiet for a few moments. "I wish you'd told us this sooner," Mom says. "But I understand why you felt like you couldn't. Why you felt like we pushed you into this. We're sorry about that."

"And I thought if I told you I wasn't interested in becoming a wedding planner, it would, I don't know, divide us as a family. That I wouldn't be welcome."

"Absolutely not," Mom says. "We love Borrowed + Blue. But we love you more. Both you and Asher. You're our daughter first, Quinn. You always have been. We hope you know that. And it doesn't make us any less of a family if you decide to do something else."

There's a strange lump in my throat that I struggle to swallow around. I've needed to hear that for a while.

"So what happens now?" Dad says. "You're done with B+B?"

There's a sense of finality in the way he says it. And as much as I've dreamed about severing myself from it, I'm not sure I can imagine a future without it, even in some small way.

"Maybe not forever," I say. "But for now, yes. I need a break. And I know I probably can't switch out of all my fall classes at this point, but I'm pretty sure I don't want to study business. Whatever

I study, I want it to be my decision. Even if I have to pay for it myself and even if I change my mind someday. And I fully intend to pay you all back. For any business you lost as a result of what happened at Victoria and Lincoln's wedding."

"Well—we appreciate that," Dad says. "But that isn't necessary. Besides, now that the promos for the wedding special are running, we've been getting quite a lot of inquiries."

"And we don't want it to be too stressful to balance a job with your freshman classes."

"I've actually been doing some other work this summer," I say, and I take the chance to tell them all about Maxine.

"You'll have to play for us sometime," Dad says. "When you're ready."

Mom is nodding along, but the expression on her face is difficult to interpret. I've never seen her like this—and I realize she might be *hurt*. This business was her dream, and maybe it doesn't feel like a family business anymore if the whole family isn't involved.

"I think it'll take me a little more time to process everything," she admits. "It's tough to hear you were so unhappy for so long."

That tugs at my heart. "Mom, no," I rush to say. "I didn't hate all of it. I swear. Remember the groom who accidentally dragged the bride down with him into a fountain when they were posing for photos? And we all had to use hair dryers to dry their clothes?"

"That poor couple," Dad says. "I forgot about that."

"Or what about that time the bride tossed her bouquet on the roof, and we had to get a ladder to get it down?" Mom says, her voice less wobbly.

"And everyone cheered when we finally rescued it," I say.

Mom laughs, and I remember how much I love that sound. "That was a good one, wasn't it?"

It was. It really was.

I've been scared of losing this, and it's true that I won't get to keep all of it. But hopefully I'll gain a lot more.

I can't wait to find out what that is.

# 29

Later that night, after a dinner with my parents during which we manage not to talk about B+B at all, I head up to the tower with Edith, who seems to have forgiven me for all the moping.

I open my laptop and flex some muscles that have been dormant since May, when I was still regularly turning in homework. I've barely glanced at anything besides Wikipedia all summer. Inspired by my conversation with Tarek that now feels eons old, I search a few things: music majors, harp construction, jobs for harpists. I learn about the harp conferences Maxine mentioned.

I have two weeks left of summer. Twenty days until Tarek goes back to UC Davis, until Julia goes to New York. Our schools have late-September starts, and I'm grateful for that, though on social media, I see that plenty of my classmates have already left. It's an odd feeling, one I'm not sure I can name. If it's nostalgia, I'm uncertain what I'm actually nostalgic *for*.

I even double-tap a photo on Jonathan Gellner's Instagram. He's wearing aviators and leaning against a suitcase, staring moodily out the window of an airport as the sun rises. And it makes me feel worse for having ignored him all summer.

With a jolt, I realize it's not entirely unlike what Tarek did to me. Even if I didn't want to have a capital-R Relationship with Jonathan, we had *something*. It was awkward and uncomfortable, but it was something. And I just brushed it off, because if I didn't think about it, I wouldn't have to feel any emotions about it.

I have not been an excellent person.

I pull up his name in my contacts, wincing at his earlier messages asking me to talk. Then I take a deep breath and write some difficult sentences I should have written a long time ago.

> I realize this is late. Too late, probably. I wouldn't blame you if you despised me at this point. I don't expect any kind of response. I just wanted to say that I'm sorry for ignoring you. So incredibly sorry about how this ended. Good luck in college—I mean that. I hope you have the best freshman year.

I wish I could make it more personal. I wish I knew more about him than the superficial, but I made sure I didn't. I steeled myself, shut out the opportunity to feel something that came so naturally with Tarek.

Something I was so scared to acknowledge the meaning of that I pushed him away.

Last summer I sat in bed just like this, reading and rereading that email before sending it to him. I remember thinking it was the scariest thing I'd done in my life.

This, I'm pretty sure, is scarier.

• • •

The summer can't end without another wedding crisis, and this time it's Asher's.

We're all in the kitchen for August work brunch, which I don't plan to stop even if I'm no longer part of Borrowed + Blue. Pancakes, pajamas, 00 DAYS WITHOUT A DAD JOKE—all of these things are so very Berkowitz without being attached to weddings.

I don't instantly have the kind of post–B+B relationship with my family that I want, but we're working on it. I've made an appointment with my old therapist for next week, and my parents asked if I wanted to join them at one of their counseling sessions, which I might do.

Progress. This is progress.

Halfway through the meal, Asher's phone buzzes on the table, and she snatches it up. "Bakery," she explains before she says hello.

Asher and I are evolving too. She asked if I'd be interested in monthly sister dates once she gets back from her Italy honeymoon, and I was so struck by her suggestion that I immediately opened my phone calendar to October so we could plan the first one: a Seattle Rock Orchestra concert.

Asher's eyes widen as she listens to whoever's on the other end. "*Oh.* Oh no . . . The whole shop . . . ? I'm so sorry."

My parents go silent, watching her carefully. By the time she hangs up, her face has gone pale.

"There was a fire at the bakery," she says, and Mom's hand flies to her mouth. "Everyone's okay, fortunately, and they have insurance. So that's a relief."

"But your cake . . . ?" Mom says, and Asher shakes her head, a strand slipping out of her topknot.

"They can't do it." Her voice wavers. "My wedding is in three days, and we don't have a cake."

"We'll reach out to all our contacts." Dad swipes through his phone, leaping into wedding-planner action mode. "Shayna, you start with the *A*s, I'll start with the *Z*s."

"It has to be gluten free," Asher says. "That was why we went with this place, because they had a gluten-free kitchen. For Gabe."

I forgot that Gabe is gluten intolerant. And really, I shouldn't have, because the gluten-free challah we had at his place for Shabbat once was the stuff of nightmares.

"That does narrow things down a bit," Dad says. "And Mansour's, they're booked?"

"We didn't go with them because they didn't have a dedicated gluten-free facility," Asher says. "So, yes. I assume they booked something else."

"Shit," Mom mutters.

The three of them scroll through their phones, and I just sit there, trying to figure out how to help.

"It'll be okay," Dad is saying to Asher, trying to reassure her.

"Tarek could do it," I say quietly.

They all pause what they're doing, three heads swiveling in my direction. "What?" Mom says.

"Tarek could do it," I repeat. "If you can't find anyone. He's never done a full cake for a wedding before"—I can't lie—"but he's done pieces of them, and he's been trying out new recipes for various allergens. He'd make sure everything was clean, no contamination."

"He's always been great at what he does," Mom agrees. "We couldn't impose like that, though. Could we?"

*He's been waiting for a chance like this*, I want to say. "It's worth a try," I say instead.

So I give Asher his number, and I wait while she makes the call. I can just barely hear his voice on the other end of the phone, and it brings back that swirly feeling I used to think was some kind of sickness.

Now I know it's something else entirely.

"He can do it," Asher says when she hangs up, letting out a long breath. Then she shakes her head and laughs a little. "Wow, he was *really* excited. He didn't even want to charge me, but I insisted. Thanks, Quinn."

And if that isn't the adorable Tarek I've always loved.

*Loved.*

With a jolt, I realize it might be true.

"I'm glad," I tell my sister, though I wish I could have witnessed that excitement for myself.

Soon, my parents will go to a final venue walk-through, and Asher to a fitting with a client. I will be alone in the house again, trying not to let it feel as lonely.

Then I have an idea. "Hey—if you all have a minute before you go back to work, could I play something for you?"

# 30

Cake ex machina. That's what Asher is calling it—cake saves the day. And she's not wrong. Tarek's cake is pretty phenomenal. Or at least it looks that way, three layers, champagne cake with buttercream frosting, dotted with dainty white sprinkles. I have a feeling it'll taste even better.

My parents tried their best not to cry during the ceremony, which was led by Gabe's rabbi, who I guess is now Asher's rabbi too. But by the time Gabe stomped on the glass and we all yelled, "Mazel tov!" neither of my parents' faces was dry. I even felt myself smiling for real when I played Etta James on the harp.

It's my last wedding with B+B. Maybe not forever, but for a while, and I wouldn't have picked any other wedding to go out with.

Now we've moved to a different part of the botanical garden for photos, and the buffet is being prepped while guests take their seats. I smooth the hem of my maid-of-honor dress, a long, flowy number with thin straps, a deep V in the back, and a gorgeous embroidered bodice. The color is technically "fog," which I only know because Asher got mad at me when I called it gray. Out here in the sun, it's not gray at all, especially when the light catches subtle hints of blue-green.

My parents are trying to enjoy themselves without rushing around behind the scenes, but they can't help it. It's a little endearing.

"Don't forget a few close-ups of the bouquet," Dad says to the photographer as we pose in the gazebo. "And the rings, too."

"Dad," Asher says. "I think they've got it."

There's nothing fake about the smile on my sister's face or how Gabe lights up when she laughs. That's all real. If her airy open-backed gown, ivory lace with flutter sleeves and a frothy train, is anything less than comfortable, I'd never know.

I'm not sure how I was ever convinced all of this was a performance when proof of the opposite is right in front of me. When maybe it's always been in front of me.

But I'm learning.

We're the last to take our seats in the garden, this area surrounded by lush trees and a hundred different flowers I'm sure my family knows all the names of. I'm tucked between Asher and my mom, who keeps fussing with Asher's veil. Every time Asher catches my eyes, she rolls hers, but I can tell she loves it. This is her day.

A few tables away are Julia and her parents. She flies out to New York tomorrow. And all the way at the back at what should be table number seventeen—but Asher tweaked the numbering so he wouldn't know he was at the reject table—is Gabe's cousin Moshe, who is under strict orders to keep his stand-up comedy to himself.

When it's time for the toasts, Gabe's best man gives a short but sweet speech about being Gabe's roommate in college and having to listen to him talk about Asher nonstop. "If you like her so much," he recalled saying to Gabe one morning, half asleep, sarcastic, "then why don't you just marry her?"

"Maybe I will," Gabe had said, and Asher laughs like she's hearing this for the first time.

When it's my turn, I lift my eyebrows at my sister, indicating that I am definitely going to embarrass her, and she waves an arm as though to say, "Go right ahead."

I unfold the piece of paper I wrote my toast on. Not the whole thing, just a few talking points. "Hi," I say into the microphone, and it squeals with feedback. An auspicious start. "Sorry. It's a little weird being on this side of things. As most of you know, I'm Asher's sister. There are seven years between us, and while that doesn't mean I'm an accident baby, it also doesn't mean I'm not an accident baby." I look directly at her. "Or it could be you, who knows."

The audience laughs a little at that.

"Asher and I have had a unique relationship. She might correct me on this, but I'm not sure if I was ever the annoying little sister. My parents used to call me her shadow; that's how much I followed her around when we were younger. I adored her—well, still do—and she was the person I most wanted to be when I grew up."

A few *aww*s. Julia flashes me a thumbs-up.

I adjust my grip on the microphone. "Asher is the kind of person who throws herself into whatever she does without hesitation. She commits. And that's an ideal trait for someone who's getting married, because I have no doubts about how deeply she's committed to Gabe. To give you a sense of how committed she is, I made this incomplete list of things she's wholeheartedly committed to over the course of her life." I continue, reading off the piece of paper: "She committed to speaking in an Australian accent for an entire month when she was thirteen and I was six, just because I told her she was horrible at it. She remains staunchly committed to not just the Bachelor franchise, but every single one of its spin-offs. And she's not watching them ironically, like I sometimes am—she truly wants everyone on that show to find love. She committed to boot-cut jeans, even when they went out of style, assuring all of us they'd come back eventually."

"And they did!" she calls. More laughter.

"In all seriousness, though, she commits to dozens of weddings a year with Borrowed + Blue. This really is her dream job, planning the best day of people's lives. For a long time, I wanted so badly to have a path for myself as right as Asher's."

As I sweep my gaze across the garden, my eyes land on Tarek, who's standing in the doorway to the kitchen. His arms are folded, but it's not an angry pose. There's a softness to his shoulders that makes me optimistic. I'm too far away to be able to interpret his expression, but that's also not exactly new with us.

"My path has been a little different," I continue. "A little rockier. But I've made some discoveries about love recently, and I wanted to share them with all of you." Nerves turn my voice shaky, and maybe that's okay. Maybe it's okay to be scared about this part. I didn't make notes past this point and had only a vague idea of what I wanted to say, but seeing Tarek makes the words come a little easier. "Love is frightening. I should know, because I keep running away from it. But someone like Asher—she loves so fully, so seemingly without fear. It's hard not to admire her for it.

"When you're in love, whether that love is platonic or romantic, you get to be the fullest version of yourself, uncertainties and mistakes and all. You *get* to be that version of yourself—because it's a privilege, really, to open up that much, even when it's challenging. And it *is* going to be challenging sometimes, especially if you're not used to being your whole self. Especially if your whole self is something of a mystery, even to you." My heart is racing, and I can't let my eyes linger on any singular person. Maybe it sounds like I'm speaking in generalities, but Tarek has to understand what I mean by this. How important he's been to me. "When you're in love, you want to spend time with that person not just on your good days, but your in-between days and your bad days too. You want to try new things and indulge in the coziness of familiar ones. And if you ever feel like you're on the verge of losing that person, you'd pull a grand gesture to get them back. The kind of grand gesture you've only seen in romantic comedies. Maybe you'd ask a guy who lives on a houseboat if he'll meet you on top of the Empire State Building, even if you've never spoken to him in real life."

When my eyes find Tarek's again, he's not laughing. His features are serious, even grim, and I clench and unclench my fist around the microphone, worried none of this is landing the way I want it to.

Still, I charge forward. "I think we all can agree that *Sleepless in Seattle* is far from a perfect film. But when you're in love, you do wild things. That love isn't always visible to the people outside of it, but *you* can feel it. And I know that's what Asher has with Gabe. It's a really special, surreal thing to find that person, and I couldn't be happier that we're all here to celebrate with you."

Asher holds a hand to her heart. *Love you*, she mouths.

I raise my glass. "To Asher and Gabe—may you always have that top-of-the-Empire-State-Building kind of love. Cheers!"

. . .

Dinner and dessert pass by in a fizzy-bright blur. It's impossible not to smile when everyone is celebrating my sister and Gabe, toasting them, praising Tarek's last-minute cake. "I can't believe this is gluten free," at least three of them proclaim. One guest asks Asher for his card, and the idea of Tarek having a business card is instantly adorable to me.

I really do feel content—mostly. Which is why I excuse myself as dessert is winding down and the band is warming up.

In the kitchen, Tarek is packaging up what's left of the cake while other servers work through a mountain of dishes. He treats the cake in this measured way, delicate but confident. I don't know how I was jealous of this because right now I'm filled with pride. This thing he loves brings joy to so many other people.

"Hey," I say, and wait for him to turn around.

It's not a smile he gives me, but it's close. "Hey."

"The cake was incredible."

"Yeah?" Now he's trying even harder to hide the smile. "You have no idea how happy I was when Asher called. Thank you for suggesting me."

"Thank *you*. You kind of saved the wedding."

"You're the one who gave me the chance." He finishes bundling a slice of cake in plastic wrap, then in aluminum foil. Always meticulous, that one. I'd be lying if I said it wasn't one of the things I loved about him. "My parents were impressed. I might get to take on another one next month."

"Tarek. That's amazing," I say. "I was hoping we could talk." I glance around the room, which isn't exactly private. "But not here.

Could you meet me out in the gazebo in . . ." I check the time on my phone. The first dance is soon, and I'll want to stick around for at least a few more. "Twenty minutes?"

His posture relaxes the tiniest bit. "Yeah. Yeah, I can do that."

Shaky legs carry me to the dance floor, something like hope hovering in my midsection. Asher and Gabe's first dance is to "You Are the Best Thing," which I give a solid seven out of ten for first-dance songs. Sappy, sure, but also kind of perfect.

The next song is customarily the father-of-the-bride dance, but they buck tradition and invite my mom and Gabe's grandparents to join in, switching partners throughout.

Then Asher nearly clobbers me in an attempt to drag me onto the dance floor. I let her take my hand in hers, resting my other one on her waist, careful with her lace bodice.

"Dress looks decent," I say as we sway back and forth.

"You little loser." With ease, she spins me around, and when we're facing each other again, she lifts an eyebrow at me. "So, that toast . . ."

I scrunch my face at her. "Was one-hundred-percent about you and Gabe."

"Right. I could tell, what with our deep personal attachment to *Sleepless in Seattle* and all." She scans the area beyond the dance floor, and I'm pretty sure she's looking for Tarek. "It was really brave, what you did."

"I'm still not sure if it worked."

"Not just the toast," she says. "Everything. This whole summer, Mom and Dad, B+B. Your lever harp."

"Not mine yet," I correct her. Because god, they're expensive. "It's just a loan. But maybe one day."

"Whatever you end up doing, I have a feeling you're going to be fantastic at it."

I have to bite the inside of my cheek to keep the emotion from leaking out. "Ugh, stop, I made a vow I wouldn't ever cry at a wedding. But I guess this is my last one. For a while, at least."

She goes quiet for a few moments. "A good one to go out on, I hope?"

I scoff at that, because how could there be any other answer? "The best." Another spin, and then I'm back in her arms. "Was it everything you wanted?"

"*Was?* It's still going on. I'm not leaving until they kick me out," she says. "There's considerably less Chris Evans than I thought there would be, but it's been incredible. I didn't think I'd get a chance to talk to everyone or to eat everything I wanted to, but Mom and Dad made it so I didn't have to worry about any of the logistics today. I could just . . . get married. And enjoy it."

"I'm so, so glad," I say, meaning it.

I tuck a loose strand of hair back into her updo, and she gives me a grateful smile.

"So. After all of that, am I going to get a Tarek update? I'll beg if I have to."

"There isn't really an update to give," I say. "At least, not yet. I asked him if he'd meet me in the gazebo so we could talk. That was about twenty minutes ago, and I asked him to meet me in twenty minutes, so—"

She lets out a yelp and nearly drops me. "And you're still dancing with me? Go! Go climb that Empire State Building!"

Then she wrinkles her nose. "Wait. Is Tarek the Empire State Building in this metaphor? Did I just tell you to go do something dirty?"

"Oh my god. I'm leaving." I pull her close, inhaling that familiar Kirschbaum shampoo I've come to associate with the people I love most. "Mazel tov, you old married lady."

# 31

I make my way deep into the garden, until I can barely hear the music. There's more green, more sprawling trees and mystery flowers, and I'm surprised to discover that Tarek beat me here. I must not have noticed when he sneaked away.

He's waiting in the gazebo, sitting with his elbows on his knees, wringing his hands, the opposite of Casual Dude Pose. I haven't seen this nervous look on him very much, and when it hits me that he's nervous because of *me*, I quicken my pace. I want to leave all my fears and uncertainties behind, but I'm sure I take a few with me.

"Thanks for meeting with me," I say, folding the skirt of my dress beneath me and sliding onto the wooden bench next to him.

"That sounds like you're interviewing me for a job."

"I could. Personal chef?"

This earns me a laugh, and I want to pluck the sound from the air and tuck it next to my heart. It's only been a couple weeks since I heard it, but it feels almost like the beginning of the summer again, like I am relearning this person who disappeared for eight months.

He toes the ground with his sensible black shoe. After a silence, he lifts his head. Those long lashes—it takes all my willpower not to reach out and touch him. "So . . . how are you doing?" he asks.

"I've been better," I admit. "You?"

"About the same."

I'm still not sure how to bring up what I asked him here to talk about, the thing that's surely on both our minds, so I start with something easier. "I changed my course schedule," I say. "I kept one of the business classes, but I'm also taking a music theory class, a gender studies class, and something about the history of theme parks." What I don't say: that he was the first person I wanted to tell. That not being able to has been torture. That the freedom is terrifying, yes, but mostly exciting.

"Maybe you'll discover a hidden talent as a roller-coaster architect."

"I'm open to it." A deep breath, a smoothing of my hands on the flowy skirt, and a summoning of courage. The antianxiety trifecta. "This isn't exactly easy for me to say, which may sound strange after the wedding toast, but . . . there it is. It's never been easy, which is part of the problem."

The slightest of nods. It's barely encouragement, but it's enough for me to keep going.

"You know I've never really dated anyone. So I assumed I could be that way with you this summer and it would be like my other relationships. No strings, no romance, no emotions. And, well, that clearly didn't work."

"I pushed you when you said you wanted to keep it casual," he says. "I take responsibility for that."

I shake my head. "I didn't want it to be casual. Not deep down. I was fighting against it, every time you brought it up. I convinced myself it was because I didn't want the kind of perfunctory romance I saw at weddings, but I think it was because I was afraid to give someone too much of myself. I had to keep one little piece of Quinn locked up where no one could find it. Sometimes, not even me." I let myself make eye contact with him, his gaze so open, so honest. It's never not been, I realize. "I've been trying this new thing where I'm, like . . . more of myself, I guess? I don't know. I'm still trying to figure out who 'myself' actually is."

"Whoever you are now isn't too bad," he says. "I want to say I've got it all figured out, but I haven't. In a lot of ways, I'm still trying."

"We're both imperfect."

"Sure," he says. "But we're learning."

I expect it to be hard to say all these things, that they'll burn as they climb up my throat and land in a pile of ash on the ground. But it's not. I told Tarek it wasn't easy to talk like this, but either I'm a liar or I'm getting better at it. Or it's the simple fact that his presence makes it easier.

There's no swelling music, no promise of scrolling end credits. Just Tarek and me and the things I have never told anyone. I am being honest with him, with myself, for the first time all summer, and it suddenly feels like the easiest thing I've ever done.

"It's also not fair for me to tell you I didn't like any of the gestures," I say. "I didn't hate everything. That's the thing. I kept telling myself I didn't want you to do these things for me, but then you'd save me a macaron, or you'd show up at my house in the rain with a homemade mug cake. Sometimes the gestures were right."

"Not everything is balloons and skywriting. I'm learning that too. Though I'm sure those have a time and a place."

I let myself crack a smile at that. "I get it, now, why my attempt at a grand gesture didn't work. You were right—that wasn't me. It didn't mean anything, me interrupting you at a wedding. I assumed I could show up and that would solve everything, but that's not what a grand gesture is about, is it? It's never one big gesture. It's a series of small ways to let someone know you care about them. Maybe I'm not cut out for a cinematic kind of romance. But what I do know is that these two weeks have been torture. What I should have done—not just then, but weeks ago, months ago—is tell you how much you mean to me. How much I like you. All the ways I'm"—I break off for a moment, draw in as much air as possible—"all the ways I'm falling for you, from your baking to the sound of your laugh to the way I feel wholly myself with you in a way I've never let myself feel before."

"Quinn," he says, and I could listen to him say my name on a loop every night before going to sleep. There's a softness there, a reverence. A thumb grazes my wrist. Then he drops his hand again, that ghost of physical contact leaving my skin aching.

"Weddings have skewed my perception of love—to the point where I didn't know what it was, or how it would feel, and that's probably why I didn't understand how I was feeling until it was too late."

"Is it?" he asks, and if I had any control over my senses right now, I might notice him inching closer to me in the gazebo. "Too late?"

"No. At least, I hope not." My voice is scratchy. I barely recognize it. "I thought I had to come up with something grand to sweep you off your feet."

He just gives me this look, like I've missed something huge, and maybe I have. "It's not about the gestures," he says. "The gesture doesn't mean anything if the couple isn't right for each other. It's about the person." A swallow, and then, as his knee taps mine: "*You* make it grand."

Oh. That's—*wow*. Okay. My heart swells, and god, we don't even need music. Not an orchestra, not a harp, just the thumping of our hearts and the sweetness of his words. If I had any concept of romance, I'd say it's the most romantic thing I've ever heard.

"I love you," I say quietly, and it's not enough, and I'm not scared anymore, so I say it again. Louder this time. "I love you, Tarek."

His whole face lights up, and I'm convinced I've never seen anything lovelier than the rich brown of his eyes. "That's a relief," he says, "because I love you too. I've loved you since—"

And I don't get to hear how long it's been because I'm pressing my lips to his, and oh, I've missed him. He is warm and solid and *I love him, I love him, I love him.* I love the way his arms wrap around me, pulling me closer. I love the way his hands map my waist and my hips. I love the way he sighs against my mouth when I break the kiss to hug him, to mold my body to his.

"Sorry, what was that?" I say next to his ear, breathless. "Something about how much you love me?"

I feel the rumble of his laugh in his throat. "I've been in love with you since last summer. I love all of you—your uncertainties and your mistakes, too, because you've sure as hell let me make mine." His hand slips through my hair, down to my shoulder, fingers brushing my collarbone. "I never wanted to freak you out. I just thought you weren't going to get there, and I was going to be fine with it . . . until I wasn't." He brushes some of my hair out of my face so he can press a kiss to my temple so tender, it nearly melts me. "I'm just . . . really glad we both made it here."

"I want to do this for real," I say. "If that's something you still want too."

"Yes. Yes, I do," he says, and reaches to slide up the droopy strap of my dress.

It's no use, because as soon as we start kissing again, it falls back down.

Eventually, we make our way back to the wedding, my fingers twined with his. I like his warmth against my palm, the way he squeezes once before he lets go.

For a moment I catch Asher's eye, and one corner of her mouth tugs up into a smile. Like she knew, in all her infinite big-sister wisdom, that this was going to happen. Or my hair is sticking up in a hundred I've-just-been-making-out directions. Probably both.

The band returns from a break, launching into something I've heard only a hundred times at a hundred different weddings.

I groan. "I hate this song."

"I love this song," Tarek says. He holds out his hand. "You should probably lead."

He tries his best not to step on my feet, and I kick off my heels, unable to stand in them a moment longer. I am dancing at my sister's wedding with my boyfriend. It's exactly where I want to be.

"I can't believe summer's almost over," I say. "Well, it's September, so I guess it *is* over."

He nudges my arm. "Right, you'll be a supercool college student soon."

"At least California's not that far." I hope he hears the subtext, that I am fully in this with him, that I'll send him letters and care packages and pick him up at the airport. Now, there's a grand gesture: waiting in SeaTac traffic.

"No," he agrees with a smile, bending to kiss the corner of my mouth, "it's not that far."

"And the quarters aren't that long."

"Quinn," he says, as though sensing I'm about to anxiety-spiral, that I'm trying to grasp on to some certainty in what might be a wholly uncertain situation. "I'm not worried about it. It took us this long to figure it out. I think we're going to be okay."

I lay my head on his shoulder. Asher said she'd stay until they kicked her out, and I can't imagine leaving anytime soon either. I'm sure my mom has plenty of extra shoes in her emergency kit. "I think so too."

And okay, maybe this song isn't that terrible when you're dancing to it. Other things that aren't terrible: his hand on my lower back, his vanilla-sugar scent, the way he whispers to me that summer was great but autumn will be so much better, his lips brushing my ear.

No, not terrible at all.

Maybe it's even a little romantic.

# ACKNOWLEDGMENTS

I'm sending the biggest, warmest thank-you to editor extraordinaire Jennifer Ung. I can't believe this marks four books and countless dog memes together. You are a tremendous force, and I'll never stop feeling lucky that my words landed on your desk in 2016. To my wonderful publicist, Lauren Carr—thank you for your boundless enthusiasm. To designer Laura Eckes and illustrator Caitlin Blunnie—thank you for this cover that so perfectly captures Quinn and Tarek.

Thank you to my agent, Laura Bradford, and at Simon & Schuster, thank you to Justin Chanda, Kendra Levin, Anne Zafian, Dainese Santos, Jenica Nasworthy, Penina Lopez, Sara Berko, Lauren Hoffman, Chrissy Noh, Lisa Moraleda, Christina Pecorale, Victor Iannone, Emily Hutton, Michelle Leo, and Anna Jarzab.

Rosiee Thor, I'm still laughing that a joke you made years ago wound up sparking this book. I just couldn't let go of the idea of a teen harpist, and I'm infinitely grateful for your wisdom and generosity. Sharon and Dave Thormahlen, thank you for welcoming me into your studio and teaching me all about lever harps! The book didn't fully click for me until that trip. I'm so honored that you shared your music and craft with me.

To my writer friends, I hope you know you're stuck with me forever. Tara Tsai and Rachel Griffin—you help make Seattle my favorite place. Auriane Desombre and Susan Lee, you can be copresidents of the Tarek fan club. Kelsey Rodkey, Sonia Hartl, Annette Christie, Andrea Contos, Carlyn Greenwald, Marisa Kanter—I love you all so much.

A huge thank-you to my street team, the Raincoats, a group

that is full of creativity and joy and kindness: Abantika Bose, Aishi Acharya, Allie Smaha, Allyson Burns, Amelie Fournier, Ari Nussbaum, Charvi Koul, Chelly Pike, Chloe Maron, Colby Wilkens, Danielle Tedrowe, Fin Daniels, Francine Puckly, Gretal McCurdy, Hallie Fields, Holly Hughes, Humnah Memon, Isabella Rangel, Jennifer Allain, Jessica Pupillo, Jordan Bishop, Jozi Bailey, Julie Martin, Kajree Gautom, Katie J. Rogers, Kayla Plutzer, Kyla Imwalle, Léa Colombo, Leïla Fournier-Parent, Lili at Utopia State of Mind, Makenna Fournier, Meghan Doberstein-Ley, Melinda Joseph-Kelly, Melissa See, Mike Lasagna, Minju Kim, Pavitra Madhusudan, Rachel Williams, Randi Muilenburg, Sarah Ann Valentini, Simant Verma, Sophie Schmidt, Sydney Springer, Tova Portmann-Bown, Trish Caragan, and Yonit Diaz.

Finally, thank you to my family, and especially to Ivan. I can't imagine doing any of this without you.

# Turn the page for a sneak peek at Rachel's next book:

"THIS HAS TO BE A MISTAKE."

I pull the extra-long twin sheets up over my ears and mash my face into the pillow. It's too early for voices. Much too early for an accusation.

As my mind unfuzzes, the reality hits me: *there's someone in my room.*

When I fell asleep last night after testing the limits of my dorm's all-you-can-eat pasta bar, which involved a stealth mission to sneak some bowls upstairs that were forbidden from leaving the dining hall, I was alone. And questioning my life choices. All those lectures about campus safety, the little red canister of pepper spray my mom made me get, and now there is a stranger in my room. Before seven a.m. On the first day of classes.

"It's not a mistake," says another voice, a bit quieter than the first, I imagine out of respect for the blanket lump that is me. "We underestimated our capacity this year, and we had to make a few last-minute changes. Most freshmen are in triples."

"And you didn't think it would be helpful for me to know that before moving in?"

That voice, the first voice—it no longer sounds like a stranger. It's familiar. Posh. Entitled. Except . . . it can't possibly belong to her. It's a voice I thought I left back in high school, along with all the teachers who heaved sighs of relief when the principal handed me my diploma. *Thank god we're done with her,* my newspaper advisor probably said at a celebratory happy hour, clinking his champagne glass with my math teacher's. *I've never been more ready to retire.*

"Let's talk out in the hall," the second person says. A moment later, the door slams, sending something crashing down.

I roll over and crack one wary eye. The whiteboard I hung on Sunday, back when I was still dreaming about the notes and doodles my future roommate and I would scribble back and forth to each other, is on the floor. A designer duffel bag has claimed the other bed. I fight a shiver—half panic, half cold. The tree blocking the window promises a lack of both heat and natural light.

Olmsted Hall is a freshmen-only dorm and the oldest on campus, scheduled for demolition next summer. "You're so lucky," the ninth-floor RA, Paige, told me when I moved in. "You're in the last group of students to ever live here." That luck oozes, sometimes even literally, from the greige walls, wobbly bookshelves, and eerie communal shower with flickering light bulbs and suspicious puddles *everywhere*. Home sweet concrete prison.

I was the first one here, and when two, three, four days passed without an appearance from Christina Dearborn of Lincoln, Nebraska, the roommate I'd been assigned, I worried there'd been a mix-up and I'd been given a single. My mom and her college roommate are still best friends, and I've always hoped the same thing would happen for me. A single would be another stroke of bad luck after several years of misfortune, though a tiny part of me wondered if maybe it was for the best. Maybe that was what the RA had meant.

The door opens, and Paige reenters with the girl who made high school hell for me.

Several thousand freshmen, and I'm going to be sleeping five feet from my sworn nemesis. The school's so huge I assumed we'd never run into each other. It's not just bad luck—it has to be some kind of cosmic joke.

"Hi, roomie," I say, forcing a smile as I sit up in bed, shoving my Big Jewish Hair out of my face and hoping it's less chaotic than it tends to be in the mornings.

Lucie Lamont, former editor in chief of the Island High School *Navigator*, levels me with an icy glare. She's pretentious and petite and terrifying, and I fully believe she could kill a man with her bare hands. "Barrett Bloom." Then she collects herself, softening her glare, as though worried how much of that conversation I overheard. "This is . . . definitely a surprise."

It's one of the nicer things people have said about me lately.

I should be wearing something other than owl-patterned pajama shorts and the overpriced University of Washington T-shirt I bought from the campus bookstore. Medieval chain mail, maybe. An orchestra should be playing something epic and foreboding.

"Aw, Luce, I've missed you, too. It's been, what, three months?" With one hand she tightens her grip on her matching designer suitcase, and with the other she white-knuckles her purse. Her auburn ponytail is coming loose—I can't imagine the stress my appearance has caused her, poor thing. "Three months," she echoes. "And now we're here. Together."

"Well. I'll leave you two to get acquainted!" Paige chirps. "Or—reacquainted." With that she gives us an exaggerated wave and escapes outside. *If there's anything you need, day or night, just come knock on my door!* she said the first night when she tricked us into playing icebreaker games by making us microwaved s'mores. College is a web of lies.

I hook a thumb toward the door. "So *she's* great. Amazing mediation skills." I hope it'll make Lucie laugh. It does not.

"This is unreal." She gazes around the room, seeming about as impressed with it as I was when I moved in. Her eyes linger on the stack of magazines I shoved onto the shelf above my laptop. It's possible I didn't need to bring all of them, but I wanted my favorite articles close by. For inspiration. "I was supposed to have a single in Lamphere Hall," she says. "They totally sprung this on me. I'm going to talk to the RD later and try to sort this out."

"You might have had better luck if you moved in this weekend, when everyone was supposed to."

"I was in St. Croix. There was a tropical storm, and we couldn't get a flight back." It's wild that Lucie Lamont, heir to her parents' media company, can get away with saying these things, and yet I was the pariah of the *Navigator*.

Also wild: the fact that for two years, she and I were something like friends.

She sets her purse down on her desk, nearly knocking over one of my pasta bowls. Spinach ravioli, from the look of it.

"There's an all-you-can-eat pasta bar." I get up to collect the bowls and stack them on my side of the room. "I thought they would cut me off after five bowls, but nope, when they say 'all you can eat,' they aren't messing around."

"It smells like an Olive Garden."

"I was going for an 'if you're here, you're family' vibe."

I take back what I said about killing a man with her bare hands. I'm pretty sure Lucie Lamont could do it with just her eyes.

"I swear, I'm usually not this messy," I continue. "It's only been me for the past few days, and all the freedom must have gone to my head. I thought I was rooming with a girl from Nebraska, but then she never showed up, so . . ."

We both go silent. Every time I fantasized about college, my roommate was someone who'd end up becoming a lifelong friend. We'd go on girls' trips and yoga retreats and give toasts at each other's weddings. I'd be shocked if Lucie Lamont went to my funeral.

She drops into her plastic desk chair and starts the breathing techniques she taught the *Nav* staff. Deep inhales, long exhales. "If this is really happening, the two of us as roommates," she says, "even if it's just until they move me somewhere else, then we'll need some ground rules."

Feeling frumpy next to Lucie and her couture tracksuit, I throw on the knitted gray cardigan hanging lopsided across my own chair. Unfortunately, I think it only ups my frump factor, but at least I'm no longer shivering. I've always felt *less* next to Lucie, like when we teamed up on an article about the misogyny of our middle school's dress code for the paper we were convinced was the epitome of hard-hitting journalism. *By Lucie Lamont,* read the byline, our teacher elevating Lucie's status above my own, and in tiny type: *with Barrett Bloom.* Thirteen-year-old Lucie had been outraged on my behalf. But whatever bond had once existed between us, it was gone by the end of ninth grade.

"Fine, I'll bring back guys to hook up with only every other night, and I'll put this sock on the door so you know the room is occupied." I reach over to the closet, which is just wider than an ironing board, and toss her a pair of knee socks that say RING-MASTER OF THE SHITSHOW. Well—just one sock. The ninth-floor dryer ate one yesterday, and I'm still in mourning. "And I'll only masturbate when I'm positive you're asleep."

Lucie just blinks a few times, which could be interpreted as lack of appreciation for my shitshow sock, a visceral fear of the *M* word, or horror that someone would want to hook up with me. Like she didn't hear about what happened after prom last year, or laugh about it in the newsroom with the rest of the *Nav.* "Do you ever think before you speak?"

"Honestly? Not often."

"I was thinking more along the lines of keeping the room clean. I'm allergic to dust. No pasta bowls or clothes or anything on the floor." With a sandaled foot, she points underneath my desk. "No overflowing trash bins."

I bite down hard on the inside of my cheek, and when I'm quiet a moment too long, Lucie lifts her thin eyebrows.

"Jesus, Barrett, I really don't think it's too much to ask."

"Sorry. I was thinking before I spoke. Was that not the right amount of thinking? Could you maybe set a timer for me next time?"

"I'm getting a migraine," she says. "And god help me for needing to acknowledge this, but I feel like it's common courtesy not to . . . you know. Indulge in that particular brand of self-love when someone else is in the room. Sleeping or not."

"I can be pretty quiet," I offer.

Lucie looks like she might combust. It's too easy, really. "I didn't realize this was so important to you."

"It's a very normal thing to need to navigate as roommates! I'm looking out for both of us!"

"Hopefully by next week, we won't be roommates anymore." She moves to her suitcase and unzips a compartment to free her laptop, then uncoils the charger and bends down to search for an outlet. Sheepishly, I show her that the sole outlets are underneath my desk, and we discover there's no way for her to type at her desk without turning the charger into a tightrope. With a groan, she returns to her suitcase. "I can only imagine what your priorities would have been as editor in chief. We're lucky we dodged that one."

With that, she unpacks a familiar wooden nameplate and sets it on her desk. EDITOR IN CHIEF, it declares. Mocking me.

It was ridiculous to think I had a chance at editor when asking people if I could interview them sometimes felt like asking if I could give them an amateur root canal.

*It doesn't matter,* I tell myself. *Later today, I'll interview for one of the freshman reporter positions on the* Washingtonian. *No one here will care about the* Nav *or the stories I wrote, and they won't care about Lucie's nameplate, either.*

"Look. I'm also not entirely enthused about this," I say. "But maybe we could put everything behind us?" I don't want to carry this into college, even if it's followed me here. Maybe we'll never be the yoga-retreat type of friends, but we don't have to be enemies. We could simply coexist.

"Sure," Lucie says, and I brighten, believing her. "We can put your attempt to sabotage our school behind us. We'll braid our hair and host parties in our room and we'll laugh when we tell people you gleefully annihilated an entire sports team and ruined Blaine's scholarship chances."

Okay, she's exaggerating. Mostly. Her ex-boyfriend Blaine, one of Island's former star tennis players, ruined his own scholarship chances. All I did was point a finger.

Besides—I'm pretty sure the Blaines of the world won in the end anyway.

"I just have one more question," I say, shoving aside the memory before it can sink its claws in me. "Is it uncomfortable to sit down?"

She looks down at the chair, at her clothes, forehead creased in confusion. "What?"

Lucie Lamont may be a bitch, but unfortunately for her, so am I.

"With that stick up your ass. Is it uncomfortable to—"

I'm still cackling when she slams the door.

ʊ ʊ ʊ

College was supposed to be a fresh start.

It's what I've been looking forward to since the acceptance email showed up in my inbox, holding out hope that a true reinvention, the kind I'd never be able to pull off in high school, was just around the corner. And despite the roommate debacle, I'm determined to love it. New year, new Barrett, better choices.

After a quick shower, during which I narrowly avoid falling in a puddle I'm only half certain is water, I put on my favorite high-waisted jeans, my knitted cardigan, and a vintage Britney Spears tee that used to be my mom's. The jeans slide easily over my wide hips and don't pinch my stomach as much as usual—this has to be a sign from the universe that I've endured enough hardship for one day. I've never been small, and I'd cry if I had to get rid of these jeans, with their exposed-button fly and buttery softness. My dark ringlets, which grow out as opposed to down, are scrunched and sulfate-free-moussed. I tried fighting them with a straightener for years to no avail, and now I must work with my BJH instead of against it. Finally, I grab my oval wire-rimmed glasses, which I fell in love with because they made me look like I wasn't from this century, and sometimes living in another century was the most appealing thing I could imagine.

It was an understatement when I told Lucie the freedom had gone to my head. Every other hour, I've been hit with this feeling that's a mix of opportunity and terror. UW is only thirty minutes from home without traffic, and though I imagined myself here for years, I didn't think I'd feel this adrift once I moved in. Since Sunday, I've been shuffling from one welcome activity to another, avoiding anyone who went to Island, waiting for college to change my life.

But here's something to be optimistic about: it doesn't seem to matter if you eat alone in the dining hall, even as I remind myself that I'm New Barrett, who's going to find some friends to laugh with over all-you-can-eat pasta and the Olmsted Eggstravaganza even if it kills her.

After breakfast, I cross through the quad, with its quaint historic buildings and cherry trees that won't bloom until spring, slackliners and skateboarders already claiming their space. This has always been my favorite spot on campus, the perfect collegiate snapshot. Past the quad is Red Square, packed with food trucks and clubs and, in one corner, a group of swing dancers. Eight in the morning seems a little early for dancing, but I give them a *you do you* tilt of my head regardless.

Then I make a fatal mistake: eye contact with a girl tabling by herself in front of Odegaard Library.

"Hi!" she calls. "We're trying to raise awareness about the Mazama pocket gopher."

I stop. "The what?"

When she grins at me, it becomes clear I've walked right into her trap. She's tall, brown hair in a topknot tied with UW ribbons: purple and gold. "The Mazama pocket gopher. They're native to Pierce and Thurston Counties and only found in Washington State. More than ninety percent of their habitat has been destroyed by commercial development."

A flyer is thrust into my hands.

"He's adorable!" I say, realizing the same image is printed on her T-shirt. "That little face!"

"Doesn't he deserve to eat as much grass as his little heart desires?" She taps the paper. "This is Guillermo. He could fit in the palm of your hand. We're hosting a letter-writing campaign to local government officials this afternoon at three thirty, and we'd love to see you there."

I'm annoyed by what *we'd love to see you there* does to my camaraderie-deprived soul. "Oh—sorry," I say. "It's not that I don't care about, um, pocket gophers, but I can't make it." My interview with the *Washingtonian*'s editor in chief is at four o'clock, after my last class.

When I try to hand her back the flyer, she shakes her head. "Keep it. Do some research. They need our help."

So I tuck it into my back pocket, promising her I will.

The physics building is much farther away than it looked on the campus map I have pulled up on my phone and keep sneaking glances at, even though every third person I pass is doing the same thing. It wouldn't be as bad if I were excited about the class. I've been planning to switch out—registration was a nightmare and everything filled up so quickly, so I grabbed one of the first open classes I saw—but damn it, New Barrett is a rule follower, so here I am, trudging across campus to Physics 101. Monday-Wednesday-Friday, eight thirty a.m.

My T-shirt is pasted to my back and my perfect jeans' perfect buttons are digging into my stomach by the time I spot the building. Still, I force myself to remain hopeful. This probably isn't an omen. I don't think omens are usually this sweaty.

In my pocket, my phone buzzes just as I'm walking up the front steps.

Mom: How do I love thee? Joss and I are wishing you SO MUCH LUCK today!

The text is time-stamped forty-five minutes ago, which I

attribute to the campus's sketchy service, and there's a picture attached: my mom and her girlfriend, Jocelyn, in the matching plush robes I gave them for Hanukkah last year, toasting me with mugs of coffee.

My mom's water broke in her sophomore year British Poetry class, and as a result, I was named after Elizabeth Barrett Browning, most famous for *How do I love thee? Let me count the ways.* College is where the two best things in my mom's life happened: me and the business degree that enabled her to open the stationery store that's supported us for years. She's always told me how much I'm going to love college, and I've held tight to the hope that at least one of these forty thousand people is bound to find me charming instead of unpleasant, intriguing instead of off-putting.

"I'm just so excited for you, Barrett," my mom said when she helped me move in. I wanted to cling to her skirt and let her drag me back to the car, back to Mercer Island, back to the HOW DO I LOVE THEE? cross-stitch hanging in my bedroom. Because even though I'd been lonely in high school, at least that loneliness was familiar. The unknown is always scarier, and maybe that's why it was so easy to pretend I didn't care when the entire school decided I wasn't to be trusted, after the *Navigator* story that changed everything. "You'll see. These four or five years—but please don't get pregnant—are going to be the best of your life."

God, I really hope she's right.

# RIVETED

BY *simon teen* ♥

BELIEVE IN YOUR SHELF

Visit RivetedLit.com &
connect with us on social to:

> **DISCOVER** NEW YA READS

> **READ** BOOKS FOR FREE

> **DISCUSS** YOUR FAVORITES

> **SHARE** YOUR IDEAS

> **ENTER SWEEPSTAKES** FOR THE CHANCE TO WIN BOOKS

Follow @SimonTeen on

to stay up to date with all things Riveted!

Leap into summer with these

# *swoon-worthy*

reads by *New York Times*
bestselling author Morgan Matson.

# WHAT IF
## ALL YOUR CRUSHES
### FOUND OUT HOW YOU FELT?

From bestselling author

# JENNY HAN

How much can you really tell about a person just by looking at them?

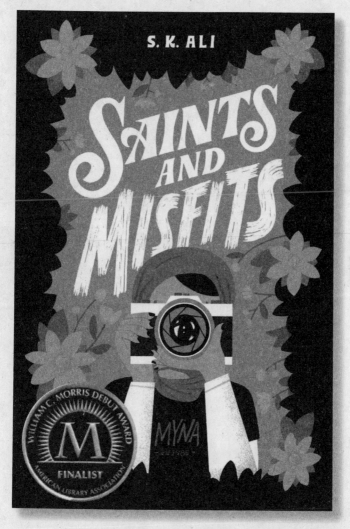